OTHER BOOKS BY THE SAME AUTHOR

Fiction

The Edible Woman
Surfacing
Lady Oracle
Dancing Girls
Life Before Man

Poetry

The Circle Game
The Animals in That Country
The Journals of Susanna Moodie
Procedures for Underground
Power Politics
You Are Happy
Selected Poems
Two-Headed Poems
True Stories

Criticism

Survival: A Thematic Guide
to Canadian Literature

Children's

Up in the Tree

BODILY HARM

■

Margaret Atwood

■

SIMON AND SCHUSTER

NEW YORK

Copyright © 1982 by O. W. Toad Ltd.
All rights reserved
including the right of reproduction
in whole or in part in any form
Published by Simon and Schuster
A Division of Gulf & Western Corporation
Simon & Schuster Building
Rockefeller Center
1230 Avenue of the Americas
New York, New York 10020
SIMON AND SCHUSTER and colophon
are trademarks of Simon & Schuster
Manufactured in the United States of America

10   9   8   7   6   5   4   3   2   1

Library of Congress Cataloging in Publication Data

Atwood, Margaret Eleanor, 1939–
   Bodily harm.

   I. Title.
PR9199.3.A8B6   1982   813'.54   81–18370
ISBN 0–671–44153–1   AACR2

Acknowledgment is made for permission to quote from Ways of Seeing by John Berger, published in 1973 by The Viking Press, Inc. Reprinted by permission of Viking Penguin Inc.

An excerpt from Bodily Harm was previously published in the Paris Review, October 1981.

ACKNOWLEDGMENTS

The author would like to thank the Canada Council and the Guggenheim Foundation for making it easier to complete this book. She would also like to thank Nan Talese, Donya Peroff, Phoebe Larmore, Michael Bradley, Jennifer Glossop, Jack McClelland, Carolyn Moulton, Rosalie Abella, Dan Green, Susan Milmoe, Carolyn Forché, and the others who are not named but whose help has been essential.

For Jennifer Rankin, 1941–1979.
For Graeme, James, and John.

A man's presence suggests what he is capable of doing to you or for you. By contrast, a woman's presence . . . defines what can and cannot be done to her.

John Berger, *Ways of Seeing*

THIS IS HOW I GOT HERE, says Rennie.

It was the day after Jake left. I walked back to the house around five. I'd been over at the market and I was carrying the shopping basket as well as my purse. There wasn't as much to carry now that Jake wasn't there any more, which was just as well because the muscles in my left shoulder were aching, I hadn't been keeping up the exercises. The trees along the street had turned and the leaves were falling onto the sidewalk, yellow and brown, and I was thinking, Well, it's not so bad, I'm still alive.

My next-door neighbor, an old Chinese man whose name I didn't know, was tidying up his front yard. The yard in front of my house had been covered over with paving stones so you could park a car on it. That meant the street was going up rather than down, and in a few years I'd have to move; though I'd stopped thinking in years. My neighbor had pulled up the dead plants and was raking the earth into a raised oblong. In the spring he'd plant things I didn't know the names for. I remember thinking it was time I learned the names, if I was going to live there.

I did notice the cruiser, which they'd left beside a meter like any other car, no flashing lights, but it was a few doors away so I didn't pay much attention to it. You see more police cars down there than you might farther north.

The front door was open, which wasn't out of place on such a warm day. The downstairs neighbor, an old woman who isn't the landlady but behaves like one, has cats and likes to leave the outside door ajar so they can get in and go through the cat door. "Cat hole," Jake calls it; used to call it.

My own door at the top of the stairs was open too. There were people inside, men, I could hear them talking, and then a laugh. I couldn't think who it could be, it wasn't Jake, but whoever it was didn't seem to care who knew they were there. The key was under the mat where I always leave it, but the edge of the doorframe was splintered, the lock was shoved right out of it. I went into the living room, which was still piled with the boxes of books Jake had packed but not collected. Nothing had been moved. Through the kitchen doorway I could see feet and legs, shining feet, pressed legs.

Two policemen were sitting at the table. I had that quick rush of fear, late for school, caught on the boys' stairs, caught out. The only thing I could think of was that they were after the pot, but there were no drawers pulled open and the tea and coffee canisters were where they should be. Then I remembered that Jake had taken the whole stash with him. Why not? It was his. Anyway, surely they'd stopped worrying about that, everyone does it now, even the police, it's almost legal.

The younger one stood up, the older one didn't. He stayed sitting down, smiling up at me as if I'd come for a job interview.

You Miss Wilford? he asked. He didn't wait. You're damn lucky. He had a massive head, with the hair clipped short like a punker's. His was left over though, from sometime in the fifties: no green highlights.

Why? I said. What's the matter?

You've got good neighbors, the younger one said. He looked like a high-school gym teacher or a Baptist, about twenty-two, earnest and severe. The one downstairs. She was the one who phoned.

Was it a fire? I said. There was no sign of it, no smell.

The older one laughed. The other one didn't. No, he said. She heard footsteps up here and she knew it wasn't you, she saw you go out, and she didn't hear anyone go up the stairs. He jimmied open your kitchen window.

I put the shopping basket on the table; then I went and looked at the window, which was open about two feet. The white paint was scratched.

You could do it with a jackknife, he said. You should get those safety locks. He heard us coming and went back out through the window.

Did he take anything? I said.

You'll have to tell us that, said the older one.

The young one looked uneasy. We don't think he was a burglar, he said. He made himself a cup of Ovaltine. He was just

18

waiting for you, I guess. There was a cup on the table, half full of something light brown. I felt sick: Someone I didn't know had been in my kitchen, opening my refrigerator and my cupboards, humming to himself maybe, as if he lived there; as if he was an intimate.

What for? I said.

The older one stood up. He took up a lot of space in the kitchen. Take a look, he said, pleased with himself, in charge. He had a present he'd been saving up. He walked past me into the living room and then into the bedroom. I was glad I'd made the bed that morning: Lately I hadn't always.

There was a length of rope coiled neatly on the quilt. It wasn't any special kind of rope, there was nothing lurid about it. It was off-white and medium thick. It could have been a clothesline.

All I could think of was a game we used to play, Detective or Clue, something like that. You had to guess three things: Mr. Green, in the conservatory, with a pipewrench; Miss Plum, in the kitchen, with a knife. Only I couldn't remember whether the name in the envelope was supposed to be the murderer's or the victim's. *Miss Wilford, in the bedroom, with a rope.*

He was just waiting for you, the younger one said behind me.

Drinking his Ovaltine, the big one said. He smiled down at me, watching my face, almost delighted, like an adult who's just said *I told you so* to some rash child with a skinned knee.

So you were lucky, the younger one said. He came past me and picked up the rope, carefully, as if it had germs. I could see now that he was older than I'd thought, he had anxious puckers around the eyes.

The big one opened the closet door, casually, as if he had every right. Two of Jake's suits were still hanging there.

You live alone, that right? the big one said.

I said yes.

These your pictures? said the big one, grinning.

No, I said. They belong to a friend of mine. The pictures were Jake's, he was supposed to take them away.

Quite a friend, said the big one.

He must've been watching you for a while, said the young one. He must've known when you'd get home. Any idea who it might be?

No, I said. I wanted to sit down. I thought of asking them if they'd like a beer.

Some nut, the big one said. If you knew what was walking around loose out there you'd never go out. You close the curtains in the bathroom when you take a shower?

There aren't any curtains in the bathroom, I said. There aren't any windows.

You close the curtains when you get undressed at night?

Yes, I said.

He'll be back, the young one said. That kind always comes back.

The big one wouldn't let up. You have men over here a lot? Different men?

He wanted it to be my fault, just a little, some indiscretion, some provocation. Next he would start lecturing me about locks, about living alone, about safety.

I close the curtains, I said. I don't have men over. I turn out the lights. I get undressed by myself, in the dark.

The big one smirked at me, he knew about single women, and suddenly I was angry. I unbuttoned my blouse and pulled my left arm out of the sleeve and dropped the slip strap over my shoulder.

What in hell are you doing? the big one said.

I want you to believe me, I said.

■

There's a two-hour stopover in Barbados, or so they tell her. Rennie finds the women's washroom in the new Muzak-slick airport and changes from her heavy clothes to a cotton dress. She examines her face in the mirror, checking for signs. In fact she looks quite well, she looks normal. Her dress is a washed-out blue, her face isn't too pale, she wears only enough makeup so she won't seem peculiar, a leftover hippie or a Plymouth Brethren or something like that. This is the effect she aims for, neutrality; she needs it for her work, as she used to tell Jake. Invisibility.

Take a chance, said Jake, during one of his campaigns to alter her, what was it that time? Purple satin with rhinestone spaghetti straps. Make a statement.

Other people make statements, she said. I just write them down.

That's a cop-out, said Jake. If you've got it, flaunt it.

Which God knows you do, said Rennie.

You're putting me down again, said Jake, affable, showing his teeth, flawless except for the long canines.

You're impossible to put down, said Rennie. That's why I love you.

In the washroom there's a blow-drier for your hands, which claims to be a protection against disease. The instructions are in French as well as English, it's made in Canada. Rennie washes her hands and dries them under the blow-drier. She's all in favor of protection against disease.

She thinks about what's behind her, what she canceled or didn't bother to cancel. As for the apartment, she just shut the door with its shiny new lock and walked out, since out was where she needed to be. It gets easier and easier, dishes in the sink for two weeks, three weeks, only a little mold on them, she hardly even feels guilty any more; one of these days it may be permanent.

Rennie's lucky that she can manage these sidesteps, these small absences from real life; most people can't. She's not tied down, which is an advantage. It's a good thing she's versatile, and it helps to know people, in this case Keith. Keith has recently come across to *Visor* from *Toronto Life*. He's a contact of hers, which is not the same as a friend. While she was in the hospital she decided that most of her friends were really just contacts.

I want to go somewhere warm and very far away, she said.

Try the Courtyard Café, he said.

No, seriously, said Rennie. My life is the pits right now. I need a tan.

Want to do The Restless Caribbean? he said. So does everyone else.

Nothing political, she said. I can do you a good Fun in the Sun, with the wine lists and the tennis courts, I know what you like.

You finked out on the last piece I wanted you to do, said Keith. Anyway, you just came back from Mexico.

That was last year, she said. Come on, we're old buddies. I need some time out.

Keith sighed and then agreed, a little too quickly. Usually he haggled more. He must have heard about the operation; maybe he even knew about Jake's leaving. He had that faint sick look in his eyes, as if he wanted to give her something, charity for instance. Rennie hates charity.

It's not a total freebie, she said. It's not as if I don't produce.

Pick an island, he said. Only it has to be someplace we haven't done. How about this one? A friend of mine went there, sort of by mistake. He says it's off the beaten track.

Rennie had never heard of it. Sounds great, she said. Ordinarily she would have done some homework, but she was in too much of a hurry. This time she's flying blind.

Rennie repacks her bag, stuffing her pantyhose into an outside pocket, the one with the clock. Then she goes to the restaurant, where everything is wicker, and orders a gin and tonic. She does not look long at the distant sea, which is too blue to be believable.

The restaurant isn't full. There are a few women alone and more in clutches, and a couple of families. There are no men by themselves. Men by themselves usually go to the bar. She knows, she's learned since Jake left, that if she spends much time gazing around the room with that slightly defiant stare adopted by women alone to indicate that they don't have to be, one of the other solitaries might join her. So instead she watches her hands and the ice cubes in her glass, which despite the air conditioning are melting almost at once.

When she goes to the gate she's told the plane is late. Lugging her bag and her camera bag, she walks among the kiosk shops: small black hand-sewn dolls, cigarette boxes and mirrors encrusted with shells, necklaces made from the teeth of sharks, porcupine fish, inflated and dried. A miniature five-piece steel band, mounted on a slab of driftwood, in which the players are toads. Looking more closely, she sees that the toads are real ones that have been stuffed and varnished. A long time ago she would have bought this monstrosity and sent it to someone for a joke.

■

Rennie is from Griswold, Ontario. Griswold is what they call her background. Though it's less like a background, a backdrop—

picturesque red Victorian houses and autumn trees on a hillside in the distance—than a subground, something that can't be seen but is nevertheless there, full of gritty old rocks and buried stumps, worms and bones; nothing you'd want to go into. Those who'd lately been clamoring for roots had never seen a root up close, Rennie used to say. She had, and she'd rather be some other part of the plant.

In an earlier phase, Rennie used to tell jokes about Griswold to amuse her friends. Such as: How many people from Griswold does it take to change a lightbulb? The whole town. One to change it, ten to snoop, and the rest of them to discuss how sinful you are for wanting more light. Or: How many people from Griswold does it take to change a lightbulb? None. If the light goes out it's the will of God, and who are you to complain?

People from bigger places, Jake in particular, think that Griswold has an exotic and primitive charm. Rennie doesn't think this. Mostly she tries to avoid thinking about Griswold at all. Griswold, she hopes, is merely something she defines herself against.

Though it's not always so easy to get rid of Griswold. For instance: When Rennie saw the piece of rope on her bed, she knew what Griswold would have had to say about it. This is what happens to women like you. What can you expect, you deserve it. In Griswold everyone gets what they deserve. In Griswold everyone deserves the worst.

■

The night before the operation Jake took Rennie out to dinner, to cheer her up. She didn't feel like going, but she knew she had been boring recently and she'd vowed, a long time ago, when she was still in her early twenties, never to be boring; a vow that had been harder to keep than she'd expected.

Rennie was an expert on boredom, having done a piece on it for *Pandora's* "Relationships" column in which she claimed that there were two people involved in boredom, not just one: the borer and the boree. Out-and-out boredom of the jaw-stiffening kind could be avoided by small shifts in attention. *Study his tie*, she recommended. *If you're stuck, make an imaginary earlobe collection and add his. Watch his Adam's apple move up and down. Keep smiling.* The assumption was that the active principle, the source of the powerful ergs of boredom, was male, and that the passive recipient was female. Of course this was unfair, but who except women would read a *Pandora* "Relationships" column? When writing for male-oriented magazines such as *Crusoe* or *Visor* she offered self-help hints: "How to Read Her Mind." *If she's looking too hard at your earlobes or watching your Adam's apple go up and down, change the subject.*

Jake took her to Fentons, which used to be more than he could afford, and they sat under one of the indoor trees. At first he held her hand, but she felt he was doing it because he thought he ought to and after a while he stopped. He ordered a bottle of wine and urged her to drink more of it than she wanted to. Perhaps he thought she would be less boring if she got drunk, but this was not the case.

She didn't want to talk about the operation but she couldn't think about anything else. Maybe it would turn out to be benign; on the other hand, maybe they would open her up and find that she was permeated, riddled, rotting away from the inside. There was a good chance she'd wake up minus a breast. She knew she ought to be thinking about how to die with dignity but she didn't want to die with dignity. She didn't want to die at all.

Jake told stories about people they knew, gossipy stories with a malicious twist, the kind she used to enjoy. She tried to enjoy them but instead she started to think about Jake's fingers: He was holding the stem of his wineglass with his left hand, lightly, but the knuckles were absolutely white. He had a habit of never throwing out empty containers; that morning she'd taken down the Shreddies box and there was nothing in it. How could she know when it was time to get more if he kept leaving empty peanut butter jars and honey jars and cocoa tins on the shelves? She refrained from mentioning this. She felt that Jake's eyes kept slipping away from her face, down to the top button of her blouse; then, as if he'd reached a line, a taboo, back up to her face again. He's fascinated, she thought.

They walked home with their arms around each other, as if they were still in love. While Jake took a shower, Rennie stood in the bedroom with the closet door open, wondering what she should put on. Two of her nightgowns, the black one with the see-through lace top and the red satin one slit up the sides, had been presents from Jake. He liked buying her things like that. Bad taste. Garters, merry widows, red bikini pants with gold spangles, wired half-cup hooker brassieres that squeezed and pushed up the breasts. The real you, he'd say, with irony and hope. Who'd ever guess? Black leather and whips, that's next.

She wanted to make it easy for him, she wanted to help him along with the illusion that nothing bad had happened to her or was going to happen. Her body was in the mirror, looking the same as ever. She couldn't believe that in a week, a day, some of it might have vanished. She thought about what they did with the parts.

In the end she wore nothing. She waited in bed for Jake to come out of the shower. He would smell of body shampoo and he would be damp and slippery. She used to like it when he slid into her wet like that, but tonight she was only waiting for a certain amount of time to be over, as if she were in a dentist's office, waiting for something to be done to her. A procedure.

At first he couldn't. It had been too sudden; she'd been told, she'd told him, the operation had been scheduled, all in the same day. She could understand his shock and disgust and the effort he was making not to reveal them, since she felt the same way. She wanted to tell him he didn't have to, not if it was too much of an effort, but he wouldn't take that well, he'd think she was being critical.

He ran his hand over her breast a couple of times, the bad one. Then he began to cry. This was what she'd been afraid she herself would do. She hugged him, stroking the back of his head.

After that he made love to her, painfully and for a long time. She could hear his teeth grinding together, as if he were angry. He was holding back, waiting for her to come. He thought he was doing her a favor. He was doing her a favor. She couldn't stand the idea of anyone doing her a favor. Her body was nerveless, slack, as if she was already under the anesthetic. As though he could sense this he gathered skin and muscle, wrenching, twisting, he hit her, not gently, shoving himself into her, trying to break through that barrier of deadened flesh. At last she faked it. That was another vow she'd made once: never to fake it.

■

By the time the flight is called it's already dark. They stand at the gate, a dozen or so of them, watching the plane land. The gate isn't even a gate but an opening in the cement wall with a chain across it. The airline officials, two kids, a light-brown girl who looks about sixteen and a boy with a set of earphones, can't decide which gate they should be standing at, so the whole group straggles back and forth several times between one hole in the wall and another. A man in tinted glasses offers to carry her camera bag for her, but Rennie refuses politely. She doesn't want anyone sitting beside her on the plane, especially a man who would wear a safari jacket. She didn't like safari jackets even when they were still possible. He's the only white man in the group.

When the hole is finally unchained, Rennie follows the others toward the plane, which is tiny and looks alarmingly homemade. Rennie tells herself that you stand a better chance in a small plane like this than in a jumbo jet. Jake has a joke about planes. He says they can't really fly, it's absurd to think a heavy piece of metal like that can fly; what keeps them up is the irrational belief of the passengers, and all plane crashes can be explained by loss of faith.

He'd have a job with this one, she thinks, anyone can see it'll never get off the ground. St. Antoine isn't a rich country, they probably buy their planes fourth-hand from other countries, then stick them together with Band-Aids and string until they fall apart irreparably. It's like the fat trade in restaurants. Rennie knows a lot about the fat trade in restaurants: the good ones selling their used fat to the second-rate ones, and so on down the line until the fat reaches the chipworks of cheap hamburger stands. Rennie's piece on the fat trade was called, "By Their Fats Ye Shall Know Them." The editor's title, not hers. She wanted to call it "Fat City."

She climbs the wobbling metal steps through the dark heat, which is doubled by the heat of the plane. The camera bag strap cuts into her shoulder and the flesh above her left breast; the scar is pulling again. When it feels like this she's afraid to look down, she's afraid she'll see blood, leakage, her stuffing coming out. It

26

isn't a very big scar as such things go; worse things happen to other people. She's lucky. Why then doesn't she feel lucky?

I don't want to have the operation, she said. She believed two things at once: that there was nothing wrong with her and that she was doomed anyway, so why waste the time? She had a horror of someone, anyone, putting a knife into her and cutting some of her off, which was what it amounted to no matter what they called it. She disliked the idea of being buried one piece at a time instead of all at once, it was too much like those women they were always finding strewn about ravines or scattered here and there in green garbage bags. Dead but not molested. The first time she'd seen that word, in a Toronto newspaper when she was eight, she'd thought a molester was someone who caught moles. A molester is someone who is indecent, said her grandmother. But since that was what her grandmother said about almost everyone, it wasn't much help. Rennie still used that word sometimes, for fun, where other people would use *gross*.

Daniel, who at that point was still Dr. Luoma, looked at her as if he was disappointed in her: Other women no doubt said similar things. This embarrassed her, since even such a short time ago she still assumed she was unique.

You don't have to, he said. Or, well, you don't *have* to do anything. Nobody's forcing you, it's your own decision. He paused here, letting her remember that the alternative he offered her was death. *Either/or*. Multiple choice: which was not what it said.

■

During the morning of the day on which she had her routine, once-a-year appointment at the gynecologist's, Rennie was working on a piece about drain-chain jewelry. You could get it for pennies at your local Woolworth's, she wrote. Buy as many lengths as you need, make the chains as long as you like with those cunning little peanut-shaped connectors, wear them on any part of your anatomy: wrists, neck, waist, even ankles, if you wanted the slave-girl effect. It was the latest Queen Street thing, she wrote, a New Wave sleaze put-on of real jewelry. Or beyond New Wave even: *nouveau wavé*.

In fact it wasn't the latest Queen Street thing. It wasn't a thing at all, it was an embellishment Rennie had spotted on one of her friends, Jocasta, who ran Ripped Off, a second-hand store on Peter Street that specialized in violently ugly clothes from the fifties, springolator pumps, tiger-stripe pedal pushers, formals with jutting tits and layers of spangles and tulle.

Jocasta was five foot nine, with the cheekbones of an ex-model. She went in for fake leopard-skin shortie coats. The women who hung out at Ripped Off were half Jocasta's age and wore a lot of black leather. They had hair dyed green or bright red, or they shaved their heads with an Iroquois fringe running down the middle. Some of them had safety pins in their ears. They looked up to Jocasta, who was right over the edge in the creative sleaze line and could carry it off, too. In her display window she made arrangements that she called Junk Punk: a stuffed lizard copulating with a mink collar in a child's rocking chair, motorized; a cairn of false teeth with a born-again tract propped against it: "How Can I Be Saved?" Once she hung a coat tree with blown-up condoms sprayed with red enamel and a sign: NATIONAL LOVE A REFUGEE WEEK.

Of course it's gross, said Jocasta. But so's the world, you know what I mean? Me, I'm relaxed. A little deep breathing, mantras of one syllable, bran for breakfast. Can I help it if I'm the wave of the future?

Jocasta wasn't Jocasta's real name: her real name was Joanne. She changed it when she was thirty-eight because, as she said, what can you do with a name like Joanne? Too *nice*. She didn't dye her hair green or wear a safety pin in her ear but calling herself Jocasta was the equivalent. Good taste kills, said Jocasta.

Rennie met Jocasta when she was doing a piece on the Queen Street renaissance for *Toronto Life*, all about the conversion of hardware stores and wholesale fabric outlets into French restaurants and trendy boutiques. She did not necessarily believe that a trendy boutique was any improvement over a wholesale fabric outlet, but she knew enough to avoid such negative value judgments in print. At first she thought Jocasta was a lesbian, because of the way she dressed, but later she decided Jocasta was merely bizarre. Rennie liked Jocasta because Jocasta was much more bi-

28

zarre than Rennie felt she herself could ever be. Partly she admired this quality, partly she felt it was dangerous, and partly, being from Griswold after all, she had a certain contempt for it.

Jocasta wore drain chains because she was miserly and they were cheap. She hadn't even bought her chains, she'd raided the sinks of neighboring restaurants for them: "All I did was take the plug off with a pair of pliers, and *voilà*." But sometimes Rennie liked to write pieces about trends that didn't really exist, to see if she could make them exist by writing about them. Six to one she'd see at least ten women with bathplug chains looped around their necks two weeks after the piece came out. Successes of this kind gave her an odd pleasure, half gleeful, half sour: People would do anything not to be thought outmoded.

Usually her articles on fake trends were just as plausible as the ones on real trends; sometimes more so, because she tried harder with them. Even the editors were taken in, and when they weren't they'd go along anyway, half believing that what Rennie had to say on subjects like this would eventually come true, even if it wasn't true at the moment. When she wasn't fooling around she was uncanny, they told each other: as if she could see into the future.

If I could see into the future, Rennie said to one of them (a man, who kept suggesting that they should have drinks sometime soon), do you think I'd waste my time on this sort of thing? The color of women's lipstick, the length of their skirts, the height of their heels, what bits of plastic or gilt junk they choose to stick on themselves? I see into the present, that's all. Surfaces. There's not a whole lot to it.

Rennie became a quick expert on surfaces when she first moved away from Griswold. (On a university scholarship: The only other respectable way out of Griswold for a young single woman, she used to say, is straight down.) Surfaces determined whether or not people took you seriously, and what was mandatory in Griswold was, more often than not, ludicrous in the real world. Griswold, for instance, was an early convert to polyester knit.

At first she'd looked in order to copy; later on she'd looked in order not to copy. After that she just looked. When Marxist college professors and hard-line feminists gave her a rough time at parties about the frivolity of her subject matter she would counter with a

29

quote from Oscar Wilde to the effect that only superficial people were not concerned with appearances. Then she would tactfully suggest certain alterations to their wardrobes that would improve their own appearances no end. They were usually vain enough to be interested: Nobody wanted to be in bad taste.

Most of the people she knew thought Rennie was way out ahead of it, but she saw herself as off to the side. She preferred it there; she'd noted, many times, the typical pose of performers, celebrities, in magazine shots and publicity stills and especially on stage. Teeth bared in an ingratiating smile, arms flung wide to the sides, hands open to show that there were no concealed weapons, head thrown back, throat bared to the knife; an offering, an exposure. She felt no envy toward them. In fact she found them embarrassing, their eagerness, their desperation, for that was what it was, even when they were successful. Underneath it they would do anything; they'd take their clothes off if there was no other way, they'd stand on their heads, anything, in that frenzied grab for attention. She would much rather be the one who wrote things about people like this than be the one they got written about.

Rennie finished the first draft of her piece on drain-chain jewelry and spent some time thinking about the title. Eventually she discarded "The Chain Gang" in favor of "Chain Reaction." The pictures would be easy to get, but she'd leave that to the magazine. She never shot high-gloss fashion, she wasn't good enough.

At eleven-thirty Jake surprised her by coming home, "for a lunchtime quickie," he said. That was fine, since she liked being surprised by him. At that time he was still inventive. Sometimes he would climb up the fire escape and in through the window instead of coming through the door, he'd send her ungrammatical and obscene letters composed of words snipped from newspapers, purporting to be from crazy men, he'd hide in closets and spring out at her, pretending to be a lurker. Apart from the first shock, none of these things had ever alarmed her.

So they had the lunchtime quickie and afterward Rennie made grilled cheese sandwiches and they ate them in bed, which wasn't as pleasant as she'd thought it would be because some of the crumbs and melted cheese got on the sheets, and Jake went back to his office. Rennie had a bath, because her background was still

with her and she felt it would be inconsiderate to go to the gynecologist right after making love without having had a bath.

Ready to have babies yet? the doctor asked, his standard opening joke as he snapped on his prophylactic gloves. You're heading
for the cutoff point. He'd been saying this for six years. Half an
hour later, everything ceased to be funny.

Though as she walked home she was still thinking in the ways
she was used to. For instance, she could do a piece on it. "Cancer,
The Coming Thing." *Homemakers* might take it, or *Chatelaine*.
How about "The Cutoff Point"?

*This is a fact, it's happened to you, and right now you can't
believe it,* she would begin. *You've been used to thinking of yourself as a person, but all of a sudden you're just a statistic.* Dying
was in bad taste, no doubt of that. But at some point it would be a
trend, among the people she knew. Maybe she was way out ahead
on that one too.

■

On the plane they serve warm ginger ale in paper cups and sandwiches wrapped in plastic film. The sandwiches are made of slices
of white bread, with slightly rancid butter and a thin piece of
roast beef between them. Rennie picks out the lettuce: She's been
to Mexico, she knows about amebic dysentery.

The seats are hard and covered with scratchy maroon plush, like
those on ancient buses. The stewardesses, two of them, one with
straightened upswept hair like Betty Grable's, one with cornrows
and beaded Rasta braids, wear hot-pink satin outfits with tiny
white aprons. They teeter up and down the narrow aisles on high-
heeled sandals, open-toed with multiple straps, magenta: Fuck-me
shoes, Jake would call them. When the plane bumps they grab for
the back of the nearest seat, but they seem used to it.

Though the plane is just half full, there's a man beside Rennie.
It isn't the white man in the safari jacket, who's sitting at the very
front reading a newspaper, but an older man, brown. He's wearing
a dark suit, despite the heat, and a tie in which a small pin shines.
She notices that he's taken only one bite of his sandwich. When
the remains of the sandwiches are being collected he speaks to
Rennie, throwing his voice above the drone of the engines.

"You are from Canada," he says, stating it rather than asking.

He's about sixty, spare-faced and tall, with a high-bridged nose; he looks vaguely Arabian. His jaw is undershot, his bottom teeth close slightly over the top ones.

"How did you know?" says Rennie.

"We get mostly Canadians," he says. "The sweet Canadians."

Rennie can't tell whether or not this is meant as irony. "We're not all that sweet," she says.

"I trained in Ontario, my friend," he says. "I was once a veterinarian. My specialty was the diseases of sheep. So I am familiar with the sweet Canadians." He smiles, speaking precisely. "They are famous for their good will. When we had our hurricane, the sweet Canadians donated a thousand tins of ham, Maple Leaf Premium. It was for the refugees." He laughs, as if this is a joke, but Rennie doesn't get it. "The refugees never see this ham," he says, explaining patiently. "Most likely they never eat ham in their lives before. Well, they miss their chance." He laughs again. "The hams turn up, surprise, at the Independence Day banquet. To celebrate our freedom from Britain. For the leading citizens only. Many of us were very amused, my friend. There was a round of applause for the sweet Canadians."

Rennie doesn't know what to say to this. She feels he's making fun of her in some obscure way, but she isn't sure why. "Was it a bad hurricane?" she says. "Was anyone killed?"

He ignores this question entirely. "Why are you coming to St. Antoine?" he says, as if it's an odd thing to be doing.

"I'm writing a piece on it," she says. "A travel piece."

"Ah," he says. "To entice the sweet Canadians."

Rennie is becoming irritated with him. She looks at the pocket in the seatback in front of her, hoping there's something she can pretend to read, an airline magazine, barf-bag mags as they're known in the trade, but there's nothing in it but the card illustrating emergency procedures. On the 707 to Barbados she had a thriller she bought at the airport, but she finished it and left it on the plane. A mistake: Now she's bookless.

"You must visit our Botanic Gardens," he says. "The British made very good ones, all over the world. For medicinal purposes, you understand. Ours is one of the oldest. It is still in good repair; they have only been gone a month. Now that we are free, we have to pull out the weeds ourselves. We have a small museum there, you must see that. Broken pots made by the Carib Indians and so forth. They did not make very accomplished pottery. We still have a few of them in our country, we have not fully modernized."

He reaches into his jacket pocket and takes out a bottle of aspirin. He taps two into his palm and offers the bottle to Rennie, as if offering a cigarette. Rennie doesn't have a headache, but feels she should take one anyway, it's the polite thing to do.

"There is a fort also," he says. "The British were proficient at that, too. Fort Industry. Under the British it was called Fort George, but our government is renaming everything." He signals the stewardess and asks for a glass of water.

"We just have ginger ale," she says.

"It will have to do," he says. His teeth clamp together in a bull-dog grin. "In my country that is a very useful phrase."

The ginger ale comes and he swallows his aspirins, then offers the Styrofoam cup to Rennie. "Thank you," says Rennie. "I'm saving mine for later." She holds the aspirin in her hand, wondering if she's just been rude, but if so he doesn't seem to notice.

"I have many statistics you might find useful," he says. "Those on unemployment, for instance. Or perhaps you would prefer the Botanic Gardens? I would be happy to escort you, I take an interest in plants."

Rennie decides not to ask him about restaurants and tennis courts. She thanks him and says she'll have a better idea of what she's looking for once she gets there.

"I think we are approaching," he says.

The plane dips. Rennie peers out the window, hoping to see something, but it's too dark. She glimpses an outline, a horizon, something jagged and blacker than the sky, but then the plane goes down at a forty-five-degree angle and a moment later they hit the ground. She jolts forward against the seat belt as the plane brakes, much too fast.

"We have a very short runway here," he remarks. "Before I tendered my regrets to the present government I attempted to have something done about it. I was at that time the Minister for Tourism." He smiles his lopsided smile. "But the Prime Minister had other priorities."

The plane taxis to a stop and the aisle jams with people. "It's been nice meeting you," Rennie says as they stand up.

33

He holds out his hand for her to shake. Rennie transfers the aspirin. "I hope you will have a pleasant stay, my friend. If you need assistance, do not hesitate to call on me. Everyone knows where I can be found. My name is Minnow, Dr. Minnow, like the fish. My enemies make jokes about that! A small fish in a small puddle, they say. It is a corruption of the French, Minôt was the original, it was one of the many things they left behind them. The family were all pirates."

"Really?" Rennie says. "That's wild."

"Wild?" says Dr. Minnow.

"Fascinating," says Rennie.

Dr. Minnow smiles. "They were common once," he says. "Some of them were quite respectable; they intermarried with the British and so forth. You have a husband?"

"Pardon?" says Rennie. The question has caught her by surprise: nobody she knows asks it any more.

"A man," he says. "Here we do not bother so much with the formalities."

Rennie wonders if this is a sexual feeler. She hesitates. "Not *with* me," she says.

"Perhaps he will join you later?" Dr. Minnow says. He looks down at her anxiously, and Rennie sees that this isn't an advance, it's concern. She smiles at him, hoisting her camera bag.

"I'll be fine," she says. Which is not what she believes.

■

When Rennie floated up through the anesthetic she did not feel anything at first. She opened her eyes and saw light green, then closed them again. She did not want to look down, see how much of herself was missing. She lay with her eyes closed, realizing that she was awake and would rather not be. She also realized, though she had not admitted it before, that she had expected to die during the operation. She'd heard stories about people going into shock or being allergic to the anesthetic. It was not out of the question.

Her left arm was numb. She tried to move it and couldn't. Instead she moved her right hand, and not until then did she understand that someone was holding it. She turned her head, forced her eyes to open, and saw, a long distance away, as if she were

34

looking through the wrong end of a telescope, the image of a man, a head surrounded by darkness, glassy and clear. Daniel.

It's all right, he said. It was malignant but I think we got it all.

He was telling her that he had saved her life, for the time being anyway, and now he was dragging her back into it, this life that he had saved. By the hand. *Malignant*, Rennie thought.

Now what, she said. Her mouth felt thick and swollen. She looked at his arm, which was bare from the elbow down and was lying beside hers on the white sheet; hair licked along the skin like dark flames. His fingers were around her wrist. She did not see hands but an odd growth, like a plant or something with tentacles, detachable. The hand moved: He was patting her.

Now you go to sleep, he said. I'll be back.

Rennie looked again and his hand attached itself to his arm, which was part of him. He wasn't very far away. She fell in love with him because he was the first thing she saw after her life had been saved. This was the only explanation she could think of. She wished, later, when she was no longer feeling dizzy but was sitting up, trying to ignore the little sucking tubes that were coming out of her and the constant ache, that it had been a potted begonia or a stuffed rabbit, some safe bedside object. Jake sent her roses but by then it was too late.

I imprinted on him, she thought; like a duckling, like a baby chick. She knew about imprinting; once, when she was hard up for cash, she'd done a profile for *Owl Magazine* of a man who believed geese should be used as a safe and loyal substitute for watchdogs. It was best to be there yourself when the goslings came out of the eggs, he said. Then they'd follow you to the ends of the earth. Rennie had smirked because the man seemed to think that being followed to the ends of the earth by a flock of adoring geese was both desirable and romantic, but she'd written it all down in his own words.

Now she was behaving like a goose, and the whole thing put her in a foul temper. It was inappropriate to have fallen in love with Daniel, who had no distinguishing features that Rennie could see. She hardly even knew what he looked like, since, during the examinations before the operation, she hadn't bothered to look at him. One did not look at doctors; doctors were functionaries, they were what your mother once hoped you would marry, they were

35

fifties, they were passé. It wasn't only inappropriate, it was ridiculous. It was expected. Falling in love with your doctor was something middle-aged married women did, women in the soaps, women in nurse novels and in sex-and-scalpel epics with titles like *Surgery* and nurses with big tits and doctors who looked like Dr. Kildare on the covers. It was the sort of thing *Toronto Life* did stories about, soft-core gossip masquerading as hard-nosed research and exposé. Rennie could not stand being guilty of such a banality.

But there she was, waiting for Daniel to appear (out of nowhere, she never knew when he would be coming, when she was having a sponge bath or struggling to the toilet, leaning on the large wattled nurse), hooked like a junkie on those pats of the hand and Rotarian words of cheer and collective first-person plurals ("We're coming along nicely"), and in a feeble rage because of it. *Shit.* He wasn't even that handsome, now that she had a good look: his proportions were wrong, he was too tall for his shoulders, his hair was too short, his arms were too long, he gangled. She sniffled with anger into the wad of Kleenex the nurse held out to her.

A good cry will do you good, said the nurse. But you're lucky, they say there's none anywhere else, some of them are full of it, they cut it out and it just pops up somewhere else. Rennie thought of toasters.

Daniel brought her a pamphlet called *Mastectomy: Answers to Down-to-Earth Questions.* Down to earth. Who wrote these things? Nobody in her position would want to think very hard about *down* or *earth. Are there any restrictions on sexual activity?* she read. The pamphlet suggested that she ask her doctor. She considered doing this.

But she didn't. Instead she asked him, How much of me did you cut off? Because she was in love with him and he hadn't noticed, her tone of voice was not all it should have been. But he didn't seem to mind.

About a quarter, he said gently.

You make it sound like a pie, said Rennie.

Daniel smiled, indulging her, waiting her out.

I guess I should be relieved, said Rennie. That you didn't hack off the whole thing.

We don't do that any more unless there's massive involvement, said Daniel.

Massive involvement, said Rennie. It's never been my thing.

He follows up, said the nurse. A lot of them, they just do their number and that's that. He likes to know how things work out, in their life and all. He takes a personal interest. He says a lot of it has to do with their attitude, you know?

Jake brought champagne and pâté and kissed her on the mouth. He sat beside her bed and tried not to look at her wrapped chest and the tubes. He spread pâté on crackers, which he'd also brought, and fed them to her. He wanted to be thanked.

You're a godsend, she said. The food here is unbelievable. Green Jello-O salad and a choice of peas or peas. She was happy to see him but she was distracted. She didn't want Daniel to walk in, trailing interns, while Jake was still there.

Jake was restless. He was healthy and healthy people are embarrassed by sickness, she could remember that. She was convinced also that she smelled peculiar, that there was a faint odor of decay seeping through the binding: like an off cheese. She wanted him to go quickly and he wanted to go.

We'll get back to normal, she told herself, though she could not remember any longer what *normal* had been like. She asked the nurse to adjust her bed so she could lie back.

That's a fine young man, the nurse said. Jake was a fine young man. He was all in place, a good dancer who hardly ever bothered to dance.

■

Rennie climbs down the steps of the plane and the heat slips over her face like thick brown velvet. The terminal is a low shed with a single turret. It looks gray under the weak lights of the runway, but as Rennie walks toward it she sees that it's really yellow. Over the doorway there's a bronze plaque thanking the Canadian government for donating it. It's odd to see the Canadian government being thanked for anything.

The immigration officer is wearing a dark-green uniform, like a soldier's, and there are two actual soldiers leaning against the wall beside him, in crisp blue shirts with short sleeves. Rennie assumes they're soldiers, since they have shoulder holsters with what look like real guns in them. They're young, with skinny innocent bodies. One of them is flicking his swagger stick against his pantleg, the other has a small radio which he's holding against his ear.

Rennie realizes she's still clutching the aspirin in her left hand. She wonders what to do with it; somehow she can't just throw it away. She opens her purse to put it with her other aspirins, and the soldier with the swagger stick saunters toward her.

Rennie feels a chill sweep down her. She's about to be singled out: Perhaps he thinks the bottle she's holding contains some kind of illegal drug.

"It's aspirin," she says, but all he wants is to sell her a ticket to the St. Antoine Police Benefit Dance, Semi-formal, Proceeds for Sports Funds. So they're only police, not soldiers. Rennie makes this out by reading the ticket, since she hasn't understood a word he's said.

"I don't have the right kind of money," she says.

"We take anything you got," he says, grinning at her, and this time she understands him. She gives him two dollars, then adds a third; possibly it's the price of admission. He thanks her and strolls back to the other one, and they laugh together. They haven't bothered with anyone else in the line.

In front of Rennie there's a tiny woman, not five feet tall. She's wearing a fake-fur shortie coat and a black wool jockey cap tilted at a rakish angle. She turns around now and looks up at Rennie.

"That a bad man," she says. "Don't you have nothin' to do with that one." She holds out to Rennie a large plastic bag full of cheese puffs. From under the brim of her jockey cap her eyes peer up out of her dark wrinkled face, she must be at least seventy but it's hard to tell. The eyes are bright, candid, sly, the eyes of a wary child.

"This my grandson," she says. She opens the coat to reveal an orange T-shirt. PRINCE OF PEACE, it says in large red letters.

Rennie has never seen a religious maniac up close before. When she was at university an economics student was rumored to have run through his dormitory one night, claiming to have given birth to the Virgin Mary, but that was put down to pre-exam tension.

38

Rennie smiles, as naturally as possible. If this woman thinks she's St. Anne or whoever, it would be best not to upset her, not in the immigration line at any rate. Rennie accepts some cheese puffs.

"It my grandson, all right," says the woman. She knows she's been doubted.

Then it's her turn, and Rennie hears her say to the immigration officer in a shrill, jocular voice, "You give me trouble, my grandson blaze your arse good for you." This seems to have the desired effect, for the man stamps her passport immediately and she goes through.

When he comes to Rennie he feels he has to be extra severe. He flips through her passport, frowning over the visas. He wears thick bifocals, and he pushes them further down on his nose and holds the passport away from him, as if it smells funny.

"Renata Wilford? That you?"

"Yes," Rennie says.

"It don't look like you."

"It's a bad picture," Rennie says. She knows she's lost weight.

"Let her in, man," one of the policemen calls, but the immigration clerk ignores him. He scowls at her, then at the picture. "What the purpose of your visit?"

"Pardon?" Rennie says. She has to strain to understand the accent. She looks around for Dr. Minnow, but he's nowhere in sight.

"What you doin' here?" He glares at her, his eyes enlarged by the lenses.

"I'm a writer," Rennie says. "A journalist. I write for magazines. I'm doing a travel piece."

The man glances over at the two policemen. "What you goin' to write about here?" he says.

Rennie smiles. "Oh, the usual," she says. "You know, restaurants, sight-seeing, that sort of thing."

The man snorts. "Sight-seein'," he says. "No pretty lights here." He stamps her passport and motions her through.

"Write it good," he says to her as she goes past. Rennie thinks he's teasing, as such a man at Heathrow or Toronto or New York would be. They would say, "Write it good, honey." Or *love*, or *sweetheart*. They would grin. But when she turns to give the required smile he's staring straight ahead, through the plateglass window to the tarmac, where the plane has already turned in the darkness and is taxiing again for take-off between the rows of white and blue lights.

Rennie changes some money, then waits while a tired uniformed woman pokes through her purse and her bags. Rennie says she has nothing to declare. The woman scrawls a chalk mark on each of her bags, and Rennie walks through a doorway into the main room. The first thing she sees is a large sign that says, THE BIONIC COCK: IT GIVES YOU SPURS. There's a picture of a rooster; it turns out to be an advertisement for rum.

There's a crowd outside the door, taxi drivers, and Rennie goes with the first one who touches her arm. Ordinarily she would talk with him, find things out: beaches, restaurants, shops. But it's too hot. She sinks into the marshmallow-soft upholstery of the car, some derelict from the fifties, while the driver goes far too fast through the winding narrow streets, honking at every bend. The car is on the wrong side of the road, and it takes Rennie a moment to remember that this is in fact the British side.

They wind up a hillside, past houses she can make out only dimly. The headlights shine on massive bushes overhanging the road, with flamboyant red and pink flowers dangling from them like Kleenex flowers at a high-school dance. Then they're in the lighted part of town. There are crowds of people on the street-corners and in front of the shops but they aren't walking, they're just standing or sitting on steps or chairs, as if they're inside a room. Music flows through the open doorways.

Some of the men wear knitted wool caps, like tea cozys, and Rennie wonders how they can stand it in the heat. Their heads turn as the taxi goes by, and some wave and shout, at the driver rather than Rennie. She's beginning to feel very white. Their blacks aren't the same as our blacks, she reminds herself; then sees that what she means by *our blacks* are the hostile ones in the States, whereas *our blacks* ought to mean this kind. They seem friendly enough.

Nevertheless Rennie finds their aimlessness disturbing, as she would at home. It's too much like teenagers in shopping plazas, it's too much like a mob. She discovers that she's truly no longer *at home.* She is away, she is *out*, which is what she wanted. The difference between this and home isn't so much that she knows nobody as that nobody knows her. In a way she's invisible. In a way she's safe.

■

When Jake moved out, naturally there was a vacuum. Something had to come in to fill it. Maybe the man with the rope hadn't so much broken into her apartment as been sucked in, by the force of gravity. Which was one way of looking at it, thought Rennie.

'Once she would have made this man into a good story; she would have told it at lunch, with the strawberry flan. She wasn't sure what stopped her, from telling anyone at all. Perhaps it was that the story had no end, it was open-ended; or perhaps it was too impersonal, she had no picture of the man's face. When she was outside, walking along the street, she looked at the men who passed her in a new way: It could be any one of them, it could be anyone. Also she felt implicated, even though she had done nothing and nothing had been done to her. She had been seen, too intimately, her face blurred and distorted, damaged, owned in some way she couldn't define. It wasn't something she could talk about at lunch. Anyway, she didn't want to become known as a man-hater, which was what happened when you told stories like that.

The first thing she did after the policemen had gone was to get the lock fixed. Then she had safety catches put on the windows. Still, she couldn't shake the feeling that she was being watched, even when she was in a room by herself, with the curtains closed. She had the sense that someone had been in her apartment while she was out, not disarranging anything, but just looking into her cupboards, her refrigerator, studying her. The rooms smelled different after she'd been out. She began to see herself from the outside, as if she was a moving target in someone else's binoculars. She could even hear the silent commentary: Now she's opening the bean sprouts, now she's cooking an omelette, now she's eating it, now she's washing off the plate. Now she's sitting down in the living room, nothing much going on. Now she's getting up, she's going into the bedroom, she's taking off her shoes, she's turning out the light. Next comes the good part.

41

She began to have nightmares, she woke up sweating. Once she thought there was someone in the bed with her, she could feel an arm, a leg.

Rennie decided she was being silly and possibly neurotic as well. She didn't want to turn into the sort of woman who was afraid of men. It's your own fear of death, she told herself. That's what any armchair shrink would tell you. You think you're dying, even though you've been saved. You should be grateful, you should be serene and profound, but instead you're projecting onto some pathetic weirdo who's never going to bother you again. That scratching you heard at the window last night wasn't coming from the outside at all.

Which was all very well, but the man existed; he was an accident that had almost happened to her; he was an ambassador, from some place she didn't want to know any more about. The piece of rope, which was evidence, which the police had taken away with them, was also a message; it was someone's twisted idea of love. Every time she went into her bedroom she could see it, coiled on the bed, even though it was no longer there.

In itself it was neutral, and useful too, you could use it for all kinds of things. She wondered whether he'd intended to strangle her with it or just tie her up. He hadn't wanted to be drunk, there had been beer and half a bottle of wine in the refrigerator, she was sure he'd looked, and he'd chosen Ovaltine. He'd wanted to know what he was doing. When he got as far as the scar perhaps he would have stopped, apologized, untied her, gone home, to the wife and children Rennie was certain he had. Or perhaps he knew, perhaps that's what turned him on. *Mr. X, in the bedroom, with a rope.*

And when you pulled on the rope, which after all reached down into darkness, what could come up? What was at the end, *the end?* A hand, then an arm, a shoulder, and finally a face. At the end of the rope there was someone. Everyone had a face, there was no such thing as a faceless stranger.

■

Rennie is late for dinner. She has to wait at the front desk while they set a table for her in the dining room. Around the corner, where she can't see, a tray of silverware hits the floor and there's an argument in low voices. After fifteen minutes a waitress comes out and says sternly that Rennie can go in now, as if it's a trial rather than a meal.

As Rennie walks toward the dining room, a woman with a tan the color of clear tea walks out of it. She has blond hair braided and wound around her head, and she's wearing a sleeveless magenta dress with orange flowers on it. Rennie feels bleached.

The woman smiles at her with fluorescent teeth, looking at her with round blue china-doll eyes. "Hi there," she says. Her friendly, glassy stare reminds Rennie of the greeting perfected by hostesses in the restaurants of Holiday Inns. Rennie waits for her to say, "Have a good day." The smile lasts a little too long, and Rennie gropes, wondering if she knows this woman. She decides with relief that she doesn't, and smiles back.

The tables are covered with starched white tablecloths and the wine glasses have linen napkins tucked into them, pleated into fans. Propped against the flower vase, one hibiscus per table, is a small typewritten card which isn't exactly a menu, since there's no choice. The food is brought by three waitresses, in light-blue full-skirted dresses and white aprons and mob caps. They are totally silent and do not smile; perhaps they've been called away from their own dinners.

Rennie begins to compose, from habit and to pass the time, though she doesn't think the Sunset Inn will find its way into her piece:

The décor is nondescript, resembling nothing so much as an English provincial hotel, with flowered wallpaper and a few prints of hunting and shooting. The ceiling fans add a pleasant touch. We began with the local bread, and butter of perhaps a questionable freshness. Then came (she consulted the menu) a pumpkin soup, which was not the bland version most North Americans may be used to. My companion. . . .

But there is no companion. It's necessary to have a companion for these excursions, always, if only a paper one. The readers would find the suggestion that you would go to a restaurant and sit there all by yourself, just eating, far too depressing. They want gaiety and the possibility of romance and a mention of the wine list.

Rennie gives up anyway when the roast beef arrives, leathery and khaki and covered with a gravy that tastes like mix. It's garnished with a cube of yam and something light green that has been boiled too long. This is the kind of food you eat only when very hungry.

Rennie is reminded of the put-on piece she did, months ago, on fast-food outlets. It was for *Pandora's* "Swinging Toronto" section. She'd once done a piece for them on how to pick men up in laundromats, unobtrusively and safely, with addresses of the good laundromats. *Check their socks. If they ask to borrow your soap flakes, forget it.* The food franchise piece was called "Sawdust Yummies" and the subtitle (not hers) read, "You better take a good thou, 'cause the bread and the wine are nowhere."

She'd covered every McDonald's and Kentucky Fried Chicken spot in the downtown core for it, dutifully taking one bite of everything. *My companion had the Egg McMuffin, which he found a trifle runny. My buns were chilly.*

Rennie picks at the alien vegetables on her plate, gazing around the room. There's only one other diner, a man, who's sitting on the far side of the room reading a paper. In front of him is a dish of what looks like whipped lime Jell-O. If this were a laundromat, would she pick him up? He turns the page of his newspaper and smiles at her, a half-smile of complicity, and Rennie looks down at her plate. She likes to stare but she doesn't like to be caught doing it.

Eye contact, that was one hint. She's not surprised when he folds the paper, gets up, and heads toward her table.

"It's kind of dumb, sitting across the room from each other like that," he says. "I think this place is empty except for us. Mind if I join you?"

Rennie says no. She has no intention of picking this man up. She never actually picked men up in laundromats, she just went through the preliminaries and then explained that she was doing research. That's what she can always say if necessary. Meanwhile, there's no reason not to be polite.

He goes to the kitchen door and asks for another cup of coffee, and one of the waitresses brings it. She also brings a dish of the green substance for Rennie, and then, instead of returning to the kitchen, sits down at the man's vacated place and finishes off his

44

dessert, staring balefully at him as she does so. The man has his back to her and can't see.

"I wouldn't eat that if I were you," he says.

Rennie laughs and looks at him more carefully. Before the operation, there was a game she used to play with Jocasta, on the street and in restaurants. Pick a man, any man, and find the distinguishing features. The eyebrows? The nose? The body? If this man were yours, how would you do him over? A brush cut, a wet suit? It was a rude game and Rennie knew it. Jocasta, for some reason, didn't. Listen, she'd say. You'd be doing them a favor.

Rennie thinks this man would resist being done over. For one thing, he's too old: he's past the Silly Putty stage. Rennie decides he must be at least forty. His tan is leathery, there are permanent white creases around his eyes. He has a light moustache and post-hippie-length hair, bottom of the earlobes in front, top of the collar in back; it's a little ragged, as if he does it himself with kitchen scissors. He's wearing shorts and a yellow T-shirt without anything written on it. Rennie approves of this. She liked T-shirts with mottoes on them when they first came out, but now she thinks they're jejune.

Rennie introduces herself and mentions that she's a journalist. She always likes to get that in first, before people mistake her for a secretary. The man says his name is Paul and he's from Iowa. "Originally," he says, implying travel. He's not staying at the hotel, he says, just eating there. It's one of the better places.

"If this is better, what's worse?" says Rennie, and they both laugh.

Rennie asks him where home is. It's all right to ask such questions, since Rennie has already decided this does not have the flavor of a pickup. File it under *attempt at human contact*. He just wants someone to talk to, he's killing time. Which is fine, that's all she's doing herself. If there's anything she doesn't need in her life right now, it's another one of what Jocasta would call *those*. Nevertheless, she's conscious of a desire to stick her head down under the tablecloth, to see what his knees look like.

"Home?" says Paul. "You mean, where the heart is?"

"Was that a personal question?" says Rennie. She starts to eat the dessert, which appears to be made of sweetened chalk.

45

Paul grins. "Most of the time I live on a boat," he says. "Over at Ste. Agathe, the harbor's better there. I'm just here for a couple of days, on business."

Rennie feels she's expected to ask what sort of business, so she doesn't. She's decided he will be boring. She's met people with boats before and all they ever talk about is boats. Boats make her seasick. "What sort of boat?" she says.

"Quite a fast one. Actually I have four of them," he says, watching her. Now she's supposed to be impressed.

"I guess that means you're filthy rich," she says.

This time he laughs. "I charter them out," he says. "They're all out now. It's a pain in the ass in some ways. I don't like tourists. They're always complaining about the food, and they throw up too much."

Rennie, who is a tourist, lets this pass. "How did you get four?" she says.

"You can pick them up cheap around here," he says, "from the dead or the disgusted, retired stockbrokers who have heart attacks or decide it's too much trouble scraping off the barnacles. There's a bit of owner piracy, too."

Rennie doesn't want to give him the satisfaction of her ignorance, but he smiles at her with his tan folding into pleats around his eyes, he wants her to ask, so she relents and asks.

"People stealing their own boats," he says. "They collect the insurance. Then they sell the boat."

"But you would never do a thing like that," says Rennie. She's paying more attention. No gold earring, no wooden leg, no hooks on the ends of the arms, no parrot. Still, there's something. She looks at his hands, square-fingered and practical, carpenter's hands, on the tablecloth, not doing anything.

"No," he says. "I would never do a thing like that."

He smiles a little, his eyes are light blue, and she recognizes something about him, a deliberate neutrality. He's doing what she does, he's holding back, and now she's really curious.

"Do you have a job?" she says.

"If you have four boats you don't exactly need a job, around here," he says. "I make enough on the charters. I used to have one, I was an agronomist with the U.S. Department of Agriculture. They sent me as an adviser. I was supposed to be telling them what else they can grow here besides bananas. I was pushing red kidney beans. The catch is, nobody really wants them to grow anything here besides bananas. But they wouldn't send me anywhere else, so I kind of retired."

"Where were you before that?" says Rennie.

"Here and there," he says. "A lot of places. I was in Vietnam, before the war, the official one that is. After that I was in Cambodia." He says this still smiling, but looking at her straight on, a little belligerently, as if he's expecting her to react, with horror or at least disgust.

"What were you doing there?" says Rennie pleasantly, putting down her spoon.

"Advising," he says. "I was always advising. It's not the same as having people do what you say."

"What about?" says Rennie; she feels now as if they're on the radio.

There's a small pause, another crinkled smile. "Rice," he says, watching her closely.

She's being asked for something, but she's not sure what it is. Not admiration, not absolution. Maybe she's not being asked for anything at all, which is just as well, since she doesn't have a whole lot of handouts left. "That must have been interesting," she says. She hasn't done profiles for nothing, she isn't stupid, she knows how to add, she knows there's an X factor. Ten years ago she would have felt entitled to moral outrage, but it's no skin off her nose. People get trapped in things that are beyond their control, she ought to know that by now.

He relaxes, leans back in his chair. She's passed the test, whatever it was. "I'll tell you about it sometime," he says, assuming the future; which is more than she can do.

■

Rennie's room at the Sunset Inn is papered with a small floral print, pink and blue; there are several pale-orange watermarks near the ceiling, which is fifteen feet high. At the end of the bed, which is single and narrow and covered with a white chenille spread, hangs a picture of a green melon cut open to reveal the seeds. Over the bed itself is a knotted mosquito net, not quite as white as the bedspread. On the night table beside the bed are a Bible, a mos-

47

quito coil in a saucer, a box of matches, Three Star, made in Sweden, and a lamp with a pleated paper shade. The lamp is a mermaid with her arms over her head, holding up the bulb. Her breasts aren't bare, she's wearing a harem jacket open at the front, its edges grazing the nipples. In the drawer of the night table are two more mosquito coils in a box labeled *"Fish Mosquito Destroyer, Blood Protection Co. Ltd."*

On the pale-green bureau there's a Thermos jug of water, a glass, and a hand-printed card warning visitors not to drink the tap water. Rennie opens the drawers. In the center one is a lime-green blanket, in the bottom one a safety pin. Rennie feels momentarily that she may be spending the rest of her life in rooms like this. Not her own.

She lights the mosquito coil, turns on the mermaid lamp, and puts her traveling alarm clock on top of the Bible. She unpacks her cotton nightgown and the zipper bag in which she keeps her toothbrush and the other pieces of cleaning and sterilizing equipment people use on their bodies. She's ceased to take such things for granted; "Prevention of Decay" is no longer just a slogan. She closes the Venetian blind on the narrow window, turns off the overhead light, and undresses. The mirror over the bureau is small, so she isn't reflected anywhere.

She takes a shower, in water that refuses to become more than lukewarm. When she comes out of the tiny bathroom, there's a green lizard sticking to the wall beside the window.

She turns down the chenille spread and the sheet and looks carefully in the bed and under the pillow, checking for wildlife. She untwists the mosquito net and tucks it around the bed. Then she crawls into the white tent, turns off the light, and moves to the center of the bed so that no part of her body is touching the net. She can see the oblong of the window, gray against the darkness, and the glowing end of the mosquito coil. The air is warm and damp, warmer and damper on her skin now than before she took the shower, and the bed smells faintly of mildew.

There are sounds from outside the window, a high cricket sound and a repeated note like a bell or a waterglass being struck, some kind of insect or frog perhaps, and beyond that the insistent syncopated music. Several minutes after she turns out the light a car backfires, or maybe it's firecrackers, and a woman screams with laughter; but that stops and the music keeps going.

Despite the heat Rennie lies with her arms folded, left hand on her right breast, right hand on the ridge of skin that slants across the side of her breast up toward her armpit. This is how she always sleeps now.

She runs the fingers of her left hand over the skin of her breast, the good one, the one she hopes is good, as she does every night. From the surface you can feel nothing, but she no longer trusts surfaces. She'd brushed her teeth and cleaned them with dental floss, prevention of decay, and rinsed out her mouth with water from the Thermos, which smelled like melted ice cubes, like the inside of a refrigerator, like cloth in a trunk. Nevertheless she can still taste the airplane sandwich, slightly rancid butter and roast beef, rotting meat.

She sleeps and wakes fitfully, listening to the music and, occasionally, a car going past in what always sounds like the wrong gear. She feels clogged and furry; she's convinced she's been snoring, though it hardly matters. At last she sinks into a heavy, damp sleep.

She wakes up suddenly. She can feel something like moist cloth, webbing, pressing down over her eyes and mouth. Her face is against the net. Through it she can see the figures on her digital clock, the dot pulsing like a tiny heart. It's six in the morning. She was dreaming that someone was climbing in through the window.

She remembers where she is and hopes she hasn't bothered anyone in the hotel by screaming. She's too warm, she's sweating, and despite the mosquito net she has several bites, from where she's rolled against the net. The muscles of her left shoulder are aching again.

There's a rooster crowing nearby and beyond that a dog, dogs. The room is growing light. Close to her ear, on the other side of the wall, there are sounds it takes her a moment to recognize, unfamiliar, archaic, the rhythmic creak of a bed and a woman's voice, wordless and mindless. Before she places it she hears it as agony. Once this intrusion would merely have irritated her, or, if she was with someone, amused or even excited her. Now it's painful to her, mournful, something lost, a voice from the past, severed from her and going on beside her in another room. Get it over, she thinks through the wall.

Oh please.

■

· II ·

ONE OF THE FIRST THINGS I can remember, says Rennie, is standing in my grandmother's bedroom. The light is coming in through the window, weak yellowish winter light, everything is very clean, and I'm cold. I know I've done something wrong, but I can't remember what. I'm crying, I'm holding my grandmother around both legs, but I didn't think of them as legs, I thought of her as one solid piece from the neck down to the bottom of her skirt. I feel as if I'm holding on to the edge of something, safety, if I let go I'll fall, I want forgiveness, but she's prying my hands away finger by finger. She's smiling; she was proud of the fact that she never lost her temper.

I know I will be shut in the cellar by myself. I'm afraid of that, I know what's down there, a single light bulb which at least they leave on, a cement floor which is always cold, cobwebs, the winter coats hanging on hooks beside the wooden stairs, the furnace. It's the only place in the house that isn't clean. When I was shut in the cellar I always sat on the top stair. Sometimes there were things down there, I could hear them moving around, small things that might get on you and run up your legs. I'm crying because I'm afraid, I can't stop, and even if I hadn't done anything wrong I'd still be put down there, for making a noise, for crying.

Laugh and the world laughs with you, said my grandmother. *Cry and you cry alone.* For a long time I hated the smell of damp mittens.

I grew up surrounded by old people: my grandfather and my grandmother, and my great-aunts and great-uncles, who came to visit after church. I thought of my mother as old too. She wasn't, but being around them all the time made her seem old. On the street she walked slowly so they could keep up with her, she raised her voice the way they did, she was anxious about details. She wore clothes like theirs too, dark dresses with high collars and small innocuous patterns, dots or sprigs of flowers.

As a child I learned three things well: how to be quiet, what not to say, and how to look at things without touching them. When I think of that house I think of objects and silences. The silences were almost visible; I pictured them as gray, hanging in the air like smoke. I learned to listen for what wasn't being said, because it was usually more important than what was. My grandmother was the best at silences. According to her, it was bad manners to ask direct questions.

The objects in the house were another form of silence. Clocks, vases, end tables, cabinets, figurines, cruet sets, cranberry glasses, china plates. They were considered important because they had once belonged to someone else. They were both overpowering and frail: overpowering because threatening. What they threatened you with was their frailty; they were always on the verge of breaking. These objects had to be cleaned and polished once a week, by my grandmother when she was still well enough and afterward by my mother. It was understood that you could never sell these objects or give them away. The only way you could ever get rid of them was to will them to someone else and then die.

The objects weren't beautiful, most of them. They weren't supposed to be. They were only supposed to be of the right kind: The standard aimed at was not beauty but decency. That was the word, too, among my mother and my aunts, when they came to visit. "Are you decent?" they would call gaily to one another before opening bedroom or bathroom doors. Decency was having your clothes on, in every way possible.

If you were a girl it was a lot safer to be decent than to be beautiful. If you were a boy, the question didn't arise; the choice was whether or not you were a fool. Clothes could be decent or indecent. Mine were always decent, and they smelled decent too, a wool smell, mothballs and a hint of furniture polish. Other girls, from families considered shoddy and loose, wore questionable clothes and smelled like violets. The opposite of decent wasn't beautiful, but flashy or cheap. Flashy, cheap people drank and smoked, and who knew what else? Everyone knew. In Griswold, everyone knew everything, sooner or later.

So you had your choice, you could decide whether people would respect you or not. It was harder if your family wasn't respectable but it could be done. If your family was respectable, though, you could choose not to disgrace it. The best way to keep from disgracing it was to do nothing unusual.

The respectability of my family came from my grandfather, who had once been the doctor. Not a doctor, the doctor: They had territories then, like tomcats. In the stories my grandmother told me about him, he drove a cutter and team through blizzards to tear babies out through holes he cut in women's stomachs and then sewed up again, he amputated a man's leg with an ordinary saw, knocking the man out with his fist because no one could hold him down and there wasn't enough whiskey, he risked his life by walking into a farmhouse where a man had gone crazy and was holding a shotgun on him the whole time, he'd blown the head off one of his children and was threatening to blow the heads off the other ones too. My grandmother blamed the wife, who had run away months before. My grandfather saved the lives of the remaining children, who were then put in an orphanage. No one wanted to adopt children who had such a crazy father and mother: Everyone knew such things ran in the blood. The man was sent to what they called the loony bin. When they were being formal they called it an institution.

My grandmother worshiped my grandfather, or so everyone said. When I was little I thought of him as a hero, and I guess he was, he was about the closest you could get in Griswold unless you'd been in the war. I wanted to be like him, but after a few years at school I forgot about that. Men were doctors, women were nurses; men were heroes, and what were women? Women rolled the bandages and that was about all anyone ever said about that.

The stories my mother and aunts told about my grandfather were different, though they never told these stories when my grandmother was there. They were mostly about his violent temper. When they were girls, whenever they skirted what he felt to be the edges of decency, he would threaten to horsewhip them, though he never did. He thought he was lenient because he didn't make his children sit on a bench all Sunday as his own father had. I found it very difficult to connect these stories, or my grandmother's either, with the frail old man who could not be disturbed during his afternoon nap and who had to be protected like the clocks and figurines. My mother and my grandmother tended him the same way they tended me, efficiently and with a lot of attention to dirt; only more cheerfully. Perhaps they really were cheerful. Perhaps it made them cheerful to have him under their control at last. They cried a lot at his funeral.

My grandmother had been amazing for a woman of her age; everyone told me that. But after my grandfather's death she began to deteriorate. That's how my mother would put it when her sisters would come to visit. They were both married, which was how they'd got away from Griswold. I was in high school by then so I didn't spend as much time hanging around the kitchen as I used to, but one day I walked in on them and all three of them were laughing, stifled breathless laughs, as if they were in a church or at a funeral: They knew they were being sacrilegious and they didn't want my grandmother to hear them. They hardly saw me, they were so intent on their laughter.

She wouldn't give me a key to the house, my mother said. Thought I'd lose it. This started them off again. Last week she finally let me have one, and I dropped it down the hot air register. They patted their eyes, exhausted as if they'd been running.

Foolishness, said my aunt from Winnipeg. This was my grandmother's word for anything she didn't approve of. I'd never seen my mother laugh like that before.

Don't mind us, my aunt said to me.

You laugh or you cry, said my other aunt.

You laugh or you go bats, said my mother, injecting a little guilt, as she always did. This sobered them up. They knew that her life, her absence of a life, was permitting them their own.

After that my grandmother began to lose her sense of balance. She would climb up on chairs and stools to get things down, things that were too heavy for her, and then she would fall. She usually did this when my mother was out, and my mother would return to find her sprawled on the floor, surrounded by broken china.

Then her memory began to go. She would wander around the house at night, opening and shutting doors, trying to find her way back to her room. Sometimes she wouldn't remember who she was or who we were. Once she frightened me badly by coming into the kitchen, in broad daylight, as I was making myself a peanut-butter sandwich after school. My hands, she said. I've left them somewhere and now I can't find them. She was holding her hands in the air, helplessly, as if she couldn't move them.

They're right there, I said. On the ends of your arms.

No, no, she said impatiently. Not those, those are no good any more. My other hands, the ones I had before, the ones I touch things with.

My aunts kept watch on her through the kitchen window while she wandered around in the yard, prowling through the frost-bitten ruins of the garden which my mother didn't have the time to keep up any more. Once it had been filled with flowers, zinnias and scarlet runner beans on poles where the hummingbirds would come. My grandmother once told me heaven would be like that: If you were good enough you would get everlasting life and go to a place where there were always flowers. I think she really believed it. My mother and my aunts didn't believe it, though my mother went to church and when my aunts visited they all sang hymns in the kitchen after supper when they were doing the dishes.

She seems to think it's still there, said my aunt from Winnipeg. Look. She'll freeze to death out there.

Put her in a home, said my other aunt, looking at my mother's caved face, the mauve half-moons under her eyes.

I can't, my mother would say. On some days she's perfectly all right. It would be like killing her.

If I ever get like that, take me out to a field and shoot me, said my other aunt.

All I could think of at that time was how to get away from Griswold. I didn't want to be trapped, like my mother. Although I admired her—everyone was always telling me how admirable she was, she was practically a saint—I didn't want to be like her in any way. I didn't want to have a family or be anyone's mother, ever; I had none of those ambitions. I didn't want to own any objects or inherit any. I didn't want to cope. I didn't want to deteriorate. I used to pray that I wouldn't live long enough to get like my grandmother, and now I guess I won't.

■

Rennie wakes up finally at eight. She lies in bed and listens to the music, which seems to be coming from downstairs now, and decides she feels much better. After a while she gropes her way through the mosquito netting and gets out of bed. She leans on the windowsill, looking out at the sunlight, which is very bright but not yet ferocious. Down below is a cement courtyard, she seems to be at the back of the hotel, where a woman is washing sheets in a zinc tub.

She considers her wardrobe. There isn't a lot of choice, since she packed the minimum.

She remembers picking out the basic functional sunbreak mix 'n' match, wrinkle-free for the most part. That was only the day before yesterday. After she'd packed, she had gone through her cupboard and her bureau drawers, sorting, rearranging, folding, tucking the sleeves of her sweaters carefully behind their backs, as if someone would be staying in her apartment while she was away and she needed to leave things as tidy and manageable as possible. That was only the clothes. The food in the refrigerator she'd disregarded. Whoever it was wouldn't be eating.

Rennie puts on a plain white cotton dress. When the dress is on she looks at herself in the mirror. She still looks normal.

Today she has an appointment with the radiologist at the hospital. Daniel made it for her weeks ago, he wants more tests. A work-up, they call it. She didn't even cancel the appointment before taking off. She knows that later she will regret this lack of courtesy.

Right now she only feels she's escaped. She doesn't want the tests; she doesn't want the tests because she doesn't want the results. Daniel wouldn't have scheduled more tests unless he thought there was something wrong with her again, though he said it was routine. She's in remission, he says. *But we'll have to keep an eye on you, we always will. Remission* is the good word, *terminal* is the bad one. It makes Rennie think of bus stations: the end of the line.

She wonders whether she's already become one of those odd wanderers, the desperate ones, who cannot bear the thought of one more useless hospital ordeal, pain and deathly sickness, the cells bombarded, the skin gone antiseptic, the hair falling out. Will she go off on those weird quests too, extract of apricot pits, medication on the sun and moon, coffee enemas in Colorado, cocktails made from the juice of cabbages, hope in bottles, the laying on of hands by those who say they can see vibrations flowing out of their fingers in the form of a holy red light? Faith healing. When will she get to the point where she'll try anything? She doesn't want to be considered crazy but she also doesn't want to be considered dead.

Either I'm living or I'm dying, she said to Daniel. Please don't feel you can't tell me. Which is it?

Which does it feel like? said Daniel. He patted her hand. You're not dead yet. You're a lot more alive than many people.

This isn't good enough for Rennie. She wants something definite, the real truth, one way or the other. Then she will know what she should do next. It's this suspension, hanging in a void, this half-life she can't bear. She can't bear not knowing. She doesn't want to know.

She goes into the bathroom, intending to brush her teeth. In the sink there's a centipede, ten inches long at least, with far too many legs, blood-red, and two curved prongs at the back, or is it the front? It's wriggling up the side of the slippery porcelain sink, falling back again, wriggling up, falling back. It looks venomous.

Rennie is unprepared for this. She's not up to squashing it, what would she use anyway? And there's nothing to spray it with. The creature looks far too much like the kind of thing she's been having bad dreams about: The scar on her breast splits open like a diseased fruit and something like this crawls out. She goes into the other room and sits down on the bed, clasping her hands together to keep them from shaking. She waits five minutes, then wills herself back into the bathroom.

The thing is gone. She wonders whether it dropped from the ceiling in the first place, or came up through the drain, and now where has it gone? Over the side onto the floor, into some crack, or back down the drain again? She wishes she had some Drano and a heavy stick. She runs some water into the sink and looks around for the plug. There isn't one.

■

There's a lounge where you can have afternoon tea; it's furnished with dark green leatherette chairs that look as if they've been hoisted from an early-fifties hotel foyer in some place like Belleville. Rennie waits on one of the sticky chairs while they set a table for her in the dining room, grudgingly, since she's half an hour late. In addition to the chairs there's a glass-topped coffee table with wrought-iron legs on which there are copies of *Time* and *Newsweek* eight months old, and a mottled plant. Gold tinsel is looped around the tops of the windows, left over from Christmas; or perhaps they never take it down.

The tablecloths from the night before have been removed; underneath, the tables are gray Formica with a pattern of small red squares. Instead of the pleated linen fans there are yellow paper napkins. Rennie looks around for Paul but there's no sign of him. The hotel seems fuller, though. There's an older woman, white, thin-faced, by herself, who stares perkily around the dining room as if expecting to be charmed by everything, and an Indian family, the wife and grandmother in saris, the little girls in frilled sundresses. Luckily, Rennie is placed one table away from the older woman, who looks unpleasantly Canadian. She doesn't want to have a conversation about scenery or the weather. The three little girls parade the room, giggling, being chased and pinched playfully by the two waitresses, who smile for them in a way they do not smile for adults.

The older woman is joined by another like herself, plumper but with hair as tight. Listening to them, watching them consult their little books, Rennie discovers that they aren't Canadian but German: one of that army of earnest travelers that is everywhere now on the strength of the Deutschmark, even in Toronto, blue-eyed, alert, cataloguing the world. Why not? thinks Rennie. It's their turn.

The waitress comes and Rennie orders yogurt and fresh fruit.

"No fresh fruit," says the waitress.

"I'll take the yogurt anyway," says Rennie, who feels she's in need of some friendly bacteria.

"No yogurt," says the waitress.

"Why is it on the menu then?" says Rennie.

The waitress looks at her, straight-faced but with her eyes narrowing as if she's about to smile. "Used to be yogurt," she says.

"When will there be some again?" Rennie says, not sure why this should all be so complicated.

"They got Pioneer Industries for dairy now," the waitress says, as if reciting a lesson. "Government thing. Dairy don't make no yogurt. Yogurt need powder milk. Powder milk outlaw, you can't buy it. The yogurt place shut down now."

Rennie feels that there are connections missing here, but it's too early in the morning to have to deal with this. "What can I have then?" she says.

"What we got," says the waitress, very patiently.

This turns out to be orange juice made from instant powder of some sort, an almost-cooked egg, coffee from a jar with tinned milk, bread with margarine, and guava jelly, too sweet, dark orange, of the consistency of ear wax. Rennie wishes she could stop reviewing the food and just eat it. Anyway, she isn't at the Sunset Inn because of the food. She's here because of the price: this time the deal isn't all-expenses. She can do the other, flossier places for lunch or dinner.

The waitress comes and takes away her plate, the runny egg in its custard cup, the pieces of bread and jam lying beside it. Like a child, she's eaten the centers and left the crusts.

After breakfast comes the rest of the day, which will surely be too long, too hot and bright, to be filled with any activity that will require movement. She wants to go to sleep in the sun on a beach, but she's prudent, she doesn't want to come out like crispy chicken. She needs suntan lotion and a hat. After that she can start going through the motions: places of interest, things to do, tennis courts, notable hotels and restaurants, if any.

She knows you become exhausted in the tropics, you lose momentum, you become comatose and demoralized. The main thing is to keep going. She has to convince herself that if she doesn't manage to complete a well-researched and cheerfully written piece on the pleasures of St. Antoine the universe will be negatively affected.

Maybe she could fake the whole article, concoct a few ravishing little restaurants, some Old World charm in the New World, throw in some romantic history, tart the whole thing up with a few photos from the lesser-known corners of, say, St. Kitts. She pictures legions of businessmen descending on St. Antoine and

61

then, in outrage, on the editorial offices of *Visor*. It won't do, she'll have to come up with something, she's overdrawn at the bank. She can always talk about development potential.

What I need is a pith helmet, she thinks, and some bearers, or are they beaters, to carry me around in a hammock, and some of what those people in Somerset Maugham are always drinking. Pink gin?

■

Rennie does what she does because she's good at it, or that's what she says at parties. Also because she doesn't know how to do anything else, which she doesn't say. Once she had ambitions, which she now thinks of as illusions: She believed there was a right man, not several and not almost right, and she believed there was a real story, not several and not almost real. But that was 1970 and she was in college. It was easy to believe such things then. She decided to specialize in abuses: Honesty would be her policy. She did a piece for the *Varsity* on blockbusting as practiced by city developers and another on the lack of good day-care centers for single mothers, and she took the nasty and sometimes threatening letters she received as a tribute to her effectiveness.

Then she graduated and it was no longer 1970. Several editors pointed out to her that she could write what she liked, there was no law against it, but no one was under any obligation to pay her for doing it, either. One of them told her she was still a southern Ontario Baptist at heart. United Church, she said, but it hurt.

Instead of writing about the issues, she began interviewing the people who were involved in them. Those pieces were a lot easier to sell. The *in* wardrobe for the picket line, the importance of the denim overall, what the feminists eat for breakfast. The editors told her she was better at that anyway. Radical chic, they called it. One day she found herself short of petty cash and did a quick piece on the return of hats with veils. It wasn't even radical, it was only chic, and she tried not to feel too guilty about it.

Now that she no longer suffers from illusions, Rennie views her kind of honesty less as a virtue than a perversion, one from which she still suffers, true; but, like psoriasis and hemorrhoids, those other diseases typical of Griswold, it can be kept under control.

62

Why make such things public? Her closet honesty is—there's no doubt about it—a professional liability.

Other people have no such scruples. Everything is relative, everything is fashion. When a thing or a person has been too widely praised, you merely reverse the adjectives. No one considers this perverse, it's simply the nature of the business, and the business runs on high turnover. You write about something until people become tired of reading about it or you become tired of writing about it, and if you're good enough or lucky enough it's the same thing. Then you write about something else.

Rennie is still close enough to Griswold to find this attitude irritating at times. Last year she went into the office of the *Toronto Star* when some of the younger staff members were making up a list. It was close to New Year's and they were drinking gallon white wine out of Styrofoam coffee cups and killing themselves laughing. The list was a regular feature. Sometimes it was called "In and Out," sometimes "Plus and Minus"; such lists reassured people, including those who wrote them. It made them think they could make distinctions, choices that would somehow vindicate them. She had once composed such lists herself.

This time the list was called "Class: Who Has It, Who Doesn't." Ronald Reagan didn't have class, Pierre Trudeau did. Jogging didn't have class, contemporary dance did, but only if you did it in jogging pants, which did, for that but not for jogging, but not in stretchy plunge-back leotards, which didn't for that but did if you went swimming in them, instead of in bathing suits with built-in bra cups, which didn't. Marilyn's didn't, the Lickin' Chicken on Bloor, which didn't sell chicken, did.

"What else for the No list?" they asked her, giggling already, anticipating her answer. "What about Margaret Trudeau?"

"What about the word *class*?" she said, and they weren't sure whether that was funny or not.

Which is a problem she has. The other problem is the reputation she's getting for being too picky. She's aware of this, she listens to gossip; people are beginning to think she won't finish assignments. There's some truth to this: Increasingly there are things she can't seem to do. Maybe it isn't *can't*, maybe it's *won't*. What she wants is something legitimate to say. Which is childish.

63

Loss of nerve, she's decided. It started before the operation but it's getting worse. Maybe she's having a mid-life crisis, way too soon. Maybe it's Griswold squeezing her head: *If you can't say anything nice, don't say anything at all.* Not that its own maxims ever stopped Griswold.

Two months ago she was offered a good piece, a profile in *Pandora's* "Women of Achievement" series. A ballet dancer, a poet, a female executive from a cheese food company, a judge, a designer who specialized in shoes with glitter faces on the toes. Rennie wanted the designer but they gave her the judge, because the judge was supposed to be hard to do and Rennie was supposed to be good.

Rennie was not prepared for the panic that overtook her the first day out. The judge was nice enough, but what did you say? What does it feel like to be a judge? she asked. What does it feel like to be anything? said the judge, who was only a year older than Rennie. She smiled. It's a job. I love it.

The judge had two wonderful children and an adoring husband who didn't at all mind the time she spent being a judge, because he found his own job so satisfying and rewarding. They had a charming house, Rennie couldn't fault the house, filled with paintings by promising young artists; the judge decided to be photographed in front of one of them. With each question Rennie felt younger, dumber, and more helpless. The judge had it all together and Rennie was beginning to see this as a personal affront.

I can't do it, she told the editor at *Pandora*. The editor's name was Tippy; she was a contact of Rennie's. She opens her mouth and out comes this ticker tape.

She's a control freak, Tippy said. She's controlling the interview. You've got to turn it around, get an angle on her. Our readers want them to be human too, a few cracks in the armor, a little pain. Didn't she have to suffer on her way up?

I asked her that, said Rennie. She didn't.

What you have to do, said Tippy, is ask her if you can just sort of hang out with her. Follow her around all day. There's a real story in there somewhere. How she fell in love with her husband, did you ask that? Look in the medicine cabinet, go for the small details, it matters what they roll on under their arms, Arrid or Love, it makes a difference. Stick with them long enough and sooner or later they crack. You've got to dig. You're not after dirt, just the real story.

Rennie looked across the desk, which was messy, at Tippy, who was also messy. She was ten years older than Rennie, her skin was sallow and unhealthy, there were pouches under her eyes. She chain-smoked and drank too much coffee. She was wearing green, the wrong color for her. She was a good journalist, she'd won all sorts of awards before she became an editor, and now she was telling Rennie to peer into other people's medicine cabinets. A woman of achievement.

Rennie went home. She looked at what she'd already written about the judge and decided that it was, after all, the real story. She tore it up and started a new page.

A profile used to mean a picture of somebody's nose seen from the side, she wrote. *Now it means the picture of somebody's nose seen from the bottom.* Which was as far as she got.

■

Rennie takes her camera, on the off chance. She's not very good, she knows that, but she forced herself to learn because she knew it would increase her scope. If you do both the pictures and the text you can go almost anywhere, or so they say.

She picks up a mimeographed map of Queenstown and a tourist brochure from the registration desk. "St. Antoine and Ste. Agathe," the brochure says. "Discover Our Twin Islands in the Sun." On the front is a tanned white woman laughing on a beach, sheathed in one-piece aqua Spandex with a modesty panel across the front. A black man in a huge straw hat is sitting on the sand beside her, handing up a coconut with a couple of straws sticking out of it. Behind him is a machete propped against a tree. He's looking at her, she's looking at the camera.

"When was this printed?" Rennie asks.

"We get them from the Department of Tourism," says the woman behind the desk. "That's the only kind there is." She's British and seems to be the manager, or perhaps the owner. Rennie is always slightly cowed by women like this, women who can wear thick-soled khaki shoes and lime-green polyester jersey skirts without being aware of their ugliness. This woman's no doubt responsible for the lounge chairs and the scabby plant. Rennie envies people who are unaware of ugliness: It gives them an advantage, they can't be embarrassed.

"I understand you're a travel writer," the woman says severely. "We don't usually have them here. You ought to be at the Drift-wood."

For a moment Rennie wonders how she knows, but then remembers that it says "freelance journalist" on her disembarkation card, which is in the office safe. Not a hard deduction. What she probably means is that Rennie can't expect special treatment because there isn't any, and in particular she's not supposed to ask for a discount.

The hotel is on the second floor of an old building. Rennie goes down the outside stone staircase, the steps worn concave in the centers, to an inner courtyard that smells of piss and gasoline, then under an archway into the street. Sunlight hits her like a wind, and she rummages in her purse for sunglasses. She realizes she's stepped over a pair of legs, trousers with bare feet at the ends, but she doesn't look down. If you look they want something. She walks along beside the wall of the hotel, patchy stucco that was once white. At the corner she crosses the main street, which is pocked with holes; thick brown sludge moves in the gutters. There aren't many cars. On the other side of the street is an overhang supported by columns, a colonnade, like the ones bordering the zócalos in Mexican towns. It's hard to tell how old things are, she'll have to find out. The tourist brochure says the Spaniards were through here, once, along with everyone else. "Leaving a charming touch of Old Spain" is how they put it.

She walks in the shade, looking for a drugstore. Nobody bothers her or even looks at her much, except for a small boy who tries to sell her some spotty bananas. This is a relief. In Mexico, whenever she left Jake at the hotel and ventured out by herself, she was followed by men who made sucking noises at her with their mouths. She buys a straw hat, overpriced, in a shop that sells batiks and shellwork necklaces made from the vertebrae of fish. It also sells bags, and because of that it's called Bagatelle. Not bad, thinks Rennie. There are familiar signs: The Bank of Nova Scotia, The Canadian Imperial Bank of Commerce. The bank buildings are new, the buildings surrounding them are old.

In the Bank of Nova Scotia she cashes a traveler's check. A couple of doors down there's a drugstore, also new-looking, and she goes into it and asks for some suntan lotion.

"We have Quaaludes," the man says as she's paying for the lotion.

"Pardon?" says Rennie.

"Any amount," the man says. He's a short man with a gambler's moustache, balding, his pink sleeves rolled to the elbows. "You need no prescription. Take it back to the States," he says, looking at her slyly. "Make you a little money."

Well, it's a drugstore, Rennie thinks. It sells drugs. Why be surprised? "No thank you," she says. "Not today."

"You want the hard stuff?" the man asks.

Rennie buys some insect repellent, which he rings up half-heartedly on the cash register. Already he's lost interest in her.

■

Rennie walks uphill, to the Church of St. Antoine. It's the oldest one left, says the tourist brochure. There's a graveyard surrounding it, the plots enclosed by wrought-iron fences, the gravestones tipping and overgrown with vines. On the lawn there's a family planning poster: KEEP YOUR FAMILY THE RIGHT SIZE. No hints about what that might be. Beside it is another poster: ELLIS IS KING. There's a picture of a fattish man, smiling like a Buddha. It's been defaced with red paint.

Inside, the church is completely empty. It feels Catholic, though there are no squat guttering red candles. Rennie thinks of the Virgins in Mexico, several of them in each church, dressed in red or white or blue or black; you chose one and prayed to it according to your needs. Black was for loss. The skirts of the Virgins had been studded with little tin images, tin arms, tin legs, tin children, tin sheep and cows, even tin pigs, in thanks for what had been restored, or perhaps only in hope that it might be. She'd found the idea quaint, then.

There's an altar at the front, a table at the back with a slotted box where you can buy postcards, and a large picture on the west wall, "by an early unknown local artist," says the brochure. It's St. Anthony, being tempted in the desert; only the desert is bursting with tropical vegetation, vivid succulent red flowers, smooth fat leaves bulging with sap, brightly colored birds with huge beaks and yellow eyes, and St. Anthony is black. The demons are noticeably paler, and most of them are female. St. Anthony is on his knees in an attitude of prayer, his eyes turned up and away from the scaly thighs, the breasts and pointed scarlet tongues of the demons. He isn't wearing one of those bedspreads she remembers from the Griswold Sunday school handouts but an ordinary shirt, white and open at the throat, and brown pants. His feet are bare. The figures are flat, as if they've been cut from paper, and they cast no shadows.

There are postcards of the painting on the table, and Rennie buys three. She has her notebook with her but she doesn't write anything in it. Then she sits down in the back pew. What part of herself would she pin on the skirt of the black Virgin now, if she had the chance?

Jake went to Mexico with her. It was their first trip together. He didn't like the churches much: Churches didn't do a whole lot for him, they reminded him of Christians. Christians have funny eyes, he said. Clean-minded. They're always thinking about how you'd look as a bar of soap.

I'm one, said Rennie, to tease him.

No, you're not, said Jake. Christians don't have cunts. You're only a *shiksa*. That's different.

Want to hear me sing "Washed in the Blood of the Lamb"? said Rennie.

Don't be perverted, said Jake. You're turning me on.

Turning? said Rennie. I thought you were on all the time.

It was a whole week. They were euphoric, they held hands on the street, they made love in the afternoons, the wooden louvers of the old windows closed against the sun, they got flea bites, there was nothing that didn't amuse them, they bought dubious cakes and strange fried objects from roadside stands, they ate them recklessly, why not? They found a sign in a little park that read, "Those found sitting improperly in the park will be punished by the authorities." It can't mean that, said Rennie. We must've translated it wrong. What is *sitting improperly*? They walked through the crowded streets at night, curious, fearless. Once there was a fiesta, and a man ran past them with a wickerwork cage balanced on his head, shooting off rockets and Catherine wheels. It's you, Rennie said. Mr. General Electric.

She loved Jake, she loved everything. She felt she was walking inside a charmed circle: Nothing could touch her, nothing could touch them. Nevertheless, even then, she could feel the circle diminishing. In Griswold they believed that everything evened out in the end: If you had too much good luck one day, you'd have bad the next. Good luck was unlucky.

Still, Rennie refused to feel guilty about anything, not even the beggars, the women wrapped in filthy rebozos, with the fallen-in cheeks of those who have lost teeth, suckling inert babies, not even brushing the flies away from their heads, their hands held out, for hours on end it seemed, in one position as if carved. She remembered stories she'd heard about people who mutilated themselves and even their children to make tourists feel sorry for them; or was that in India?

At the end of the week Jake got a case of Montezuma's Revenge. Rennie bought a bottle of sweet pink emulsion for him at the corner *farmacia*, running the gantlet of sucking mouths, and he allowed himself to be dosed. But he wouldn't lie down. He didn't want her to go anywhere without him, he didn't want to miss anything. He sat in a chair, clutching his belly and limping to the bathroom at intervals, while Rennie consulted him about her piece. "Mexico City on Less Than You'd Think."

I'm supposed to be doing this other piece too, she said, for *Pandora*. It's on male pain. How about it? What's the difference?

Male what? Jake said, grinning. You know men don't feel pain. Only when they cut themselves shaving.

It's just been discovered that they do, she said. Tests have been done. Papers have been presented. They wince. Sometimes they flinch. If it's really bad they knit their brows. Come on, be a nice guy, give me a few hints. Tell me about male pain. Where do you feel it the most?

In the ass, Jake said, during conversations like this. Enough with the instant insight.

It's a living, she said, it keeps me off the streets. Where would I be without it? You wouldn't feel so much pain in the ass if you'd take the poker out.

That's not a poker, it's a backbone, he said. I got it from pretending to be a goy. Girls can never tell the difference.

Only between the backbone and the front bone, she said. She sat down on his lap, one leg on either side of him, and began to lick his ear.

Have a heart, he said, I'm a sick man.

Beg for mercy, she said. Do boys cry? We have ways of making you talk. She licked his other ear. You're never too sick, she said. She undid the buttons on his shirt and slid her hand inside it. Anyone as furry as you could never be too sick.

Enough with the voracious female animalistic desires, he said. You should all be locked in cages.

He put his arms around her and they rocked slowly back and forth, and outside the wooden shutters a bell rang somewhere.

■

Rennie walks back on the shadow side. After a few blocks she realizes she's not entirely sure where she is. But she came up to get to the church, so now all she has to do is head down, toward the harbor. Already she's coming to some shops.

Someone touches her on the shoulder, and she stops and turns. It's a man who has once been taller than he is now. He's wearing worn black pants, the fly coming undone, a shirt with no buttons, and one of the wool tea-cozy hats; he has no shoes on, the trouser legs look familiar. He stands in front of her and touches her arm, smiling. His jaw is stubbled with white hairs and most of his teeth are missing.

He makes his right hand into a fist, then points to her, still smiling. Rennie smiles back at him. She doesn't understand what he wants. He repeats the gesture, he's deaf and dumb or perhaps drunk. Rennie feels very suddenly as if she's stepped across a line and found herself on Mars.

He runs the fingers of his right hand together, he's getting impatient, he holds out his hand, and now she knows, it's begging. She opens her purse and gropes for the change purse. It's worth a few cents to be rid of him.

But he frowns, this isn't what he wants. He repeats his series of gestures, faster now, and Rennie feels bewildered and threatened. She gets the absurd idea that he wants her passport, he wants to

70

take it away from her. Without it she could never get back. She closes her purse and shakes her head, turning away and starting to walk again. She's being silly; in any case, her passport is in the safe back at the hotel.

Wherever that is. She can feel him behind her, following her. She quickens her pace; the slip-slop of his bare feet speeds up too. Now she's almost running. There are more people on the street, more and more as she runs downhill, and they notice this little procession of two, this race, they even stop to watch, smiling and even laughing, but nobody does anything to help her. Rennie is close to panic, it's too much like the kind of bad dream she wishes she could stop having, she doesn't know why he's following her. What has she done wrong?

There are crowds of people now, it looks like a market, there's a widening that in Mexico would be a square but here is an amorphous shape, the edges packed with stalls, the center clogged with people and a few trucks. Chickens in crates, fruit stacked into uneasy pyramids or spread out on cloths, plastic pails, cheap aluminum cookware. It's noisy, dusty, suddenly ten degrees hotter; smells engulf her. Music blares from tiny shops crammed with gadgets, the spillover from Japan: cassette players, radios. Rennie dodges among the clumps of people, trying to lose him. But he's right behind her, he's not as decrepit as he looks, and that's his hand on her arm.

"Slow down," says Paul. And it is Paul, in the same shorts but a blue T-shirt, carrying a string bag full of lemons. The man is right behind him, smiling again with his gaping jack-o'-lantern mouth.

"It's okay," says Paul. Rennie's breathing hard, her face is wet and must be red, she probably looks demented and certainly inept. "He just wants you to shake his hand, that's all."

"How do you know?" says Rennie, more angry now than frightened. "He was chasing me!"

"He chases women a lot," says Paul. "Especially the white ones. He's deaf and dumb, he's harmless. He only wants to shake your hand, he thinks it's good luck."

Indeed the man is now holding out his hand, fingers spread.

"Why on earth?" says Rennie. She's a little calmer now but no cooler. "I'm hardly good luck."

"Not for him," says Paul. "For you."

Now Rennie feels both rude and uncharitable: He's only been trying to give her something. Reluctantly she puts her hand into the outstretched hand of the old man. He clamps his fingers around hers and holds on for an instant. Then he lets her go, smiles at her again with his collapsing mouth, and turns away into the crowd.

Rennie feels rescued. "You need to sit down," says Paul. He still has his hand on her arm, and he steers her to a storefront café, a couple of rickety tables covered with oilcloth, and inserts her into a chair next to the wall.

"I'm all right," says Rennie.

"It takes a while for your body to adjust to the heat," says Paul. "You shouldn't run at first."

"Believe me," says Rennie, "I wasn't doing it on purpose."

"Alien reaction paranoia," says Paul. "Because you don't know what's dangerous and what isn't, everything seems dangerous. We used to run into it all the time."

He means in the Far East, he means in the war. Rennie feels he's talking down to her. "Those for scurvy?" she says.

"What?" says Paul.

"On your pirate boats," Rennie says. "The lemons."

Paul smiles and says he'll go inside and order them a drink.

It isn't just a market. Across from the café they've set up a small platform: orange crates stacked two high, with boards across the top. A couple of kids, fifteen or sixteen at the oldest, are draping a bedsheet banner on two poles above it: PRINCE OF PEACE, it says in red. A religious cult of some kind, Rennie decides: Holy Rollers, Born Againers. So the woman in the airport with the Prince of Peace T-shirt wasn't a maniac, just a fanatic. She knows about those: Griswold had its lunatic fringe, women who thought it was a sin to wear lipstick. Then there was her mother, who thought it was a sin not to.

There's a man sitting on the edge of the platform, directing the kids. He's thin, with a riverboat moustache; he slouches forward, dangling his legs. Rennie notices his boots, riding boots, cowboy boots almost, with built-up heels. He's the first man she's seen here wearing boots. Why would anyone choose to? She thinks briefly of his feet, stifled in humid leather.

He sees her watching him. Rennie looks away immediately, but

72

he gets up and comes toward her. He leans his hands on the table and stares down at her. Up close he looks South American.

Now what? thinks Rennie. She assumes he's trying to pick her up, and she's stuck here, wedged in between the table and the wall. She waits for the smile, the invitation, but neither comes, he just frowns at her as if he's trying to read her mind or impress her, so finally she says, "I'm with someone."

"You come in on the plane last night?" he says.

Rennie says yes.

"You the writer?"

Rennie wonders how he knows, but he does, because he doesn't wait for her to answer. "We don't need you here," he says.

Rennie's heard that the Caribbean is becoming hostile to tourists, but this is the most blatant sign she's seen of it. She doesn't know what to say.

"You stay around here, you just mess things up," he says.

Paul is back, with two glasses full of something brown. "Government issue," he says, putting them down on the table. "Something the matter?"

"I don't know," says Rennie. "Ask him." But the man is already sauntering away, teetering a little on the uneven ground.

"What did he say to you?" says Paul.

Rennie tells him. "Maybe I'm offending someone's religion," she says.

"It's not religion, it's politics," says Paul, "though around here it's sometimes the same thing."

"Prince of Peace?" says Rennie. "Politics? Come on."

"Well, his name's Prince, really, and the one you just met is Marsdon. He's the campaign manager," says Paul, who doesn't seem to find any of this odd. "They're the local excuse for communists, so they stuck the *Peace* on for good measure."

Rennie tastes the brown drink. "What's in it?" she says.

"Don't ask me," says Paul, "it's all they had." He leans back in his chair, watching not her but the space in front of them. "They're having an election, the first since the British pulled out," he says. "This afternoon they'll make speeches, all three parties, one after the other. Prince, then Dr. Minnow, that's his corner over there. After that the Minister of Justice. He's standing in for Ellis, who never goes outside his house. Some say it's because he's always too

73

drunk; others say he's been dead for twenty years but no one's noticed yet."

"Dr. Minnow?" says Rennie, remembering the man on the plane. With a name like that there can't be two of them.

"The fish," says Paul, grinning. "They use pictures here, it gets around the illiteracy."

The signs and banners are going up everywhere now. ELLIS IS KING. THE FISH LIVES. Everything looks homemade: It's like college, like student elections.

"Will there be trouble?" says Rennie.

"You mean, will you get hurt?" says Paul. "Yes, there will be trouble. No, you won't get hurt. You're a tourist, you're exempt."

There's a truck making its way through the crowd now, slowly; in the back is a man wearing a white shirt and mirror sunglasses, barking at the crowd through a bullhorn loudspeaker. Rennie can't understand a word he's saying. Two other men flank him, carrying placards with large black crowns on them. ELLIS IS KING. "The Minister of Justice," says Paul.

"What sort of trouble?" says Rennie, wondering if she can get a refund on her excursion ticket if she goes back early.

"A little pushing and shoving," says Paul. "Nothing to get excited about."

But already people are throwing things at the truck; fruit, Rennie thinks, they're picking it up from the stacks on the sidewalk. A crumpled beer can hits the wall above Rennie's head, bounces off.

"They weren't aiming at you," says Paul. "But I'll walk you back to the hotel. Sometimes they get into the broken glass."

He moves the table to let her out, and they push their way through the crowd, against the stream. Rennie wonders if she should ask him about tennis courts and restaurants but decides not to. Her image is fluffy enough already. Then she wonders if she should ask him to have lunch with her at the hotel, but she decides not to do that either. She might be misunderstood.

■

Which is just as well, considering the lunch. Rennie has a grilled cheese sandwich, burned, and a glass of grapefruit juice out of a tin, which seems to be all there is. After the Jell-O pie she takes out the map of Queenstown and pores over it with vague desperation; she has the unpleasant feeling that she's already seen just about everything there is to see. There's a reef, though, on the other side of the jetty that marks off the harbor; you can go out in a boat and look at it. The picture in the brochure shows a couple of murky fish. It doesn't look too promising, but it might yield a paragraph or two.

The map shows a shortcut to the sea. Rennie envisioned a road, but it's only a rudimentary path; it runs behind the hotel, beside something that looks like a sewage pipe. The ground is damp and slippery. Rennie picks her way down, wishing her sandals had flat soles.

The beach isn't one of the seven jewel-like beaches with clean sparkling iridescent sand advertised in the brochure. It's narrow and gravelly and dotted with lumps of coagulated oil, soft as chewing gum and tar-colored. The sewage pipe runs into the sea. Rennie steps over it and walks left. She passes a shed and a hauled-up rowboat where three men are cutting the heads off fish, gutting them, and tossing them into a red plastic pail. Bladders like used condoms litter the beach. One of the men grins at Rennie and holds up a fish, his finger hooked through the gills. Rennie shakes her head. She might take their picture and write something about the catch fresh from the sea and down-to-earth lifestyles. But then she would have to buy a fish, and she can't carry a dead fish around with her all day.

"What time you meet me tonight?" one of the men says behind her. Rennie ignores this.

In the distance there are two boats with awnings, more or less where the map says they should be. She plods along the beach; when she's well past the fish heads she takes off her sandals and walks on the wet packed sand near the water. To the left she can now see the mountains, rising steeply behind the town, covered with uniform nubbled green.

The boats don't leave until high tide. She buys a ticket from the owner of the nearest and newest-looking one, *The Princess Anne*, and sits on the raspy grass in the shade of a bush. The other boat is called *The Princess Margaret*. There's hardly a lineup: a gray-haired couple with binoculars and the ingenuous, eager-to-be-pleased look of retired Americans from the Midwest, and two girls in their teens, white and speckled. They're both wearing T-shirts with mottoes: TRY A VIRGIN (ISLAND), PROPERTY OF ST. MARTIN'S COUNTY JAIL. There's half an hour to wait. The girls peel off their T-shirts and shorts; they're wearing bikinis underneath. They sit out on the filthy beach, rubbing oil on each other's parboiled backs. Skin cancer, thinks Rennie.

Her own dress comes up to her neck. Although it's sleeveless she's already too warm. She gazes at the deceptively blue sea; even though she knows what kind of garbage runs into it nearby, she longs to wade in it. But she hasn't been swimming since the operation. She hasn't yet found a bathing suit that will do: This is her excuse. Her real fear, irrational but a fear, is that the scar will come undone in the water, split open like a faulty zipper, and she will turn inside out. Then she would see what Daniel saw when he looked into her, while she herself lay on the table unconscious as a slit fish. This is partly why she fell in love with him: He knows something about her she doesn't know, he knows what she's like inside.

■

Rennie takes the three postcards out of her purse, "St. Anthony by an early unknown local artist." She addresses one of them to her mother in Griswold. Her mother still lives in Griswold, even though her grandmother is dead and there's no reason at all why her mother can't move, travel, do something else. But she stays in Griswold, cleaning the red brick house that seems to get bigger and both emptier and more cluttered every time Rennie visits it. Where else would I go? says her mother. It's too late. Besides, my friends are here.

One of Rennie's less pleasant fantasies about the future, on nights when she can't sleep, is that her mother will get some lingering disease and she'll have to go back to Griswold to take care of her, for years and years, for the rest of her life. She'll plead illness, they'll have a competition, the sickest one will win. That's how it's done in Griswold, by the women at any rate. Rennie can remember her mother's church group in the front parlor, drinking tea and eating small cakes covered with chocolate icing and poisonous-looking many-colored sprinkles, discussing their own and each other's debilities in hushed voices that blended pity, admiration,

76

and envy. If you were sick you were exempt: other women brought you pies and came to sit with you, commiserating, gloating. The only thing they liked better was a funeral.

On the card Rennie writes that she's well and is having a nice relaxing time. She hasn't told her mother about Jake leaving, since it was hard enough to get her to accept the fact that he'd moved in. Rennie would have dodged that one if she could, but her mother was fond of phoning her early in the morning, at a time when she thought everyone ought to be up, and the phone was on Jake's side of the bed. It would have been better if Jake weren't in the habit of disguising his voice and saying things like "The White House" and "Fiedlefort's Garage." Rennie finally had to explain to her mother that it was only one male voice she was hearing, not several. Which was only marginally acceptable. After that, they didn't discuss it.

Rennie hasn't told her mother about the operation, either. She stopped telling her mother bad news a long time ago. As a child, she learned to conceal cuts and scrapes, since her mother seemed to regard such things not as accidents but as acts Rennie committed on purpose to complicate her mother's life. What did you do *that* for, she would say, jabbing at the blood with a towel. Next time, watch where you're going. The operation, too, she would see as Rennie's fault. Cancer was a front-parlor subject, but it wasn't in the same class as a broken leg or a heart attack or even a death. It was apart, obscene almost, like a scandal; it was something you brought upon yourself.

Other people think that too, but in different ways. Rennie used to think it herself. *Sexual repression. Couldn't act out anger.* The body, sinister twin, taking its revenge for whatever crimes the mind was supposed to have committed on it. Nothing had prepared her for her own outrage, the feeling that she'd been betrayed by a close friend. She'd given her body swimming twice a week, forbidden it junk food and cigarette smoke, allowed it a normal amount of sexual release. She'd trusted it. Why then had it turned against her?

Daniel talked about the importance of attitude. It's mysterious, he said. We don't know why, but it helps, or it seems to.

77

What does? she said.

Hope, he said. The mind isn't separate from the body; emotions trigger chemical reactions and vice versa, you know that.

So it's my fault if there's a recurrence? I have cancer of the mind? said Rennie.

It isn't a symbol, it's a disease, said Daniel patiently. We just don't know the cure yet. We have a few clues, that's all. We're looking for the X factor. But we'll get it sooner or later and then people like me will be obsolete. He patted her hand. You'll be fine, he said. You have a life to go back to. Unlike some. You're very lucky.

But she was not fine. She was released from the hospital, she went back to the apartment, she still wasn't fine. She longed to be sick again so that Daniel would have to take care of her.

She constructed a program for herself: schedules and goals. She exercised the muscles of her left arm by lifting it and pressing the forearm against the wall, she squeezed a sponge ball in her left hand twenty times a day. She went to movies with Jake to cheer herself up, funny movies, nothing heavy. She began to type again, a page at a time, reworking her drain-chain jewelry piece, picking up where she'd left off. She learned to brush her hair again and to do up buttons. As she did each of these things, she thought of Daniel watching her and approving. Good, he would say. You can do up buttons now? You can brush your own hair? That's right, go to cheerful movies. You're doing really well.

She went for an examination and to get the stitches out. She wore a red blouse, to show Daniel what a positive attitude she had, and sat up straight and smiled. Daniel told her she was doing really well and she began to cry.

He put his arms around her, which was what she'd wanted him to do. She couldn't believe how boring she was being, how stupid, how predictable. Her nose was running. She sniffed, blotted her eyes on Daniel's pocket, in which, she noted, he kept several cheap ballpoint pens, and pushed him away.

I'm sorry, she said. I didn't mean to do that.

Don't be sorry, he said. You're human.

I don't feel human any more, she said. I feel infested. I have bad dreams, I dream I'm full of white maggots eating away at me from the inside.

He sighed. That's normal, he said. You'll get over it.

Stop telling me I'm fucking *normal*, she said.

Daniel checked his list of appointments, looked at his watch, and took her down for a swift coffee in the shopping arcade below his office, where he delivered an earnest lecture. This was the second part of her life. It would be different from the first part, she would no longer be able to take things for granted, but perhaps this was a plus because she would see her life as a gift and appreciate it more. It was almost like being given a second life. She must stop thinking of her life as over, because it was far from over.

When I was a student I used to think I would be able to save people, he said. I don't think that any more. I don't even think I can cure them; in this field you can't afford to think that. But in a lot of cases we can give them time. A remission can last for years, for a normal lifespan even. He leaned forward slightly. Think of your life as a clean page. You can write whatever you like on it.

Rennie sat across the table from him, white Formica with gold threads in it, thinking what a lot of facile crap he was talking and admiring his eyes, which were an elusive shade between blue and green. Where does he get this stuff, she thought, *The Reader's Digest*?

How many times have you used that one? she said. Are you just saying that because I'm a journalist? I mean, if I were a dentist, would you say, Your life is like an empty tooth, you can fill it with whatever you like?

Rennie knew you weren't supposed to say things like this to men you were in love with, or to men in general, or to anyone at all for that matter; making fun was rude, especially when the other person was being serious. But she couldn't resist. He would have had a right to be angry, but instead he was startled. He looked at her for a moment almost slyly; then he began to laugh. He was blushing, and Rennie was entranced: The men she knew didn't blush.

I guess you think that's pretty corny, he said.

Corny. My God, thought Rennie, I'm caught in a time warp, it's nineteen fifty-five again. He's from another planet.

I'm sorry, she said. I get pretty surly at times. It's just that, what am I supposed to do with it? All this time I've got. Sit around waiting till it gets me? You know it's going to, sooner or later.

He gazed at her sadly, disappointed again, as if she were talking like a spoiled child. Do what you want to, he said. What you really want to.

What would you do? she said. She fought the impulse to interview him. "When Doctors Get Sick."

He looked down at his hands. What I'm doing now, I guess, he said. That's about all I know anything about. But you have an interesting life.

This was the first clue Rennie had that Daniel thought she was interesting.

Rennie looks at the other two postcards. She addresses one to Jake, it would be a courtesy to let him know where she is, but she doesn't write anything on it because she can't think of anything she wants to say to him. The third one she leaves empty. Empty is not the same as clean. She bought the third one for Daniel but she decides not to send it. She'll send it later, when she can say, *I'm fine.* That's what he would like to hear: that she's fine, that everything is fine, that he's done no damage.

∎

Rennie feels a darker shadow fall over her. "Hi there," says a flat nasal voice, mildly familiar. It's the woman who passed her in the hotel last night. She now sits down beside Rennie uninvited and takes a pack of cigarettes out of her bag. Rennie puts away her postcards.

"You smoke?" says the woman. The fingers holding the cigarette are bitten to the quick, stub-tipped, slightly grubby, the raw skin around the nails nibbled as if mice have been at them, and this both surprises Rennie and repels her slightly. She wouldn't want to touch this gnawed hand, or have it touch her. She doesn't like the sight of ravage, damage, the edge between inside and outside blurred like that.

"No, thanks," says Rennie.

"My name's Lora," says the woman, "With an o, not the other way. Lora Lucas. *L*'s run in our family, my mother's name was Leona." Now that she's talking, the illusion shatters: "Hi there" is about the only thing she's learned to fake, the rest is natural. She's not as young as she looked in the dim light of the hotel. Her hair is down today, flower-child length, dry as hay. She's wearing an above-the-knee oblong of orange knotted across her large breasts.

Her eyes are scanning, all the time, back and forth, taking everything in. "You just come in, eh?" she says, and Rennie thinks, *Canadian.*

"Yes," says Rennie.

"You got to watch it around here," says Lora. "People see you don't know what you're doing, they rip you off. How much he soak you from the airport last night?"

Rennie tells her and she laughs. "You see?" she says.

Rennie immediately resents her, she resents the intrusion. She wishes she had a book; then she could pretend to read.

"You should watch your stuff, that camera and all," says Lora. "There's been some break-ins around here. A girl I know, she woke up in the middle of the night and there was this black guy in a bathing suit holding a knife to her throat. Nothing sexual, he just wanted her money. Said he'd kill her if she told anyone. She was afraid to go to the police."

"Why?" Rennie says, and Lora grins at her.

"She figures he was the police," she says.

In response to some signal Rennie hasn't caught, she stands up and brushes the sand from her orange tie-dye. "Boat time," she says. "If that's what you're here for."

It seems they're expected to wade out to the boat. The old couple with the matching binoculars go first. They're both wearing wide-legged khaki shorts, which they roll up even farther, exposing stringy whitish legs which are surprisingly muscular. Even so, the drooping bottoms of their shorts are wet through by the time they reach the boat's ladder. The two speckled pink girls make it with a lot of shrieking. Lora unties her tie-dye, under which she's wearing a black bikini half a size too small, and drapes it around her neck. She holds the purple cloth bag she's carrying at shoulder height and surges into the water; surf breaks around her thighs, which bulge out of the bikini like caricatures of thighs, like the thighs on humorous cocktail napkins.

Rennie considers her options. She can either hitch up her dress and tuck it into her underpants, with everyone watching her, or get it wet and smell like seaweed for the rest of the day. She compromises, hiking her skirt halfway up and draping it through the sash tie. It gets wet anyway. The man who appears to own the boat smiles widely as the swell hits her. He reaches out a long ropy arm, a hand like a clamp, to help her up. At the last moment, when the motor is already running, five or six children come screaming and laughing out through the waves and swarm onto the boat, clambering up onto the awning, which Rennie now sees is wooden rather than cloth.

"Mind yourself, you fall off," the owner yells at them.

Rennie sits on the wooden bench, dripping, while the boat goes up and down and the exhaust blows into her face. Lora has gone up on top where the kids are, probably to work on her tan. The two girls are flirting with the man running the boat. The old couple are looking at sea birds through their binoculars, murmuring to each other in what sounds like a secret language. "Booby," the old woman says. "Frigate," the man replies.

In front of Rennie is a raised ledge bordering an oblong piece of glass almost the length of the boat. Rennie leans forward and rests her arms on it. Nothing but grayish foam is visible through the glass. She's doing this, she reminds herself, so she can write about how much fun it is. *At first you may think you could get the same effect for a lot less money by putting a little Tide in your Jacuzzi. But wait.*

Rennie waits, and the boat stops. They're quite far out. Twenty yards from them, surf crashes over an invisible wall, each wave lifting the boat. In the furrows between the waves they sink down until they're only a foot from the reef. It's an illusion, Rennie thinks. She prefers to believe that people who run things know what they're doing, and these people surely would not do anything so dangerous. She doesn't like the idea of a prong of coral suddenly bursting through the glass.

Rennie looks, which is her function. The water is clouded with fine sand. At the edges of the glass oblong, dark shapes flit and are hidden. Below her, so encrusted in purplish coral that its shape is almost obscured, is a soft-drink bottle. A tiger-striped fish swims near it.

"It's not so great today, it's been too windy, and this one's not such a great one anyway," Lora says to her. She's come down from the roof and is kneeling beside Rennie. "The reef's getting all messed up by the oil and junk from the harbor. What you need is a snorkel and stuff, over at Ste. Agathe. That's where I live, you'd like it a lot better than here."

Rennie doesn't say anything; she doesn't seem expected to. Also she doesn't want to start a conversation. Conversations lead to acquaintances, and acquaintances are too easy to make on these trips. People mistake them for friendships. She smiles and turns back to the glass oblong.

"You write for the magazines, eh?" the woman says.

"How did you know that?" Rennie asks, a little annoyed. This is the third time today.

"Everyone knows everything around here," the woman says. "Word of mouth, the grapevine you might say. Everyone knows what's happening." She pauses. She looks at Rennie, scanning her face as if trying to see through the blue lenses of her sunglasses. "I could tell you stuff to write about," she says darkly. "The story of my life, you could put it in a book all right. Except no one would believe it, you know?"

Rennie is instantly bored. She can't remember how many people have said this to her, at parties, on airplanes, as soon as they've found out what she does. Why do they think their own lives are of general concern? Why do they think that being in a magazine will make them more valid than they are? Why do they want to be *seen*?

Rennie switches off the sound and concentrates only on the picture. Lora could definitely be improved. She would benefit greatly from a good cut and shape, for instance, and she should grow her eyebrows in, just a little. Plucking them fine like that broadens her face. Rennie arranges her into a Makeover piece, before and after, with a series of shots in between showing the process, Lora being tweezed and creamed and colored in and fitted with a Norma Klein sweater. After that you could take her to lunch at Winston's and all you'd have to teach her would be how to keep her mouth shut.

■

They're sitting under a metal umbrella at one of the round white tables on the patio at the Driftwood, Lora with the sun on her back, Rennie in the shade. The other tables are thinly scattered with white people in various phases of hot pink, and one couple who seems to be Indian. The waiters are black or brown; the architecture is roadside modern, the balconies have plastic panels, green and blue. At the edge of the patio there's a tree covered with red flowers, huge lobed blossoms like gigantic sweet peas; a dozen hummingbirds swarm around them. Below, on the other side of the curving stone wall, the surf crashes against the rocks just as it is supposed to, and a fresh wind blows off the Atlantic. To the right is a wide beach devoid of fish heads. There's nobody on it.

Lora orders another piña colada. Rennie is only halfway through hers, but she orders another one anyway.

"Who's paying for this?" Lora asks, too innocently.

"I will," says Rennie, who has always known she would.

"You can put it on your whatchamacallit," Lora says. "Don't they pay for everything, those magazines?"

"Not always," says Rennie, "but I can write it off as an expense. We can pretend I was interviewing you."

"Write it off," says Lora. "Jesus." Rennie can't tell whether she's impressed or disgusted.

"This is where people like you stay, most of the time," says Lora.

Rennie dislikes having these kinds of assumptions made about her, she dislikes being lumped in with a fictitious group labeled *people like you.* She can't stand the self-righteousness of people like Lora, who think that because they've had deprived childhoods or not as much money as everybody else they are in some way superior. She feels like using one of her never-fail ploys. She'll lean across the table, take off her sunglasses, gaze into Lora's round blue-china eyes, eyes that manage to look at the same time aggrieved and secretly delighted, and say, "Why are you being so aggressive?" But she has a feeling this wouldn't work on Lora.

She thinks about unbuttoning her dress and displaying her scar. If they're having a poor-me contest, that should be good for a few points; but she doesn't want to turn into one of those people who use their physical disabilities for social blackmail.

She knows she shouldn't have allowed herself to be picked up on the reef boat, she shouldn't have expressed interest in seeing the other hotels, she should have insisted on a taxi instead of listening

84

to Lora, who said she knew people and why get ripped off when you could get a free ride? "Free rides, that's my motto," she said. Rennie's mother used to say there was no such thing as a free ride.

The free ride turned out to be a battered pickup truck with two yellow eyes painted on the hood. It was delivering toilet paper, and they had to sit on the boxes in the back, perched up there like float queens; groups of people waved and yelled at them as they went past. Outside the town the road got steadily worse, dwindling finally into a two-wheel track of cracked and disintegrating concrete. The driver went as fast as possible, and every time they hit a gap in the concrete Rennie could feel the top of her spine being rammed up into her skull.

She doesn't want to face the ride back, but she doesn't want to stay here either. If she isn't careful she'll be trapped into having dinner. Lora, she's decided, is one of those women you meet in bars in foreign countries who seem not to have chosen anything but merely ended up wherever they happen to be, and it's too much effort for them to go home. Rennie can't imagine why Lora has been so insistent about coming with her. They have nothing in common. Lora says she has nothing else to do at the moment so she might as well show Rennie around, but Rennie doesn't believe this. She resolves to finish her drink and then go. If she's lucky it will rain: Promising clouds are already piling up.

Now Lora opens her purple bag and rustles through it, and suddenly everything falls into place. What she takes out is a poly bag of grass, about an ounce, Rennie guesses. She wants Rennie to buy it. The price, by Toronto standards, is ridiculously low.

"The best," she says. "Colombian, it just came in."

Rennie of course refuses. She's heard about dope laws in foreign countries, she knows about being set up, she has no intention of spending any time at all growing fungus in the local jail while the local bureaucrats try, unsuccessfully, to put the squeeze on her mother. Her mother is a firm believer in taking the consequences for your actions. And who else would get her out? Who would even try?

Lora shrugs. "It's cool," she says. "No harm in asking."

Rennie looks around to see what has become of Lora's drink, and feels herself turn cold.

"My God," she says.

There are two policemen in the bar, they're going from table to table, it looks as if they're asking questions. But Lora stares calmly over at them, she doesn't even put the dope away, she just moves her cloth bag so it's covered. "Don't look so weird," she says to Rennie. "It's cool. I wouldn't say it was cool if it wasn't."

And it turns out after all that they're just selling tickets to the Police Benefit Dance. Rennie thinks she recognizes them from the airport, but she's not sure. One sells, the other stands behind him, dangling his swagger stick and checking out the scene. She produces her own ticket from her purse. "I already have one," she says, a little too smugly because the one selling grins at her and says, "You need two, man. One for your boyfriend. Some things you can't do by yourself."

The second one laughs, a high giggle.

"That's a real good idea," says Lora, smiling a little tightly, her Holiday Inn smile; so Rennie pays.

"We see you there," says the first policeman, and they saunter off.

"If there's one thing I hate it's cops," says Lora, when they're hardly out of earshot. "They're all in the business if you ask me, one way or another, I've got nothing against that but they take advantage. It's unfair competition. You ever been stopped by a cop? For speeding or anything? Back home I mean, around here they don't bother that much about speeding."

"No," says Rennie.

"They look at your driver's license. Then they use your first name. Not Miss or Mrs. or anything, your first name, and you've got no way of knowing any of their names at all. You ever have that happen to you?"

In fact Rennie hasn't. She's having trouble paying attention, there's too much rum in the drinks. Lora, however, has just signaled for another one, it's not bothering her.

"That's where it begins," says Lora. "Where they can use your first name and you can't use theirs. Then they think they've got you, they can look down on you, like. Sometimes they give you a choice, fork out or put out."

"Sorry?" says Rennie.

"You know, pay the fine or go down on them. They always know where the vacant lots are, eh?"

86

Lora looks at her slyly and Rennie knows she's supposed to be shocked. "Really," she says, as if she's been through it herself, dozens of times.

The Women's Movement would have loved Lora, back in the old days, back in the early seventies when they were still doing pieces about the liberating effects of masturbation. They'd have given her ten out of ten for openness, a word that always made Rennie think of a can of worms with the top off. Nevertheless, Rennie did several pieces on the movement back then, until its media potential burned out. Then she did a piece called "Burned Out": interviews with eight women who'd explained why they'd gone into weaving placemats and painting miniature landscapes on bottles, instead. It was the infighting, they said. The bitching. The trashing. Other women were just so difficult to work with, you never knew where you stood with them. And it all went on behind your back. At least with men it was out on the table, they said; and Rennie busily wrote it all down.

Great stuff, said the editor. It's about time someone had the courage to speak out.

Lora smiles but she's not fooled; she can tell this is one of the things Rennie doesn't know. But she's generous, she's willing to share. Ten out of ten for sharing.

"Listen," she says, "at least you have the choice. You can always say you're worth more than a speeding ticket. I don't know which is worse though, no choice at all or just a lot of bad ones. At least when you don't have a choice you don't have to think, you know? The worst times in my life I had choices all right. Shit or shit."

Rennie doesn't want to hear about the worst times in Lora's life, so she doesn't say anything.

"Anyway, why dwell on it?" says Lora. "That's what my mother used to say. There's enough bad things in the world, there's no shortage, so why dwell on it, there's better things to talk about."

Rennie wonders what these may be, since Lora can't seem to think of any. She slurps at the bottom of her glass with the two plastic straws. "You like maraschino cherries?" she says. "I can't stand them."

Rennie hesitates. She does like maraschino cherries, but she isn't sure she wants to eat the one Lora is now poking around for at the bottom of the glass with her bitten fingers. However, she's about to be rescued, because Paul has just stepped out onto the patio and is standing there scanning the tables as though he's looking for someone.

Rennie knows it's her. She waves, and he strolls over to their table.

"What have you been up to?" he says, smiling at her.

"Research," says Rennie, smiling back.

"You're late," Lora says to him. "I've been here for hours."

"I'll get myself a drink," he says, and walks over to the bar.

"Just a sec," says Lora. "Would you mind keeping an eye on my bag?" She stands up, pushes back her hair, straightens up so her breasts stick out more, and walks over to join Paul. They stand there talking, for a lot longer than Rennie wants them to.

The third piña colada comes, the one for Lora, and Rennie drinks some of it, for something to do.

■

Lora comes back from the bar and sits down. Her drink is there but she doesn't touch it. Something has happened, her face is no longer a dollface. Rennie notices the skin under her eyes, too much sun, in a few years she'll shrivel up like an apple. She looks at Rennie, dolefully as a spaniel.

"What's wrong?" says Rennie, knowing as she says it that she shouldn't have asked. To ask is to get involved.

"Look," says Lora, "can you do me a big favor?"

"What?" says Rennie, on guard.

"Elva's sick," she says, "that's Prince's grandmother. Over on Ste. Agathe."

"Prince?" says Rennie. There can't be two of them.

"The guy I live with," Lora says.

"The one in the election?" says Rennie, who can't quite put it together.

"That's why he can't go over to Ste. Agathe," says Lora, "he's making a speech today, so I have to, she sort of lives with us. She's eighty-two, it's her heart, and there's no doctors over there and nobody to, you know. So I have to get over there right away." Is it possible she's almost crying?

"What can I do?" says Rennie. In Griswold it would be cup-

88

cakes or a pumpkin pie. This is familiar ground. She's friendlier toward Lora now that she knows Lora's living with someone. Who is not Paul.

"There's this box coming into the airport tomorrow," says Lora, "you think you can pick it up for me?"

Rennie is immediately suspicious. "What's in it?" she says.

Lora looks at her and manages a grin. "Not what you think," she says. "There's one thing around here you don't have to get mailed in from New York, that's for sure. It's her heart medicine. She's got this daughter there sends it to her all the time. You can't get stuff like that here. She ran out of it, that's why she got sick."

Rennie does not want the death of an eighty-two-year-old grandmother on her hands. What can she say but yes? You're too distrustful, Jake used to tell her. Try the benefit of the doubt, for once in your life.

Paul walks over, he's taking his time, he never seems to move very fast. He puts his half-empty drink on the table and sits down. He smiles, but Lora doesn't even look at him.

"What you need to do," Lora says, "you need to go there tomorrow morning around eight, the window that says Customs. Here, you need this thing here. It has to be around eight." She rummages in her purple bag, she can't seem to find it. Finally she takes out a creased and folded piece of paper. "Right," she says. "Just say she sent you and give them this. You ask for this fellow called Harold, he should be there; if he's not you have to wait."

Rennie takes the paper; it's a simple customs notice. There's nothing to pay, no complications. "Why can't I just hand it in at the window?" she says. "Anyone should be able to deal with this."

Lora gives her a patient but exasperated look. "You don't know how they do things around here," she says. "He's the one I gave the bribe to. If you don't do that, they just open it up and keep half the stuff. Or they might keep all of it and never tell you it got here, you know? Sell it on the black market."

"Really?" says Rennie.

"Every place has a different system," says Lora. "But they've all got one. You just need to figure out how it works." She's more relaxed now, she siphons up the rest of her piña colada and stands, scraping back the metal chair. "I got to go to the can," she says, and disappears into the main building.

Rennie and Paul are left sitting together. "Can I get you another?" Paul says.

"No thanks," says Rennie. She's on the edge of being quite drunk. "How do I get back from here?" She realizes this sounds like a request. "I'll call a taxi," she says.

"Taxis don't like to come out here," Paul says. "The roads are too bad, they don't like to wreck their springs. Anyway, you'd have to wait for hours. I'll give you a lift, I've got a jeep out front."

"Only if you're going back anyway," says Rennie.

He stands up, he's ready to leave right now. "What about Lora?" says Rennie. She doesn't want to ride back with Lora, but it would be rude to leave her stranded.

"She'll get back on her own all right," Paul says. "She knows a lot of people."

On the way out Rennie sees Lora, who isn't in the can after all but is standing near the kitchen door, talking with one of the waiters. Rennie goes over to say good-bye.

"Have a nice time," Lora says, with her Holiday Inn smile. She presses something into Rennie's hand; it feels like a wad of Kleenex. "It's a gift," she says. "You're doing me a favor."

"Is Lora a friend of yours?" Rennie asks when they're outside, walking across the Driftwood's thick lawn.

"How do you mean?" says Paul.

Rennie founders. She doesn't want to reveal jealousy or even interest, though she suddenly realizes that she feels both. "I mean, do you know her very well?"

"Well enough," says Paul. "She's been around for a while."

"She seems to be living with some man, over on Ste. Agathe," Rennie says.

"Prince?" Paul says. "Not exactly. Off and on, the way they do. He's into politics, she's not."

"She seems to be into just about everything else," says Rennie.

Paul doesn't say anything, he's staying completely neutral. Rennie's real question hasn't been answered and she can see it won't be.

They reach the driveway and find the jeep, which is small and battered, with open sides and a canvas top. "Is it yours?" Rennie says.

"Friend of mine's," says Paul. He doesn't open the door for her and it takes her a while to get it open for herself. She's definitely had too much to drink. Paul takes out a pair of mirror sunglasses and puts them on. Then he turns the key. The jeep scoots backward into the ditch, which seems to be the only way to turn around, then accelerates forward, wheels spinning in the mud. Rennie clamps her right hand to the metal frame at the top, her left to the seat, which is also metal. There are no safety belts.

They drive through the forest that surrounds the Driftwood, huge hothouse trees draped with creepers, giant prehistoric ferns, obese plants with rubbery ear-shaped leaves and fruit like warts, like glands. Some of the trees have toppled over, tearing up swaths of earth, their thick snarled roots in the air now.

"Allan," Paul yells over the noise of the Jeep.

"What?" says Rennie.

"The hurricane."

Now they're in a coconut plantation. It seems to be abandoned, some of the trees are dead, the coconuts are everywhere, on the road even, the road is worse here, they're hitting every pothole. Rennie's hands are cold, she's sweating, she no longer feels drunk but she thinks she's going to be sick.

"Could you stop?" she shouts.

"What?" says Paul.

"Stop!" she says. "Please stop!"

He looks over at her, then pulls the jeep off to the side of the road. Rennie puts her head down on her knees; she'll be all right if she can just stay like this for a minute. It's a drag, stopping like this, she feels silly, but it's better than vomiting on him. "Throwing Up in the Sun," she thinks briefly. Tippy would say everything's raw material, you just have to know how to work it in.

Paul touches her back. "Any better?" he says. "I guess I was driving too fast for you."

With her head down Rennie listens, she can hear birds, thin shrill voices like fingernails, raucous croaks, insects, her heart going too fast. After a while, she doesn't know how long, she lifts her head. Paul is looking at her, his face is right there, she can see two little faces, white and tiny, reflected back at her from his sunglasses. Without his eyes his face is expressionless, he's a faceless stranger. She's aware of his arm lying across the back of the seat.

"Could you take off your sunglasses, please?" she says.

"Why?" he says, but he does.

Rennie turns her head away from him. It's late, the sun is slanting down through the long spokes of the palm trees, the coconuts lie rotting in their husks; here and there something, an animal, has made large burrows in the ground.

"What lives in the holes?" says Rennie.

"Landcrabs," Paul says. "Big white buggers. They only come out at night, you hunt them with a flashlight and a big stick. You shine the light in their eyes, that stops them, and then you pin them down with the stick."

"Can you eat them?" Rennie says. She's still not connecting very well: the outlines are too clear, the sounds too sharp.

"Sure, if you want to," Paul says. "That's why you hunt them."

He turns her around to face him, he's smiling, he kisses her, more exploration than passion. After a minute Rennie puts her hand on the back of his neck; the hair is soft, she can feel the muscles under it, the ropes, the knots. His hand moves toward her breast, she takes hold of it, slides her fingers between his own. He looks at her and nods a little. "Right," he says. "Let's go back." The rest of the way he drives slowly; it's dark by the time they reach the town.

Rennie wants everything to be easy, why not? Once it would have been, there would have been nothing to it. She likes him, well enough but not too well, she knows nothing about him, she doesn't need to know anything, he knows nothing about her, it's perfect. She walks down the wooden corridor, past the chilly eyes of the Englishwoman, he's just behind her, this is something she wants to do, again, finally, she wants it so much her hands are shaking.

But at the door of her room she turns, without unlocking the door, she can't do it. She can't take that risk.

"I take it I'm coming in?" he says.

She says no, but there's nothing more she can say.

He shrugs. "Up to you," he says. She has no idea what he thinks. He kisses her on the cheek, a peck, and walks away down the green corridor.

■

92

Rennie goes into her room, locks the door, and sits down on the edge of the bed. After a while she opens her purse. From the zipper compartment at the back she takes out the Kleenex package Lora handed her and unwraps it. Inside, there's what she knew there would be, five joints, tightly and expertly rolled. She's grateful.

She picks one and lights it with a wooden Swedish match. She smokes a little of it, just enough to relax, puts it out, and slides the remaining half and the other four joints between the folds of the green blanket in the middle drawer of the bureau. She lies down on the bed again, hearing the blood running through her body, which is still alive. She thinks of the cells, whispering, dividing in darkness, replacing each other one at a time; and of the other cells, the evil ones which may or may not be there, working away in her with furious energy, like yeast. They would show up hot orange under one kind of light, hot blue under another, like the negative print of the sun when you close your eyes. Beautiful colors.

They use it now in hospitals for terminal cases, it's the one thing that can stop the nausea. She pictures all those Baptists and Presbyterians, no longer sitting in their upright pews but laid out in rows in clean white crank-up beds, stoned to the gills. Of course they call it something else, some respectable Latin name. She wonders how much pain she could take before she would give herself up, give herself over again to the probers, the labelers and cutters. *Doctored*, they say of drinks that have been tampered with, of cats that have been castrated.

You just feel this way about me because I'm your doctor, Daniel said. I'm a fantasy for you. It's normal.

I don't mean to be rude, said Rennie, but if I was going to have a fantasy why would I pick you?

It would be nice to have someone on the bed with her. Almost anyone, as long as he would keep still. Sometimes she wanted just to be still.

You're using me for a teddy bear, Jake said. Why don't you go back to sucking your thumb?

You wouldn't like the substitution, she said. Is there something wrong with quiet companionship?

No, he said, but not every night.

Sometimes I think you don't like me very much, she said.

Like? he said. Is that all you want to be? Liked? Wouldn't you rather be passionately and voraciously desired?

Yes, she said, but not every night.

That was before. After, he said, You're cutting yourself off.

That's a bad pun, she said.

Never give a sucker an even break, he said. What can I do if you won't let me touch you? You don't even want to talk about it.

What aspect of it would you like to discuss? she said. Instances of recurrence? My chances of survival? You want statistics?

Stop talking like a sick joke, he said.

It may be a sick joke but it's what I'm stuck with, she said. That's why I don't want to discuss it. I *know* it's a sick joke. So I'd rather not, if you don't mind.

How you feel, he said. Try that.

How I feel? Great. I feel great. I feel like the body beautiful. How do you want me to feel?

Come on, he said. So it's the end of the world?

Not yet, she said. Not for you.

You're relentless, Jake said.

Why? she said. Because I don't feel like it in the same way any more? Because I don't believe you do either?

She used to think sex wasn't an issue, it wasn't crucial, it was a pleasant form of exercise, better than jogging, a pleasant form of communication, like gossip. People who got too intense about sex were a little *outré*. It was like wearing plastic spikes with rhinestones and meaning it, it was like taking mink coats seriously. What mattered was the relationship. A good relationship: that was what she and Jake were supposed to have. People commented on it, at parties, as if they were admiring a newly renovated house.

That was what it had been at first: no mess, no *in love*. By the time she met Jake she'd decided she didn't much like being in love. Being in love was like running barefoot along a street covered with broken bottles. It was foolhardy, and if you got through it without damage it was only by sheer luck. It was like taking off your clothes at lunchtime in a bank. It let people think they knew something about you that you didn't know about them, it gave them power over you. It made you visible, soft, penetrable; it made you ludicrous.

There was no question about love with Jake, at first. Not that he wasn't attractive, not that he wasn't possible. He wasn't deformed or a fool and he was good at what he did, he was even good enough to have started his own small company by the time he was thirty. This was how she'd met him: She'd been doing a piece for *Visor* on men who had started their own small companies by the time they were thirty. "The Young and the Solvent," it was called. They'd used Jake for the full-page picture facing the title, and when she thought about him that was the first image she always saw: Jake, "saturnine" she'd called him in the piece, with his dark skin and white teeth and narrow muzzle, grinning like a fox, perched with jaunty irony at his drawing board, wearing a navy blue three-piece suit to prove you didn't have to be afraid of suits. That was about the year the tide was turning, on suits.

A prick, the photographer said to Rennie. He was an old pro, that's what he called himself, the mournful kind, balding and a little seedy. He wore vests with no jacket and his shirt sleeves rolled up. They used him a lot for indoor shots, but only the black and white ones that were supposed to be the subject's real life. For the color they used a fashion photographer.

How can you tell? asked Rennie.

I can just tell, the photographer said. Women can't tell.

Oh, come on, said Rennie.

Or maybe they can tell, said the photographer. The thing about women is they prefer guys who treat them like shit. A nice guy like me never gets a chance. There's only two kinds of guys, *a prick* and *not a prick*. Not counting fags.

You're jealous, Rennie said. You wish you had teeth like that. He's good at what he does.

Watch out, said the photographer. He's still a prick.

What Jake did was design. He was a designer of labels, not just labels but the total package: the label, the container, the visuals for the advertising. He was a packager. He decided how things would look and what contexts they would be placed in, which meant what people would feel about them. He knew the importance of style, so he didn't sneer at Rennie for doing pieces on the return of the open-toed spike-heel sandal.

Better than that, he liked her body and said so, which Rennie found refreshing. Most of the men she knew used the word *person*, a little too much, a little too nervously. A *fine* person. It was a burden, being a fine person. She knew she was not as fine a person as they wanted her to be. It was a relief to have a man say, admit, confess, that he thought she had a terrific ass.

What about my mind? she said. Aren't you going to tell me I have an interesting mind?

Screw your mind, Jake said. Both of them laughed. No, he said, I couldn't screw your mind even if I wanted to. You're a tough lady, you've got your legs crossed pretty tight. You can't rape a woman's mind without her consent, you know that.

You can try, Rennie said.

Not me, Jake said. I'm not a mind man. I'm more interested in your body, if you want the truth.

When they'd moved in together, they'd agreed to keep their options open. That was another phrase she'd had to translate for Daniel; by that time she'd had trouble explaining what it meant.

It took her more time than it should have to realize that she was one of the things Jake was packaging. He began with the apartment, which he painted several shades of off-white and filled with forties furniture, chrome for the kitchen and a deep-pink bulgy chair and sofa for the living room, "like thighs," he said, with a real trilight he'd picked up at the Sally Ann. Wicker and indoor plants had been done, he said, and he got rid of the benjamin tree, Rennie suspected, by pouring his leftover coffee into it when she wasn't looking.

Then he started on her. You have great cheekbones, he said. You should exploit them.

Oppressed cheekbones? said Rennie, who was slightly embarrassed by compliments; they'd been rare in Griswold.

Sometimes I feel like a blank sheet of paper, she said. For you to doodle on.

Screw that, said Jake. It's all there underneath. I just want you to bring it out. You should enjoy it, you should make the most of it.

Aren't you afraid packs of ravening, lustful other men will storm in and snatch me away from you? said Rennie. If I make the most of it.

Not a chance, said Jake. Other men are wimps. He believed this, which was one of the things Rennie liked about him. She didn't have to stroke his ego, he did that for himself.

He decided she should wear nothing but white linen jumpsuits, with shoulder pads. The Rosie the Riveter look, he said.

They make my ass look big, she said.

Rennie drew the line at *nothing but*—Let's not be absolutist, she said—but she got one, to please him, though she refused to wear it out on the street. In the living room he hung blowups of Cartier-Bresson photographs, three Mexican prostitutes looking out of wooden cubicles, their eyebrows plucked thin and drawn into exaggerated bows, their mouths clown-mouths, an old man sitting in a field of deserted chairs.

That was the daytime. When he had that arranged, he started on the night. In the bedroom he hung a Heather Cooper poster, a brown-skinned woman wound up in a piece of material that held her arms to her sides but left her breasts and thighs and buttocks exposed. She had no expression on her face, she was just standing there, if anything a little bored. The picture was called *Enigma*. The other picture in the bedroom was a stylized print of a woman lying on a forties puffy sofa, like the one in their own living room. She was feet-first, and her head, up at the other end of the sofa, was tiny, featureless, and rounded like a doorknob. In the foreground there was a bull.

These pictures made Rennie slightly nervous, especially when she was lying on their bed with no clothes on. But that was probably just her background.

Put your arms over your head, Jake said, it lifts the breasts. Move your legs apart, just a little. Raise your left knee. You look fantastic.

A secure woman is not threatened by her partner's fantasies, Rennie told herself. As long as there is trust. She'd even written that, or something like it, in a piece on the comeback of satin lingerie and fancy garter belts. And she was not threatened, not for some time.

You're so closed, Jake said once. I like that. I want to be the one you open up for.

But she could never remember afterward what he had actually said. Perhaps he'd said, I want to be the one who opens you up.

■

MY FATHER CAME HOME every Christmas, says Rennie. He always spoke of it as coming home, though it became obvious at last, even to me, that his home was elsewhere. He'd gone to Toronto soon after I was born, he'd been in the war and got university free as a veteran. He studied chemical engineering. He stayed there, everyone said, because the jobs were there. We couldn't go because my grandfather got sick and my grandmother needed the help, that's what they said, and after my grandfather died my grandmother could not be left alone. People in Griswold had a great fear of being left alone. It was supposed to be bad for you, it made you go funny, it drove you bats. Then you had to be put in the loony bin.

So my father would turn up every Christmas. He would stay in one of the guest bedrooms, we had a lot of them, bedrooms that had once been for children and now stood empty, dustless and smelling of lavender and dead air. These visits of his, I was told later, were for my sake. My father and I would be bundled up and sent for walks on the icy streets; both of us would be told not to fall down. He would ask me how I was doing at school and tell me that soon I would be able to come and visit him. Neither of us believed this. On the main street people's heads would turn, not too abruptly, as we went past, and I would know that we were being looked at and discussed.

When I was in grade six, two girls, the kind from loose families, spread the story that my father was living with another woman in Toronto, and that was the real reason my mother didn't go to join him. I didn't believe this, but I didn't ask my mother about it either, so I probably did believe it after all. Just as well, because it was true, and when my mother finally told me I wasn't surprised. She waited until my thirteenth birthday, two weeks after my first period. She must have felt I was ready for pain.

I think she wanted sympathy, she felt that at last I would understand what a hard life she had led and what sacrifices she had been forced to make. She hoped I would blame my father, see him in his true light. But I was unable to feel what I was supposed to; instead I blamed her. I was angry with him, not for leaving—I could see why he would have wanted to do that—but for leaving me behind.

By that time he'd stopped coming back for Christmas, though he still sent cards, to me but not to her, and I didn't see him again until I moved to Toronto to go to university. For years he'd been married to someone I thought of only as *her*, because that's what my mother called her. I'd forgotten what he looked like.

I visited them at their apartment. I had never been in an apartment before. That was the first time I'd ever seen a house plant that wasn't an African violet or a poinsettia. They had a lot of plants, hanging all over the southern windows, things I didn't know the names for. There was space between the furniture in their apartment, a lot more space than I was used to. The first thing he said to me was *You look like your mother.* And that was the end of him.

■

When I was growing up, says Lora, we lived in cellars. We lived in the cellars of apartment buildings; they were always dark, even in summer, and they smelled like cat piss, partly because of Bob's cats, he never emptied the litter box even though they were his cats, and partly because those kinds of places always smell like cat piss anyway. Bob got the apartments for next to nothing, they were the caretaker's apartments, he was supposed to take out the garbage and mop the floors and fix people's toilets, but he was never much good at that, or maybe he didn't want to, which is why we were always moving.

His war buddy Pat used to say that wasn't how Bob really made his money anyway. He said Bob made his money by catching things that fell off the backs of lorries. I didn't figure out for a while that *lorry* was the English word for *truck*, Pat was from England, and then I didn't believe it, because I knew Bob didn't chase after trucks waiting for stuff to fall off them. He was home most of the time, sitting at the kitchen table in his old gray cardigan, and besides he couldn't run because of his limp. This was lucky for me: If I could keep him from grabbing me I could always outrun him, but he was fast with the hands, he'd pretend he was looking the other way and then snatch, and when I was small he could keep hold of me with one hand while he got his belt off with the other. I guess that's partly what made me so quick on my feet.

He said he got the limp in the war and it was typical of the government that they wouldn't give him a pension. He was against the government, whoever was in, he said it didn't matter a tinker's piss, but don't get the wrong idea, he was death on communism too. He couldn't stand the idea of welfare, that was communism as far as he was concerned. Bob's war buddy Pat used to talk about the working class, he used to say that's what they were, the both of them, but that was always a big joke to me. Working class my ass. Bob worked as little as he could. His whole thing was how you could avoid working, he thought anyone with a steady job was the world's number-one dummy. He was dead against the unions too, he had no sympathy for them at all, he said they just made things more expensive for everybody else. When there were strikes on the TV he would cheer on the police, which was something, because the rest of the time he was dead against them too.

Anyway, it took me a long time to figure out why we would suddenly have five television sets, then none, then eight radios, then only one. Sometimes it was toasters, sometimes it was record players, you never knew. Things appeared and disappeared around our place like magic. I got the belt for bragging at school that we had five television sets, I brought one of the kids over to see, which made Bob mad as hell. This'll teach you to keep your fuckin' lip zipped, he said.

A lot of things made him mad as hell. It was like he spent the whole day sitting at that table, smoking Black Cat cigarettes the way he did and waiting for something to come along and make him mad, and my mother spent the whole day trying to guess what it would be so she could stop it from happening.

Go around him, she told me. Why do you have to walk right into him all the time? Pretend he's a closed door. You wouldn't walk right into a door if you could help it, would you? I thought when she said stuff like this she was taking his side, but now I see she was just trying to keep me from getting beat up too much.

I hated him more than anything. I used to lie awake at night thinking up bad things that could happen to him, like falling down a sewer or getting eaten by rats. There were rats in our apartments too, or anyway mice, and Bob wouldn't let my mother put out poison because the mice might eat it and then his cats might eat the mice, though his cats never ate any mice that I ever saw. When he wasn't there, which wasn't all that often, I used to step on the cats' tails and chase them around with the broom. I couldn't do anything to him but I sure could make life miserable for his bloody cats. I still can't stand to have a cat near me.

It was mean on the cats, but I think I did stuff like that so I wouldn't have to be so scared of him. Remember that story in the papers, six, seven years ago? It was about this woman with a little boy, who married this man, and after a while the two of them killed the little boy, out in the woods. They said they were taking him on a picnic. There was a picture of the little boy that broke my heart. The man just didn't want him around, I guess, and the mother went along with it. I was grown up by the time I read that. I was almost thirty, but it put me in a cold sweat and I dreamed about it off and on for weeks. It was like something that almost happened to me and I didn't even know it at the time, like you're sleepwalking and you wake up and you're standing on the edge of this cliff. I was always more scared of Bob when he was trying to be nice than when he was mad. It's like knowing there's someone in the closet waiting for you but not being able to see in.

My mother remarried Bob after my father died, that would be when I was around four. I don't know why she married him. My mother wasn't religious or anything, we didn't go to church, but she had this belief that things were ordered, meant to be she would say. When I asked her why she married Bob she would say it was meant to be. I don't know who by, somebody with a pretty poor sense of humor if you ask me. She never did figure out that some things are just accidents. When I was twelve or so I decided that was about the best way to think of Bob: He was an accident that happened to me, like getting run over by a truck, I was just in the way. I had to live with him, but like a broken leg, not like a person. I stopped trying to work out in advance what would make him happy or not or mad or not, because I never would be able to work it out, and I stopped thinking it had a whole lot to do with me. If he hit me it was like the weather, sometimes it rains, sometimes it doesn't. He didn't hit me because I was bad, like I used to think. He hit me because he could get away with it and nobody could stop him. That's mostly why people do stuff like that, because they can get away with it.

My mother was full of schemes. She was always reading the back pages of magazines, those ads that tell you how to start your own business in your home and make thousands of dollars. She tried a lot of them too, she addressed envelopes, she sold magazine subscriptions and encyclopedias and stuff like that door to door, she even tried arts and crafts, putting together dried flower arrangements out of the raw materials they'd send to her. Once she even rented a knitting machine. That one died a quick death.

But it was no use, she never did get rich the way they promised, you'd have to work forty-eight hours a day anyway on most of those things just to break even, and she'd lose interest pretty fast. She didn't have the business sense to handle things that really would work, like Tupperware parties. Not that we lived in Tupperware country, no way she could've had one of those parties in any of our apartments, with the cat litter box in the kitchen and the lightbulbs with no shades and the red stains down the backs of the toilets and that smell, and Bob sitting there in his cardigan with the ravelly cuffs and his cigarette cough, like his insides were going to come up any minute. That and chip dip and salads with baby marshmallows in them don't mix, you know?

She was more interested in reading the ads anyway, and sending off the first letter. That always excited her. For her it was like gambling, she wanted to believe in fate, she wanted to believe that some day the wheel would come around and it would be her turn, not for anything she'd done that would make her deserve it, but just because it was her turn. She never said so, she used to say we should make the most of what we had and be thankful for our blessings, but underneath it I think she hated those cellars and the smell of cat piss and maybe even Bob as much as I did. But she didn't know what else to do, she didn't know how to get out.

Where there's life there's hope, that's what my mother would say. She had to believe good luck was out there somewhere and it was waiting for her. All those years I didn't see her I used to send her a Loto Canada or a Wintario ticket for her birthday, sometimes a book of them when I had the money, but she never won.

■

Rennie's dreaming, she knows it, she wants to wake up.

She's standing in her grandmother's garden, around at the side of the house, she knows this garden disappeared a long time ago, I can't take care of everything, said her mother, but here it is, back in place, everything is so bright, so full of juice, the red zinnias, the hollyhocks, the sunflowers, the poles with scarlet runner beans, the hummingbirds like vivid bees around them. It's winter though, there's snow on the ground, the sun is low in the sky; small icicles hang from the stems and blossoms. Her grandmother is there, in a white cotton dress with small blue flowers on it, it's a summer dress, she doesn't seem to mind the cold, and Rennie knows this is because she is dead. There's an open window, through it Rennie can hear her mother and her aunts singing hymns in the kitchen while they do the dishes, three-part harmony.

Rennie puts out her hands but she can't touch her grandmother, her hands go right in, through, it's like touching water or new snow. Her grandmother smiles at her, the hummingbirds are around her head, lighting on her hands. Life everlasting, she says.

Rennie struggles to wake up, she doesn't want to be in this dream, and finally she makes it. She's lying in her bed, the sheet's twisted around her, she thrashes and untangles herself and pushes herself upright. Outside the window it's gray, the room is dim, perhaps it's not yet morning. There's something she has to find. She stands up, in her bare feet, she's wearing a long white cotton gown, it ties at the back, but this is not a hospital. She gets to the other side of the room and pulls open her bureau drawers, one after another, rummaging through her slips, scarves, sweaters with their arms tucked carefully behind them. It's her hands she's looking for, she knows she left them here somewhere, folded neatly in a drawer, like gloves.

Rennie opens her eyes; this time she's really awake. It's dawn, the noises are beginning, the mosquito netting hangs around her in the warm air like mist. She sees where she is, she's here, by herself, she's stranded in the future. She doesn't know how to get back.

■

What do you dream about? Rennie asked Jake, a month after they'd started living together.

You sound like my mother, Jake said. Next thing you'll want to know about my bowel movements.

Jake was in the habit of making Jewish-mother jokes, which Rennie felt was just a way of not really talking about his mother. She resented all jokes about mothers, even the ones she made about her own. Mothers were no laughing matter. You don't have a monopoly on mothers, she said. And I'm not yours. You should be flattered that I'm even interested.

Why does every woman in the world need to know that? said Jake. A few good fucks and they have to know what you dream. What difference does it make?

I just want to know you better, said Rennie. I want to know everything about you.

I'd have to be crazy to tell you anything at all, said Jake. You'd use it against me. I've seen those notebooks of yours. You'd keep lists. I bet you go through the trash can when I'm out.

Why are you so defensive? said Rennie. Don't you trust me?

Do chickens have lips? said Jake. Okay, here's what I dream about. I dream about your bum, a hundred times lifesize, floating in the sky, covered with neon lights and flashing on and off. How's that?

Don't put me down, said Rennie.

I like you down, said Jake. Flat on your back. He rolled over on top of her and started biting her neck. I'm uncontrollable, he said. I'm an animal in the dark.

Which one? said Rennie. A chipmunk?

Watch it, pussycat, said Jake. Remember your place. He got hold of her two hands, held her wrists together, shoved himself in between her thighs, squeezing her breast harder than he needed to. Feel that, he said. That's what you do to me, the fastest erection in the West. Pretend I just came through the window. Pretend you're being raped.

What's pretend about it? said Rennie. Stop pinching.

Admit it turns you on, said Jake. Admit you love it. Ask for it. Say please.

Fuck off, said Rennie. She kicked him on the backs of his legs with her heels, laughing.

Jake laughed too. He liked it when she swore; he said she was the only woman he knew who still pronounced the g in *fucking*. This was true enough: swearing was one of the social graces Rennie hadn't learned early in life, she'd had to teach herself.

You have a dirty mouth, Jake said. It needs to be washed out with a tongue.

What do you dream about? Rennie asked Daniel.

I don't know, said Daniel. I can never remember.

■

Last night Rennie set her alarm for seven. She lies in bed, waiting for it to be seven. When the alarm goes off she claws her way through the mosquito netting and pushes the off button.

If it weren't for Lora and the grandmother with the bad heart, she wouldn't have to get up at all. She considers staying in bed, she could always say she slept in. But Griswold is ingrained in her. If you can't keep your word, don't give it. Do unto others. She struggles out through the cocoon of moldy-smelling gauze, feeling not virtuous but resentful.

She wants to have breakfast before taking a taxi to the airport, but the Englishwoman says breakfast isn't ready yet, it won't be for another hour. Rennie can't wait. She decides to have coffee and a doughnut at the airport. She asks the Englishwoman to call for a taxi for her and the Englishwoman points to the phone. "You don't need to call for one," she says, "they're always hanging around down there." But Rennie calls anyway.

The car's interior is upholstered in mauve shag, the kind they use for bedroom slippers and toilet seat covers. A St. Christopher doll and a pair of rubber dice swing from the mirror. The driver is wearing purple shorts and a T-shirt with the sleeves ripped off, and a gold cross on a chain around his neck. He's young, he turns the music up as loud as it can go. It's a noxious capon-like rendering of "I Saw Mommy Kissing Santa Claus," and Rennie wonders what month they're in; already she's lost track. She's far too cowardly to ask him to turn it down, and she clenches her teeth against the adenoidal soprano as they drive into town, much too fast, he's doing it on purpose. They pass a clump of people, gathered outside a store for no discernible purpose, and he honks the horn, a long drawn-out blare, drawing attention to them as if it's a wedding.

At the airport Rennie wrestles with the door, gets it open, and climbs out. The driver makes no move, so she goes around to his side.

"How much?" she says.

"You leavin' us?" he says.

"No, I'm just picking up a package," says Rennie, and realizes immediately that she's made a mistake, because he says, "I wait for you here."

"That's all right," says Rennie. "I may be a while."

"Nothin' else to do," he says cheerfully.

The airport is almost empty. Rennie looks around for the snack bar and finds it, but it's closed. The customs window is closed too. There's a large poster taped to the glass: ELLIS IS KING.

It's a quarter to eight. Rennie sits down on a bench to wait. She hunts through her purse, looking for Lifesavers, cough drops, anything she could eat, but there's nothing. Beside the bench is a photo machine, a booth with a curtain and a slot for the coins. Rennie considers this, but it takes only American quarters. She stares across at the poster, the one with the rooster on it. THE BIONIC COCK. IT GIVES YOU SPURS. "Prince of Peace," someone has scrawled across it.

At eight-thirty the window slides up, there's someone behind it. Rennie digs the crumpled customs form out of her purse and goes over.

"I'm looking for Harold," she says, feeling very silly, but the man behind the counter isn't surprised.

"Yeah," he says. He disappears into a back room. Rennie thinks he's gone to find Harold, but he returns with a large oblong box.

"Are you Harold?" she says.

He regards this as a stupid question and doesn't answer it. "That must be one fat old lady," he says. "She get six parcel this month.

From New York. Food, it say. What she needin' all this food for?"

He looks at her slyly, smiling as if he's told a joke. The box is too big to go through the window, so he unlocks the door at the side.

Rennie was expecting something more like a package. "Isn't that the wrong box?" she says. "I'm looking for a smaller one. It's just some medicine."

"That in here too," he says airily, as if he's been through the contents himself. "This the one, ain't no other box I see."

Rennie is dubious. She reads the label, which indeed has the right name on it. "You forgot this," she says, handing him the customs form. He glances at it with contempt, then tears it in two.

"Shouldn't I sign something?" says Rennie, whose sense of correct procedure is being violated. He scowls at her.

"You tryin' to get me in trouble?" he says. "You take that and go on out of here." He locks himself in his cubicle and turns his back on her.

The box weighs a ton. Rennie has to drag it. It occurs to her that she has no idea where Lora lives or where the grandmother lives, or how she's supposed to deliver the box to either of them. The address is typed clearly enough, but all it says is Elva, Ste. Agathe. There isn't any last name. What next? She feels she has been either duped or used, but she isn't sure which or how. She makes it through the front door and looks for her taxi. It's nowhere in sight and there isn't another; probably they come to the airport only when there's a plane. There's a single car parked across the street but it isn't a taxi, it's a Jeep. There's a policeman sitting in it, smoking a cigarette and talking with the driver, and Rennie realizes with a small shock that the driver is Paul. He doesn't see her, he's facing straight ahead, listening to the policeman. Rennie thinks of asking him for a lift; he could carry the box up those stairs for her and then they could have breakfast together. But she's embarrassed, she can't ask him to do that. After the way she's behaved. Chickening out on friendly sex with no explanation at all is socially gauche, inexcusable really: She treated him as if she thought he had genital wens. He'd be right to be angry.

She'll have to lug the box back into the terminal building and phone for another taxi; then she'll have to wait for it to arrive. While she's sifting through her purse for pay-phone change, a taxi pulls up, the original. The driver is eating a huge roti; filling drips down his wrist, meat sauce. The smell reminds Rennie that she's nearly faint with hunger, but she can hardly ask for a bite. That would be borderline familiar.

The box is too big to fit into the trunk. The driver tosses the remains of his roti on the sidewalk, wipes his hands carefully on his shorts so as not to damage his mauve upholstery, and helps Rennie slide the box into the back seat. Rennie sits beside him in the front. This time the music is Nat King Cole, singing "I'm Dreaming of a White Christmas," which is better.

"How much?" Rennie asks again, outside the hotel.

"Twenty E.C.s." he says promptly. Rennie knows this is outrageous.

"It's only seven one-way from the airport," she says.

"The extra for waitin'," he says, grinning at her.

Before, on a trip like this, Rennie would have haggled; once she prided herself on her haggling. Now she doesn't have the energy, and he knows it, they all know it, they can smell it on her. She gives him twenty-three and goes around to haul out the box.

To her surprise, the driver gets out of the car, though he doesn't help her, he just watches.

"You a friend of Miss Lora's?" he says. "I see you with her. Everyone know Miss Lora."

"Yes," says Rennie, to avoid explanations. She's grappling with the box; the end slides off the back seat and hits the street.

"She a nice lady," he says softly. "You a nice lady too, like her?" Two other men, also with the sleeveless T-shirts, have stopped and are leaning against the wall.

Rennie decides to ignore this. There's an innuendo but she can't interpret it. She smiles, politely she hopes, and retreats toward the inner courtyard, dragging the box with what she hopes is dignity. Laughter trails her in.

At the foot of the stairs the deaf and dumb man is curled, asleep and snoring, drunk most likely. His fly is open, revealing torn cloth, gray; there's a recent cut across his cheek, the white stubble on his face is now half an inch long. Rennie can't get the box up the stairs without moving his legs, so she moves them. When she's setting down his feet, bare and crusted with drying mud, he opens his eyes and smiles at her, a smile that would be innocent, blissful even, if it weren't for the missing teeth. She's afraid he will want to shake her hand again, but he doesn't. Maybe he thinks she has enough good luck already.

Rennie negotiates the stairs, hugging the box, lifting it one stair at a time. It's too hot to be doing this; she's an idiot for getting herself into it, for saying she would.

When she reaches the front desk the Englishwoman informs her that it's now too late for breakfast.

"What can I have then?" says Rennie.

"Tea and biscuits," says the Englishwoman crisply.

"Can't I have some toast?" says Rennie, trying not to whine.

The Englishwoman gives her a contemptuous look. "You might find something else," she says, "out there." Her tone implies that anything eaten out there will result in cholera or worse.

Rennie orders the tea and biscuits and pulls the box along the hall to her room. By now it's almost like another person, a body, a dancing partner who's passed out cold. There's no place to put it, it won't fit into the bureau and there's no closet. Rennie slides it under the bed, and she's still on her knees when one of the waitresses brings the tea and biscuits, on a plastic tray with a picture of Windsor Castle on it.

Rennie clears the Bible and her clock off the night table so the waitress can set the tray down. The bed hasn't been made. When the waitress has gone Rennie bundles the mosquito netting into a loose knot and sits down on the twisted sheets.

The tea is made with a Tetley's teabag and water that was obviously not boiling. The biscuits are arrogantly English, flat beige ovals with the edges stamped into a Victorian-ceiling design and the centers dabbed with putty-like red jam. They look like enlarged corn plasters. Rennie bites into one. It's uncompromisingly stale, it tastes like a winter foot, like a cellar, like damp wool. Rennie wants to go home.

■

Rennie sits by the window, staring at her notebook, in which she's managed to write four words: "Fun in the Sunspots." But why worry? The editors always change her titles anyway.

There's a knock at the door. A man, says the maid, is waiting for her at the front desk. Rennie thinks it must be Paul; she checks her face in the small mirror. Now she will have to explain.

But it's Dr. Minnow, in a khaki shirt and immaculate white shorts, looking even neater than he did on the plane.

"You are enjoying your stay?" he asks, smiling his crooked smile. "You are learning about local customs?"

"Yes," says Rennie, wondering what he wants.

"I have come to take you to the Botanic Gardens," he says. "As we arranged."

Rennie can't remember having arranged any such thing, but perhaps arrangements are more casual here. She also can't remember having told him where she's staying. The Englishwoman is looking at her from behind the desk. "Of course," says Rennie. "That would be very nice."

She collects her camera, just in case, and Dr. Minnow ushers her to his car. It's a maroon Fiat with an ominous dent in the left fender. When Rennie is strapped in, Dr. Minnow turns to her with a grin that verges on slyness. "There are things more useful for you to see," he says. "We will go there first."

They drive, alarmingly fast, along the main street, away from the bankers' end. The road ceases to be mostly paved and becomes mostly unpaved; now they're in the market. The signs are still up here and there but the orange-crate platforms are gone.

Dr. Minnow hasn't slowed down as much as Rennie thinks he ought to. People stare at them, some smile. Dr. Minnow has rolled down his window and is waving. Voices call to him, he answers, everyone seems to know who he is.

Palms press flat against the windshield. "We for you," someone shouts. "The fish live!"

Rennie's beginning to be worried. The crowd around the car is too thick, it's blocking the car, not all of these people are smiling. Dr. Minnow honks his horn and revs the engine and they move forward.

"You didn't tell me you were still in politics," Rennie says.

"Everyone is in politics here, my friend," says Dr. Minnow. "All the time. Not like the sweet Canadians."

They turn uphill, away from the center of the town. Rennie grips the edge of the seat, her hands sweating, as they careen along the road, barely two lanes and switchbacked up a steep hill. She looks at the ocean, which is below them now, too far below. The view is spectacular.

They bump at a forty-five-degree angle through an arched stone gateway. "Fort Industry," says Dr. Minnow. "Very historical, built by the English. You will want to take some pictures." There's a field of sorts, rutted partially dried mud with a little grass growing on it, and a number of tents, not tents really, pieces of canvas held up by poles. Dr. Minnow parks the car on the near side of the tents and gets out, so Rennie gets out too.

Even outside there's a smell of bodies, of latrines and lime and decaying food. There are mattresses under the canvas roofs, most without sheets. Clothing is piled on the beds and hangs from ropes running from pole to pole. Between the tents are cooking fires; the ground around them is littered with utensils, pots, tin plates, pans. The people here are mostly women and young children. The children play in the mud around the tents, the women sit in the shade in their cotton dresses, talking together and paring vegetables.

"They from the hurricane," says Dr. Minnow softly. "The government have the money to rebuild their houses, the sweet Canadians send it to them. Only it has not yet happened, you understand."

An old man comes over to Dr. Minnow, an older woman, several younger ones. The man touches his arm. "We for you," he says gently. They look sideways at Rennie. She stands awkwardly, wondering what she's supposed to do or say.

Across the field, walking away from them, there's a small group of people, white, well dressed. Rennie thinks she recognizes the two German women from the hotel, the old couple from the reef boat, binoculars pointed. That's what she herself must look like: a tourist. A spectator, a voyeur.

Near her, on a mattress that's been dragged out into the sun, a young girl lies nursing a baby.

"That's a beautiful baby," Rennie says. In fact it isn't, it's pleated, shriveled, like a hand too long in water. The girl says nothing. She stares woodenly up at Rennie, as if she's been looked at many times before.

Should we have a baby? Rennie said to Jake, only once.

You don't want to limit your options too soon, said Jake, as if

114

it was only her options that would be limited, it had nothing to do with him. Maybe you should postpone it for a while. You want to get the timing right.

Which was true enough. What about you? said Rennie.

If you don't like the road, don't go, said Jake, smiling at her. I'm not too good at lifetime goals. Right now I like the road.

Can I have a baby? Rennie said to Daniel, also only once.

Little boys say *Can I,* said her grandmother. Little girls are more polite. They say *May I.*

Do you mean right now? said Daniel.

I mean ever, said Rennie.

Ever, said Daniel. *Ever* is a pretty big word.

I know. Big words get you in trouble, said Rennie. They told me that at school.

It's not a question of whether you can or not, said Daniel. Of course you can, there's nothing physical that would stop you. You could probably have a perfectly normal, healthy baby.

But? said Rennie.

Maybe you should give yourself some time, said Daniel. Just to adjust to things and consider your priorities. You should be aware that there are hormonal changes that seem to affect the recurrence rate, though we don't really know. It's a risk.

God forbid I should take a risk, said Rennie.

The girl pulls the baby off her breast and switches it to the other side. Rennie wonders if she should give her some money. Would that be insulting? Her hand moves toward her purse, but now she's surrounded by a mob of children, seven or eight of them, jumping excitedly around her and all talking at once.

"They want you to take their pictures," says Dr. Minnow, so Rennie does, but this doesn't seem to satisfy them. Now they want to see the picture.

"This isn't a Polaroid," says Rennie to Dr. Minnow. "It doesn't come out," she says to the children. It's hard to make them understand.

■

It's noon. Rennie stands under the violent sun, rubbing lotion on her face and wishing she had brought her hat. Dr. Minnow seems to know everything there is to know about this fort, and he's going to tell it all to her, brick by brick, while she dehydrates and wonders when she'll faint or break out in spots. What does he want from her? It must be something. "You shouldn't take the time," she's protested, twice already. But he's taking it.

The number of things Rennie thinks ought to happen to her in foreign countries is limited, but the number of things she fears may happen is much larger. She's not a courageous traveler, though she's always argued that this makes her a good travel writer. Other people will want to know which restaurant is likely to give you the bends, which hotel has the cockroaches, she's not the only one. Someday, if she keeps it up, she'll find herself beside a cauldron with an important local person offering her a sheep's eye or the boiled hand of a monkey, and she'll be unable to refuse. The situation has not reached that point. Nevertheless she's a captive; though if worse comes to worst she can always get a lift back with the other tourists.

Now Dr. Minnow is speculating on the methods of sanitation used by the British. It's almost as if they're extinct, a vanished tribe, and he's digging them up, unearthing their broken Queen Anne teacups, exhuming their garbage dumps, exclaiming with wonder and archeological delight over their curious customs.

The fort itself is standard Georgian brickwork, falling into decay. Although it's listed in the brochure as one of the chief attractions, nothing has been done to improve it or even to keep it in repair. Below is the muddy open space cluttered with tents, and beyond that a public toilet that's ancient and wooden and looks temporary. The only new structure is a glassed-in cubicle with an antenna of some sort on top.

"They have a high-power telescope in there," Dr. Minnow tells her. "They can see everything that comes off the boats. When it is not so hazy you can see Grenada." Beside the cubicle is a square hut that Dr. Minnow says is the prison bakery, since the fort is used as a prison. A goat is tethered beside the toilets.

Dr. Minnow has scrambled up the parapet. He's remarkably active for a man of his age. He seems to expect Rennie to climb up there too, but it's a sheer drop, hundreds of feet to the sea. She stands on tiptoe and looks over instead. In the distance, there's a blue shape, long and hazy, an island.

Dr. Minnow jumps down and stands beside her.

"Is that Grenada?" says Rennie.

"No," says Dr. Minnow. "Ste. Agathe. There, they are all sailors."

"What are they here?" says Rennie.

"Idiots," says Dr. Minnow. "But then, I am from Ste. Agathe. The British make a big mistake in the nineteenth century, they put us all together in one country. Ever since then we have trouble, and now the British have got rid of us so they can have their cheap bananas without the bother of governing us, and we have more trouble."

He's watching something below them now, his head with its high-bridged nose cocked to one side like a bird's. Rennie follows his gaze. There's a man moving among the refugees, from group to group, children following him. He's handing something out, papers, Rennie can see the white. He's wearing boots, with raised heels, cowboy boots: When he pauses before a trio of women squatting around their cooking fire, a small child runs its hands up and down the leather.

Dr. Minnow is grinning. "There is Marsdon," he says. "That boy always busy, he's working for the Prince of Peace. They're making the leaflets in the People's Church, there is a machine. They think they have the one true religion and you go to hell if you don't believe, they be glad to send you. But with these people they will not get far. You know why, my friend?"

"Why?" says Rennie, humoring him. She's tuning out, it's too much like small-town politics, the tiny feuds in Griswold, the grudges, the stupid rivalries. Who cares?

"Always they hand out papers," says Dr. Minnow. "They say it explain everything, why the sun shine, whose arse it shine out, not mine I can assure you of that." He chuckles, delighted with his own joke. "But they forget that few can read."

The children caper in Marsdon's wake, holding the squares of paper up in the air by their corners, waving them, white kites.

Another car drives into the muddy space and parks in front of the bakery; there are two men in it but they don't get out. Rennie can see their upturned faces, the blank eyes of their sunglasses.

"Now we have the whole family," says Dr. Minnow. "This kind does not hand out papers."

117

"Who are they?" says Rennie. His tone of voice is making her jumpy.

"My friends," he says softly. "They follow me everywhere. They want to make sure I am safe." He smiles and puts his hand on her arm. "Come," he says. "There is more to see."

He steers her down some steps to a stone corridor, where at least it's cooler. He shows her the officers' quarters, plain square rooms with the plaster falling away from the walls in patches.

"We wanted to have a display here," he says. "Maps, the wars between the French and English. And a gift shop, for the local arts and culture. But the Minister for Culture is not interested. He say, 'You can't eat culture.'" Rennie wants to ask what the local arts and culture are, but decides to wait. It's one of those questions to which she's already supposed to know the answer.

They go down more stone stairs. At the bottom there's a line of fresh washing, sheets and flowered pillowcases hung out to dry in the sun. Two women sit on plastic-webbed chairs; they smile at Dr. Minnow. One of them is making what looks like a wall-hanging from shreds of material in pastel underwear colors, peach, baby-blue, pink; the other is crocheting, something white. Perhaps these are the local arts and culture.

A third woman, in a brown dress and a black knitted hat, comes from a doorway.

"How much?" Dr. Minnow says to the woman who's crocheting, and Rennie can see that she's expected to buy one of the white objects. So she does.

"How long did it take you to make it?" Rennie asks her.

"Three days," she says. She has a full face, a pleasant direct smile.

"That if your boyfriend not around," says Dr. Minnow, and everyone laughs.

"We here to see the barracks," Dr. Minnow says to the woman in brown. "This lady is from Canada, she is writing about the history here." He's misunderstood her, that's why he's showing her all this. Rennie doesn't have the heart to correct him.

The woman unlocks the door and ushers them through. She has a badge pinned to her shoulder, Rennie sees now. MATRON.

"Do those women live here?" she asks.

"They are our women prisoners," Dr. Minnow says. "The one you buy the thing from, she chop up another woman. The other one, I don't know." Behind her the matron stands beside the open door, laughing with the two women. It all seems so casual.

They're in a corridor, with a row of doors on one side, a line of slatted windows on the other, overlooking a sheer drop to the sea. They go through a doorway; it leads to another corridor with small rooms opening off from it.

The rooms smell of neglect; bats hang upside down in them, there are hornets' nests on the walls, debris rotting in the corners. *Down with Babylon*, someone has scrawled across one wall. *Love to All*. The rooms farthest from the sea are damp and dark, it's too much like a cellar for Rennie.

They go back to the main corridor, which is surprisingly cool, and walk toward the far end. Dr. Minnow says she should try to imagine what this place was like with five hundred men in it. Crowded, thinks Rennie. She asks if this is the original wood.

Dr. Minnow opens the door at the end, and they're looking at a small, partly paved courtyard surrounded by a wall. The courtyard is overgrown with weeds; in a corner of it three large pigs are rooting.

In the other corner there's an odd structure, made of boards nailed not too carefully together. It has steps up to a platform, four supports but no walls, a couple of crossbeams. It's recent but dilapidated; Rennie thinks it's a child's playhouse which has been left unfinished and wonders what it's doing here.

"This is what the curious always like to see," Dr. Minnow murmurs.

Now Rennie understands what she's being shown. It's a gallows.

"You must photograph it, for your article," says Dr. Minnow. "For the sweet Canadians."

Rennie looks at him. He isn't smiling.

■

Dr. Minnow is discoursing on the Carib Indians.

"Some of the earlier groups made nose cups," he says, "which they used for taking liquid narcotics. That is what interests our visitors the most. And they took drugs also from behind. For religious purposes, you understand."

"From behind?" says Rennie.

Dr. Minnow laughs. "A ritual enema," he says. "You should put this in your article."

Rennie wonders whether he's telling the truth, but it's too grotesque not to be true. She's not sure the readers of Visor will want to hear about this, but you never know. Maybe it will catch on; for those who cough when smoking.

Dr. Minnow has insisted on taking her to lunch, and Rennie, hungry enough to eat an arm, has not protested. They're in a Chinese restaurant, which is small, dark, and hotter than the outside sunlight. Two ceiling fans stir the damp air but do not cool it; Rennie feels sweat already wetting her underarms and trickling down her chest. The table is red Formica, spotted with purplish brown sauce.

Dr. Minnow smiles across at her, kindly, avuncular, his bottom teeth clasped over the top ones like folded hands. "There is always a Chinese restaurant," he says. "Everywhere in the world. They are indefatigable, they are like the Scots, you kick them out in one place, they turn up in another. I myself am part Scottish, I have often considered going to the Gathering of the Clans. My wife say this is what makes me so pig-headed." Rennie is somewhat relieved to hear that he has a wife. He's been too attentive, there must be a catch.

A waiter comes and Rennie lets Dr. Minnow order for her. "Sometimes I think I should have remained in Canada," he says. "I could live in an apartment, or a split-level bungalow, like all the sweet Canadians, and be a doctor of sheep. I even enjoy the snow. The first time it snowed, I ran out into it in my socks, without a coat; I danced, it made me so happy. But instead I come back here."

The green tea arrives and Rennie pours it. Dr. Minnow takes his cup, turns it around, sighs. "The love of your own country is a terrible curse, my friend," he says. "Especially a country like this one. It is much easier to live in someone else's country. Then you are not tempted."

"Tempted?" says Rennie.

"To change things," he says.

Rennie feels they're heading straight toward a conversation she doesn't really want to have. She tries to think of another topic.

At home there's always the weather, but that won't do here, since there is no weather.

Dr. Minnow leans across the table toward her. "I will be honest with you, my friend," he says. "There is something I wish you to do."

Rennie isn't surprised. Here it comes, whatever it is. "What's that?" she says warily.

"Allow me to explain," says Dr. Minnow. "This is our first election since the departure of the British. Perhaps it will be the last, since it is my own belief that the British parliamentary system will no longer work in this place. It works in Britain only because they have a tradition, there are still things that are inconceivable. Here, nothing is inconceivable." He pauses, sips at his tea. "I wish you to write about it."

Whatever Rennie's been expecting, it isn't this. But why not? People are always coming on to her about their favorite hot topic. She feels her eyes glaze over. *Great*, she should say. *Good idea.* Then they're satisfied. Instead she says, "What on earth could I write about it?"

"What you see," says Dr. Minnow, choosing not to pick up on her exasperation. "All I ask you to do is look. We will call you an observer, like our friends at the United Nations." He gives a small laugh. "Look with your eyes open and you will see the truth of the matter. Since you are a reporter, it is your duty to report."

Rennie reacts badly to the word *duty*. Duty was big in Griswold. "I'm not that kind of reporter," she says.

"I understand, my friend," says Dr. Minnow. "You are a travel writer, it is an accident you are here, but you are all we can turn to at the moment. There is no one else. If you were a political journalist the government would not have been happy to see you, they would have delayed your entry or expelled you. In any case, we are too small to attract the attention of anyone from the outside, and by the time they are interested it will be too late. They always wait for the blood."

"Blood?" says Rennie.

"News," says Dr. Minnow.

The waiter brings a platter of tiny corncobs and some things that look like steamed erasers, and another of greens and squid. Rennie picks up her chopsticks. A minute ago she was hungry.

"We have seventy percent unemployment," says Dr. Minnow. "Sixty percent of our population is under twenty. Trouble happens when the people have nothing left to lose. Ellis knows this. He is using the foreign aid money from the hurricane to bribe the people. The hurricane was an act of God, and Ellis thinks that too. He hold out his hands to heaven and pray for someone up there to save his ass from him, and bang, all that money from the sweet Canadians. This is not all. He is using threats now, he says he will take away the jobs and maybe burn down the houses of those who do not vote for him."

"He's doing this openly?" says Rennie.

"On the radio, my friend," says Dr. Minnow. "As for the people, many are afraid of him and the rest admire him, not for this behavior, you understand, but because he can get away with it. They see this as power and they admire a big man here. He spends their money on new cars and so forth for himself and friends, they applaud that. They look at me, they say, 'What you can do for us?' If you have nothing you are nothing here. It's the old story, my friend. We will have a Papa Doc and after that a revolution or so. Then the Americans will wonder why people are getting killed. They should tell the sweet Canadians to stop giving money to this man."

Rennie knows she's supposed to feel outrage. She remembers the early seventies, she remembers all that outrage you were supposed to feel. Not to feel it then was very unfashionable. At the moment though all she feels is imposed upon. Outrage is out of date.

"What good would it do, even if I wrote it?" says Rennie. "I couldn't get it published here, I don't know anyone."

Dr. Minnow laughs. "Not here," he says. "Here there is one paper only and Ellis has bought the editor. In any case, few can read. No, you should publish it there. This will be of help, they pay attention to the outside, they are sensitive about their foreign aid. They would know they are being watched, that someone knows what they are doing. This would stop excesses."

Rennie wonders what an excess is. "I'm sorry," she says, "but I can't think of anyone who would touch it. It isn't even a story yet, nothing's happened. It's hardly of general interest."

"There is no longer any place that is not of general interest," says Dr. Minnow. "The sweet Canadians have not learned this yet. The Cubans are building a large airport in Grenada. The CIA is here, they wish to nip history in the bud, and the Russian agents. It is of general interest to them."

Rennie almost laughs. The CIA has been done to death; surely by now it's a joke, he can't be serious. "I suppose they're after your natural resources," she says.

Dr. Minnow stares across at Rennie, smiling his cramped smile, no longer entirely kind and friendly. "As you know, we have a lot of sand and not much more. But look at a map, my friend." He's no longer pleading, he's lecturing. "South of St. Antoine is Ste. Agathe, south of Ste. Agathe is Grenada, south of Grenada is Venezuela with the oil, a third of U.S. imports. North of us there is Cuba. We are a gap in the chain. Whoever controls us controls the transport of oil to the United States. The boats go from Guyana to Cuba with rice, from Cuba to Grenada with guns. Nobody is playing."

Rennie puts down her chopsticks. It's too hot to eat. She feels as if she's stumbled into some tatty left-liberal journal with a two-color cover because they can't afford three colors. She's allowed this conversation to go on too long, a minute more and she'll be hooked. "It's not my thing," she says. "I just don't do that kind of thing. I do lifestyles."

"Lifestyles?" says Dr. Minnow. He's puzzled.

"You know, what people wear, what they eat, where they go for their vacations, what they've got in their living rooms, things like that," says Rennie, as lightly as she can.

Dr. Minnow considers this for a moment. Then he gives her an angelic smile. "You might say that I also am concerned with lifestyles," he says. "It is our duty, to be concerned with lifestyles. What the people eat, what they wear, this is what I want you to write about."

He's got her. "Well, I'll think about it," she says limply .

"Good," says Dr. Minnow, beaming. "This is all I wish." He picks up his chopsticks again and scrapes the rest of the squid into his bowl. "Now I will give you a good piece of advice. You should be careful of the American."

"What American?" says Rennie.

"The man," says Dr. Minnow. "He is a salesman."

He must mean Paul. "What does he sell?" says Rennie, amused. This is the first she's heard of it.

"My friend," says Dr. Minnow, "you are so very sweet."

■

There's a small stationery shop across the street from the hotel, and Rennie goes into it. She passes over the historical romances, imported from England, and buys a local paper, *The Queenstown Times*, which is what she's come to the shop for. Guilt impels her: She owes at least this much to Dr. Minnow.

Though it's becoming clear to her that she has no intention of doing what he wants her to do. Even if she wanted to, she could hardly run all over the place, talking to men in the street; they don't understand the convention, they'd think she was trying to pick them up. She can't do proper research, there are no books in the library here; there's no library. She's a hypocrite, but what else is new? It's a Griswold solution: If you can't say anything nice, don't say anything at all. I'm dying, she should have told him. Don't count on me.

She orders tea and biscuits and takes the paper into the leatherette lounge. What she really wants is to lie down and sleep, and if she goes back to her room she knows she will. She's trying to resist that; it would be so easy here to do nothing but eat and sleep.

The Englishwoman brings the tea tray herself and slams it down in front of Rennie. "I don't know where *they've* gone to," she says.

Rennie expects her to go away, but instead she hovers. "There's no water," she says. "They should have it fixed in a few hours." Still she lingers.

"May I offer you some advice?" she says at last. "Don't have anything to do with that man."

"What man?" says Rennie. The Englishwoman's voice suggests some violation of sexual morality, and Rennie wonders what she's done to deserve this.

"That man," says the Englishwoman. "Calls himself a doctor."

"He just wanted to show me the Botanic Gardens," says Rennie, conscious of a slight lie. She waits for the woman to tell her that Dr. Minnow is really a notorious sexual molester, but instead she says, "The trees have signs on them. You can read them yourself, if that's what you want."

"What's the matter with him?" says Rennie. Now she expects racial prejudice.

"He stirs people up for nothing," says the Englishwoman.

This time the biscuits are white and sprinkled with sand. The tea is lukewarm. Rennie fishes the teabag out by its string. She doesn't want to leave it on her saucer, it's too much like a dead mouse, so after some thought she conceals it in the earth around the mottled plant.

The editorial is about the election. Dr. Minnow, it seems, is almost as bad as Castro, and Prince Macpherson is worse. If anyone at all votes for either of them, they are likely to combine forces and form a coalition, and that will be the end of the democratic traditions that St. Antoine has cherished and protected for so long, says the editor.

On the front page there's a story about the new sugar factory Prime Minister Ellis is planning, and an article about road repairs. There's a picture of Ellis, the same picture that's everywhere on the posters. The Canadian High Commissioner has recently paid a visit from his base in Barbados, and a reception was given for him at Government House. Canada is sponsoring a diver training program for lobster fishermen on Ste. Agathe, where most of the fishermen live. The inhabitants of Songeville will be pleased to learn that the United States has contributed an extra five hundred thousand dollars to the hurricane relief fund, which will be used to repair roofs and fix the schoolhouse. Those still living in temporary camps and in churches will soon be able to return to their homes.

The Englishwoman comes back in, white-faced, tight-lipped, dragging an aluminum step ladder which screeches on the wooden floor. "If you want it done, do it yourself," she announces to Rennie. She sets the ladder up, climbs it, and starts taking down the tinsel festoons, her solid white-marbled calves two feet from Rennie's head. There's a strong smell of women's washrooms: tepid flesh, face powder, ammonia. Rennie tries to read a story about the sudden increase in petty thievery, but the Englishwoman is making her feel lazy and selfish. In a minute she'll offer to help and then she'll be stuck, catching those fuzzy fake poinsettias as the Englishwoman tosses them down and putting them away in that tatty cardboard box. She folds up her newspaper and retreats to her room, carrying her cup of cold tea.

"What to Do If the Thief Visits You," she reads. "1. Have a flashlight by your bed. 2. Have a large can of Baygon or other insect spray. 3. Shine the flashlight into his face. 4. Spray the Baygon into his face. 5. Go to the police, make a statement." Rennie wonders what the thief is supposed to do while you're spraying the Baygon into his face, but doesn't pursue this further. Like everything else she's been reading, the instructions are both transparent and impenetrable.

She skips the column entitled "Spiritual Perspectives," toys with the idea of doing the crossword puzzle but discards it; the answers are on page ten and she knows she'll cheat. The "Housewives' Corner" has nothing in it but a recipe for corn fritters. The "Problem Corner" is by Madame Marvelous.

Dear Madame Marvelous:

I am in love with a boy. Both of us are Christians. Sometimes he asks me for a kiss, but I have read that kissing before marriage is not right because it arouses passions that lead to sex. But he does not believe that sex before marriage is wrong. The Bible says fornication is wrong, but he says fornication is not sex. Please explain this in a clear way.

Worried.

Dear Worried:

My dear, love is the full expression of oneself. As long as you remember this you will not go wrong. I do hope I have helped you.

Madame Marvelous.

Rennie closes her eyes and pulls the sheet up over her head. She doesn't have the strength to untangle the mosquito netting.
Oh please.

■

Rennie lies in bed and thinks about Daniel. Which is hopeless, but wasn't it always? The sooner she stops the better. Still, she keeps on.

It would be easier if Daniel were a pig, a prick, stupid or pompous or even fat; especially fat. Fat would be a big advantage. Unfortunately Daniel is thin. Also he loves Rennie, or so he said, which is no help at all. (Though what did it amount to? Not much, as far as Rennie could see. She isn't even sure what it meant, this love of his, or what he thought it meant; which may not be the same thing.)

Rennie once spent a lot of time trying to figure out what Daniel meant. Which was difficult, because he wasn't like any of the people she knew. The people she knew spoke of themselves as bottoming out and going through changes and getting it together. The first time she'd used these phrases with Daniel, she'd had to translate. Daniel had never bottomed out, as far as she could tell, and apparently he'd never felt the need to get it together. He didn't think of himself as having gone through changes. In fact he didn't seem to think of himself much in any way at all. This was the difference between Daniel and the people she knew: Daniel didn't think of himself.

This sometimes made it hard for Rennie to talk to him, since when she asked him questions about himself he didn't know the answers. Instead he acted as if he'd never even heard the questions. Where have you been for the past twenty years? she wanted to ask him. Etobicoke? It was more like Don Mills, but Daniel didn't seem to care where he lived. He didn't care what he ate, he didn't care what he wore: His clothes looked as if they'd been picked out by his wife, which they probably had been. He was a specialist, he'd been immersed, he knew only one thing.

He thought Rennie knew things he didn't know but ought to; he thought she lived in the real world. It pleased him to believe this, and Rennie wanted him to be pleased, she liked to amuse him, though she was afraid that sooner or later he would decide that the things she knew weren't really worth knowing. Meanwhile he was like a Patagonian in Woolworth's, he was enthralled by trivia. Maybe he's having a mid-life crisis, thought Rennie. He was about that age. Maybe he's slumming.

Sometimes they had lunch together, but not very often because most of Daniel's life was spoken for. At lunch Rennie did tricks, which was easy enough with Daniel: He could still be surprised by things that no longer surprised anyone else. She deduced the customers from their clothes, she did them over for him in front of his very eyes. This one, she said. A receptionist at, let's see, Bloor and Yonge, but she'd like you to think she's more. Overdid it on the eyeshadow. The man with her though, he's a lawyer. At the next table, middle management, probably in a bank. I'd redo the cuffs on the pants, the lawyer's, not the other one. On the other one, I'd redo the hair.

I don't see anything wrong with his hair, said Daniel.

You don't understand, Rennie said. People love being redone. I mean, you don't think you're finished, do you? Don't you want to change and grow? Don't you think there's more? Don't you want me to redo you? It was one of Rennie's jokes that the perfect magazine title would be "Sexual Makeovers." People thought of their lives as examinations they could fail or pass, you got points for the right answers. Tell them what was wrong, preferably with them, then suggest how to improve it. It gave them hope: Daniel should approve of that.

How would you redo me? said Daniel, laughing.

If I could get my hands on you? said Rennie. I wouldn't, you're perfect the way you are. See how good I'd be for your ego, if you had one?

Daniel said that he did have one, that he was quite selfish in fact, but Rennie didn't believe him. He didn't have time for an ego. During lunch he looked at his watch a lot, furtively but still a lot. "Romance Makes a Comeback," thought Rennie. She kept hoping she'd see enough of him so she'd begin to find him boring; talking with Daniel was a good deal like waltzing with a wall, even she knew that. But this failed to happen, partly because there wasn't a whole lot of him to see. When he wasn't at the hospital he had family obligations, as he put it. He had a wife, he had children, he had parents. Rennie had trouble picturing any of them, except the parents, whom she saw as replicas of American Gothic; only Finnish, which was what they were. They didn't have a lot of money and they were very proud of Daniel, who wasn't any more Finnish than she was except for the cheekbones. Sundays the parents got him; Saturdays were for the kids, evenings for the wife. Daniel was a dutiful husband, a dutiful parent, a dutiful son, and Rennie, who felt she had given up being dutiful some time ago, found it hard not to sneer and hard not to despise herself for wanting to.

She wasn't jealous of his wife, though. Only of his other patients. Maybe I'm not the only one, thought Rennie. Maybe there's a whole lineup of them, dozens and dozens of women, each with a bite taken out of them, one breast or the other. He's saved all our lives, he has lunch with us all in turn, he tells us all he loves us. He thinks it's his duty, it gives us something to hold onto. Anyway he gets off on it, it's like a harem. As for us, we can't help it, he's the only man in the world who knows the truth, he's looked into each one of us and seen death. He knows we've been resurrected, he knows we're not all that well glued together, any minute we'll vaporize. These bodies are only provisional.

At the beginning, when she still believed she could return to normal, Rennie thought that they would see each other a certain number of times and then they would have an affair; naturally; that's what people did. But this also failed to happen. Instead, Daniel spent one whole lunch explaining, earnestly and unhappily, why he couldn't go to bed with her.

It would be unethical, he said. I'd be taking advantage of you. You're in an emotional state.

What is this, thought Rennie, Rex Morgan, M.D.? People she knew prided themselves on taking emotional risks. She couldn't decide whether Daniel was being wise, principled, or just a coward.

Why is it such a big deal? she said. Once wouldn't kill you. Behind a bush, it would only take five minutes.

It wouldn't be once, he said.

Rennie felt suspended; she was waiting all the time, for something to happen. Maybe I'm an event freak, she thought. The people she knew, Jocasta for instance, would have regarded it all as an experience. Experiences were like other collectibles, you kept adding them to your set. Then you traded them with your friends. Show and tell. But Rennie had trouble thinking of Daniel as just an experience; besides, what was there to tell?

What do you get out of this? she said. What do you want?

Does there have to be something? he said. I just want it to go on the way it is.

But what *is* it? she said. It isn't anything. There's nothing to it.

He looked hurt and she was ashamed of herself. What he probably wanted was escape, like everyone else; a little but not too much, a window but not a door.

I could ask you the same thing, he said.

I want you to save my life, thought Rennie. You've done it once, you can do it again. She wanted him to tell her she was fine, she wanted to believe him.

I don't know, she said. She didn't know. Probably she didn't really want him to go to bed with her or even touch her; probably she loved him because he was safe, there was absolutely nothing he could demand.

Sometimes they held hands, discreetly, across the table in the corners of restaurants; which, in those weeks and then those months, was about as much as she could stand. Afterward she could feel the shape of his hand for hours.

∎

There's someone knocking at the door. The room is dark. Whatever sings at night is singing outside her window, and there is the same music.

The knocking goes on. Perhaps it's the maid, coming far too late, to make up the bed. Rennie pulls off the damp sheet, walks to the door in her bare feet, unlocks it, opens it. Paul is there, one shoulder leaning against the wall, looking not at all like a salesman.

"You shouldn't unlock your door like that," he says. "It could be anyone." He's smiling though.

Rennie feels at a disadvantage without her shoes on. "I'm lucky this time," she says. She's glad to see him: He's the closest facsimile here to someone she knows. Maybe they can just skip yesterday and start again, as if nothing at all has happened. Which is true enough, since nothing has.

"I thought you might like dinner," he says, "some place with real food."

"I'll put on my shoes," says Rennie. She turns on the mermaid lamp. Paul comes into the room and closes the door, but he doesn't sit down. He just stands, gazing around as if it's an art gallery, while Rennie picks up her sandals and purse and goes into the bathroom to see what she looks like. She brushes her hair and sticks on a little blue eyeliner pencil, not too much. She thinks about changing her dress but decides against it; it might look anxious. When she comes out he's sitting on the edge of her bed.

"I was having a nap," says Rennie, feeling she has to explain the unmade bed.

"I see you got Lora's box for her all right," he says. "Any problems?"

"No," says Rennie, "except it was a little bigger than I thought, and now I don't know what to do with it." It occurs to her that she may be able to fob the box off on Paul, since he knows Lora. "I don't know where this woman lives," she says, as helplessly as she can.

"Elva?" says Paul. "You just take it over to Ste. Agathe, there's a boat every day at noon. Once you get there anyone can tell you." He doesn't offer to take it himself.

Rennie turns off the mermaid lamp and locks the door and they walk out past the front desk and the Englishwoman's laser-beam gaze, and Rennie feels she's sneaking out of the dorm.

"The dinner's part of the plan," says the Englishwoman behind them.

"Pardon?" says Rennie.

"If you don't eat it you pay for it anyway. It's part of the plan."

"I realize that," says Rennie.

"We lock up at twelve," says the Englishwoman.

Rennie's beginning to understand why she dislikes this woman so much. It's the disapproval, automatic and self-righteous, it's the ill-wishing. Rennie knows all about that, it's part of her background. Whatever happens to Rennie the Englishwoman will say she was asking for it; as long as it's bad.

They go down the stone steps and through the damp little courtyard and step out into the musical night. Paul takes hold of Rennie's arm above the elbow, his fingers digging in. "Just keep going," he says. He's steering her.

Now she sees what he's talking about. A little way up the street, in the dim light over by the stationery store, two of the blue-shirted policemen are beating a man up. The man is on his knees in the potholed road and they're kicking him, in the stomach, on the back. All Rennie can think of is that the two policemen are wearing shoes and the man isn't. She's never seen anyone being beaten up like this before, only pictures of it. As soon as you take a picture of something it's a picture. Picturesque. This isn't.

Rennie has stopped, though Paul is pushing her, trying to keep her moving. "They don't like you to stare," he says. Rennie's not sure who he means. Does he mean the policemen, or the people they beat up? It would be shaming, to have other people see you so helpless. There are other people on the street, the usual clumps and knots, but they aren't staring, they're looking and then looking away. Some of them are walking, nobody is doing anything, although the walking ones deflect themselves, they go carefully around the man, who is now doubled over.

"Come on," says Paul, and this time Rennie moves. The man is struggling onto his knees; the policemen are standing back, watching him with what seems like mild curiosity, two children watching a beetle they've crippled. Perhaps now they will drop stones on him, thinks Rennie, remembering the schoolyard. To see which way he will crawl. Her own fascination appalls her. He lifts his face and there's blood streaming down it, they must have cut his head, he looks directly at Rennie. Rennie can remember drunks on Yonge Street, men so drunk they can't stand up, looking up at her like that. Is it an appeal, a plea for help, is it hatred? She's been seen, she's being seen with utter thoroughness, she won't be forgotten.

It's the old man. He can't be totally mute because there's a sound of some kind coming out of him, a moaning, a stifled reaching out for speech which is worse than plain silence.

They reach the Jeep and this time Paul opens the door and helps her in, he wants her in there as fast as possible. He closes the door carefully, tests it to make sure it's really shut.

"Why were they doing that?" Rennie says. She's pressing her hands together, she refuses to shake.

"Doing what?" says Paul. He's a little sharp, a little annoyed. She stalled on him.

"Come on," says Rennie.

Paul shrugs. "He was drunk," he says. "Or maybe they caught him thieving. He was hanging around the hotel when I came in, they don't like people bothering the tourists. It's bad for business."

"That was horrible," says Rennie.

"Up north they lock them up, down here they just beat them up a little. I know which I'd choose," says Paul.

"That wasn't a little," says Rennie.

Paul looks over at her and smiles. "Depends what you think a lot is," he says.

Rennie shuts up. She's led a sheltered life, he's telling her. Now she's annoyed with herself for acting so shocked. Squealing at mice, standing on a chair with your skirts hitched up, that's the category. *Girl*.

Paul drives through the darkness with elaborate slowness, for her benefit. "You can go faster," she says. "I'm not about to throw up." He smiles, but he doesn't.

■

The Driftwood at night is much the same as the Driftwood by day except that it's floodlit. There's a half-hearted steel band and two couples are dancing to it. The women are wearing shirts made from fake flour sacks; the blonde is taking pictures with a flashcube camera, the brunette is wearing a captain's cap, backward. One of the men has a green shirt with parrots on it. The other one is shorter, fatter, with the fronts of his legs so badly burned that the skin is peeling off in rags. He's wearing a red T-shirt that says BIONIC COCK. It's the usual bunch, from Wisconsin Rennie decides, dentists and their wives fresh off the plane, their flesh like uncooked Dover sole, flying down to run themselves briefly under the grill. The dentists come here, the dental assistants go to Barbados, that's the difference.

Rennie and Paul sit at a metal table and Rennie orders a ginger ale. She's not going to get sick in the Jeep again, once was enough. She's thinking about the man on his knees in the dark road, but what is there to think? Except that she's not hungry. She watches the awkward stiff-legged dancers, the steel-band men, who are supple, double-jointed almost, glancing at them with a contempt that is almost but not quite indifference.

"Dentists from Wisconsin?" she says to Paul.

"Actually they're Swedes," he says. "There's been a rash of

Swedes lately. Swedes tell other Swedes, back in Sweden. Then all of a sudden the place is swarming with them."

"How can you tell?" says Rennie, impressed.

Paul smiles at her. "I found out," he says. "It's not hard. Everyone finds out about everyone else around here, they're curious. It's a small place, anything new or out of the ordinary gets noticed pretty fast. A lot of people are curious about you, for instance."

"I'm not out of the ordinary," says Rennie.

"Here you are," he says. "You're at the wrong hotel, for one thing. It's mostly package tours and little old ladies who stay there. You should be at the Driftwood." He pauses, and Rennie feels she has to supply an answer.

"Pure economics," she says. "It's a cheap magazine."

Paul nods, as if this is acceptable. "They wonder why you aren't with a man," he says. "If you'd come on a boat they'd know why, they'd figure you're just boat-hopping. Girls do that quite a bit here, it's like hitchhiking, in more ways than one. But you don't seem the type. Anyway, they know you came in on the plane." A smile, another pause. It occurs to Rennie that it may not be *they* who want to know these things about her, it may only be Paul. A small prickle goes down her spine.

"If they know so much, they must know what I'm doing here," she says, keeping her voice even. "It's business. I'm doing a travel piece. I hardly need a chaperone for that."

Paul smiles. "White women have a bad reputation down here," he says. "For one thing, they're too rich; for another, they lower the moral tone."

"Come on," says Rennie.

"I'm just telling you what they think," says Paul. "The women here think they spoil the local men. They don't like the way white women dress, either. You'd never see a local woman wearing shorts or even pants, they think it's degenerate. If they started behaving like that their men would beat the shit out of them. If you tried any of that Women's Lib stuff down here they'd only laugh. They say that's for the white women. Everyone knows white women are naturally lazy and they don't want to do a woman's proper work, and that's why they hire black women to do their work for them."

He looks at her with something between a challenge and a smirk, which Rennie finds irritating.

"Is that why you like it here?" she says. "You get your grapes peeled for you?"

"Don't blame it on me," Paul says, with a little shrug. "I didn't invent it."

He's watching her react, so she tries not to. After a minute he goes on. "They also think you aren't only a journalist. They don't believe you're really just writing for a magazine."

"But I am!" says Rennie. "Why wouldn't they believe that?"

"They don't know much about magazines," says Paul. "Anyway, almost nobody here is who they say they are at first. They aren't even who somebody else thinks they are. In this place you get at least three versions of everything, and if you're lucky one of them is true. That's if you're lucky."

"Does all this apply to you?" says Rennie, and Paul laughs.

"Let me put it this way," he says. "For ten thousand dollars you can buy a St. Antoine passport; officially, I mean, unofficially it costs more. That's if you've got the right connections. If you want to, you can open your own private bank. The government even helps you do it, for a cut of the action. Certain kinds of people find it very convenient."

"What are you telling me?" says Rennie, who senses increasingly she's been asked out to dinner for a reason, which is not the same as the reason she had for accepting. She looks into his light-blue eyes, which are too light, too blue. They've seen too much water. Burned out, she thinks.

Paul smiles, a kindly, threatening smile. "I like you," he says. "I guess I'm trying to tell you not to get too mixed up in local politics. That is, if you really are writing a travel piece."

"Local *politics*?" says Rennie, taken by surprise.

Paul sighs. "You remind me of a certain kind of girl back home," he says. "The kind who move to New York from the Midwest and get jobs on magazines."

"In what way?" says Rennie, dismayed.

"For one thing you're nice," says Paul. "You'd rather not be, you'd rather be something else, tough or sharp or something like that, but you're nice, you can't help it. Naïve. But you think you have to prove you're not merely nice, so you get into things you shouldn't. You want to know more than other people, am I right?"

"I don't have the faintest idea what you're talking about," says

Rennie, who feels seen through. She wonders if he's right. Once he would have been, once there were all kinds of things she wanted to know. Now she's tired of it.

Paul sighs. "Okay," he says. "Just remember, nothing that goes on here has anything to do with you. And I'd stay away from Minnow."

"Dr. Minnow?" says Rennie. "Why?"

"Ellis doesn't like him," says Paul. "Neither do some other people."

"I hardly know him," says Rennie.

"You had lunch with him," says Paul, almost accusingly.

Rennie laughs. "Am I going to get shot, for having *lunch*?"

Paul doesn't think this is funny. "Probably not," he says. "They mostly shoot their own. Let's go get something to eat."

Under an open-sided hut with fake thatching there's a buffet laid out, bowls of salad, platters of roast beef, lime pies, chocolate cakes with hibiscus flowers stuck into them. As much as you can eat. There are more people now, piling food high on their plates. To Rennie, they all look Swedish.

She takes her plate to the table. Paul is silent now and absent. It's almost as if he's in a hurry to get away. Rennie sits across from him, eating shrimp and feeling like a blind date, the comic-book kind with buck teeth and pimples. In situations like this she reverts to trying to please, or is it appease? Maybe he's with the CIA, it would all fit in, the warning and the neo-hippie haircut, camouflage, and the time in Cambodia, and the boats he shouldn't be able to afford. The more she thinks about it the more sense it makes. She's innocent, she doesn't want him to get the wrong impression, he might end up putting some kind of weird drug into her guava jam. Does he think she's a dangerous subversive because she had lunch with Dr. Minnow? She wonders how she can convince him that she is who she is. Would he believe drain-chain jewelry?

Finally she asks him about tennis courts. She wants things to return to normal; she wants the situation to normalize, as they say on the news. "Tennis courts?" Pauls says, as if he's never heard of them.

Rennie feels that she's been investigated and dismissed, she's been pronounced negligible, and this is either because Paul believes her or because he doesn't. Which is worse, to be irrelevant or to be dishonest? Whichever it is has erased her as far as he's concerned. As for her, all she can think of is how to recapture his interest, now that it's no longer there. She's almost forgotten there's some of her missing. She realizes she was looking forward, though to what she doesn't know. An event, that's all. Something. She's had enough blank space recently to last her for a long time.

■

Rennie and Jocasta were trying on used fur coats in the Sally Ann at Richmond and Spadina. According to Jocasta this was the best Sally Ann in the city. It was really Jocasta who was trying them on, since Rennie didn't have much interest in used fur coats, she stuck to her classic down-fill from Eddie Bauer's. They were supposed to be shopping for Rennie; Jocasta thought it would make her feel better if she went out and bought something. But she should have known. With Jocasta you always ended up in the Sally Ann.

I won't wear seal though, said Jocasta. I draw the line. Look at this, what do you think it is?

Dyed rabbit, said Rennie. You're safe.

Jocasta turned the pockets inside out. There was a stained handkerchief in one of them. What I'm really looking for, she said, is a black hat with a pheasant feather, you know those curved ones? Gloria Swanson. How's everything?

I'm having a thing with this man, said Rennie, who had resolved many times never to discuss this with anyone, especially Jocasta.

Jocasta looked at her. The pause was just a little too long, and Rennie could hear Jocasta wondering how much of her was gone, chopped away; under all that, you couldn't tell really. A thing with a man. *Bizarre.* Possibly even gross.

That's wizard, said Jocasta, who liked resurrecting outmoded slang. Love or sex?

I'm not sure, said Rennie.

Love, Jocasta said. Lucky you. I can't seem to get it up for love any more. It's such an effort.

She slipped her arms into a late forties lantern-sleeve muskrat, while Rennie held it for her. A little tatty around the collar, but not bad, said Jocasta. So it's walking-on-air time, a little pitty-pat of the heart, steamy dreams, a little how-you-say purple passion? Spots on the neck, wet pits? Buying your trousseau yet?

Not exactly, said Rennie. He's married.

Before Daniel, Rennie had never paid much attention to married men. The mere fact that they were married ruled them out, not because they were off-limits but because they had demonstrated their banality. Having a married man would be like having a Group of Seven washable silkscreen reproduction in your living room. Only banks had those any more, and not the best banks, either.

Lately, though, she'd been seeing it from a different angle. Maybe Daniel wasn't an afterglow from the past; maybe he was the wave of the future. As Jocasta said about her wardrobe, save it up. Never throw anything away, because time is circular and sooner or later it all comes around again. Maybe experiments in living, trying it out first, and infinitely renegotiable relationships were fading fast. Soon Daniel would be *in*, limited options would be *in*. No way out would be *in*. Group of Seven silkscreens were coming back too, among the ultra *nouveau wavé*, but they had to be washable.

Sometimes married is better than not married, Jocasta said. They've got their own lives, they don't need to muck up yours. You can do it in the afternoon, have a nice fuck, hear all about how important you are in their life, listen to their little troubles, their mortgage, the way their kid grinds chewed-up caramels into the shag, how they had to get the clutch on the Volvo replaced, and then you can go out with someone fun at night. I used to like stoles, but you know those little shortie jackets they used to wear with formals? With the handkerchief pocket. They're better.

You don't quite see it, said Rennie. He's *really* married. He thinks of himself as married.

You mean he says stuff like his wife doesn't understand him, Jocasta said. That can be boring. Usually their wife understands them backward, that's the problem. I went through all that ten years ago, when I was still a junior buyer for Creeds. Every time I had to go to New York; it was the goddamn supervisor. He thought I was so *dirty*, you know? *Turkeyville!* I must have been desperate, I hadn't discovered cucumbers then. What they usually mean is

138

that their wives won't go down on them, as far as I can figure out. Kids? Let me guess. Two.

Three and a half, Rennie said.

You mean one's brain-damaged? said Jocasta, looking over her shoulder in the mirror. Waltz length. Remember waltz length?

No, said Rennie. His wife's pregnant again.

And he loves his wife, of course, said Jocasta. And she loves him. Right?

I'm afraid so, said Rennie.

Daniel had not said *I'm afraid so*. He'd said *I think so*.

You mean you don't know? said Rennie.

We don't talk about it, he said. I guess she does. She does.

So sit back and enjoy it, said Jocasta. What do you have to worry about? Except Jake, but he's cool.

Rennie wondered how cool Jake actually was. She hadn't told him about Daniel. Daniel, however, asked about Jake almost every time they saw each other. How's Jake? he would say hopefully, and Rennie would always say, Fine. She knew about bookends, she knew that one wouldn't work without the other. Any damage to Jake and Daniel would be off and running. He wouldn't want to be stuck with the whole package. She might be the icing on his cake but she sure as hell wasn't the cake.

Jake's a grown-up, she said. *Open-ended* is one of his favorite words.

Well, there you go, said Jocasta. Nifty. Two's better than one any day, as long as you don't go all soft and grubby and Heartbreak Hotel.

You still don't see it, said Rennie. Nothing's happening.

Nothing? said Jocasta.

Unless you count some pretty frantic hand-holding, said Rennie. She was embarrassed to have to admit this, she knew how abnormal it was, but she wasn't as embarrassed as she would have been once. The fact was that she wasn't sure whether she wanted it or not, an affair with Daniel. It would not be what you would call relaxed, it wouldn't be very much fun. Pulling the plug on all that repression. It would be like going over Niagara Falls in a spin-drier, you could get injured that way.

Why not? said Jocasta.

I told you, said Rennie. He's too married.

They looked at one another. Nothing, said Jocasta. Weird. She put her hand on Rennie's shoulder. Listen, she said, it could be worse. Look at it this way. I mean, an affair's just another affair, what else is new? It's like one chocolate bar after another; you start having these fantasies about being a nun, and you know what, they're enjoyable. But nothing, that's kind of romantic; he must think a lot of you. There's something to be said for nothing.

■

After the chocolate cake they drive back, straight back, no stopping in the woods this time. Rennie sits jolting in the front seat, trying not to feel disappointed. What does she need it for anyway? It's foolishness, as her grandmother would say. Her mother too. They all have the category, it gets passed down like a cedar chest, though they each put different things into it.

When they reach the hotel Paul doesn't touch her, not even a peck on the cheek. He opens his door and gets out, whistling through his teeth. He doesn't take her hand to help her down, he takes her arm, and he doesn't go as far as her room. He waits at the bottom of the stone stairs until she reaches the top, that's all.

Rennie walks down the green wooden corridor, feeling very tired. What is she supposed to make of all this? Why is she trying to make anything? He asked her for dinner and dinner is what she got. She remembers seeing a film, years ago, about the effects of atomic radiation on the courtship instincts of animals: birds ignoring each other or attacking instead of dancing, fish going around in lopsided circles instead of spawning, turtles leaving their eggs to fry in the sun, unfertilized anyway. Maybe this is what accounts for the New Chastity: a few too many deadly rays zapping the pineal gland. The signals are all screwed up and nobody understands any more what they used to mean.

What she remembers most clearly about the evening is not even Paul. It's the deaf and dumb man on his knees in the street, the two men kicking at him, then watching him with that detachment, that almost friendly interest.

A long time ago, about a year ago, Jocasta said, I think it would be a great idea if all the men were turned into women and all the women were turned into men, even just for a day. Then they'd all know exactly how the other ones would like to be treated. When they got changed back, I mean. Don't you think that's a great idea?

It's a great *idea*, said Rennie.

But would you vote for it? said Jocasta.

Probably not, said Rennie.

That's the problem with great ideas, said Jocasta. Nobody votes for them.

Jocasta thinks it would be a great idea if all the men were changed into women and all the women were changed into men for a week. Then they'd each know how to treat the other ones when they got changed back, said Rennie.

Jocasta's full of crap, said Jake. And too bony. Bony women shouldn't wear V-necks.

What's the matter with it? said Rennie. Wouldn't you like to know how women want to be treated? Wouldn't it make you irresistible?

Not if everyone else knew it too, said Jake. But first of all, that isn't what would happen. The women would say, Now I've got you, you prick. Now it's my turn. They'd all become rapists. Want to bet?

What would the men say? said Rennie.

Who knows? said Jake. Maybe they'd just say, Oh shit. Maybe they'd say they don't feel like it tonight because they're getting their periods. Maybe they'd want to have babies. Myself, I could do without it. Feh.

That would take more than a week, said Rennie.

Anyway, said Jake, do you really know how you want to be treated? You ever met anyone who does?

You mean any women, don't you, said Rennie.

Skip the semantics, said Jake. Tell the truth. Tell me how you want to be treated. In twenty-five words or less. You say it, I'll do it.

Rennie began to laugh. All right, she said. Is that a promise?

Later she said, It depends who by.

■

Rennie unlocks the door of her room. The mermaid lamp is on, and for a moment she can't remember whether or not she turned it off when she left. She could swear she did. There's a smell in the room that wasn't there before.

She sees her notebook, laid out on the bed, with the material she's been collecting, maps and brochures, neatly beside it. Someone's been in here. Rennie senses an ambush. She had her purse with her, the camera and lenses are at the front desk, there's nothing anyone would want. Is there? She opens the bureau drawer and hunts for the joints but they're safely in place.

In the bathroom her cosmetic bag has been emptied into the sink: toothbrush, toothpaste, Love deodorant, dental floss, bottle of aspirins, the works. Two of the glass louvers have been slid out of the metal frame that holds them in place. They're nowhere in sight, they must be outside somewhere, on a balcony, a fire escape, the ground, who knows what's out there, and there's no way of putting them back. That is how he got in, sliding himself into the bathroom like an anonymous letter. The man in the bathing suit. She thinks of herself standing there with a flashlight and a can of insect spray. God knows what he'd do, she's glad she wasn't here.

But it's only a thief, there are worse things. Whatever he wanted, which was probably only money, he didn't get: nothing is missing. She moves her notebook, *Fun in the Sunspots*, and sits down on the bed. Then she looks under it.

The box is there all right, but it's been opened, the packing tape slit neatly. Styrofoam beads leak out onto the floor. Perhaps he's made off with the heart medicine. She slides the box out, lifts the flap, and thrusts her hand into the fake snow.

At first there's nothing. Then there are two tins of smoked oysters, which Rennie sets on the floor, and after that her hand hits something that is in no way like a tin of anything at all, except that it's hard and metallic. Rennie pulls and it comes toward her, scattering Styrofoam beads. This is something else she's only seen pictures of. It's the front end of a small machine gun.

Rennie shoves it back, replaces the smoked oysters and the Styrofoam beads, and closes the flap. She wonders if the Englishwoman has any tape. She pushes the box as far under the bed as it will go and rearranges the chenille coverlet, spreading it so it hangs to the floor.

This, thinks Rennie, is an exceptionally tacky movie. What next, what now? It's not even a good lunchtime story, since the main point of it would have to be her own stupidity. Dumb, gullible, naïve, to believe people; it came from drinking too much. Now she must try not to panic.

Everything, especially this room, is now unsafe, but it happens to be the middle of the night and there's no way she can move. She can't report the break-in to the police or even to the English-woman: She may be naïve but it's not terminal. No one would believe she didn't know what was in the box when she picked it up at the airport. Lora knows, of course: That's why she sent Rennie instead of picking it up herself. Who else knows? Whoever sent the box. Harold the customs official, maybe. And now another man, possibly in a bathing suit. A faceless stranger. *Mr. X, in the bedroom, with a knife.*

Rennie goes to the bathroom door, closes it, tries to lock it. She doesn't want anyone else coming in through the bathroom window while she's asleep. The lock is broken. She opens the bureau drawer again, takes out Lora's joints, crumbles them into the toilet, and flushes them down. She refolds her mix 'n' match wardrobe and packs it into her bag. She cleans her things out of the bathroom. Then she lies down on the bed in her clothes and turns out the light. She wants somebody to be with her, she wants somebody to be with. A warm body, she doesn't much care whose.

■

·IV·

In the summer, soon after she'd come out of the hospital, Rennie called up Jocasta and asked if they could have lunch. She wanted some support. *Support* was what the women she knew said to each other, which had once made Rennie think of stretch stockings for varicose veins. Firm support, for life crises or anything else you could mention. Once Rennie had not intended to have life crises and she did not feel in need of support. But now she did. Jocasta was a little too surprised to hear from her, a little too pleased.

Rennie made it to the restaurant in the usual way, one foot in front of the other on a sidewalk that wasn't really there; but it was important to keep your balance, it was important to behave normally. If you did that enough, Daniel said, sooner or later you would begin to feel normal.

Jocasta drank red wine and Perrier and gobbled up her spinach salad in no time flat. Then she started on the bread. She didn't ask Rennie how she was, she didn't ask her anything. Politely, elaborately, she avoided the subject of Rennie. If anyone brought it up it wouldn't be her.

Rennie picked at her quiche, watching Jocasta's angular face with the huge mime's eyes. She wondered whether she herself would be that odd at forty. She wondered whether she would ever be forty. She wanted Jocasta to reach across the table, past the breadbasket and the blue silk rose in the bud vase, and put her hand on top of Rennie's and say that everything was going to be fine. She wanted to tell Jocasta she was dying.

Jocasta had just moved in with someone, or was it out on someone? Go with the flow, said Jocasta. She did a lot of moving. She was talking much too fast, Rennie embarrassed the hell out of her. Rennie concentrated on behaving normally. If she drank just enough but not too much, she could do it.

Who knows what goes on in their heads? said Jocasta. They were well into the second carafe of wine. Not me, I've stopped even trying. It used to be women that were so mysterious, remember? Well, not any more, now it's men. Me, I'm an open book. All I want is a good enough time, no hassle, a few laughs, a little how-you-say romance, I'll take the violins if they're going around, dim lights, roses, fantastic sex, let them scrape the pâté off the rug in the morning, is that too much to ask? Are they afraid of my first name or something, is that it? Remember when we all batted our eyes and pretended not to know what dirty jokes meant and crossed our legs a lot and they chased around like pigs after a truffle and God did they complain. Frigid, cock teaser, professional virgin, remember those? Remember panty girdles, remember falsies, remember Peter Pan brassieres in the front seat after the formal, with your wires digging into his chest?

Rennie didn't remember these things too well. But she didn't say so, she didn't want to remind Jocasta about her age.

There's probably men still around who don't think a woman's a woman unless she feels like a car grille or the insides of a toaster, said Jocasta. Not the back seat though, God forbid the word should get around you were an easy out.

Well, so two months ago this man, a nice enough man, nice shoulders, said why didn't we go out for dinner. I've known him a while, I like him okay, he's fine, nothing wrong with him, not ultra bright but not a nylon stocking murderer either, and I've always felt I wouldn't mind, you know. If the occasion should arise. Well, it looked as if it was arising, pardon the pun, so I tarted myself up, nothing too obvious, I just bought this fabulous black knitted sheath for the store, remember bat wings?

So out we go, he was paying it seems, though I did offer, it's a new place over on Church, not too many of those damn asparagus ferns shedding down your back, I had the quails, which was a mistake, gnawing those tiny bones and trying to look soignée. But everything was going fine, a lot of eye contact, we talked about his career, he's into real estate, doing up downtown houses. All he has to do is beat off the Marxists, the ones that rent rather than owning. The ones that own don't care, it jacks up their property values.

So I admire him some and he asks me back to his place, and we sit on the broadloom drinking white wine, and he puts on a record,

Bartok, which I thought was a little heavy for the occasion but never mind, and he wants to talk about himself some more. Okay, I don't mind listening, but all this time he doesn't touch me. What's the matter, you think I have vaginal warts, I want to ask him, but I'm doing some serious listening, it's all about his two business partners and how they can't express anger. I personally think it's just dandy when people can't express anger, there's enough of it in the world already.

So nothing happens and finally I say, I'm really tired, this certainly has been nice but I've got to get home, and he says, Why don't you stay the night? Funny you should ask, I think, though I don't say it, so we go into the bedroom and I swear to God he turns around so his *back* is to me and he takes off all his clothes. I can't believe it, I stand there with my mouth open, and before you know it he's all tucked into his side of the bed, he was practically wearing striped flannelette pajamas if you know what I mean. He asks if I want the light on or off, and by this time I'm so freaked I say *off*, so he turns it off and there I am, taking my clothes off all by myself in the dark. If I was smart I'd have left them on and headed fast for the down elevator, but you know me, Little Mary Sunshine, ever hopeful, so I climb into the bed, expecting to be embraced passionately, maybe he's just afraid of the light, but he says good night and turns over and goes to sleep!

Talk about feeling like an asshole. Now if a girl did that, what would she be called? There I was, horny as hell from looking at his *shoulders* for about five hours, and he's sleeping away like a baby. So I got up and spent the night on his sofa.

In the morning he waltzes in, all bright and shiny in his brown velour dressing gown with the monogram on the pocket, with two glasses of fresh orange juice, and he says, "Where did you go last night? When I woke up this morning you weren't there."

He hadn't even noticed, he hadn't noticed all night that I was gone.

I'm sorry, I said, but I think we have a semantic problem. A problem in communications, or maybe it's linguistics. What does *spending the night* usually mean to you? I mean, I'm not knocking the orange juice but I don't have to spend the night on the sofa to get it, I can squeeze it myself, you know what I mean?

Well, it turns out he's having an identity crisis, boy, am I sick of those. Before this he's only made it with younger, dumber chicks, women who're easy to impress, he says, and he's never tried it with someone like me, notice he meant old and wise, like an owl maybe. If you have to be a bird, which would you rather be, a chick or an owl? He's not sure someone like me would think he has anything to offer besides sex, and he wants to be valued for himself, whatever that is. Chinese! He wants a long-term meaning-ful relationship. I can tell he was a bedwetter as a child. Maybe still is for all I know.

I'm sitting there with my hair not brushed and I really have to pee, but I don't want to interrupt him because he obviously finds this important, and I'm thinking, I've heard this before, only it used to be women saying it to men. I can't believe it! And I'm thinking, do I want a long-term meaningful relationship with this guy? And then I'm thinking, does he have anything to offer be-sides sex?

Well, the answer was no. But that didn't used to matter, did it? How come it matters all of a sudden? Why do we have to start respecting their minds? Who keeps changing the rules, them or us? You know how many times that's happened to me since then? Three more times! It's an epidemic! What do they want?

My theory is that when sex was such a big deal, above the waist, below the waist, with stages of achievement marked on it like the United Appeal thermometer, they wanted it that way because you could measure it, you could win, scoring, you know? Our team against their team. Getting away with it. One in the teeth for Mummy. So we said, you want it, fine, we want it too, let's get together, and all of a sudden millions of pricks went limp. Nationwide! That's my theory. The new scoring is not scor-ing. Just so long as you keep control. They don't want love and understanding and meaningful relationships, they still want sex, but only if they can take it. Only if you've got something to lose, only if you struggle a little. It helps if you're eight years old, one way or another. You follow me?

Jocasta paid for Rennie's lunch. That meant she thought Ren-nie was in terrible shape, on the brink of death in fact, since ordinarily she never paid for anything if she could help it.

I'm hardly dead yet, Rennie wanted to say. But she was touched by this gesture, it was support after all, Jocasta had done what she could. She had paid for the lunch, which was a big thing, and she'd been as amusing as possible, a cheerful bedside visit in the terminal ward. Talk about your own life, life after all goes on, shun morbid subjects. A positive attitude does wonders for out-of-control cell division.

Rennie walked back to the apartment, unsupported, one foot in front of the other, keeping her balance. When she got there Jake was sitting in the living room. There were two beer bottles, Carlsberg, on the floor beside the plump pink chair. Ordinarily he never drank from the bottle. He didn't get up.

Once Rennie would have known why he was there, in the middle of the day. But he would not have been sitting in a chair, he would have been hiding behind the door, he'd have grabbed her from behind.

What's wrong? she said.

Jake looked up at her. His eyes were puffy, he hadn't been sleeping well lately. Neither had Rennie, as far as that went, but every time she mentioned it it turned out he'd slept even worse than she had. They were competing for each other's pity, which was too bad bcause neither of them seemed to have a lot of it lying around, they'd been using it up on themselves.

Rennie went over and kissed Jake on the top of the head. He looked so awful.

He took her hand, held on to it. We should try again, said Jake.

■

If I could do it over again I'd do it a different way, said Lora, God knows. Except maybe I wouldn't, you know? Look before you leap, my mother used to say, not that she ever did, she never had the time. When they're right behind you you don't look, you only leap, you better believe it, because if you don't leap that's fucking it, eh? Just keep moving, is my motto.

The year I turned sixteen my mother got a job selling Avon door to door, so she wasn't there in the afternoons when I got home. I didn't like being there in the cellar with just Bob, he gave me the creeps, so I used to hang out after school with Gary, that's my boyfriend. Sometimes we'd skip after lunch, and we'd have a few beers in his car, he sure loved that car, and then we'd neck afterward. We never went all the way. Everyone thought it was the girls like me and Marie who went all the way, but mostly it was the nice girls. They figured it was okay if you were going with the guy and you were in love with him. Sometimes they'd get caught, that was before the Pill was a big thing or abortions either, and Marie and me would kill ourselves laughing, because we were the ones always getting accused of it.

At that high school they thought we were the tough girls and I guess we thought that too. We wore this heavy eye makeup and white lipstick, I guess we were something. But I never let myself get too drunk or carried away or anything. When the nice girls got in trouble their parents bought them trips to the States to get fixed up, but I knew what happened to you if you couldn't afford it. Somebody's kitchen table. There was one girl a couple of grades ahead of us at school, she tried it herself with a knitting needle only it didn't work. The teachers told us it was some kind of a rare disease but everyone knew the truth, it got around. As for me, I knew Bob would make sure I'd be out on my ass just as soon as he could throw me out, and that would be it.

Gary liked me to stop him, he said he respected me for it. He wasn't the motorcycle type, he had a job too on weekends. It was the other kind you had to look out for, the ones with money. No one at our school was a millionaire or anything but some had more money than others and they thought they were the cat's ass. I never went out with them, they'd never ask me anyway except to somewhere like the back of the field hut. It was all how much money you had. If you had enough you could get away with anything, you know?

Whenever I'd come in late Bob would be there, sitting at the kitchen table with his cardigan sleeves coming unraveled, and he'd look at me like I was dirt. He didn't slap me around any more though; I was too big for that. I used to get Gary to park right in front of the kitchen window, it was half below street level because we lived in a cellar, and we'd neck away like crazy right where Bob could hear us and maybe see us too if he looked out.

Then I quit school and started working full-time, at the pizza takeout, it was no great hell but it was money. I figured I'd have enough soon to move into my own place, and Gary said, Why don't we get married. That was what I wanted then, I wanted to get married, have kids; only I wanted to do it right, not like my mother.

It was pretty soon after that I let him go all the way, it was okay because we were getting married anyway. It just happened that way, we didn't have a safe or anything. It was in the back seat of his car, right in broad daylight behind this reservoir where we used to go. It was uncomfortable as hell, and I kept thinking someone would come along and look in the window. There wasn't all that much to it, except it hurt, not a lot though, and I couldn't figure out what they were always making so much fuss about. It was like my first cigarette, I was sick as a dog, though I ended up smoking in a big way.

We didn't have any Kleenex or anything so we had to use this old undershirt he had in the trunk, to polish the car with, he made some joke about running me through the car wash. When he saw the blood though he stopped laughing, he said everything would be okay, he'd take care of me. What he meant was we were still getting married.

I had to go to work that night, I was working three evenings with two afternoons off, so I got Gary to drop me off at the apartment so I could change into my uniform. After I did that I went into the kitchen to make myself some dinner, I could get free pizza at the shop but by that time I couldn't stand the sight of it. You don't like it so much once you know what they put into it. Bob was in there as usual, smoking and finishing off a beer. I guess by that time my mother was supporting him because he didn't seem to be in the television business any more.

His damn cats came over right away and began rubbing on my legs, they must've smelled it, like I was a raw steak or a fish or something. It was the same when I got the curse, when I started using Tampax they'd fish the used ones out of the garbage and go around with the strings hanging out of their mouths, the first time Bob saw that he was so proud, he thought they'd finally caught a mouse and those were the tails. When he found out what it really was he was mad as hell.

I kicked one of the cats away from my legs and he said, Cut that out. I started opening a can of soup, like nothing was happening, Campbell's Chicken Noodle, and I could feel Bob looking at me and all of a sudden I was scared of him again just like when I was little.

Then he stood up and took hold of my arm and pulled me around, he hadn't tried the belt routine for a while, he hadn't put a hand on me for years, so I wasn't expecting it. I slammed into the refrigerator and this bowl on top of it fell off, my mother was keeping the used lightbulbs in it, she had the idea she was going to paint them and make Christmas tree ornaments out of them and sell them but she never did, it was the same as her other ideas. Anyway the lightbulbs broke and the bowl too. I thought he was going to slap me around but he didn't. He just smiled down at me with those gray teeth of his with the fillings showing and the black gums around the edges. If there's anything I can't stand it's bad teeth. Then he put his other hand right on my tit. He said, Your mother won't be home till six, and he was still smiling. I was really scared, because I knew he was still stronger than me.

I thought about screaming, but there was a lot of screaming around there and people had this thing about minding their own business. I reached behind me and picked up the can opener from the kitchen table, it was that kind with the prong, you know? And I shoved it into him as hard as I could, and at the same time I brought my knee up right into his balls. So it wasn't me that screamed. He fell onto the floor, right onto the lightbulbs and the dish of cat food, I heard that sound of glass breaking, and I ran like hell out of there, I didn't care if I'd killed him or not.

I phoned my mother the next day and told her why I wasn't coming back. She was really mad, not at him but at me. It wasn't that she didn't believe me, she did and that was the trouble. You're asking for it, she said, you flaunt it around enough, it's a wonder every man in the city didn't do the same thing a long time ago. Later on I thought maybe I shouldn't of told her. She didn't have that much in life and God knows he wasn't much either but at least she had him. You won't believe this, but I guess she thought I was trying to take him away from her. She wanted me to apologize for sticking the can opener into him, but I wasn't sorry.

■

There's a line between being asleep and being awake which Rennie is finding harder and harder to cross. Now she's up near the ceiling, in the corner of a white room, beside the air-conditioning unit, which is giving out a steady hum. She can see everything, clear and sharp, under glass, her body is down there on the table, covered in green cloth, there are figures around her, in masks, they're in the middle of a performance, a procedure, an incision, but it's not skin-deep, it's the heart they're after, in there somewhere, squeezing away, a fist opening and closing around a ball of blood. Possibly her life is being saved, but who can tell what they're doing, she doesn't trust them, she wants to rejoin her body but she can't get down. She crawls through the gray folds of netting as if through a burrow, sand in her eyes, blinking in the light, disoriented. It's far too early. She takes a shower, which helps a little, and gets dressed. Routines are calming.

The box under her bed is making her very nervous. She doesn't want to let it out of her sight, but she can hardly take it to breakfast with her. She locks it in the room, convinced that once she's around the corner it will hatch and something unpleasant will emerge. All the time she's eating, watery scrambled eggs, she worries about it. She could check out of the hotel and leave it behind in the room, she could try for the next flight out, but that would be risky. The Englishwoman would be into it before she was down the stairs, and there's no doubt about it, she's the police-phoning type. She'd make sure Rennie got arrested at the airport. The only thing to do with it is to get the box to Elva as quickly as possible and then forget about it.

After breakfast she walks across the street to the stationery store and buys a roll of packing tape. She goes back to her room and tapes the box shut, trying to make it seem as much as possible like the original job. If the box doesn't look opened she can always plead ignorance. She orders tea and biscuits in her room and puts in some time looking at her watch. Then she goes to the front desk and tells the Englishwoman she'll be over at Ste. Agathe tonight but she wants the room held for her.

"You have to pay for it, you know," the Englishwoman says. "Even if you're not in it."

Rennie says she's aware of this. She considers haggling about the meals, but drops the idea. It's what the Englishwoman is expecting her to do, she's tapping her pencil on the edge of the desk, waiting for it. Rennie's not up to that gooseberry stare.

She lugs the box out of her room and props it against the front desk. She goes back for her bags and checks her camera out of the safe; she leaves the passport, it's safer here. Then she goes down the stone stairs to look for a taxi.

There are no taxis, but there's a boy with a wheelbarrow. He looks about eight, though he's probably older, and after hesitating a moment Rennie hires him. She sends him upstairs for the box, which she doesn't want to touch any more than she has to. The boy is shy and doesn't talk much. He loads all her things, even her purse, into the wheelbarrow and sets off along the pockmarked road in his bare feet, almost running.

At first Rennie thinks he's going this fast because he has some notion of making off with her possessions. She hurries behind him, sweating already and feeling not very dignified. But then she notes his thin arms and decides that he's like rickshaw drivers, he had to go this fast to keep up the momentum. He takes her a back way, between two ramshackle wooden buildings, along a rutted path too narrow and muddy for cars, cluttered with discarded cardboard boxes. Then there's a tiny house with a family of chickens scratching around it, then a storage warehouse piled with sacks and they come out onto the pier.

The boy, who has not looked back once, speeds up on the level ground, heading for the boat, which must be the one at the end. Rennie sees the virtue of arriving at the same time he does. Even if he's honest the others may not be, and there are several of them now, a whole group of young boys, running beside the wheelbarrow, calling out things she can't understand, grinning back at her as she jogs, puffing now, the edges of her straw hat flapping, chasing her own purse as it flees ahead of her down the pier, around piles of wooden crates, parked trucks covered with tarpaulins, small mounds of fruit and unknown vegetables discarded and rotting. Opposite the boat the boy stops and waits for her with a smile she can't interpret, and the other boys draw back into a circle, leaving a gap for her to enter. Is he making fun of her?

"How much?" she says.

"What you wish," he answers. Of course she overpays him, she can tell by his grin and those of the other boys, delighted and mocking. They want to put things on the boat for her, they're grabbing for the purse, the camera bag, but she fends them off, she's had enough of that. She piles her things on the dock and sits down on top of them, feeling like a hen. Now, of course, there's no way she can leave the pile to ask about the fare and the departure time, and the boy has already run off with his wheelbarrow. She sees why he was going so fast. He wants to get in as many trips as possible before the boat leaves.

Rennie catches her breath. Nobody is watching her, she's avoided suspicion. She remembers the time Jake got pulled over for speeding, with some hash in the glove compartment. Act normal, he said to her quickly before rolling down the window, and Rennie had to think about that. Normal for her would be getting out of the car and walking as fast as possible in any direction as long as it was away. But she sat there without saying anything at all, and that was acceptable enough, though she'd felt guilt shining around her like a halo.

As she does now. She decides to act like a journalist, for the benefit of anyone watching but also for her own. If she goes through the motions, takes a few pictures, a few notes, maybe she'll convince herself. It's like making faces: Her mother used to say she shouldn't do that or her face would stay that way permanently. Is that what happened to you? she'd said once, when she was thirteen, the backchat age her mother called it. But she said it under her breath.

She looks around her for possible subjects, takes out her camera, fiddles with the lens. There's the boat, for instance, which is tied to the pier with looped ropes thick as a wrist. It was black once but is now mottled with rusty brown where the paint has weathered. The name is fading on the bow: Memory. Rennie feels about it much as she felt about the plane she came on: Can it really float? But it makes the trip, twice a day, to the blue shape in the distance, there and back. Surely people would not use it if it weren't safe.

The deck is a jumble of wicker hampers, suitcases, and bundles. Several men are tossing cardboard boxes aboard and stowing them through the open hatchway and under the outside benches. Rennie takes a picture of them, shooting into the sun, catching a box in midair with two pairs of outstretched arms framing it, thrower's and catcher's. She hopes the picture will look dramatic, though she knows that when she tries for such effects they usually don't turn out. Overexposure, Jake says. On Ste. Agathe she'll take pictures of the restaurants, if any, and of old women sitting in the sun peeling lobsters, or peeling anything within reason. She knows there will be old women peeling things but she's not dead certain about the lobsters.

There's a hand on her shoulder and Rennie freezes. She's been watched, they know, she's been followed. But then she hears the voice, "Hi there," and it's Lora, in cerise today with blue orchids, smiling away as if she's supposed to be here.

Rennie stands up. "I thought you were over on Ste. Agathe," she says. It will take a moment but very soon she'll be angry.

"Yeah, well, I got held up," says Lora. She's glancing around, down, she's already checked out the box, swiftly and casually. "I missed the boat. Anyway, Elva got better."

Both of them know this is a lie. But what should she do now? One question too many may take her somewhere she definitely doesn't want to go. There's no way she wants Lora to find out that she knows what's in the box, that she knows she's been used. The less she admits to knowing the better. When people play with guns, sooner or later they go off, and she would rather be somewhere else at the time.

Lora's scanning the pier now, noting who's there, who isn't. "I see you got Elva's box okay," she says.

"No problem," says Rennie, amiably, neutrally. "I guess we can just have it put down there in the hold?"

"Keep it with you," says Lora. "Things disappear around here. Anyway Elva always comes down for her box, she gets impatient if she has to wait around for them to unload all that stuff. She hates standing out in the sun."

Lora doesn't offer to take charge of the box. She does however get it lifted on board and stowed under the seat, Rennie's seat, the wooden bench running along the side. "Upwind," says Lora, "and outside. That way you don't get wet and it's not smelly." "Never sit in the cabin," she says. "You just about choke to death. If we're lucky they'll only use the sails."

"Where do we pay?" says Rennie.

"They collect once you're on," says Lora. She's looking around the pier again.

Without any signal people begin to board. They wait until the boat rocks toward them, then jump the gap of water where seaweed washes out from underneath the pier, swatches of rubber hair. When it's Rennie's turn one of the men grabs her purse, wordlessly, then grips her arm to pull her across.

The deck fills with people, most of them brown or black. They sit on the benches, on the crates and canvas-covered baggage, anywhere, and Rennie begins to remember stories about overloaded boats capsizing. The two German women from the hotel appear, looking around for seats. The retired American couple from the reef boat climb on board too, still wearing their baggy wide-legged shorts, but they choose to stand. Already they're peering up into the sky.

"Is it usually this crowded?" Rennie asks.

"This is extra," Lora says. "They're going home to vote. The election's tomorrow."

The men are casting off, there are legs and feet beside Rennie's head, the thick ropes come aboard. A pink-faced fattish man in a greasy white hat and a dark blue jacket has come up through the hatchway, which they're now closing, pulling a tarp over it; he shoves himself among the people, squeezing past legs, climbing over bodies, collecting the money. Nobody is giving orders, least of all him, though suddenly there are about ten men all undoing knots. The edge of the pier is crowded, everyone's shouting. Water grows between the boat and the shore, a split, a gap.

Behind the line of people a maroon car is driving slowly out onto the pier. It stops, a man gets out, then another; their mirror sunglasses are turned toward the boat. Lora bends down, scratching at her ankle. "Damn fleas," she says. The motor starts and the cabin immediately fills with smoke.

"See what I mean?" says Lora.

■

Ste. Agathe emerges out of the blue hazy sky or sea, rising slowly, sinking slowly, at first only an indistinct smudge, then clearer, a line of harsh vertical cliffs flat-topped and scrubby past the glassy slopes of waves. It looks dry, not like St. Antoine, which from this distance is a moist green, its outline a receding series of softly rounded cones. Queenstown is now just a sprinkling of white. Rennie decides the pale oblong on the hill above it must be Fort Industry. From here the whole place looks like a postcard.

They've turned off the motor and are coasting, the three sails bellying out like old sheets on a line, patched and stained, revealing too many secrets, secrets about nights and sicknesses and the lack of money. They remind Rennie of the lines of washing seen from trains, the trains she used to take for Christmas visits home during university, since no planes go to Griswold. Driers were invented not because they were easier but because they were private. She thinks about her mother's red knuckles and her phrase for disreputable stories: *dirty laundry*. Something you weren't supposed to hang out in public. Her mother's red knuckles were from hanging the sheets out on the line, even in winter, to get the sun she said, but of course her sheets were always very clean.

Lora says this is a calm day, but Rennie feels queasy anyway; she wishes she'd had the foresight to take something, there must be a pill. The people sitting on the downwind side get the occasional bucketful of spray as the boat creaks and lurches heavily into a trough.

Lora is sitting beside her; she's taken a small loaf of bread out of her purple bag and is breaking pieces off of it and chewing them. At their feet four men are lying on the floor, half on top of the canvas-covered suitcases, passing around a bottle of rum. They're already quite drunk and they're getting drunker, they're laughing a lot. The bottle sails past Rennie's head into the sea, they've already got another one. Lora offers the bread silently to Rennie, who says no thanks.

"It'll help you out," says Lora. "If you're not feeling too good. Don't look down, look out at the horizon."

Right beside them there's a small boat, no bigger than a rowboat it seems to Rennie, with a reddish-pink sail; two men are on it, fishing. The boat rolls and tips, it looks very unsafe.

"It's boats like that they hunt the whales in," Lora says.

"You're joking," says Rennie.

"Nope," says Lora. She tears another piece off the loaf. "They have a lookout, and when they see a whale they get into those boats and row like shit. Sometimes they even catch one, and then there's a big feast." Rennie doesn't want to think about anyone eating anything.

Down by their feet there's more laughter. One of the men, Rennie sees now, is the deaf and dumb man, the man they were beating up. He has a cut on his forehead, but apart from that he doesn't seem any worse off than the others, he's drunk as a skunk and grinning away, no teeth at all now. The old American couple in their wide-legged shorts step carefully over the bodies on their way to the stern. "Careful, Mother," says the man, gripping the thin freckled elbow. Laughter rises around their four white chicken-shank legs. Rennie tugs at her skirt, pulling it down over her knees.

And then Paul comes out of the cabin. He too pushes past the knees, picks his way over the lolling bodies. He nods to Rennie and Lora but keeps on going, he's in no hurry, he wanders back to the stern, ducking under the mainsail boom. Rennie didn't see him get on. He must have been down there all the time, when the boat was tied up at the pier.

Suddenly she's hungry, or at least the rocking emptiness, the absence of a center of gravity, feels now like hunger. She never liked roller coasters either. "I'll take you up on the bread," she says.

"Have the rest," says Lora handing her the heel of the loaf. "It swells up inside, you know?" She gets out her cigarettes and lights one, tossing the match over the side.

"Can I ask you something?" says Rennie. She's almost finished the bread. It works, already she feels better.

"Sure," says Lora, looking at her with what Rennie is almost sure is amusement. "You want to know if I'm making it with Paul, right? The answer is, Not any more. Help yourself, be my guest."

This is not what Rennie thought she wanted to know, nor does she appreciate Lora's generosity; nor is Paul a buffet casserole or a spare room, Occupied or Vacant as the case may be. "Thanks," she says, "but really I wanted to ask you something quite different. Is he working for the CIA?"

"The CIA?" says Lora. "Him?" She begins to laugh, throwing her head back, showing all her white teeth. "Hey, that's great! Wait'll he hears that! Is that what he told you?"

"Not exactly," says Rennie, who now feels foolish, and annoyed because of it. She turns away, watching the scrubby cliffs as they slide too slowly past the boat.

"Listen, if that's what he told you," says Lora, "who am I? Hey, maybe he thinks it turns you on!" She laughs some more, until Rennie is ready to shake her. Then she stops. "You want to know who the CIA really is around here?" she says. "Look down there." She points to the old American couple standing in the stern, harmless and implausible in their khaki shorts. They're flipping through their bird book now, heads together, like eager children. "They are," says Lora. "Both of them."

"I can't believe that," says Rennie, who can't. Surely these people are the embodiment of midwestern innocence, not at all the kind; though she's no longer sure what the kind is. After all, she was willing to believe Paul was; and if him, why not anyone?

Lora laughs again. She's delighted, as if the whole thing is a joke she's telling. "It's great," she says. "I love it. It's them all right, everyone knows. Prince always knows which one's the CIA. When you're in local politics you have to know."

"Aren't they too old?" says Rennie.

"They don't have much of a budget for down here," says Lora. "Listen, who's complaining? Everyone tells them stuff just to keep them happy; if they didn't have anything to put in their reports someone up there might get the idea they're senile or something and send down somebody heavy. Of course they're supposed to support Ellis, that's the official line, so Ellis loves them, and Prince loves them because they're so dumb; even Minnow doesn't mind them all that much. Sometimes he takes them out to lunch and tells them all this stuff about what the U.S. should be doing to avoid a revolution, and they write it all down and send it off, it keeps them busy. As for them, they haven't had so much fun since they got to go through the wastebaskets in Iceland, that was their last posting. They tell everyone he's a retired bank manager."

Maybe he is, thinks Rennie. Lora is laughing too much. "So who is he really?" she says. Paul, she means, and Lora picks that up too quickly, she's been waiting for it, the shrug and the answer are right there. "A guy with four boats and some money," she says. "Guys with boats and some money are a dime a dozen down here. It's the ones with boats and no money you've got to look out for."

Rennie eats the rest of the bread, slowly, feeling more and more dim-witted. She may not have asked the wrong question, but she's asked the wrong person. She knows she should pretend to believe the answer, that would be clever, but she just can't manage it.

Lora must sense this; she lights another cigarette from the butt of the first and leans forward, resting her elbows on her spread knees. "I didn't mean to laugh," she says, "except it's so funny, when you really know."

The boat is pulling around into the harbor, out of the wind, and they turn on the smelly motor. Around Rennie people are stirring, gathering up small parcels, stretching their legs out. The harbor seems crowded, small fishing boats, a police launch, yachts at anchor, sails furled, bright flags fluttering from their masts. The *Memory* threads through them, trailing gray smoke. Ahead the pier swarms with people, waving, calling.

"They come down for the eggs," Lora says. "And the bread. There's never enough eggs and bread here. You'd think someone would get a bright idea and start a bakery or something."

"When you know what?" says Rennie.

Lora looks at her with that posed smile, then leans over and forward, getting into the right position for the truth, the confidence. "Who he really is," she says. "Really, he's the connection."

■

The *Memory* hits with a soft thud; there's a line of tractor tires nailed along the dock to keep it from scraping. Already there are men roping the boat to the shore. Rennie's caught in the scramble, legs around her head, it's like a football team walking across her. There's a lot of shouting, friendly she thinks. In self-defense she stands up, then feels it will be safer sitting down; but Lora's pulling at her arm and there's a man on his knees in front of her, digging for the box. She stands up again and hands reach for her, she makes the leap, she's been landed.

Right in front of her there's a small woman, not five feet tall. She's wearing a pink cotton skirt with red flamingoes on it and a black jockey cap, and a red T-shirt with PRINCE OF PEACE on it in white. Now Rennie remembers her.

"You got my food?" she says, not to Lora but directly to Rennie herself. She says nothing at all about heart medicine. It's an old face, but her black hair is in pigtails today; they stick out sideways from under the jockey cap.

"It's here," says Lora, and it is, she's holding the box upright, steadying it with one hand.

The woman ignores her. "Good," she says, to Rennie alone. She takes the box by its sides and lifts it onto her head, much more easily than Rennie could have done, balancing it on the woolly jockey cap. She steadies it with one hand and marches off without another word to either of them. Rennie, who's been expecting a cross between Aunt Jemima and a basket case, watches her go. What will happen when she opens the box? Rennie can hardly believe she knows what's in it. But if Rennie can believe the geriatric CIA she can believe anything. Possibly this woman's the local gun runner.

Still, Rennie can't quite imagine her opening the box, unpacking the gun, assembling it if it needs assembling, and then what? Does she sell them, and if so, who's buying? What are they used for, here? But these questions are not ones Rennie needs the answers for. Yesterday she would have asked; today she knows it's safer not to. The box is off her back, which is where it should be: off.

She looks around for Paul but he's gone already; she spots him up on the road, getting into a Jeep, with another man and the driver. Elva's on the beach, walking along with the machine-gun box on her head, as if that's the most normal thing in the world.

"She's amazing," Rennie says to Lora. "That's a heavy box. I thought you said she had a heart condition," she adds. Now that she's safe she can risk it.

"That's the other grandmother," says Lora, lying without much energy.

"And they're both called Elva," says Rennie.

"Yeah," says Lora, "this place is crawling with grandmothers. The old bitch, you see the way she didn't speak to me? She hates it that I'm living with Prince, but she also hates it that we don't have kids. Around here, if you don't have kids you're nothing, that's what she keeps telling me. She wants me to have a son for Prince, so she can have a great-grandson. For Prince, that's what she says. 'You too smart to make babies?' she says. At the same time she hates it that I'm white; but she thinks she's practically related to the Royal Family, my Princess Margaret, my Prince Charles, last time I heard they were all white, eh? You figure it out."

"Maybe she's just old," says Rennie.

"Sure," says Lora. "Why not. Where you staying?"

Rennie hasn't considered this. She's just assumed there would be a hotel.

"But it's the election," says Lora. "They might be full up. I can ask for you, though."

When they step onto the beach Lora takes off her shoes, so Rennie does too. Lora's carrying her camera bag for her. They walk along the packed sand, under the trees, palm trees. The beach is wider than the one on St. Antoine and it's fairly clean. Boats are hauled up on it, turned over. Above the beach the town begins, one main road, a couple of foreign banks, a couple of stores, all two-story and white; a church, then square houses, white and pastel, scattered up the hillside.

They come to a cliff jutting into the sea and wade around it, hitching up their skirts. Then there's more beach and more palm trees, and finally a stone wall and some steps. There's a sign, seashells glued on wood: THE LIME TREE. The hotel's hardly bigger than a house.

"The food's not bad here," Lora says. "Only, Ellis is trying to squeeze them out. He wants to buy it and put in his own people. Funny thing, their electricity keeps going off."

"Why?" says Rennie. "Why would he want to do that?"

"Politics, is what they say," says Lora. "They're for Minnow. What I figure is, he hates anyone making money. Except him, of course."

165

"If this man is so terrible," says Rennie, "why does he keep getting elected?"

"Search me," says Lora. "I'll see about the room." She walks off toward the main building.

Rennie's standing in a beach bar, surrounded by low wooden tables and chairs with people in them. She sits down and piles her bags on the chair beside her and orders a rum and lime. She drinks it, looking out at the boats in the harbor, the flags: Norway, she thinks, Germany, France for sure, and some others.

The rum is going right into her, smoothing her down from the inside. She can relax now, she's off the hook. One hook at any rate.

At the table beside her there's a young couple, the girl brown-haired, lightly tanned, in a white dress, the man in jogging shorts, his nose peeling. The man is fooling with his camera, expensive enough but jammed. "It's the light meter," he says. They're people like her, transients; like her they can look all they want to, they're under no obligation to see, they can take pictures of anything they wish.

■

There's a small dock in front of the Lime Tree, and on it there's a man, shouting and waving his arms. Rennie watches him for a moment and decides that he's teaching three girls to wind-surf: there they are, out in the harbor. "Upright!" the man shouts, lifting both arms like an orchestra conductor. "Bend the knees!" But it's no use, the sails collapse and the girls topple almost in unison into the sea. In the distance the two German women from the hotel are wading around the cliff, their skirts hitched up, carrying their suit-cases. One of their sunhats has blown off into the water.

Rennie wonders where Lora is. She orders a cream cheese and banana bread sandwich from the bar, and another rum and lime. She goes back to her chair and moves it so it's out of the sun.

"May we sit here?" says another voice, a woman's. Rennie looks up. It's the old American couple, in their adventurous shorts, their binoculars hanging like outsized talismans around their necks. Each of them is carrying a glass of ginger ale. "There don't seem to be any other chairs."

166

"Of course," Rennie says. "I'll move my things for you."

But the old man insists on doing it himself. "My name is Abbott," he says, "and this is Mrs. Abbott." He holds the chair for his wife, who sits down and fixes Rennie with eyes round as a baby's.

"That's very nice of you, dear," she says. "We saw you on the reef boat. Disappointing, we thought. You're Canadian, aren't you? We always find the Canadians so nice, they're almost like members of the family. No crime rate to speak of at all. We always feel quite safe when we go up there. We go to Point Pelee, for the birds. Whenever we can, that is."

"How did you know?" says Rennie.

Mrs. Abbott laughs. "It's a very small place," she says. "You hear things."

"Nice though," says her husband.

"Oh yes. The people are so lovely. So friendly, not like a lot of places." She sips her ginger ale. "So independent," she says. "We have to go back soon, we're getting too old for it. It's a little primitive down here, on Ste. Agathe especially, they don't have many of the conveniences. It's all right for younger people but it's sometimes difficult for us."

"When you can't get toilet paper," says Mr. Abbott.

"Or garbage bags," says his wife. "But we'll be sorry to leave it."

"You don't see many beggars," says Mr. Abbott, who is looking at something in the harbor through his binoculars. "Not like India."

"Do you travel a lot?" says Rennie politely.

"We love to travel," says Mrs. Abbott. "It's the birding, but we like the people too. Of course with the exchange rate these days it's not as easy as it used to be."

"You're right about that," says her husband. "The U.S. borrowed too much money. That's the whole problem in a nutshell. We should stop living beyond our means."

"He ought to know," says Mrs. Abbott, proudly and fondly. "He's a retired bank manager." Mr. Abbott now has his head tilted back and is looking straight up.

Rennie decides that Lora must be wrong. Surely two such innocuous, kindly, boring people cannot possibly be CIA agents. The question is, how can she get rid of them? They appear to have

167

settled in for the afternoon. Rennie waits for the pictures of the grandchildren to make their appearance, out of Mrs. Abbott's sensible canvas shoulder bag.

"Do you see that man over there?" says Mrs. Abbott, pointing toward the bar, which is more crowded than when Rennie first arrived. Rennie isn't sure which one, but she nods.

"He's an international parrot smuggler," says Mrs. Abbott, dropping her voice.

"A parrot smuggler?" says Rennie faintly.

"Don't laugh," says Mrs. Abbott. "It's a big business. In Germany you can get thirty-five thousand dollars for a mated pair."

"The Germans have too much money," says Mr. Abbott. "It's coming out of their ears. They don't know what to do with it."

"It's the St. Antoine parrot," says Mrs. Abbott. "They're very rare, you know. You don't find them anywhere but on St. Antoine."

"It's disgusting," says Mr. Abbott. "They give them drugs. If I ever caught him with one of those little parrots I'd wring his neck."

From the horror in their voices, they could be talking about a white-slave ring. Rennie concentrates on taking this seriously.

"How do they smuggle them?" she says.

"On the yachts," says Mr. Abbott, "like everything else around here. We made it our business to find out about him. He's not from here, he's from Trinidad."

"Then we reported him to the association," says Mrs. Abbott, pleased. "It didn't stop him but it slowed him down. He didn't know it was us, though. Some of them are dangerous and we really aren't equipped to deal with that sort of thing."

"Not at our age," says Mr. Abbott.

"Which association?" says Rennie.

"The International Parrot Association," says Mrs. Abbott. "They're quite good, but they can't be everywhere at once."

Rennie figures she'd better have another drink. If surrealism is taking over the world, she might as well enjoy it. She asks the Abbotts if they would like another ginger ale, but they say they're quite happy. In any case it will soon be dusk.

"Roosting time," says Mr. Abbott happily, as he stands up.

■

This is Rennie's third rum and lime. She's fuzzy, but not too fuzzy. It's occurred to her several times that there's no boat back and she doesn't have a place to stay. She supposes there's always the beach.

It isn't dark yet, but beneath the overhanging porch roof the waitresses are setting the tables for dinner, lighting the candles inside the little red glass chimneys. The tables outside are full now, with yacht people, and the bar is lined with men, brown and black mostly. Some of them look familiar, but maybe they aren't. She spots a pair of boots, that one she knows anyway, the man with the South American moustache. This time he's ignoring her. There are a few white men with the leathery dull skin and the dry albino hair of those who spend constant time in the sun.

While she's walking back from the bar, Dr. Minnow steps onto the patio. He hasn't come along the beach but down through the garden behind the hotel. He's with three other men; two of them are wearing T-shirts that say THE FISH LIVES, with a picture of a whale, and, underneath, VOTE JUSTICE PARTY. The third man is white and thin; he's wearing a safari jacket and tinted glasses. He stays a little behind.

Dr. Minnow spots Rennie and comes over to her at once. The two men head for the bar, but the third hesitates a moment and then comes over too.

"Well, my friend," says Dr. Minnow, "I see you are covering the election after all." He smiles his crooked smile.

Rennie smiles back. She thinks he's treating it as a joke now, and she can handle that. "From a bar," she says. "All good journalists cover elections from bars."

"I'm told it is the best place," says Dr. Minnow. His accent is broader here, he's less controlled. Rennie thinks he's had a few himself. "Everyone is here. For instance, that is our Minister of Justice over there. He is preparing himself for his defeat." He laughs. "You will excuse me for talking sedition," he says to the white man with him. "This is a compatriot of yours, my friend. He is with the Canadian High Commissioner in Barbados; he comes here to see why no one attend the diving program sponsored by the sweet Canadians."

Rennie doesn't catch the name, it's something Middle European, she thinks. A multiculturalism functionary. The man shakes her hand.

"I understand you're a journalist," he says. He's nervous.

"I just do food," says Rennie, to make him feel better. "Things like that."

"What could be more important?" he says politely. They both sit down.

"I tell you why, my friend," Dr. Minnow says. "The sweet Canadians wish to teach the fishermen how to dive so they don't get the bends and come up crippled. What do they do? They hire an expert who comes just at the lobster season when the fishermen all have to be out fishing. That's the money they live on. There is no conspiracy, it is all very simple. Tell them next time they should ask first. Ask someone who knows."

The man smiles and takes out a cigarette, a brown one, and screws it into a black holder. Rennie decides this is pretentious. It embarrasses her that her country's representative is wearing a safari jacket. Where does he think he is, Africa? He could at least have chosen a different color: The beige should not wear beige.

"You know what they're like," he says. "Governments have to deal with governments in power, which does not always produce the most accurate information."

"Are you going to win?" Rennie says to Dr. Minnow.

"Yesterday," Dr. Minnow says conversationally, his eye on the Canadian, "the government offer me a large sum of money to go over to their side. Minister of Tourism, they offer me."

"I take it you didn't accept," says Rennie.

"Why cut your own throat?" says Dr. Minnow, who seems very pleased. "I have not read Machiavelli for nothing. If they offer, it means they are scared, they think they could lose. So I turn them down, and today they are slandering me in a new way. Before it was Castro, now they say I am in the pocket of the Americans and the plantation owners. They should make up their minds, one way or the other. It confuses the people: They may think I am neither, which would be the truth. If we begin to believe the truth here, that would be the end of Ellis, and also of the Prince of Peace, as he calls himself. He think he got the true religion, all right." He stands up.

170

"Tomorrow I will make a speech on the problems of garbage collection, among other things," he says. "It is one of our most urgent problems on these islands, what to do with the garbage. You should attend, my friend." He bestows one more smile upon Rennie and moves away toward the bar, the neutral-colored Canadian trailing.

■

As she's coming back from the bar again, Rennie sees the two German women climbing the stone steps. The bottoms of their dresses are dripping wet and their hair has come unglued and is hanging in wisps and strands; their faces are dangerously pink. They seem to have abandoned their suitcases. One of them is supporting the other, who is limping and uttering little shrieks of pain. Both have been crying, but as they enter the bar and the ring of curious faces that quickly surrounds them, they pull themselves together. Someone offers a chair.

"What on earth?" says Rennie, to no one in particular. Everyone in the place is peering at the German woman's foot, plump and white and pink-toed, stuffed-looking, which her friend holds up like a trophy.

"She stepped on a sea urchin," says Lora, who's back again. "They always do it, they should watch where they're going. It hurts at first but it's no big deal."

The woman is lying back with her eyes closed; her foot sticks straight out. After a few minutes Elva comes through the doorway that leads to the kitchen; she no longer has the box, she's wearing a red and white checked apron and carrying a lime and a candle. She kneels in front of the outstretched foot, appropriates it, peers at the toes. Then she begins rubbing with the cut lime. The German woman screams.

"Keep still," says Elva. "It nothin'. This will be gone tomorrow."

"Can you not take them out?" says the other woman. She's anxious, she's almost incoherent. This is not according to schedule.

"They break off and poison you," Elva says. "You got matches?"

There's no doubt who's in charge. Someone from the circle produces a box of matches and Elva lights the candle. She tilts it and drops the hot wax over the toes, rubbing it in. "You should

171

of pee on it," she says to the other woman. "When this happen here, the boy pee on the girl's foot or the girl pee on the boy's. That take away the pain."

The German woman opens her eyes and gazes at Elva. Rennie recognizes the look, it's a look you can give only to a foreigner, a look of hope, a desperate clinging to the illusion that it's all a translation problem and you haven't really heard what you know you've just heard.

Several people laugh, but not Elva. She's got the other foot now, the uninjured one, she's digging her thumbs into it. The German woman gasps and looks around for help: She's been invaded, this is the wrong foot. She has the controlled, appalled expression of a visiting duchess who knows she must not openly disparage the local customs, however painful or revolting.

Elva digs harder. She's smug now, she has an audience, she's enjoying herself. "Your veins block," she says. "I unblock your veins, the blood carry the poison away."

"I wouldn't let her near me," says Lora. "She's got thumbs like hammers. She'll total your back as soon as look at you. She says she can cure just about anything but I'd rather be sick, thank you very much."

There's an audible snapping sound; the tendons, Rennie thinks. The German woman's face is twisted, her eyes are screwed up, she's not going to yell or moan, she's determined to preserve her dignity. "You hear the veins cryin' out?" says Elva. "That the gas, movin' in them. You feel lighter?"

"There's no rooms," Lora says to Rennie. "It's full up, it's the election."

"Maybe I should phone the other hotels," says Rennie, who is still watching Elva.

"Phone?" says Lora. "Other hotels?" She laughs a little.

"There aren't any other hotels?" says Rennie.

"There used to be," says Lora, "but they're closed down now. There's one for the locals, but I wouldn't stay there. A girl could get seriously misunderstood. I'll try somewhere else for you."

"It in the hands," says Elva to the onlookers. "It a gift, I have it from my grandmother, she give me that when I small. She pass it to me. You feel this lump?"

The German woman nods. She's still wincing, but not as much.

"Your mama give you a blow when you small," Elva says. "You too small that time, you don't remember. The blood lie down, it make a lump. Now it have to move or the poison grow into a cancer." She digs in both thumbs again. "The pain is your youth, risin' up now."

"The old fake," says Lora. "Give her a tourist and she's happy as a pig in shit. Even if they don't believe her they have to act like they do. There's no doctor around here anyway, so they don't have a whole lot of choice; if you sprain your ankle it's her or nothing."

"I think this is maybe enough," says the other woman, who's been hovering around like a concerned parent.

Elva gives her a look of contempt. "I say when I done," she says. The foot cracks, bends in her hands like rubber.

"Now," Elva says, sitting back on her heels. "Walk on it."

Tentatively the German woman puts both feet on the ground. She stands up.

"The pain gone," says Elva, looking around the circle.

The German woman smiles. "It is remarkable," she says.

Rennie, watching, wants to hold out her own foot, even though there's nothing wrong with it, even though it will hurt. She wants to know what it feels like, she wants to put herself into the care of those magic hands. She wants to be cured, miraculously, of everything, of anything at all.

■

Paul is standing in the kitchen doorway, looking without hurry; Rennie sees him, but decides not to wave. He comes over anyway.

"Taking it easy?" he says to Rennie. "Lora says you don't have a place to stay. I've got space, if you like."

"On a boat?" Rennie says dubiously. She ought to have said thank you first.

"I have a house too," Paul says, smiling. "Two bedrooms. Two beds."

Rennie's not sure what is being offered, but suspects it's not much. There's some room in this world for face value.

"Well," she says, "if you're sure it's all right."

"Why wouldn't it be?" says Paul.

They walk back through the garden. It's full of trees, flowering, overgrown, limes and lemons and something else, odd reddish-orange husks split open to show a white core and three huge black seeds like the eyes of insects. There are a lot of things here that Rennie has no names for.

At the back of the garden there's a five-foot stone wall. Paul lifts her camera bag and her other bag to the top, hoists himself up, and reaches down for her. She takes hold of his hands; she doesn't know where they're going.

■

Rennie and Daniel were sitting in Daniel's car, which was an unusual thing for them to be doing. It was night, which was also unusual, and it was raining, which was par for the course. When they were together it always seemed to be raining.

They'd just had dinner, dinner, not lunch. Rennie wondered whether Daniel was about to do something out of character.

Well, how about it? she said to him. A little reckless hand-holding? Want to roll around on the gear shift?

I know I can't offer you much, he said.

He looked so miserable that she felt she ought to express compassion, she ought to comfort him, she ought to tell him everything was fine. Instead she said, You're right. You can't offer me much.

Daniel looked at his watch, then out the window at the rain. There were cars going by but nobody walking on the street. He took hold of Rennie's shoulders and kissed her gently on the mouth. He ran the ends of his fingers over her lips.

I'm very fond of you, he said.

Flamboyant adjectives will be your downfall, said Rennie, who couldn't resist.

I know I don't express myself very well, Daniel said. Rennie wasn't sure she could take that much sincerity all at once. He kissed her again, quite a lot harder. Rennie put her face against his neck and the collar of his shirt. He smelled like laundry. It was

174

safe enough, he could hardly take off her clothes or his in a parked car on a street with two-way traffic.

She wanted him to though, she wanted to lie down beside him and touch him and be touched by him; at the moment she believed in it, the touch of the hand that could transform you, change everything, magic. She wanted to see him lying with his eyes closed, she wanted to see him and not be seen, she wanted to be trusted. She wanted to make love with him, very slowly, she wanted it to last a long time, she wanted the moment just before coming, helplessness, hours of it, she wanted to open him up. There was such a gap between what she wanted and where she was that she could hardly stand it.

She pulled back. Let's go home, she said.

It's not that I don't want to, he said. You know that.

His face for a moment was like a child's looking up, he was so sweet it hurt, and Rennie felt brutal. He had no right to appeal to her like that, to throw himself on her mercy. She wasn't God, she didn't have to be understanding, which was a good thing because she was rapidly understanding less and less about this and soon she wouldn't understand anything at all. Rennie liked to know the names for things and there was no name for this.

What do you do afterward, she said, go home and jerk off? Or maybe you go home and stick your hand into the job jar. Don't tell me you haven't got one, I know you do. What else would you do with your spare time?

He put his hand gently on the back of her neck. What would you like to do? he said. If you really want to, we'll check into a hotel somewhere. I can only stay an hour, that's all I've got, and then what? Would that be love? Is that what you want?

No, said Rennie. As usual she wanted everything, which was in short supply.

I'm not good at that sort of thing, Daniel said. I'd resent you for it and I don't want that. I care about you, I care what happens to you. I guess I think I can do more for you as your doctor; I'm better at it. He looked down at his hands, which were on the steering wheel now.

Why not both? said Rennie.

That's the way I am, said Daniel. There are some things I just can't do.

175

It struck Rennie that Daniel was a lot like Griswold, not as it was but as it would like to be. Ordinary human decency, a fine decent man they would say, with a list of things you just couldn't do. This insight did not fill her with joy. He was normal, that was what she'd fallen in love with, the absolutely ordinary raised to the degree of X. What you were supposed to be. He did make his living cutting parts off other people's bodies and patting their shoulders while they died, he used the same hands for both, but nobody considered that unusual. He was a good man, a mystery, Rennie wanted to know why. Maybe it was habit.

What do you believe in? she said to him. I mean, what keeps you ticking over? What makes you get up in the mornings? How do you know what kinds of things you can do and what kinds you can't do? Don't tell me it's God. Or maybe you've got those things in the job jar, along with the jobs. Saying this, she felt like a troll, but Daniel took it straight.

I don't know, said Daniel. I've never thought that much about it.

Rennie felt cold, she felt she was dying and Daniel knew it, he just hadn't told her about it yet. But making love for an hour in a hotel room with Daniel would not work, she could see that now. They would go in and close the door and take off their damp coats and he would sit down on the edge of the bed. Seeing him with his head bent, dutifully undoing his shoelaces: this would be too much for her, it would be too sad. You don't have to, she would say. She would hold onto his hands and cry and cry.

She no longer expected Daniel to save her life. She no longer expected Daniel. Maybe that was the right way to do it, never to expect anything.

Let's go home, she said.

∎

Rennie lay on the bed, their bed, stiff as plaster, waiting for Jake to come out of the shower. They'd talked about it enough. The truth was that she didn't want him to touch her and she didn't know why, and he didn't really want to touch her either but he wouldn't admit it.

You have to try, he said. You won't let me try.

You sound like the little engine that could, she said. I think I can, I know I can.

You really are relentless, he said.

So they were going to try. She'd stood in front of her open closet, wondering what you should wear to try, to a trial. A trial of strength. She wanted to wear something and knew she had to; these days she always wore something to bed. She didn't want to be seen, the way she was, damaged, amputated.

Once he'd given her a purple one-piece number that snapped together at the crotch and they'd got very high on some top-grade Colombian, and at the crucial moment neither of them could get the snaps undone. They'd hugged each other, rolling around and laughing so much they almost fell off the bed. So much for sexy underwear, she'd said.

She decided on black, two pieces, he'd given that to her a while ago. He could leave the top part on if he wanted to. She lit some candles and lay down on the bed, raising one knee, arranging herself. It was no good.

She tried to think about Daniel, lying here beside her instead, hoping that would make her feel better, softer, but she couldn't. She could hardly imagine him without clothes. All she could imagine were his hands, hands with thin fingers and with the marks of a slow dark burning on their backs. In the Middle Ages they'd painted pictures of souls, the souls of the dying leaving their bodies, and for a long time they'd argued about what part of the body the soul inhabited when you were alive. There was no doubt about Daniel at all: His soul was in his hands. Cut them off and he'd be a zombie.

One man I'm not allowed to touch, she thought, and another I won't allow to touch me. I could write a piece on it: "Creative Celibacy." "Sexual Abstinence, the Coming Thing." Except it's been done. What's supposed to come next? Sublimation? Ceramics? Devotion to a good cause?

Jocasta would have advised her to try masturbation. That too was once supposed to be the wave of the future. *Listen, when all else fails let your fingers do the walking.* But masturbation didn't interest her, it would be like talking to yourself or keeping a journal. She'd never been able to understand women who kept journals. She already knew what she would be likely to say. Unlikely things could only be said by other people.

Jake came in from the shower with a blue towel tucked around his waist. He sat down on the bed beside her and kissed her gently on the mouth.

I'd like the candles out, she said.

No, he said, leave them on. I want to see you.

Why? she said.

You turn me on, he said.

She didn't answer. He ran his hand up her right leg, across her belly, down the left thigh, over the bent knee. He did that again, moving the black cloth down. He didn't go above the waist. Upsidedown high school, Rennie thought. He moved his hand between her legs, bent to kiss her navel.

Maybe we should smoke some dope, he said.

To help me relax? she said, watching him from her head, which was up there on the pillow at the other end of her body. She felt her eyes sparkling like those of some small malicious animal, a weasel or a rat. Red, intelligent, in a sharp little face with tiny incisors. Cornered and mean.

That's right, he said. He brought the tea canister in and opened it and rolled a joint and lit it and passed it to her. I love you, he said, but you can't believe it.

What's the difference between a belief and a delusion? she said. Maybe you just think you ought to. Maybe I make you feel guilty. You've always told me guilt was a big thing with Jewish mothers.

You aren't my mother, he said. A good thing, too.

How could I be? she said. I'm not Jewish.

Nobody's perfect, he said. You're my golden *shiksa*. We all have to have at least one, it's obligatory.

So that's what I am, said Rennie. I guess that's it for my identity crisis. It's nice to know who you are. But I'm hardly golden.

Gilt-edged security, anyway, said Jake.

Is that a pun? said Rennie.

Don't ask me, said Jake, I'm a functional illiterate and proud of it.

But up and coming, said Rennie.

As often as possible, said Jake. You think we could set this to music?

This isn't a forties movie, said Rennie.

You could have fooled me, said Jake.

Rennie felt she was going to cry. What she couldn't bear was the effort he was making to pretend nothing was different, the effort she was making to help him pretend. She wanted to say, I'm dying, but that would be melodrama, and anyway she probably wasn't.

Jake began rubbing her left thigh, slowly up and then down. I feel awkward, he said. I feel you don't want me to be doing this.

She was watching him but she didn't know how to help him. I can't believe, she thought. Why not? The words in her head came one at a time, as if they were being spoken by someone else. She watched them form, rise, burst. It was strong grass.

You don't have to be perfect, he said.

He bent down and kissed her again, supporting himself with his arms so his torso didn't touch her. He's doing this for me, she thought. It's not for him, he doesn't want to.

He lifted her and slid the black satin shorts down and put his mouth on her.

I don't want that, she said. I don't need charity. I want you inside me.

Jake paused. He raised her arms, holding her wrists above her head. Fight me for it, he said. Tell me you want it. This was his ritual, one of them, it had once been hers too and now she could no longer perform it. She didn't move and he let go of her. He put his face down on her shoulder; his body went limp. Shit, he said. He needed to believe she was still closed, she could still fight, play, stand up to him, he could not bear to see her vulnerable like this.

Rennie knew what it was. He was afraid of her, she had the kiss of death on her, you could see the marks. Mortality infested her, she was a carrier, it was catching. She lay there with his face against her neck, thinking of something she'd seen written in a men's washroom once when she was doing a piece on graffiti. *Life is just an-*

other sexually transmitted social disease. She didn't blame him. Why should he be stuck with it? With her.

After a while he raised his head. I'm sorry, he said.

So am I, said Rennie. She waited. You're having a thing with someone else, aren't you?

It's not important, said Jake.

Is that what you say about me? Rennie said. To her?

Look, said Jake, it's either that or a warm wet washcloth. You won't let me touch you.

Touch, said Rennie. Is that all? Does it matter that much? Isn't there any more to it than that?

She stroked the back of his neck and thought of the soul leaving the body in the form of words, on little scrolls like the ones in medieval paintings.

Oh please.

■

They walk inland, uphill. Rennie tries to think of something neutral to say. He's carrying her camera bag and the other bag. It's the minimum, but she shouldn't have brought so much.

It's about five-thirty and although the asphalt road is hot it's not too hot, the trees cast shadows. There are little houses set back from the road, people are sitting out on their porches, the women wear print dresses, some of the older ones have hats on, and Paul nods to them, they nod back, they don't stare but they look, taking note. A group of girls passes, going down the hill, fifteen- or sixteen-year-olds in white dresses, some with bows or flowers in their hair, which is braided and pinned up; they look oddly old-fashioned, costumed. They're singing, three-part harmony, a hymn. Rennie wonders if they're going to church.

"It's up here," Paul says. The house is concrete block like the others and only a little bigger, painted light green and raised on stilts above the rainwater tank. There's a rock garden covering the hill, cactus and rubbery-looking plants. The shrubs at the gateway are dying though, there's a many-stranded yellow vine covering them like a net, like hair.

"See that?" Paul says. "Around here they break pieces of that off and throw it into the gardens of the people they don't like. It grows like crazy, it strangles everything. Love vine, they call it."

"Are there people here who don't like you?" Rennie says.

"Hard to believe, isn't it?" he says, grinning at her.

Inside, the house is neat, almost blank, as if no one is actually living in it. The furniture is noncommittal, wood-frame chairs of the kind Rennie has seen in the beach bars. Beside one of the chairs there's a telescope on a tripod.

"What do you watch through it?" says Rennie.

"The stars," says Paul.

On the wall above the sofa there's a map, on the wall facing it another, island after island, navigational maps with the soundings marked. There are no pictures. The kitchen is an open counter with appliances behind it, a stove, a refrigerator, no clutter. Paul takes ice cubes from the refrigerator and fixes two drinks, rum and lime. Rennie looks at the maps; then she goes out through the double doors, there's a porch with a hammock, and leans on the railing, looking down over the road to the tops of the trees and then the harbor. There's a sunset, as usual.

The bed is expertly made, hospital corners firmly tucked in. Rennie wonders where he learned to do that, or maybe someone comes in to do it for him. Perhaps this is the spare bedroom, it's empty enough. There are two pillows, though nobody lives with him. He untwists the mosquito net, spreads it over the bed. "We can go for dinner, if you like," he says.

Rennie's wearing a white shirt and a wrap skirt, also white. She wonders which she should take off first. What will happen? Maybe there's no point to taking off anything, maybe she should offer to sleep in the other bed. All he said was that he had room.

Nevertheless she's afraid, of failure. Maybe she should be fair, maybe she should warn him. What can she say? I'm not all here? There's part of me missing? She doesn't even have to do that, failure is easy to avoid. All you have to do is walk away.

Then she realizes she doesn't care. She doesn't care what he thinks of her, she never has to see this man again if she doesn't want to. She never has to see anyone again if she doesn't want to.

She's been hoping for some dope, he's in the business, he must have some; it would help, she thought, she'd be able to relax. But she doesn't need it; already she feels light, insubstantial, as if she's died and gone to heaven and come back minus a body. There's nothing to worry about, nothing can touch her. She's a tourist. She's exempt.

He's standing in front of her, in the half light, smiling a little, watching her to see what she'll do.

"I thought you didn't want that," he says.

He doesn't touch her. She undoes the buttons on the blouse, he's watching. He notes the scar, the missing piece, the place where death kissed her lightly, a preliminary kiss. He doesn't look away or down, he's seen people a lot deader than her.

"I was lucky," she says.

He reaches out his hands and Rennie can't remember ever having been touched before. Nobody lives forever, who said you could? This much will have to do, this much is enough. She's open now, she's been opened, she's being drawn back down, she enters her body again and there's a moment of pain, incarnation, this may be only the body's desperation, a flareup, a last clutch at the world before the long slide into final illness and death; but meanwhile she's solid after all, she's still here on the earth, she's grateful, he's touching her, she can still be touched.

■

· V ·

JAKE LIKED to pin her hands down, he liked to hold her so she couldn't move. He liked that, he liked thinking of sex as something he could win at. Sometimes he really hurt her, once he put his arm across her throat and she really did stop breathing. Danger turns you on, he said. Admit it. It was a game, they both knew that. He would never do it if it was real, if she really was a beautiful stranger or a slave girl or whatever it was he wanted her to pretend. So she didn't have to be afraid of him.

A month before the operation Rennie had a phone call from *Visor*. Keith, the managing editor, thought it would be sort of fun to do a piece on pornography as an art form. There had already been a number of anti-porno pieces in the more radical women's magazines, but Keith thought they were kind of heavy and humorless. They missed the element of playfulness, he said. He wanted a woman to write it because he thought they'd crack the nuts of any guy who tried to do it. Rennie tried to find out who he meant by "they," but he was vague. Tie it in with women's fantasy lives, if you can, he said. Keep it light. Rennie said she thought the subject might have more to do with men's fantasy lives, but Keith said he wanted the woman's angle.

Keith fixed it up for her to interview an artist who lived and worked in a warehouse down off King Street West and did sculptures using life-sized mannequins. He was making tables and chairs from the mannequins, which were like store mannequins except that the joints had been filled in and plastered over to make them smooth. The women were dressed in half-cup bras and G-string panties, set on their hands and knees for the tables, locked into a sitting position for the chairs. One of the chairs was a woman on her knees, her back arched, her wrists tied to her thighs. The ropes and arms were the arms of the chair, her bum was the seat.

It's a visual pun, said the artist, whose first name was Frank. He had one woman harnessed to a dogsled, with a muzzle on. It was called *Nationalism Is Dangerous*. There was another one with a naked mannequin on her knees, chained to a toilet, with a Handy Andy between her teeth like a rose. It was called *Task Sharing*, said Frank.

If a woman did that, said Rennie, they'd call it strident feminism.

That's the breaks, said Frank. Anyway, I don't just do women. He showed her a male figure sitting in a swivel chair with a classic blue pinstripe business suit on. Frank had glued nine or ten plastic dildos to the top of his head, where they stood out like pigtails or the rays of a halo. *Erogenous Zone Clone Bone*, it was called.

You're going to find this boring, said Rennie, but your work doesn't exactly turn me on.

It's not supposed to turn you on, said Frank, not offended. Art is for contemplation. What art does is, it takes what society deals out and makes it visible, right? So you can see it. I mean, there's the themes and then there's the variations. If they want flower paintings they can go to Eaton's.

Rennie remembered having read these opinions already, in the file on Frank given to her by *Visor*. I guess I see your point, she said.

I mean, said Frank, what's the difference between me and Salvador Dali, when you come right down to it?

I'm not sure, Rennie said.

If you don't like my stuff, you should see the raw material, he said.

That was the other part of Keith's plan, the raw material. The Metro Police had a collection of seized objects, Keith said; it was called Project P., P for pornography, and it was open to the public. Rennie took Jocasta with her, not because she didn't think she could get through it on her own, she felt she was up to almost anything. Still, it didn't seem like the kind of thing you would do by yourself if you could help it. Someone might see you coming out and get the wrong idea. Besides, it was Jocasta's kind of thing. Bizarre. Human ingenuity, that's what you should stress, said Keith. Infinite variety and all that.

The collection was housed in two ordinary rooms at the main police building, and this was the first thing that struck Rennie:

the ordinariness of the rooms. They were rectangular, featureless, painted government gray; they could have been in a post office. The policeman who showed them around was young, fresh-faced, still eager. He kept saying, Now why do you think anyone would want to do *that*? Now what do you think *that* could be for?

Rennie made it through the whips and the rubber appliances without a qualm. She took notes. How do you spell the plural of *dildo*? she asked the policeman. With or without an *e*? The policeman said he didn't know. Probably like *tomatoes*, Rennie thought. Jocasta said it all looked very medical to her and she understood that in England it was the truss shops that used to sell under-the-cover bondage magazines, before sex supermarkets came in. The policeman said he wouldn't really know about that. He opened a cupboard and took out something even the police hadn't been able to figure out. It was a machine like a child's floor polisher, with an ordinary-looking dildo on the handle. He plugged it into a wall socket and the whole machine scooted around the floor, with the handle plunging wildly up and down.

But what's it *for*? Jocasta said, intrigued.

Your guess is as good as mine, the policeman said. It's too short for anyone standing up, and there's no place on it to sit down. Anyhow, the way it runs around the room like that you couldn't keep up with it. We've got a private bet on here. Anyone comes up with some use for it that wouldn't take your guts out, we give them a hundred dollars.

Maybe it's for very active midgets, Jocasta said.

Maybe the police made a mistake, Rennie said. Maybe it really is just a floor polisher, with kind of a strange handle. Next thing you know you'll be raiding General Electric and seizing pop-up toasters.

Fifty percent of fatal accidents occur at home and now we know why, said Jocasta.

The policeman somehow did not like them laughing. He disapproved of it. He took them into a third room, which was set up with black-out windows and a video viewer and showed them some film clips, a woman with a dog, a woman with a pig, a woman with a donkey. Rennie watched with detachment. There were a couple of sex-and-death pieces, women being strangled or bludgeoned or having their nipples cut off by men dressed up as Nazis, but Rennie felt it couldn't possibly be real, it was all done with ketchup.

This is our grand finale, the policeman said. The picture showed a woman's pelvis, just the pelvis and the tops of the thighs. The woman was black. The legs were slightly apart; the usual hair, the usual swollen pinkish purple showed between them; nothing was moving. Then something small and gray and wet appeared, poking out from between the legs. It was the head of a rat. Rennie felt that a large gap had appeared in what she'd been used to thinking of as reality. What if this is normal, she thought, and we just haven't been told yet?

Rennie didn't make it out of the room. She threw up on the policeman's shoes. Sorry, she said, but he didn't seem to mind. He patted her on the back, as if she'd passed a test of some sort, and took her arm, leading her from the darkened room. Politely, he did not look down at his shoes.

I thought that one would get to you, he said. A lot of women do that. Look at it this way, at least it's not for queers.

You need your head repaired, said Jocasta, and Rennie said she thought maybe it was time to leave. She thanked the policeman for being so cooperative. He was annoyed with them, not because of his shoes but because of Jocasta.

I can't do this piece, Rennie told Keith.
Why not? he said, disappointed in her.
It's not my thing, she said. I'll stick to lifestyles.
Maybe it is a lifestyle, he said.

Rennie decided that there were some things it was better not to know any more about than you had to. Surfaces, in many cases, were preferable to depths. She did a piece on the return of the angora sweater, and another one on the handknit-look industry. That was soothing. There was much to be said for trivia.

For a couple of weeks after that she had a hard time making love with Jake. She didn't want him grabbing her from behind when she wasn't expecting it, she didn't like being thrown onto the bed or held so she couldn't move. She had trouble dismissing it as a game. She now felt that in some way that had never been spelled out between them he thought of her as the enemy. Please don't do that any more, she said. At least not for a while. She didn't want to be afraid of men, she wanted Jake to tell her why she didn't have to be.

I thought you said it's okay if you trust me, he said. Don't you trust me?

It's not you, she said. It's not you I don't trust.

Then what is it? he said.

I don't know, she said. Lately I feel I'm being used; though not by you exactly.

Used for what? said Jake.

Rennie thought about it. Raw material, she said.

Later on, she said, If I had a rat in my vagina, would it turn you on?

Dead or alive? said Jake.

Me or the rat? said Rennie.

Feh, said Jake. You sound like my mother. Always worrying about the dustballs under the bed.

No, seriously, she said.

El sleazo, he said. Come on, don't confuse me with that sick stuff. You think I'm some kind of a pervert? You think most men are like that?

Rennie said no.

■

I ran into Paul in Miami, said Lora. At first he told me he was in real estate. I was down there with some guy, that was after me and Gary split up, and around that time if there was a free weekend going I took it. It wasn't the sex. I couldn't have cared less if a man ever touched me again or not, that's how I felt then. With Gary it was never that great anyway, it was a lot like going through a revolving door, in and out before you know it and if you sneezed it was all over except for washing the sheets.

Maybe I wanted it that way, maybe I wanted to be able to take it or leave it. Maybe I thought if I got to like it too much I'd be stuck. I wanted to think, Chuck you, Farley, there's nothing much I need you for, if I want to I can turn around and walk right through that door and the only one who'll be missing a thing is you. I thought it was just something you let men do to you. I don't think most of them even liked it very much either. They only did it because you were supposed to.

I guess I just wanted to be with someone. It wasn't the nights that were bad, it was the mornings. I didn't like to wake up in the morning and have nobody there. After a while you just want someone to like you. You want someone to maybe have breakfast with, go to the movies with, stuff like that. I used to say there's only two things that matter, is he nice or is he rich. Nice is better than rich but take it from me, you can't have both, and if you can't get nice take rich. Sometimes I said it the other way around. Not that there's a whole lot of either one hanging out there on the trees, you know?

At first I thought Paul was only nice. He wasn't mean like a lot of them, he was easy to be with, he wasn't a pain in the ass, you know? Then I figured it out that he was rich, too. He had this boat, he only had the one then, and he said why didn't I come down here for a couple of weeks, get a tan, relax, and there wasn't any good reason not to. Once I got down here I couldn't see any good reason to leave. Around that time I found out what he really did.

I worked on the boats for a while. Most of these boats have two or three crew and a cook, they really do run charters on the boats, it would look funny if they didn't, and the crew all knew what he was doing, they were in for a percentage, he had people he could trust. I was supposed to be the cook, what I knew about cooking on a boat you could stick in your ear, it's not like cooking in a real kitchen, but I picked it up. I was seasick as hell at first, I puked my guts out, but I figure you can get used to almost anything if you have to and when you're out in the middle of the ocean there's only one way off the boat, eh?

A lot of girls work the boats here, the straight boats as well, though you never really know if the boat's straight or not, you learn not to ask what they've got in the hold. Whoever runs the boat expects you to make it with them; if you don't like it you can always get off the boat. I never made it with the charters though, that wasn't part of the deal. It's always them that get the maddest about it too. They think if they're renting the boat they're renting everything on it. Maybe I'm for sale, I'd tell them, but

I'm sure as hell not for rent. How much? one of them said, an asshole. Hot-shot lawyer or something. You couldn't afford it, I said. Funny, you look pretty cheap to me, he said. I may be pretty but I'm not cheap, I said. I'm like a lawyer, what you're paying for is the experience.

Anyway you only had to do a few charters, maybe once a month, you could survive on that. The rest of the time I was living with Paul. Or anyway that's what it was called. We slept in the same bed and all, but there was something missing in him, it was like being with someone who wasn't there, you know? He didn't care what I did, anything I wanted to do was okay with him, other men, anything, as long as it didn't interfere with him. Deep down inside he just didn't give a shit. You know what the locals say about him? *He does deal.* With the devil, is what they mean, they don't mean the business. It's what they say about loners.

About the only thing that really turned him on was danger, as far as I could figure out. Once in a while he'd do this really dangerous stuff.

Like, a couple of months after I came down here there was this thing with Marsdon. That was before Marsdon went to the States. He was living with this woman, and he came home one day and caught her in the sack with one of his cousins, I forget which one. It could be anybody, sooner or later they all turn out to be cousins if you study it hard enough.

Of course Marsdon beat her up. If he hadn't beat her up, the other men would have laughed at him and so would the women. They expect it, for being *bad*, which is what they call it. But he went too far, he made her take off all her clothes, not that she had that many on when he found her, and then he covered her with cow-itch. That's like a nettle, it's what you do to people you really don't like a whole lot. Then he tied her to a tree in the back yard, right near an anthill, the stinging kind. He stayed in the house, drinking rum and listening to her scream. He left her there five hours, till she was swollen up like a balloon. A lot of people heard her but nobody tried to untie her, partly because he had a mean reputation and partly because it was a man-woman thing, they don't think that's anyone else's business.

Paul heard about it and he walked into the back yard and cut the rope. You just don't do that. Everyone waited to see what

Marsdon would do, but he didn't do anything. He's hated Paul ever since. It was after that he went to the States and got into the army, or that's what he said he was doing. I wish he'd stayed there.

Paul didn't know the woman, he wasn't being noble as far as I could tell. He did it because it was dangerous; he did it because it was fun. Some fun if you ask me. You'd never know when he was going to pull one of those, you'd be washing your hair and you'd look out the window and there he'd be swinging from some goddamn tree, like Tarzan. He was like a little boy that way. He always said he knew what he was doing, but I knew some day he'd try it once too often and that would be that.

That's one of the reasons I stopped working on his boats. He was taking too many chances.

The stuff comes from Colombia, on the freighters. For the government there it's just another cash crop. Nobody can do anything about the freighters and once they're out in the ocean nobody can do anything about that either, except maybe hijack the boat. People have tried that but it's not too safe any more, they're shooting back. The U.S. knows which boats it's on, they follow everything by satellite, they can track the big boats by the sound of the motors; so they can't get it into the States that way. They bring it here, to one of these islands, and they split it up and put it onto yachts or private planes, they're using those more now, and they take it up to Miami or maybe in through the Virgin Islands. It's not just the U.S. and Cuba trying to control it here. The third group is the mob, and they're spending more money. It's a guaranteed multimillion-dollar business, so they can afford a top-level lobby in Washington, to keep them from legalizing it. Nobody wants it legalized, then you could grow it right there in your own back yard, the bottom would fall out of the market.

Ellis never stopped them, they were paying him off, but that may be changing, he may want in on the ground floor. He just made a big bust in the harbor over at St. Antoine. It seems some locals were growing it up there behind the bananas and smuggling it out on the fishing trawlers. A medium-sized operation but the big ones don't want any competition, and Ellis doesn't want the peasants marketing it themselves, he'd lose his cut. I'd guess it was the mob who put Ellis up to making the bust. Two to one he'll resell it himself.

At first they were just hiring Paul's boats, piecework, to make the run up from here to Miami. But then he went down there himself and bought his own army general. He figured why should he be the middleman when he could buy wholesale himself and sell retail, which makes sense except that then he had them all down his back, the CIA, the mob, Ellis, the works. No thanks, I said, I like my skin the way it is, only the holes God gave me. I told him I'd do the tourists, they'd trust me more because I was white and a woman, as long as he bought a few local cops for me, I'd do retail, but none of that other stuff.

The second reason I stopped was Prince. I just met him in a beach bar and it was love at first sight, that never happened to me before. I know you think it's weird because he's so much younger than me but that's the way it happened. I don't know what it was, maybe it was the eyes. He looked at you straight on, you felt that everything he was saying just had to be the truth. It wasn't always, I found that out, but he always believed it was. He even believed all that communist stuff, he really believed he could save the world. He couldn't tell you something and not believe it himself. He was so sweet. I was a real sucker for that.

He didn't want me going out on the boats with Paul, he didn't want me having anything to do with Paul in that way any more, he was jealous as hell. I guess I was a sucker for that, too. He wanted me all to himself, nobody else ever wanted that. He wanted us to have a baby. I never felt that important before.

As for Paul, you know what he did? He shook hands with me. That was all. I thought I was going to cry but instead I laughed. And I thought, that's what it's been like all along, sleeping with him and everything, there's been nothing more to it than that. Shaking hands.

■

Rennie wakes up in the middle of the night and Paul is still there, she can hardly believe it; he's even awake, he's a shape in the darkness, above her, resting on one elbow; is he watching her?

"Is that you?" she says.

"Who else would it be?" he says. She doesn't know. She reaches out for him and he's tangible, he doesn't go away.

It's early morning. Rennie can hear a sound outside the window, a bleating. She gets out of bed and looks: It's a goat, right beside the house, with a chain around its neck attached to a stone so it can't wander off. She wishes it would shut up. Two men are nearby, hacking at the shrubs with machetes. Gardeners. One of them has a transistor radio, which is thinly playing a hymn. Paul is still asleep, he must be used to it. She was dreaming there was another man in the bed with them; something white, a stocking or a gauze bandage, wrapped around his head.

When she wakes again Paul is gone. Rennie gets up and puts on her clothes, then wanders through the house looking for him. It's nobody's house, it could be a motel, it's empty space and he's left no footprints. It occurs to her that she's just spent the night with a man about whom she knows absolutely nothing at all. It seems a foolhardy thing to have done.

She goes outside. There's a tree beside the porch, covered with pink flowers, a swarm of hummingbirds around it. It looks arranged. The too-bright sunshine, the rock garden, the road below it along which two women are walking, one carrying a large tree limb balanced on her head, the foliage and then the blue harbor dotted with postcard boats, the whole vista is one-dimensional this morning, a scrim. At any moment it will rise slowly into the air and behind it will appear the real truth.

There's a noise coming from behind a clump of trees to the east, a desolate monotonous wail, a child. It goes on and on, as if this is a natural form of speech, almost like breathing. A woman's voice rises, there are thumps; the child's howling changes in intensity but not in rhythm.

Rennie looks through the telescope, which is focused on one of the yachts. There's a woman in a red bikini, lowering herself into the water; the telescope is so strong that even the roll of fat above the bikini bottom, even the striations on her belly are visible. Is this Paul's hobby, peering at distant flesh? Surely not. Yet the telescope confers furtive power, the power to watch without being watched. Rennie's embarrassed by it and turns away. She swings herself in the hammock, trying not to think. She feels deserted.

When Paul still doesn't come back, she goes into the house. She checks out the refrigerator for something to eat, but there's not much. Ice cubes in the ice cube tray, a tin of condensed milk with holes punched in the top, a small paper bag full of sugar, some yellowing limes, a pitcher of cold water. Noodles in the cupboard, a bottle of rum, a packet of coffee, some Tetley's teabags, a tin of Tate & Lyle golden syrup with a string of ants undulating around the lid. They skipped dinner last night and she's starving.

The logical explanation is that Paul has gone for food, since there isn't any. She wishes he'd left a note for her, but he doesn't seem like the note-leaving type. The house is very empty. She walks through the living room again; there aren't even any books or magazines. Maybe he keeps his personal things on the boat, the boats. She goes into the bedroom and looks into the closet: a couple of shirts, a spear gun and a mask and flippers, jeans folded on a hanger, that's it.

In the bureau there are some T-shirts, neatly stacked, and stuck at the back of the top drawer a couple of photos: color snapshots, a white colonial house with a double garage, a green lawn, a yellow-haired woman in a shirtwaist dress, smiling to reveal slightly buck teeth; hair short and close to the head, an unsuccessful permanent growing out, two little girls, one blonde, one reddish-brown, both in pigtails with ribbons, it must have been a birthday. The mother's hands on their shoulders. The sun casts shadows under their eyes so that even though they're smiling they look slightly disappointed, the disappointment of ghosts. In the other picture Paul is there too, much younger, a crewcut but it must be him: a shirt and tie and pants with sharp creases, and beneath his eyes the same shadows.

Rennie feels she's prying but she's into it now, she might as well go on. It's not as if she'll use it for anything: she just wants to know, she wants to find something that will make Paul real for her. She goes into the bathroom and looks through the medicine cabinet. The brand names are unrevealing: Tylenol in a large bottle, Crest toothpaste, Elastoplast, Dettol. Nothing unusual.

There's another bedroom, or she assumes it's a bedroom. The door's closed but not locked: It opens as easily as all the other doors. It is a bedroom, or at least there's a bed in it. There's also a table, with what looks like a radio on it, a complicated-looking one, and some other equipment she can't identify. In the closet there's a large cardboard box standing on end. The address label's been torn off. It's full of Styrofoam packing beads, but otherwise empty. It looks very familiar.

There's someone in the house, walking across the wooden floor. She feels as if she's been caught in a forbidden room, though Paul hasn't forbidden anything. Still, it isn't nice to snoop in other people's houses. She comes out, closing the door behind her as quietly as she can. Luckily there's a hallway: She can't be seen.

But it's not Paul, it's Lora, in a fresh pink dress with bare shoulders. "Hi there," she says. "I brought you some stuff." She's at the kitchen counter, taking it out of a straw basket: bread, butter, a carton of long-life milk, even a tin of jam. "He never has anything in the house. I'll make us some coffee, okay?"

She gets out the electric kettle, the coffee, the sugar; she knows exactly where everything is. Rennie sits at the wooden table, watching her. She knows she should feel thankful for all this attention, thoughtfulness, but instead she's irritated. This isn't her kitchen and she doesn't live here, so why should it bother her that Lora is acting as if she owns the place? And how did Lora know she'd be here? Maybe she didn't know it. Maybe she's in the habit.

"Where's Paul?" says Lora.

"I don't know," Rennie says. She's on the defensive: Shouldn't she know, shouldn't he have told her?

"He'll turn up," says Lora lightly. "Here today, gone tomorrow, that's Paul."

Lora brings the coffee, a cup for each of them, and sets it down on the table. Rennie doesn't want to ask for food, though she's ravenous; she doesn't want to tell Lora about missing dinner. She doesn't want to tell Lora anything. She would like Lora to vanish, but instead Lora sits down at the table, settling in. She sips her coffee. Rennie watches her hands, the squat fingers, the rough gnawed skin around the nails.

"I wouldn't get too mixed up with Paul if I was you," she says. Here it comes, thinks Rennie. She's going to tell me something for my own good. In her experience, things that people told you for your own good were always unpleasant.

"Why not?" she says, smiling as neutrally as possible.

"I don't mean you can't," says Lora. "Hell, why not, it's a free country. Just, don't get mixed up, is all. Not that he gets that mixed up with most people anyway. Easy come, easy go. Around here there's a high turnover."

Rennie isn't sure what she's being told. Is she being warned off or just warned? "I guess you've known him a long time," she says.

"Long enough," says Lora.

Now there are footsteps and a shadow falls on the front window, and this time it is Paul, coming across the porch. He walks through the door smiling, sees Lora, blinks but keeps on smiling.

"I went for eggs," he says to Rennie. "I thought you'd be hungry." He sets a brown paper bag down on the table, proud of himself.

"Where in hell did you get any eggs, at this time of day?" says Lora. "The eggs aren't in yet." She's getting up, to go Rennie hopes, she sets down the coffee mug.

Paul grins. "I've got connections," he says.

■

Paul scrambles the eggs, quite well, they're not too dry; Rennie gives him three and a half stars for the eggs. They eat them with jam and toast. There's a toaster, though the only way you can get it to work, says Paul, is by short-circuiting it with a paring knife. He keeps meaning to get a new one, he says, but new toasters are smuggled in and none have come in lately.

After breakfast Rennie thinks she should offer to wash the dishes, since Paul did the cooking. "Forget that," says Paul. "Someone comes in." He takes her hands and pulls her to her feet and kisses her, his mouth tasting of buttered toast. Then he leads her into the bedroom. This time he takes off her clothes, not too quickly, without fumbling. She takes his hands with their blunt practical fingers, guides him, they slide onto the bed, it's effortless.

Rennie comes almost at once, they're both slippery with sweat, it's luxurious, indulgent, gleeful as rolling around in warm mud, the muscles of her thighs are aching. He pauses, goes on, pauses, goes on until she comes again. He's skilled and attentive, he's good at it. Maybe she's just a quick fuck for him, a transient, maybe they're both transients, passing through, is that what Lora was trying to say? But she can live with that, it's something, and something is better than nothing after all.

After a long time they get up and take a shower; together, but Paul is absent-minded as he soaps her back and then her breasts, carefully enough but he's already thinking about something else. She passes her hands over his body learning him, the muscles, the hollows. She's looking for something, his presence in his own body beneath the tangible one, but she can't reach him, right now he's not there.

Paul takes Rennie's arm above the elbow as they step out into the white light. She wants to ask what they're going to do now, but she doesn't, because it doesn't seem to matter. Go with the flow, Jocasta would say, and she's going. She feels lazy and unhurried; the future, which contains among other things an overdraft at the bank, seems a long way from here. She knows she's fallen right into the biggest cliché in the book, a no-hooks, no-strings vacation romance with a mysterious stranger. She's behaving like a secretary, and things must be bad, because it isn't even bothering her. As long as she doesn't fall in love: That would be more than secretarial, it would be unacceptable. Love or sex? Jocasta would ask, and this time Rennie knows. Love is tangled, sex is straight. High-quality though, she'd say. Don't knock it.

They walk down to the sea and along the beach. By now he's remote but friendly, like a tour guide. Part of a package.

"See that building?" he says. He's pointing to a low shed-like structure. It's painted green and has three doors. "That made a lot of trouble here a couple of years ago. Ellis built it, it was supposed to encourage the tourists."

"What is it?" Rennie asks, unable to see why it would be encouraging.

"Now they use it to store fishnets in," says Paul, "but it used to be a can. A public can; Men, Women, and Tourists. The idea was that the tourists would get off the boat and need a place to shit, and it would be right there handy for them. But the people here didn't think a thing like that should be down on the beach,

198

out in the open like that. They thought it was indecent. They filled it up with stones, Tourists first." He smiles.

"They don't like tourists?" says Rennie.

"Let's put it this way," says Paul. "When the tourists come in, the prices go up. The big election issue this year is the price of sugar. They say it's getting too high, the people can't afford it."

"Just as well, it's bad for you," says Rennie, who believes in roughage, more or less.

"That depends on what else you have to eat," says Paul.

■

There's music, coming along the beach, wooden flutes and a drum. It's a parade of some sort, a mob of people walking along on the sand. Even though it's morning they have torches, cloth wrapped on sticks and soaked in kerosene, Rennie can smell it. Behind the adults in the crowd, around the edges, children are jumping and dancing in time to the music. Two kids are carrying a banner made from an old sheet: PRINCE OF PEACE: HE WORKS FOR YOU NOT YOU FOR HIM. Out front is Elva, chin up, strolling rather than marching. She has a white enamel potty in one hand and an unfurling roll of toilet paper in the other. She holds these objects high, as if they're trophies.

Rennie and Paul stand to the side as the parade goes past. At the very end comes Marsdon, still in his boots; the heels sink into the sand, it's hard for him to walk. He sees the two of them but does not acknowledge them.

"What does it mean?" says Rennie. "The toilet paper."

"It's aimed at the government," says Paul. "It's what they'll need after the election."

"I don't understand," says Rennie.

"They'll be so scared they'll shit their pants," says Paul. "Roughly translated." He's indulging her again.

They walk up the beach to the main road of the town. The parade has turned around now and is coming back; people have stopped to watch it. There's a car parked also, with two men in mirror sunglasses in the front and a third in the back. He's wearing a black suit, like an undertaker.

"The Minister of Justice," says Paul.

Paul says a lot of the stores are closed because of the election. Knots of men are gathered here and there; sun glints on the bottles as they pass from hand to hand. Some of the men nod to Paul. Not to Rennie: Their attention slides over her, around her, they see her but only from the corners of their eyes.

They go up the hill and along a back street. There's a persistent hum; as they walk north it becomes a throb, a steady heartbeat. Metal, a motor of some kind.

"The power plant," says Paul. "It runs on oil. That's the poor end of town."

They go into a store called The Sterling Emporium. Paul asks for some long-life milk, and the woman gets it for him. She's about forty-five, with huge muscled arms and a small neat head, the hair screwed into lime-green plastic curlers. She brings out a brown paper bag from under the counter. "I save it for you," she says.

"Eggs," Paul says. He pays. Rennie can't believe how much they cost.

"If they're that hard to get," she says, "why doesn't someone start a chicken farm?"

"You'd have to ship in the feed," says Paul. "They don't grow it here. The feed weighs more than the eggs. Besides, the eggs come in from the States."

"What's that got to do with it?" says Rennie. Paul only smiles.

"They catch the thief," the woman says to Paul as they're heading for the door. "The police take him on the boat today."

"He's lucky then," Paul says to her.

"Lucky?" says Rennie, when they're outside.

"He's still alive," says Paul. "They caught another man, last month, stealing pigs up at one of the villages; they pounded him to death, no questions asked."

"The police?" says Rennie. "That's terrible."

"No," says Paul. "The people he was stealing the pigs from. It's a good thing for this one he only stole from tourists. If it was locals they'd have kicked his head in or taken him out and dumped him into the sea. As far as they're concerned, stealing's worse than murder."

"I can't believe that," says Rennie.

"Look at it this way," says Paul. "If you get angry and chop up

200

your woman, that's understandable; a crime of passion, you might say. But stealing you plan beforehand. That's how they see it."

"Is there a lot of that?" says Rennie.

"Stealing?" says Paul. "Only since the tourists came in."

"Chopping up your woman," says Rennie.

"Less than you might think," says Paul. "Mostly they beat or slice rather than chop." Rennie thinks of cookbooks. "There's no shooting at all. Not like in, say, Detroit."

"Why is that?" says Rennie, hot on the sociological trail.

Paul looks at her, not for the first time, as if she's a charming version of the village idiot. "They don't have any guns," he says.

■

Rennie is sitting on a white chair in the beach bar of the Lime Tree, where Paul has left her. Parked her. Stashed her. He has a boat coming in in a few days, he said, there are some things he has to take care of. Rennie feels peripheral.

Is there anything you need? he asked before he went off.

I thought most of the stores were closed, she said.

They are, he said.

Something to read, she said, with a touch of malice. If he's so good at it let him try that.

He didn't miss a beat. Anything in particular?

Anything you think I'd like, said Rennie.

Which will at least make him think about her. She sits at the wooden table, eating a grilled cheese sandwich. What could be nicer? What's wrong anyway? Why does she want to go, if not home, at least away? Paul doesn't love her, that's why, which ought to be irrelevant.

Don't expect too much, he said last night.

Too much of what? said Rennie.

Too much of me, said Paul. He was smiling, calm as ever, but she no longer found this reassuring. Instead she found it a symptom. Nothing could move him. He kissed her on the forehead, as if she were a child, as if he were kissing her goodnight.

Next you're going to tell me there isn't very much, said Rennie. Right?

Maybe there isn't, said Paul.

Rennie didn't know she was expecting anything until she was told not to. Now they seem vast, sentimental, grandiose, technicolor, magical, ridiculous, her expectations.

What am I doing here? thinks Rennie. I should take my body and run. I don't need another man I'm not supposed to expect anything from.

She's a tourist, she can keep her options open. She can always go somewhere else.

■

"I am disturbing you?" It's a statement, with the force of a question. Rennie looks up: It's Dr. Minnow, in a white shirt open at the throat, balancing a cup of coffee. He sits down without waiting for an answer.

"You are enjoying yourself at the home of your American friend?" he says slyly.

Rennie, who believes in personal privacy, is annoyed. "How did you know I'm staying there?" she says. She feels as if she's been caught by a high-school teacher, necking under the boys' gym stairs. A thing she never did.

Dr. Minnow smiles, showing his skewed teeth. "Everyone knows," he says. "I am sorry to interrupt you, but there are some things I must tell you now. For the article you are writing."

"Oh yes," Rennie says. "Of course." Surely he doesn't still believe she's going to do this, now or in the future; but apparently he does, he's looking at her with candor and assurance. Faith. "I don't have my notebook with me," she says, feeling more and more fraudulent.

"You can remember," says Dr. Minnow. "Please, continue with your lunch." He's not even looking at her, he's glancing around them, noting who's there. "We are seeing how the election is going, my friend," he says.

"Already?" says Rennie.

"I do not mean the results," says Dr. Minnow. "I mean the practices of this government. Ellis is winning, my friend. But not honestly, you understand? This is what I wish you to make clear: that Ellis will not have the support of the people." It's the same measured tone of voice he's always used, but Rennie can see now that he's far from calm. He's enraged. He sits with his thin hands placed one on the other, on top of the wooden table, but the hands are tense, it's as if he has to hold onto them to keep them from moving, lifting, striking out.

"The only votes Ellis is getting are the ones he buys. First they bribe the people with the foreign aid money from the hurricane," he says. "This I can prove to you, I have witnesses. If they are not afraid to come forward. He give out the roofing materials too, the sewage pipes, the things donated. On St. Antoine this bribery is effective, but here on Ste. Agathe it does not work. Here the people take the money from Ellis but vote for me anyway; they think this is a good joke. Ellis knows this trick will not work here on Ste. Agathe, he knows the people are for me. So he has been playing with the voters' list. When my people go to vote today, they find they are not recorded. Even some of my candidates have been removed, they cannot cast a vote in their own favor. 'Sorry,' they tell them. 'You cannot vote.' You know who he put on? Dead people, my friend. Half the people on the voters' list are dead. This government is being elected by corpses."

"But how could he do that?" says Rennie. "Didn't your party see the lists before the election?"

Dr. Minnow smiles his crooked smile. "This is not Canada, my friend," he says. "It is not Britain. Those rules no longer apply here. Nevertheless I will do what the sweet Canadians would do. I will challenge the results of the election in the courts and demand another vote, and I will call for an independent inquiry." He laughs a little. "It will have the same results here as it has there, my friend. None at all. Only there it takes longer."

"Why do you bother?" Rennie says.

"Bother?" says Dr. Minnow.

"If it's as rotten as you say," says Rennie, "why do you bother trying to do anything at all?"

Dr. Minnow pauses. She's shaken him a little. "I agree with you that it seems illogical and futile for me to do so," he says. "But this is why you do it. You do it because everyone tell you it is not possible. They cannot imagine things being different. It is my duty to imagine, and they know that for even one person to imagine is very dangerous to them, my friend. You understand?"

He's about to say something else, but there are screams, from over near the kitchen door, the yacht people at the tables are looking, getting up, already there's a cluster of them.

Rennie stands up, trying to see what it is. It's Lora. She has one arm around Elva, whose eyes are closed, who's silently crying. There are red splotches on her PRINCE OF PEACE T-shirt. Her face is streaked, mapped, caked, dark red.

■

Lora sits at a table, one leg crossed, ankle on her knee. In front of her is a rum and lime and a glassful of ice cubes and a white enamel basin full of dark pink water. Elva is sitting beside her, still crying, her hands in her lap. Lora is washing away the blood with a blue washcloth from the hotel.

"Maybe I should lie her down," she says to Rennie. "What do you think?"

"God," says Rennie. "What happened?"

"I don't really know," says Lora. "I hardly saw it, it was too fast. One minute Prince was outside this polling station, just talking to the people, and the next thing there was all this shouting. It was two policemen with guns and the Minister of Justice. They just pushed in and started hammering Prince. Don't ask me why."

"Is he all right?" says Rennie.

"I don't even know that," says Lora. "I don't know where he went. He'll turn up, he usually does."

"Did she get knocked down by accident or something?" Rennie says.

"Her?" says Lora. "Hell no. She had her hands around the Justice Minister's neck, she damn near strangled him. They hit her on the head with a pistol butt to make her let go."

"Is there anything I can do?" says Rennie, who isn't too comfortable: The sight of the blood in the white basin is making her feel sick. Maybe she can go for Band-Aids and then she'll be off the hook.

"Get me some cigarettes," says Lora. "Over at the bar, Benson and Hedges. Maybe we should take her home."

"Marsdon," says Elva. "Some time I kill that boy."

"What?" says Lora. "What's she saying?"

"Marsdon start it," says Elva. She stops crying and opens her eyes. "I hear him. He call the Justice Minister a bad name. Why he need to do that?"

"Shit," says Lora. "Marsdon thinks everybody has to die for the revolution. *His* revolution, is what he means. He'll do just about anything to make sure they do. I wish he'd take off those stupid cowboy boots, I bet he sleeps in them. He thinks he's God's gift, ever since he came back from the States. He was in the army up there, it did something to him. He saw too many movies and now he thinks he's a hero. If Prince gets elected, Marsdon gets to be the Minister of Justice. Shit, can you picture that?"

"I better now," says Elva. She takes an ice cube out of the glass and pops it into her mouth.

"She's still bleeding," says Rennie, but Elva's already walking away, steadily, as if there's nothing wrong with her. "Shouldn't you go with her?"

Lora shrugs. "What makes you think she'd let me?" she says. "She does what she likes. When you get to be her age around here nobody can tell you a thing."

"Does she have somewhere to go?" Rennie says. "Someone who can take care of her?"

"She has daughters," Lora says. "She has grandchildren. Not that she needs taking care of, mostly she takes care of them. This whole place runs on grandmothers."

A girl from the hotel comes and takes away the basin. Rennie feels a little better, now that there's no actual blood. The people are back in their chairs, voices are normal, the sun shines on the boats in the harbor. Lora has her cigarettes now; she lights one, blowing the smoke out through her nostrils in a long gray sigh.

"The whole thing was Marsdon's idea," she says. "Prince running in the election. He never would of thought it up himself. Marsdon would run for God if it was open, except who would vote for him? Nobody likes him, everybody likes Prince, so he had to talk Prince into doing it for him. Prince thinks the sun shines right out of Marsdon's ass and nobody can tell him any different, so what can you do?"

"Do you think he'll win?" Rennie says.

"Christ, I hope not," Lora says. "I hope he loses. I hope he loses so bad he never even thinks of doing it again. Then maybe we can get back to some kind of a normal life."

Rennie trudges up the road toward Paul's house, because where else is there? She wishes Paul had told her when he was coming back, but she's hardly in a position to demand it. She's only a sort of house guest. A visitor.

There's no cool side of the road, and the asphalt is so hot it's almost melting. No one is sitting on the porches at this time of day; nevertheless, Rennie feels she's being watched. Halfway up the hill she's overtaken by a crowd of schoolgirls, ten or twelve of them, different sizes but all in heavy black skirts and white long-sleeved blouses, white bows in their hair, bare feet for the most part. Without asking or saying anything two of them take her hands, one on either side. The rest of them laugh and mill around her, examining her dress, her sandals, her purse, her hair.

"Do you live near here?" she asks one of them, the one holding her right hand. She's about six, and now that Rennie's speaking directly to her she's shy; but she doesn't let go of the hand.

"You have a dollar?" says the one on the left. But an older girl puts a stop to that. "Don't be so bold," she says.

"Are you cousins?" asks Rennie. One of them attempts to explain: some are sisters, others cousins, others cousins of some but not of others. "Her daddy the same, her mother different." When they reach Paul's gateway they let go of her hands without being told: They already know she's staying there. They watch as she goes up the steps, giggling behind her.

Rennie has no key, but the door isn't locked. Until recently, Paul said, you never had to lock your door, and he's still not in the habit. She goes out to the hammock and rocks herself, waiting for time to pass.

Half an hour later a short brown woman in a green print dress with large yellow butterflies walks in through the door. She nods at Rennie but takes no notice of her after that. She wipes off the table, washes the dishes and dries them and puts them away, cleans off the top of the stove, and sweeps the floor. Then she goes into the bedroom and brings the sheets out. She carries them into the garden at the side of the house, where she washes them, by hand, in a big red plastic pail, using water from a small tap that comes out of the water tank. She rinses them and wrings them out and hangs them up. She disappears into the bedroom again, to make up the bed, Rennie assumes. Rennie swings herself in the hammock, watching. She ought to pretend to be doing something important, but she can't, she's too uneasy, she can almost smell what it feels like to be cleaning up after other people's feeding and sex. She feels superfluous and both invisible and exposed: something so much there that nobody looks at it. The woman comes out of the bedroom with Rennie's pink bikini underpants from the day before. Presumably she's going to wash them.

"I'll do that," says Rennie.

The woman gives her a sideways glance, of contempt, puts the underpants on the kitchen counter, nods again, and goes down the steps to the road.

Rennie gets up and locks the doors of the house and mixes herself a drink. She lies down on the bed, under the mosquito net, meaning to take only a short nap. Then someone is touching her neck. Paul. A faceless stranger.

■

It's raining; heavy drops like tacks patter on the tin roof. The huge leaves outside the window move in the wind, making a sound like the dragging of thick cloth across a floor. Something's loose out there.

Rennie's both avid and melancholy, as if it's the last time. More and more the emptiness of this house reminds her of a train station. Terminal, the place where you go to say good-bye. Paul is being too tender, it's the tenderness of a man boarding a troop ship. A man who can hardly wait. *Wait for me* would be the proper thing for him to say; he'd have no intention of doing the same himself. But she doesn't know where he's going. He's not giving anything away.

"If I were noble," says Paul, "I'd tell you to get the next boat out to St. Antoine and get the next plane out to Barbados and get the hell back home."

Rennie's kissing him beside the ear. His skin is dry, salty, the hair graying there. "Why would you do that?" she says.

"Safer," says Paul.

"Who for, you or me?" says Rennie. She thinks he's talking about their relationship. She thinks he's admitting something. This cheers her up.

"You," he says. "You're getting too involved, it's bad for you."

Rennie stops kissing. *Massive involvement*, she thinks. He smiles at her, looking down at her with his too-blue eyes, and she wonders whether she can believe a word he says.

"Take the plane, lady," he says, very sweetly.

"I don't want to go back," Rennie says.

"I'd like you to," says Paul.

"Are you trying to get rid of me?" says Rennie, smiling, fearing it.

"No," says Paul. "Maybe I'm just being stupid. Maybe I want there to be something good I've done."

Rennie feels she can make her own choices, she doesn't need to have them made for her. In any case she doesn't want to be something that Paul has done. Good or otherwise.

She thinks about going back. There will be the hedgehopper to Barbados, the wait in the steamy airport among the secretaries, just-arrived or in transit, lonely and hopeful, with their vague expectations; then the monotonous jet and then the airport, sterile and rectilinear. It will be cold outside and gray, and the wind will smell of diesel fuel. In the city, people will be hunched into their winter coats, scuttling heads-down along the sidewalks, their faces not flat and open like the faces here but narrow and pallid and pushed into long snouts, like the snouts of rats. No one will even glance at anyone else. What does she have to look forward to?

■

Jake came over to pick up his suits and his books and pictures. He had his new lady's car downstairs, his own was on the fritz. He didn't say whether or not the new lady was in it, and Rennie didn't ask. *Lady* was his own term, a recent one. He had never called Rennie his lady.

He made several trips, up the stairs and down again, and Rennie sat at the kitchen table and drank coffee. From the hooks above the stove there were now things missing, pots, frying pans, which had left round halos of lighter yellow on the wall, penumbras of grease. From now on she would have to decide what to eat. Jake decided before: Even when it was her turn to cook he decided. He brought home all kinds of things: bones, wrinkled old sausages filmed with powdery mold, rank and horrible cheeses which he insisted she had to try. Life is an improvisation, he said. Exploit your potential.

Rennie's potential had been exploited, she didn't have any left. Not for Jake, who stood awkwardly in the doorway, holding a dark blue sock, asking if she'd seen the other one. Domesticity still hung in the air around them, like dust in sunlight, a lingering scent. Rennie said she hadn't, but he might try the bathroom, behind the laundry hamper. He went out and she could hear him rummaging. She should have gone somewhere else, not been here, they should have arranged things differently.

She tried not to think of the new lady, of whom it was not right to be jealous. She didn't know what the new lady looked like. To Rennie she was just a headless body, with or without a black nightgown. As perhaps she was to Jake. What is a woman, Jake said once. A head with a cunt attached or a cunt with a head attached? Depends which end you start at. It was understood between them that this was a joke. The new lady stretched out before her, a future, a space, a blank, into which Jake would now throw himself night after night the way he had thrown himself into her, each time extreme and final, as if he was pitching himself headlong over a cliff. It was for this she felt nostalgia. She wondered what it was like to be able to throw yourself into another person, another body, a darkness like that. Women could not do it. Instead they had darkness thrown into them. Rennie couldn't put the two things together, the urgency and blindness of the act, which had been urgent and blind for her too, and this result, her well-lit visible frozen pose at the kitchen table.

Jake was in the doorway again. Rennie did not want to look at him. She knew what she would see, it would be the same thing he saw when he looked at her. Failure, of a larger order than they would once have thought possible. But how could there be failure, since failure had been outside their terms of reference? No strings, no commitments, that's what they'd said. What would success have been?

Rennie thought of telling him about the man with the rope. Meanly, since it would only make him feel guilty and that was why she would be doing it. What would Jake make of it, the sight of one of his playful fantasies walking around out there, growling and on all fours? He knew the difference between a game and the real thing, he said; a desire and a need. She was the confused one.

Rennie did not say anything, nor did she stand up and throw her arms around Jake's neck, nor did she shake hands with him. She didn't want charity so she didn't do anything. She sat with her hands clenched around the coffee cup as if it was a bare socket, live electricity, and she couldn't move. Was this open, was it grief? What had become of them, two dead bodies, what could you do without desire, without need, what was she supposed to feel, what could be done? She pressed her hands together to keep them still. She thought of her grandmother, hands together like that, head bowed over the joyless Christmas turkey, saying grace.

Keep well, said Jake, and that was the whole problem. He could not admit she wasn't. No fun playing games with the walking wounded. Not only no fun, no fair.

■

The day after Jake was gone, for good, Rennie did not get up in the morning. There did not seem to be any point. She lay in bed thinking about Daniel. It was true he was a fantasy for her: a fantasy about the lack of fantasy, a fantasy of the normal. It was soothing to think of Daniel, it was like sucking your thumb. She thought about him waking up in the morning, rolling over, turning off the alarm clock, making love with his pregnant wife, whose face Rennie did not picture, carefully and with consideration but somewhat quickly because it was morning and he had other things to do. His wife didn't come but they're both used to that, they love each other anyway. She'll come later, some other day, when Daniel has more time. Taking a shower, drinking a cup of coffee, black, no sugar, which is handed to him by his wife through the bathroom door, looking in the mirror while he shaves and not seeing at all what she saw when she looked at him. Daniel getting dressed, in those mundane clothes of his, tying his shoelaces.

At three in the afternoon Rennie called Daniel, at the office, where she thought he would be. She left her number with the nurse: She said it was an emergency. She had never done such a thing before. She knew she was being wicked, but thinking about Daniel brought out in her whatever notions of wickedness were left over from her background. Daniel himself had such clean fingernails, such pink ears, he was so *good*.

Daniel called her back fifteen minutes later, and Rennie did her best to give the impression of someone on the verge of suicide. She never actually said it, she could not go so far, but she knew the only way she could entice Daniel over would be to give him a chance to rescue her. She was crying though, that was real enough.

She wanted Daniel to hold her hand, pat her on the back, comfort her, be with her. That was what he was good at. She had given up expecting anything else. She got dressed, made the bed, brushed her teeth and hair, being a good child at least to this extent. When Daniel came he would give her a gold star.

He knocked at the door, she opened it, he was there. What she saw was not someone she knew. Anger and fear, and something else, a need but not a desire. She'd pushed it too far.

Don't do that again, he said, and that was all for the time being. She thought he knew what was inside her. No such luck.

After a while Rennie was lying on her own bed, which was still more or less made, and Daniel was putting on his shoes. She could see the side of his head, the bent back. The fact was that he had needed something from her, which she could neither believe nor forgive. She'd been counting on him not to: She was supposed to be the needy one, but it was the other way around. He was ashamed of himself, which was the last thing she'd wanted. She felt like a vacation, Daniel's, one he thought he shouldn't have taken. She felt like a straw that had been clutched, she felt he'd been drowning. She felt raped.

This is what *terminal* means, she thought. Get used to it.

■

After they make love Rennie wraps a towel around herself and goes out to the kitchen. There's a lizard, sand-colored, with huge dark eyes, hunting the ants that file toward the cupboard where the golden syrup is kept. Rennie eats three pieces of bread and jam and drinks half a pint of long-life milk. Paul says some people here think that because it says Long Life on the carton, you'll have a long life if you drink it.

She goes back to the bedroom and steps over the clothes entwined on the floor. Paul is lying with his hands behind his head, legs flung out, looking up at the ceiling. Rennie climbs in under the mosquito net and curls beside him. She licks the hollow of his stomach, which is damp and salty, but he hardly twitches. Then she runs her hand over him, stroking. He blinks and smiles a little. The hair on his chest is gray, and Rennie finds it comforting, this sign of age: It's possible after all for people to grow older, change, weather. Without deteriorating; up to a point. It's the past, it's time that's stained him.

She wants to ask about his wife. It must be a wife, the house and the lawn and the shirtwaist dress wouldn't go with anything else. But she doesn't want to admit she's been going through the bureau drawers.

"Were you ever married?" she asks.

"Yes," says Paul. He doesn't volunteer anything else, so Rennie keeps on going. "What happened?"

Paul smiles. "She didn't like my lifestyle," he says. "She said there wasn't enough security. She didn't mean financial. After the Far East, I tried to go back and settle down, but when you've been living that way, day to day, never knowing when someone's going to blow you into little pieces, that other kind of life seems fake, you can't believe in it. I just couldn't get too excited about taking the car in for the winter tune-up or any of that. Not even my kids."

"So you're a danger freak," says Rennie. "Is that why you run dope?"

Paul smiles. "Maybe," he says. "Or maybe it's the money. It beats selling real estate. Second biggest dollar import commodity in the States; oil's the first. I don't take unnecessary risks though." He takes her hand, moves it down, closes his eyes. "That's why I'm still alive."

"What do you dream about?" says Rennie after a while. She wants to know, which is dangerous, it means she's interested.

Paul waits before answering. "Not a hell of a lot," says Paul finally. "I think I gave it up. I don't have time for it any more."

"Everyone dreams," says Rennie. "Why don't men ever want to say what they dream about?"

Paul turns his head and looks at her. He's still smiling, but he's tightened up. "That's why I couldn't hack the States," he says. "When I went back there, the women were talking like that. That's how they began all their sentences: *Why don't men. . . .*"

Rennie feels she's been both misinterpreted and accused. "Is there something wrong with saying that?" she says. "Maybe we want to know."

"There's nothing wrong with saying it," says Paul. "They can say it all they like. But there's no law that says I have to listen to it."

Rennie continues to stroke, but she's hurt. "Sorry I asked," she says.

Paul puts a hand on her. "It's not that I've got anything against women," he says. Rennie supplies: *In their place.* "It's just that when you've spent years watching people dying, women, kids, men, everyone, because they're starving or because someone kills them for complaining about it, you don't have time for a lot of healthy women sitting around arguing whether or not they should shave their legs."

Rennie's been outflanked, so she retreats. "That was years ago," she says. "They've moved on to other issues."

"That's what I mean," says Paul. "Issues. I used to believe in issues. When I first went out there I believed in all the issues I'd been taught to believe in. Democracy and freedom and the whole bag of tricks. Those gadgets don't work too well in a lot of places and nobody's too sure what does. There's no good guys and bad guys, nothing you can count on, none of it's permanent any more, there's a lot of improvisation. Issues are just an excuse."

"For what?" says Rennie. She leaves her hand on him but stops moving it.

"Getting rid of people you don't like," says Paul. "There's only people with power and people without power. Sometimes they change places, that's all."

"Which are you?" says Rennie.

"I eat well, so I must have power," says Paul, grinning. "But I'm an independent operator. Freelance, same as you."

"You don't take me very seriously, do you?" says Rennie sadly. She wants him to talk to her, about himself.

"Don't start that," says Paul. "You're on vacation." He rolls over on top of her. "When you go back home, I'll take you seriously."

Once upon a time Rennie was able to predict men; she'd been able to tell exactly what a given man would do at a given time. When she'd known that, when she was sure, all she had to do was wait and then he would do it. She used to think she knew what most men were like, she used to think she knew what most men wanted and how most men would respond. She used to think there was such a thing as most men, and now she doesn't. She's given up deciding what will happen next.

She puts her arms around him. She's trying again. She should know better.

■

From the refrigerator Paul takes two fish, one bright red, the other blue and green, with a beak like a parrot's. He cleans them with a large black-handled knife, kneeling by the tap in the garden. Rennie can smell the fish from where she lies in the hammock; it's not her favorite smell. It strikes her that she hasn't yet been to the beach here. She would like to lie on the sand and let the sun wash out her head so that nothing is left in it but white light, but she knows the consequences, a headache and skin like a simmered prune's. She's gone so far as to put on a pair of shorts though.

There's a vine over the porch, large cream-white flowers, cup-shaped and unreal. From the porch railing two blue-green lizards watch her. The road below is empty.

Paul leaves the fish on the porch and shinnies up a nearby tree, coming down with a papaya. Rennie can't help it, but all this activity reminds her of Boy Scouts. Next thing you know he'll be showing her how well he can tie knots.

There's a sunset, a quick one; it's getting dark. Rennie goes inside. Paul is cooking the fish, with onions and a little water, but he won't let her help.

They sit across from each other at the wooden table. Rennie gives him four out of five on the fish. He's even got candles; a huge green locust has just singed itself in one of them. Paul picks it up, still perking, and throws it out the door.

"So you thought I was with the CIA," he says, as he sits down again.

Rennie is not so much embarrassed as startled. She isn't ready for it, she drops her fork. "I suppose Lora told you that," she says.

Paul is having fun. "It's a strange coincidence," he says, "because we thought you were, too."

"What?" says Rennie. "You must be crazy!" This time it's not surprise, it's outrage.

"Look at it from our point of view," says Paul. "It's a good front, you have to admit. The travel piece, the camera. This just isn't the sort of place they do a lot of travel pieces about. Then the first person you connect with happens to be the man who has the best chance of defeating the government in the election. That's Minnow. Nobody watching would call that an accident."

"But I hardly know him," says Rennie.

"I'm just telling you what it looks like," says Paul. "Spot the CIA, it's a local game; everyone plays it. Castro used tourists a lot, and now all kinds of people are using them. The CIA is using non-Americans a lot; it's a better cover. Locals and foreigners. We know they're sending someone else in; they may be here already. There's always one or two here, and in my business you like to know who it is."

"So it wasn't the Abbotts after all," says Rennie. "I didn't think so, they were just too old and nice."

"As a matter of fact it was," says Paul. "But they've been recalled. Whoever comes in next will be taking a more active role. It could be anyone."

"But me," says Rennie. "Come on!"

"We had to check it out," says Paul.

"Who is we?" she says. "Lora, I suppose." Things are coming clear. They picked her up almost as soon as she was off the plane. First Paul in the hotel dining room; so much for eye contact. Then Lora, the next day on the reef boat. Between the two of them they'd hardly let her out of their sight. There must have been someone following her around and reporting back to them so they'd know where she was heading.

"Lora comes in handy," says Paul.

"Who went through my room?" says Rennie. It couldn't have been him, since he was having dinner with her at the Driftwood.

"Did someone go through your room?" asks Paul. Rennie can't tell if his surprise is real or not.

"Everything," she says. "Including the box. The one in your spare bedroom."

"I don't know who it was," says Paul. "I'd like to though."

"If you thought I was the CIA, why did you send me to pick up the box?" says Rennie.

"First of all," says Paul, "they don't care that much about the dope trade. They like to know what you're up to so they can maybe use it on you to get you to do something for them, but apart from that they don't care. It's the political stuff they care about. But the police hanging around the airport are something else. They'd seen Lora too many times, that was the sixth box we'd run through. We needed someone else and I didn't want it to be me. It's always better to use a woman, they're less likely to be suspected. If you weren't an agent, no harm done; unless you got caught, of course. If you were, you'd already know what was in the box but you'd pick it up anyway, you wouldn't want to lose contact by refusing. Either way, I'd have the gun."

"It was for you?" says Rennie.

"In my business you need them," Paul says. "People shoot at you and you have to be able to shoot back. I had some coming up from Colombia, you can often pick them up down there, serial numbers filed off, but they're U.S. Army equipment, military aid, you get them from crooked generals who want to make a little money on the side. But I lost that boat and I lost the connection at the same time. Elva's the contingency plan. She really does have a daughter in New York, so it was easy enough to fly her there with the money. Those people like cash. She didn't know what it was for though. She didn't know what was in the boxes."

"Lost?" says Rennie.

"The boat got sunk, the general got shot," says Paul. "I've just replaced both of them but it took me a while."

"Who's shooting at you?" says Rennie, who is trying very hard not to find any of this romantic. Boys playing with guns, that's all it is. Even telling her about this is showing off; isn't it? But she can't

216

help wondering whether Paul has any bullet holes in him. If he has, she'd like to see.

"Who isn't?" says Paul. "I'm an independent. They don't like people like me, they want a monopoly."

Rennie picks up her fork again. She lifts her fish, separating the bones.

"So that's what all this was about," she says.

"All what?" says Paul.

"All this fucking," says Rennie, pronouncing the g despite herself. "You were checking me out."

"Don't be stupid," says Paul. "It was mostly Marsdon's idea anyway, he's paranoid about the CIA, it's like a monomania with him. He wanted us to get you out of here as fast as possible. I never believed it myself."

This isn't the answer Rennie wants. She wants to be told she's important to him. "Why not?" she says.

"You were too obvious," Paul says. "You were doing everything right out in the open. You were too nice. You were too naïve. You were too easy. Anyway, you wanted it too much. I can tell when a woman's faking it."

Rennie puts her fork down carefully on her plate. Something is being used against her, her own desire, she doesn't know why. "I'll do the dishes," she says.

∎

Rennie fills the sink with hot water from the teakettle. Paul is in the second bedroom, with the door closed. He says he's trying to find out who's winning the election. Local politics, he's told her. Nothing to do with her. She can hear blurred voices, the crackle of static.

She's scraping the fishbones off the plates when she hears footsteps on the porch. There are a lot more footsteps than she's prepared to deal with. Wiping her hands on the dishtowel, she goes to the second bedroom and knocks at the door. "Paul," she says. Feeling like a wife. Incapable.

Rennie's in the bedroom, which is where she wants to be and where Paul wants her to be. Out there, in the living room, there's a loud meeting going on. The results of the election are in, Ellis has seven seats, Minnow has six, and Prince has two, and Rennie can add. So can everyone in the living room, but so far six and two still only make six and two.

It's nothing to do with her though. Paul said that and she believes it. She's reading the books he got for her somewhere, God knows where since they're museum pieces, Dell Mysteries from the forties, with the eye-and-keyhole logo on the cover, the map of the crime scene on the back, and the cast of characters on the first page. The pages are yellowed and watermarked and smell of mold. Rennie reads the casts of characters and tries to guess who gets murdered. Then she reads up to the murder and tries to guess who did it, and then she turns to the back of the book to see if she's right. She doesn't have much patience for the intricacies of clues and deductions.

"You goin' to let that bastard win?" It's Marsdon, almost a shriek. "You let him fool you? So many years he betray the people, you goin' to betray the people too?"

Dr. Minnow is making a speech; his voice rises and falls, rises and falls. He, after all, has more experience as well as more seats, he will be the leader of the opposition, if nothing else. Why should he back down in favor of Prince? He cannot let the Justice Party swing in the direction of Castro.

"Castro!" Marsdon yells. "All you tell me is Castro! Prince no Castro!"

Why here? Rennie asked. I'm the connection, Paul told her. Rennie wishes they would turn down the volume. She's not doing too well with the murderers, but she's eighty percent on the victims: two blondes with pale translucent skin, mouths like red gashes and swelling breasts bursting through their dresses, two tempestuous redheads with eyes of green smoldering fire and skin like clotted cream, each carefully arranged on floor or bed like a still life, not quite naked, clothing disheveled to suggest rape, though there was no rape in the forties, finger-marks livid around the throat—they loved *livid*—or a wound still oozing, preferably in the left breast. Dead but not molested. The private eyes finding them (two hot-tempered Irishmen, one Greek, two plain Americans) describe each detail of the body fully, lushly, as if running their tongues over it; all that flesh, totally helpless because totally dead. Each of them expresses outrage at the crime, even though the victim provoked it. Rennie finds it curiously innocent, this hypocritical outrage. It's sweetly outmoded, like hand-kissing.

■

After a while Rennie hears the sound of chairs being scraped back, and then it's quiet. Then Paul comes into the room and starts taking off his clothes, as if nothing at all has happened. He peels the T-shirt off first, drops it to the floor. Already it seems to her a familiar gesture. Rennie counts: She's known him five days.

"What happened?" she says. "What were they doing?"

"Dealing," says Paul. "Minnow won. As of fifteen minutes ago, he's the new prime minister. They've all gone off to have a party."

"Marsdon backed down?"

"No," says Paul. "He didn't exactly back down. He said he was doing it for the good of the people. There was some disagreement about who *the people* were, but you have to expect that."

"Did Prince just sort of abdicate?" says Rennie.

"Prince didn't do anything," Paul says. "Marsdon did it for him. Marsdon's going to be Minister of Tourism, and they sawed off at Justice Minister for Prince. That's why Marsdon didn't struggle too hard. He wants to see the look on the face of the current Justice Minister. They hate each other like shit."

He disappears into the bathroom and Rennie can hear him brushing his teeth. "You don't seem too happy," she calls.

Paul comes out again. He walks flat-footed, heavily toward the bed. He's older than she thought. "Why should I be?" he says.

"Dr. Minnow's a good man," says Rennie. This is true, he is a good man, and it's not his fault that goodness of his kind makes her twitchy. It's like being with someone on a diet, which always makes her lust for chocolate mousse and real whipped cream.

"Good men can be a pain in the ass," says Paul. "They're hard to deal with. He's a politician so he's a user, they have to be, but he's less of a user than most. He believes in democracy and fair play and all those ideas the British left here along with cricket, he really does believe that shit. He thinks guns are playing dirty."

"What do you think?" says Rennie. She's back to interviewing him.

Paul's sitting on the edge of the bed, as if reluctant to get into it. "It doesn't matter what I think," he says. "I'm neutral. What matters right now is what the other side thinks. What Ellis thinks."

"What does Ellis think?" says Rennie.

"That remains to be seen," says Paul. "He's not going to like it."

"What about Prince?" says Rennie.

"Prince is a believer," says Paul. "He supplies the belief. He thinks that's all you need."

Now at last he does get into the bed, crawling under the mosquito net, tucking it in before turning to her. He's tired, no doubt of that, and Rennie suddenly finds this very suburban. All he needs are some striped pajamas and a heart attack and the picture will be complete. He's not the one who's giving that impression though. It's her own solicitude, faked. She knows something he doesn't know, she knows she's leaving. She'll be on the afternoon boat tomorrow, and everything in between is just filler. Maybe she'll tell him she has a headache. She could use some sleep.

Still, doubt is what you should give other people the benefit of, or that's the theory. She owes him something: He was the one who gave her back her body; wasn't he? Although he doesn't know it. Rennie puts her hands on him. It can be, after all, a sort of comfort. A kindness.

"What do you dream about?" Rennie says. It's her last wish, it's all she really wants to know.

"I told you," Paul says.

"But you lied," says Rennie.

For a while Paul doesn't say anything. "I dream about a hole in the ground," he says finally.

"What else?" says Rennie.

"That's all," says Paul. "It's just a hole in the ground, with the earth that's been dug out. It's quite large, there are trees around it. I'm walking toward it. There's a pile of shoes off to the side."

"Then what?" says Rennie.

"Then I wake up," says Paul.

■

Rennie hears it before she realizes what it is. At first she thinks it's rain. It is rain, but something more. Paul is out of the bed before she is. Rennie goes into the bathroom for a large towel, which she wraps around her. The pounding at the door goes on, and the voice.

When she gets to the living room what she sees is Paul, stark naked, and Lora with her arms around him. She's dripping wet.

Rennie stands with her mouth open, holding her towel around her, while Paul grapples with Lora, pushing her away from him, holding her at arms' length, shaking her. She's crying. "Oh God, oh Christ," she says.

"What is it?" says Rennie. "Is she sick?"

"Minnow's been shot," Paul says, over the top of Lora's head.

Rennie goes cold. "That's incredible!" she says. She feels as if someone's just told her the Martians have landed. It must be a put-on, an elaborate joke.

"They shot him from behind," says Lora. "In the back of the head. Right out on the road and everything."

"Who would do it?" Rennie says. She thinks of the men, the followers, the ones with mirror sunglasses. She tries to focus on something useful she could do. Maybe she should make some tea, for Lora.

"Get your clothes on," Paul says to her.

Lora starts to cry again. "It's so crummy," she says. "The fuckers. I never thought they'd go that far."

■

Dr. Minnow is in a closed coffin in the living room. The coffin is dark wood, plain; it rests on two kitchen chairs, one at either end. On top of the coffin there's a pair of scissors, open, and Rennie wonders whether they are part of some ritual, some ceremony she doesn't know about, or whether someone's just forgotten them.

The coffin is like a stage prop, an emblem out of some horrible little morality play; only they've forgotten to say what the moral is. At any moment the lid will pop up and Dr. Minnow will be sitting there, smiling and nodding, as if he's pulled off a beautiful joke. Only this does not happen.

Rennie is in the living room with the women, who sit on chairs or on the floor, children sleeping in their laps, or stand against the wall. It's one o'clock at night. There are other women in the kitchen, making coffee and setting out plates for the food that the women have brought: Rennie can see them through the open doorway. It's a lot like Griswold, it's a lot like her grandmother's funeral, except in Griswold you ate after the burial, not before, and you did the hymn singing in church. Here they do it whenever they feel like it: one starts, the others join in, three-part harmony. Someone's playing the mouth organ.

Dr. Minnow's wife has the place of honor beside the coffin; she cries and cries, she makes no attempt to hide it, nobody disapproves. This, too, is different from Griswold: Sniffling was all right, into a handkerchief, but not this open crying, raw desolation, this nakedness of the face. It wasn't decent. If you went on like that they gave you a pill and told you to go upstairs and lie down.

"Why this happen?" the wife says, over and over again. "Why this happen?"

Elva is sitting beside her, holding her hand, which she rubs gently between her own two hands, massaging the fingers. "I see him into this world," she says. "Now I see him out of it."

Two women come out of the kitchen, carrying a tray with mugs of coffee. Rennie takes one, and some banana bread and a coconut cookie. It's her second mug of coffee. She's sitting on the floor, her legs are going to sleep beneath her.

She feels guilty and useless, guilty because useless. She thinks of all the history that's lying there in the coffin, wasted, a hole blown through it. It seems to her a very tacky way to die. Now she knows why he wanted her to write about this place: so there would be less chance of this happening, to him.

"Should we be doing anything?" she whispers to Lora, who's sitting beside her.

"Who knows?" says Lora. "I never went to one of these before."

"How long does it go on?" says Rennie.

"All night," says Lora.

"Why this happen?" says the wife again.

"It was his time," says one of the women.

"No," says Elva. "A Judas here."

The women stir uneasily. Someone begins to sing:

> Blessed assurance, Jesus is mine,
> Oh what a foretaste of Glory divine,
> Perfect salvation, sent from above,
> Washed in his goodness, lost in his love.

Rennie is uneasy. It's hot in the room and too crowded, it smells of cinnamon and coffee and sweat, a sweet, stuffy, unhealthy smell, clogged with emotion, and it's getting so much like Griswold she can't bear it. *What did she die of? Cancer, praise the Lord.* That was the kind of thing they said. She stands up, as unobtrusively as she can, and edges toward the porch, out the door that stands mercifully open.

The men are outside, on the concrete porch that runs around three sides of the house. The drink here is not coffee; in the dim porch light the bottles gleam, passing from hand to hand. There are more men, down below in the garden, there's a crowd, gathering, some of them have torches, there are voices, tense, rising.

Paul is out there, a conspicuous white face, standing to one side. He spots Rennie and pulls her back against the wall beside him. "You should be in with the women," he says.

Rennie chooses to take this not as a put-down but as a social hint. "I couldn't breathe," she says. "What's going on down there?"

"Nothing yet," says Paul. "They're mad as hell though. Minnow was from Ste. Agathe. A lot of people here are related to him."

Someone's carrying a chair over to the porch railing. A man climbs up on it and looks down at the upturned faces. It's Marsdon. The voices quiet.

"Who kill this man?" he says.

"Ellis," someone calls, and the crowd chants, "Ellis, Ellis."

"Judas," says Marsdon, almost a shout.

"Judas. Judas."

Marsdon raises his hands and the chanting stops.

"How many more times?" he says. "How much more, how many more dead? Minnow a good man. We are going to wait till he kill all of us, every one? We been asking, many times, we get nothing. Now we gonna take."

There's shouting, an enraged cheer, then one clear voice: "*Tear down Babylon!*" In the dark below, bodies begin to move. Marsdon bends, stands up again; in his hands is a compact little machine gun.

"Shit," says Paul. "I told them not to do that."

"Do what?" says Rennie. "What are they going to do?" She can feel her heart going, she doesn't understand. *Massive involvement.*

"They don't have enough guns," says Paul. "It's as simple as that. I don't know where Prince is, he'll have to stop them."

"What if he can't?" says Rennie.

"Then he'll have to lead them," says Paul. He pushes off from the wall. "Go back to the house," he says.

"I don't know the way," says Rennie. They came in a Jeep.

"Lora does," says Paul.

"What about you?" says Rennie.

"Don't worry," says Paul. "I'll be fine."

■

They go by the back streets, Lora first, then Rennie. The only place to be, in Lora's opinion, is out of the way. It's muddy here from the rain but they don't bother to pick their way around the water-filled potholes, there's no time and it's hard to see. The only light comes from the small concrete-block houses set at intervals back from the road. The road is deserted, the action is a couple of streets farther down toward the sea. They hear shouting, the smash of glass.

"Bank windows," says Lora. "I bet you anything."

They cross a side street. For a moment there's a glimpse of torches. "Don't let them see you is my motto," says Lora. "In the dark anyone's fair game. They can apologize afterward but who cares, eh? There's going to be a few old scores settled, no matter what else they do."

Now they can hear gunfire, irregular and staccato, and after a minute the feeble lights in the houses flicker and go out, the underlying hum in the air shudders and cuts. "There goes the power plant," says Lora. "They'll take over that and the police station, there's only two policemen on Ste. Agathe anyway so it shouldn't be that hard. There isn't a hell of a lot else to take over around here. Maybe they'll smash up the Lime Tree and get drunk on the free booze."

"I can't see," says Rennie. Her sandals are muddy, the bottom of her skirt is dripping; she's more disgusted than frightened. Window-breaking, juvenile delinquency, that's all it is, this tiny riot.

"Come on," says Lora. She gropes for Rennie's arm, pulls her

224

along. "They'll be up here in a minute, they'll be after Ellis's people. We'll take the path."

Rennie stumbles after her. She's disoriented, she has no idea where they are, even the stars are different here. It's slow going without a moon. Branches heavy with damp flowers brush against her, the smells are still alien. She pushes through the leaves, slipping on the wet earth of the path. Below them is the road. Through the undergrowth she can see moving lights now, flashlights, torches, and hurrying figures. It's almost like a festival.

When they finally reach the house it's completely dark.

"Damn," says Rennie. "We locked it when we went out and Paul's got the key. We'll have to break in."

But Lora's already at the door, pushing. "It's open," she says.

As soon as they're inside the door there's a sharp glare, sudden, against their eyes. Rennie almost screams.

"It's only you," says Paul. He lowers the flashlight.

"How in shit did you get back here ahead of us?" says Lora.

"Took the Jeep," says Paul. To Rennie he says, "Get your things."

"Where's Prince?" says Lora.

"Down there being a hero," says Paul. "They've got the two policemen tied up with clothesline, and they're declaring an independent state. Marsdon's writing a proclamation and they want to send it out over my radio. They're asking Grenada to recognize them. There's even some talk of invading St. Antoine."

"You've got to be kidding," says Lora. "How the shit would they do that?"

"In the fishing boats," says Paul, "plus whatever other boats they can grab. They've got a bunch of Swedish tourists in the police station, and those two German women, who are making one hell of a fuss. They've requisitioned them. Hostages."

"Can't you stop them?" says Lora.

"You think I haven't tried?" says Paul. "They won't listen to me any more. They think they've won. It's way out of control. Go into the bedroom," he says to Rennie, "and get your stuff. There's a candle in there. I'm taking you over to St. Antoine, you can get the morning plane out. If you were smart," he says to Lora, "you'd go with her. You've still got your passport." Rennie lets herself be ordered. This is his scene after all, his business; he's the one who's supposed to know what to do next. She hopes he does.

She feels her way along the hall into the bedroom. There isn't much to pack. It might as well be a hotel room; it has the same emptiness, the same melancholy aura of a space that has been used but not lived in. The bed is tangled, abandoned. She can't remember having slept in it.

■

The Jeep is parked on the road in front of the house. They go down the stone steps, hurrying, their feet in the strong beam of the flashlight.

Paul has one of the small machine guns; he carries it casually, like a lunch pail. To Rennie it looks like a toy, the kind you aren't supposed to give little boys for Christmas. She doesn't believe it could go off, and surely if it did nothing would come out of it but rubber bullets. She's afraid, but even her fear seems inappropriate. Surely they are not in any real danger. She tries hard for annoyance: Perhaps she should feel interrupted.

Just before they climb into the Jeep Paul heaves something overarm into the darkness of the rock garden.

"What was that?" says Lora.

"I killed the radio," says Paul. "I called my boats first. They're staying away. I don't want anyone calling St. Antoine, I don't want any welcoming committees in the harbor when we get there."

"Who'd do that?" says Lora.

"I've got a few ideas," says Paul.

The motor catches and the headlights go on and they drive down the road, which is empty. Paul doesn't go all the way into the town. Instead he parks beside a stone wall.

"Go down to the shore and wait beside the pier," he says. "I'll pick you up there in about fifteen minutes. I'll get us a boat."

"Your boats are all out," says Lora.

"I didn't say mine," says Paul. "I'll jump the motor."

He's younger, alive in a way he hasn't been before. He loves it, thinks Rennie. That's why we get into these messes: because they love it.

He helps them over the stone wall and passes Rennie's bags

down to her. She feels stupid lugging her camera: What is there to take pictures of now?

"Don't talk," says Lora. Rennie sees where they are: They're in the garden at the back of the Lime Tree. They find the path and feel their way down it. The hotel is dark and silent; behind a few of the windows candles flicker. The bar is deserted, the patio littered with broken glass. Along the beach, toward the town, they can hear singing. It's men, it's not a hymn.

The tide's going out, there are several yards of wet beach. The waves are strangely luminous. Rennie wants to look at this, she's heard about it, phosphorescence.

"Crawl under the dock," Lora whispers.

"For heaven's sake," says Rennie, who doesn't like the idea of crabs and snails.

"Do it," Lora says; it's almost a hiss. This, apparently, is serious.

The dock is built on a foundation of split rocks that have not yet been smoothed by the sea; the space between the rocks and the wooden slats of the dock is only two feet high. They crouch together, doubled over. Rennie's still clutching her bags and her purse. She doesn't know who they're supposed to be hiding from.

The moon comes up, it's almost full; the gray-white light comes through the slats of the dock, throwing bars of shadow. Rennie thinks how nice it would be to have a warm bath and something to eat. She thinks about having lunch with someone, Jocasta maybe, and telling this story. But it's not even that good a story, it's about on the level of being stopped at customs, since nothing more than inconvenience has happened to her.

At last they can hear a motor, turning over, starting up, moving toward them.

"That's him," says Lora, and they back out from under the dock.

Marsdon is sitting in one of the wooden chairs up on the patio, one leg bent, the ankle resting on his knee to show off his boots. He's got his machine gun pointed right at them. Two men stand silently behind him.

"Where you think you goin'?" he says.

The St. Antoine police motor launch is tied at the end of the Lime Tree pier, where it bobs gently up and down in the swell.

Paul sits at the round wooden table facing Marsdon. He's soaking wet, from swimming out to the launch. Between them there's a bottle of rum. Each of them has a glass, each of them has a machine gun; the machine guns are on the ground under the table, but within reach. The two other men are over at the bar. There's a woman with them, very drunk, she's lying on the patio near them, in the broken glass, humming to herself, her skirt up over her thighs, opening and closing her legs. Rennie and Lora sit in the other two chairs.

Paul and Marsdon are arguing about them. Paul wants to take Rennie to St. Antoine, Marsdon doesn't want him to. Marsdon doesn't want anyone leaving the island. Also, Marsdon wants more guns. Paul promised him more, says Marsdon, they've been paid for; now he should deliver. He's the connection.

"I told you about the problem," Paul said. "You should have waited. Next week I have some coming."

"How can we wait?" Marsdon says impatiently. "When they hear on St. Antoine that Minnow is shot, they goin' to blame us anyway." Slyly, he offers to trade Paul's own machine gun for a safe exit. Slyly, Paul refuses.

Rennie can see what she is now: She's an object of negotiation. The truth about knights comes suddenly clear: The maidens were only an excuse. The dragon was the real business. So much for vacation romances, she thinks. A kiss is just a kiss, Jocasta would say, and you're lucky if you don't get trench mouth.

She listens, trying to follow. She feels like a hostage, and, like a hostage, strangely uninvolved in her own fate. Other people are deciding that for her. Would it be so bad if she stayed here? She could hole up in the Lime Tree, call herself a foreign correspondent, send out dispatches, whatever those are. But maybe Paul just wants to leave, get out; maybe she's just the occasion.

"You think I'm more important than I am," she says to Marsdon.

"Don't bug him," Lora says in a low voice. Marsdon looks at Rennie, seeing her this time. His movements are slow enough, outwardly calm, but he's excited, his eyes gleam in the moonlight. Fragmentation, dismemberment, this is what he sees when he looks at her. Then he's ignoring her once more.

"You bring the guns, you can take her," he says.

"No deal," says Paul.

There are more men now, coming along the beach from the town; several carry torches. One of them comes over to the table and puts his hand on Marsdon's shoulder.

"I am ready to make the broadcast now," he says, and Rennie realizes that this must be Prince. She's never seen him before. His face is in shadow, but the voice is young, younger than she thought, he sounds about nineteen.

"I wouldn't do that yet," says Paul, "if I were you."

Prince's head turns toward him in the shadows. "Why?" he says.

"Have you any idea of what's going to happen next?" Paul says.

"We have won the revolution," says Prince, with the placid confidence of a child reciting a lesson. "Grenada has recognized us. They are sending men and guns, in the morning."

"Where did you hear that?" says Paul.

The outline of Prince's head turns toward Marsdon.

"The radio," Marsdon says.

"Did you hear it yourself?" Paul says to Prince.

Marsdon pushes his chair back. "You calling me a liar," he says. There are more men now, a circle; tension draws them in.

"Take a boat to Grenada," Paul says to Prince. "Anything you can get. Right now, before morning. If you're lucky they'll let you stay there."

"You an enemy of the revolution," says Marsdon.

"Bullshit," says Paul. "You just want an excuse to blow my head off the way you blew off Minnow's."

"What you tellin' me?" says Prince.

"Put it together," says Paul. "He's the new agent. You've been set up, right from the beginning."

There's a pause. Rennie closes her eyes. Something with enormous weight comes down on them, she can hardly breathe. She hears the night sounds, the musical waterdrip, the waves, going on as usual. Then everything starts to move.

Oh God, thinks Rennie. Somebody change the channel.

■

Rennie walks along the pier at St. Antoine. She's safe. It's almost dawn. The power plant here isn't on the fritz and there's a string of feeble bulbs to see by. She feels dizzy and nauseated, an hour and a half in the launch, not rolling with the waves but smashing into them, a collision, a sickening lurch downward, then up like a roller coaster, thud, crunch of her bones, backbone against backbone, stomach lurching inside her with its own motion. She'd hung on, trying to think of something serene, keeping her head up, eyes on the moon, on the next wave, the water glowed when it moved, phosphorescent, sweating all over her body despite the wind, wondering when she was going to throw up, trying not to. After all she was being rescued.

Can't you slow down? she called to Paul.

It's worse that way, he called back, grinning at her. Even now he found her funny.

At the dock he idled the motor and practically threw her onto the shore, her and her luggage, before backing the boat out and turning toward the sea. No good-bye kiss and just as well, she didn't want anything against her mouth just now. They touched hands for a moment, that was all. What bothers her is that she forgot to thank him.

He's not going back to Ste. Agathe, he's heading south. He'll meet one of his boats, he says. There are other harbors.

What about Lora? said Rennie.

She had the chance, said Paul. She wanted to stay with Prince. I can't fight off the entire St. Antoine police force just for Lora. She can take care of herself.

Rennie doesn't understand anything. All she knows is that she's here and there's a plane at six and she wants to be on it, and she can't keep walking. She sits down on the pier with her head between her knees, hoping that the rolling under her feet will stop.

She can hear the sound of the motor launch, receding, no more significant than the drone of a summer insect. Then there's another sound, too loud, like a television set with a cop show on it heard through a hotel room wall. Rennie puts her hands over her ears. In a minute, when she's feeling better, she'll go to the Sunset Inn and pick up her passport and see if she can get a cup of coffee, though there's not much chance of that. Then she'll take a taxi to the airport and then she'll be gone.

She sits there until she's ready, ready enough; then she starts walking again. There are a few people about, men; only one of them tries to stop her, a simple request for fornication, and he's pleasant enough when she says no. There's no war on here, possibly they haven't heard anything about it yet, everything seems normal. Then there are more men, running past her toward the end of the pier.

It's light; close by there are roosters. After what seems a very long time she reaches the Sunset Inn and goes in through the archway. She climbs the stairs; now she will have to sign her name for all the time she hasn't spent here, all the meals she hasn't eaten. She won't even argue, she'll put it on her charge card. Enjoy now, pay later.

The Englishwoman is up and dressed, in an avocado-green shirtwaist, behind the counter as usual. Possibly she never sleeps.

"I'd like to check out," says Rennie, "and I'd like my passport, please, it's in the safe. And I'd like to call a taxi."

The Englishwoman looks at her with the gloating, almost possessive stare of one who enjoys giving unwelcome news. "Are you thinking of taking that morning plane?" she says.

Rennie says yes.

"It's been canceled," says the Englishwoman. "All the planes have been canceled. The airport's been shut down."

"Really?" says Rennie, cold within.

"We're in a state of emergency," says the Englishwoman proudly. "There's been an uprising on Ste. Agathe. But you must know all about that. Didn't you just come from there?"

Rennie lies on her bed. At least it's a bed. She's fallen on it without even taking off her clothes but she's too exhausted to sleep. Now she will have to stay here, at the Sunset Inn, home of beige gravy, until they start the planes again. She feels marooned.

Then it's full of daylight and the door, which was shut and locked, is open. Two policemen are standing in the doorway. Grins, drawn guns. Behind them is the Englishwoman, her arms folded across her chest. Rennie sits up. "What?" she says.

"We arrestin' you," says one of the policemen, the pinkish one.

"What for?" says Rennie. She feels she ought to act like an outraged tourist.

231

"Suspicion," says the other policeman.

"Suspicion of what?" says Rennie, who is still half asleep. "I haven't done anything." It can't be the box with the gun, they haven't mentioned it. "I'm writing a travel piece. You can phone the magazine and check," she adds. "In Toronto, when they're open. It's called *Visor*." This sounds improbable even to her. Does Toronto exist? They won't be the first to wonder. She thinks of her blank notebook, no validation there.

The two policemen come forward. The Englishwoman looks at her, a look Rennie remembers from somewhere, from a long time ago, from a bad dream. It's a look of pure enjoyment. *Malignant*.

■

·VI·

"I THOUGHT IT WAS DUMB," says Lora. "I always thought it was dumb. Anyone who'd die for their country is a double turkey as far as I'm concerned. I mean any country, but this one, well, that would make you a triple one. Shit, it's only three miles long. I thought they were all nuts, but what can you tell them, eh?

"You may think Ellis is an old drunk, I told Prince, you may think he's harmless because nobody's seen him for twenty years, but if you think he's just going to let you take over without a squeak, you're out of your mind. But then Marsdon would start talking about sacrifice for the good of all, and that stuff would get to Prince every time. He's a sweet guy, he's soft-hearted, it appealed to him, and though I wouldn't want to be part of a country Marsdon was the leader of, he's no dummy, he knew he was making me look like a selfish white bitch who didn't care and only wanted Prince to screw around with.

"Maybe I should of left, but the truth is I thought they were just having a good time, sneaking around at night, having secrets, sort of like the Shriners, you know? I never thought they'd do anything.

"Change the system, Marsdon used to say. Why would I want to do that? I said. It's working just fine for me. Stuff politics, I'd tell him. As far as I'm concerned the world would be a lot better off if you took the politicians, any kind at all, and put them in the loony bin where they belong. You can tell that junk to Prince if you want to but don't tell it to me, because I know what you really want. You want to shoot people and feel really good about it and have everyone tell you you're doing the right thing. You'd get a kick out of that. You make me sick.

"I always knew Marsdon would shove a knife in me as soon as look at me if he got the chance, or in anyone else for that matter, he's a mean bugger, but I guess if you want to start a war you have to have someone who doesn't give that much of a piss about killing people, you can't make an omelette without breaking eggs.

"There just weren't enough of them and they weren't ready.

They wouldn't of been ready in a month of Sundays. Paul used to tell Marsdon he just wanted to be Castro without putting in the time, and it would get to him because that was about the size of it. They wouldn't of even had any guns if Paul hadn't brought some in for them. That was Marsdon's idea too, the guns. Paul didn't know he was an agent. I don't think he knew, not until Minnow got shot.

"If you're thinking of hiding out in the hills, forget it, Paul said. Two helicopters and that's it, this is a dry island, you know there's no cover up there, it's just scrub. But they seemed to think it was enough for them to be right. Getting rid of Ellis, that was the point. Nobody's denying it would've been nice, but there's real life, you know? I mean, I used to think I'd like to fly like a bird but I never jumped off any roofs. I once heard of a man who blew himself up in the toilet because he was sitting on the can and he lit a cigarette and he threw the match in, except his wife had just dumped some paint remover into it. I mean, that's what it was like. Though once in a while I thought, well, they might just do it. You know why? They're crazy enough. Sometimes crazy people can do things other people can't. Maybe because they believe it."

Rennie wonders where her passport is. She feels naked without it, she can't prove she is who she says she is. But she believes that other people believe in order, and in the morning, once they find out she's in here, once they realize who she is, they'll let her out.

Lora slaps at herself. "Fucking bugs," she says. "They like some people and not others. You think you'd get used to them, but you never do. Anyway, we've got a roof over our head. There's lots worse things."

Rennie decides not to think about what these may be.

■

"There was a little shooting at the police station," says Lora, "but not that much, and the power plant was empty. The police did a sweep of the island, it's not that hard because it's not that big, and they picked up anyone they found hiding or running or even walking on the road. They had the names of the main ones and they wanted everyone related to them too but that would've been

236

everyone on the island, everyone's related to everyone else around here.

"They tied the men up with ropes, those yellow nylon ropes they used a lot around here for boats and stuff, they tied them together in bundles of three or four and threw them on top of each other in the ship, down in the hold, like they were cargo. The women they just tied their hands together, behind their backs, two together, they let them stand up. When we got over to St. Antoine there was a big crowd at the dock already, the radio had been full of it all morning, communists and all that, they hauled the bundles of men off the boat and the people in the street were screaming *Hang them! Kill them!* It was like wrestling.

"The police took us to the main station, down in the cellar where there's a cement floor, and they tied the men together in a long line, there must've been fifty or sixty people, and they beat them up, sticks and boots, the works. The women they beat up some too but not as much. I wasn't there for that part of it, they had me in another room, they were asking me questions about Prince. They've got him in here somewhere.

"Then they threw buckets of cold water over them and locked them up, they were wet and cold, nowhere to piss, nothing to eat, and then they brought them here. They didn't lay any charges because they hadn't figured out what charges to lay. The Justice Minister went on the radio and said there hadn't been any violence, the people got the cuts and bruises from falling down when they were running away. And then they declared a state of emergency, which made everything legal. They can take anything of yours they want to, your car, anything, and there's a curfew too. Nobody knows for how long.

"They said Minnow was shot by the rebels, they said Prince killed him. People believe what they hear on the news and who's going to tell them any different? They'll believe Ellis because it's easier to believe Ellis.

"It's perfect for Ellis: Now he's got an excuse to do it to everybody he doesn't like, plus nobody's going to say anything against him, for years. And think of all the foreign aid he'll get now. The hurricane was all right but this is a lot better.

"We're lucky. The others are all seven or eight to a cell. Some of these people have no idea why they're here, all of a sudden these police with guns just bashed into their houses and grabbed them. They didn't know what was happening, they don't have a clue, they were just in the way."

∎

The room they're in is about five feet by seven feet, with a high ceiling. The walls are damp and cool, the stone slick to the touch as if something's growing on it, some form of mildew. The back of Rennie's shirt is damp, from the wall. This is the first time she's been cold since coming down here.

The floor is stone too and wet, except for the corner they've been sitting in. There's a barred metal door fitted into the end wall and opening onto the corridor, which is lighted; the light shines in on them through the bars. Someone has written on the walls: *Down with Babylon. Love to All.* In the wall opposite the door, higher up, there's a small window with a grating. Through this window they can see the moon. There's nothing in the room with them except a bucket, red plastic, new, empty. Its use is obvious but neither of them has used it yet.

"How long do you think they'll keep us in here?" says Rennie.

Lora laughs. "You in any hurry?" she says. "If you are, don't tell them. Anyway it's not how long you're in, it's what they do to you." She inhales, then blows the smoke out. "Well, this is it," she says. "Tropical paradise."

Rennie wonders why they've left Lora her cigarettes and especially the matches. Not that there's anything here that could burn down, it's all stone.

Rennie wishes they had a deck of cards or a book, any book at all. It's almost bright enough to read. She can smell the smoke from Lora's cigarette and beneath that a faint aftersmell, stale perfume, underarm deodorant wearing off; it's from both of them. She's starting to get a headache. She'd give anything for a Holiday Inn. She longs for late-night television, she's had enough reality for the time being. Popcorn is what she needs.

"You got the time?" says Lora.

"They took my watch," says Rennie. "It's probably about eleven."

"That all?" says Lora.

"We should get some sleep, I guess," Rennie says. "I wish they'd turn out the lights."

"Okay," says Lora. "You sleepy?"

"No," says Rennie.

■

They're scraping the bottom of the barrel. Rennie thinks of it as the bottom of the barrel, Lora thinks of it as the story of her life. This is even what she calls it. "The story of my life," she says, morosely, proudly, "you could put it in a book." But it's one way not to panic. If they can only keep talking, thinks Rennie, they will be all right.

Lora takes out her cigarettes, lights one, blows the smoke out through her nose. "You want a cigarette? I've got two left. Oh, I forgot, you don't smoke." She pauses, waiting for Rennie to contribute something. So far most of the contributing has been done by Lora. Rennie is having a hard time thinking up anything about her life that Lora might find interesting. Right now, her life seems like a book Jocasta once lent her, very *nouveau wavé*, it was called *Death by Washing Machine* although there were no washing machines in the book. The main character fell off a cliff on page sixty-three and the rest of the pages were blank.

Rennie tells Lora about the man with the rope. She's certain that Lora will be able to produce something much heavier, a multiple ax murder at the least.

"Sick," Lora says. "They shouldn't even put those guys away, they should just hang a few cement blocks around their legs and drop them in the harbor, you know? Let them out in twenty years and they just do it again. I once knew this guy who wanted to tie me to the bedpost. No way, I said. You want to tie somebody up, I've got a few suggestions, but you're not starting with me. Try a sheep and a pair of rubber boots and work your way up. He come back?"

"No," says Rennie.

"I'd rather be plain old raped," says Lora, "as long as there's nothing violent."

Rennie feels there's been a communications breakdown. Then she realizes that Lora is talking about something that has actually happened to her. Without any warning at all.

"God," she says, "what did you do?"

"Do?" says Lora. "He had a knife. I was just lucky he didn't mess anything up, including me. I could of kicked myself for not having a better lock on the window."

Rennie sees that Lora is pleased to have shocked her. She's enjoying the reaction; it's as if she's displaying something, an attribute somewhere between a skill and a deformity, like double-jointedness; or a mark of courage, a war wound or a dueling scar. The pride of the survivor.

Rennie knows what she's supposed to feel: first horror, then sympathy. But she can't manage it. Instead she's dejected by her own failure to entertain. Lora has better stories.

∎

Rennie watches Lora's mouth open and close, studies the nicotine stains on her once perfect teeth, it's a movie with the sound gone. She's thinking that she doesn't really like Lora very much; she never has liked her very much; in fact she dislikes her. They have nothing in common except that they're in here. There's nobody here to look at but Lora, nobody to listen to but Lora. Rennie is going to like her a whole lot less by the time they get out.

"But, Jesus, will you listen to me," says Lora. "Here we are, just sitting around on our asses talking about men, fucking men, pardon my French, like at high school only then it was boys."

"What else do you suggest we do?" says Rennie, with sarcasm; after all, it's Lora's fault they're in here. But it's lost on Lora.

"If it was two guys in here," she says, "you think they'd be talking about women? They'd be digging a tunnel or strangling the guards from behind, you know? Like at the movies." She stands up, stretches. "I need to pee," she says. "At least we don't have to do it on the floor, though ten to one somebody already has, it smells like it." She slips off her underpants, spreads her purple skirt over the red bucket like a tent, squats down. Rennie stares at the wall, listening to the patter of liquid against plastic. She doesn't want to know what Lora will wipe herself with; there are only two choices, hands or clothing.

Rennie has her knees drawn up, she's cold. If they lie down they'll be wet, so they're still sitting, backs against the wall. The light comes through the door, endlessly, it's impossible to sleep. She puts her forehead on her knees and closes her eyes.

"I bet you could see out the window," says Lora, "if I gave you a leg up."

Rennie opens her eyes. She fails to see the point, but it's something to do. Lora bends and cups her hands, Rennie puts her right foot into them and Lora hoists, and Rennie manages to reach up and grab the bars. She pulls herself up, she can raise her head to the opening.

It's a courtyard of sorts, with a wall around it and another building on the other side. Her eyes are almost at ground level; it's overgrown with weeds, a white jungle in the moonlight. The gallows platform rises out of the weeds, a derelict tower. Rennie knows where they are. On three sides of the courtyard it's a sheer drop to the sea, and the building they're in is the fourth side. There's a faint smell of pigs. No one is out there.

"There's nothing to see," she says when she's back down.

Lora rubs her hands together. "You're heavier than I thought," she says.

They sit down again. After five minutes or half an hour there's a sound above them, outside the window. A scuttling, a squeak.

"Rats," says Lora. "Around here they call them coconut rodents. Mostly they just eat coconuts."

Rennie decides to concentrate on something else. She closes her eyes: She knows that there are some things she must avoid thinking about. Her own lack of power, for instance; what could be done to her.

She can feel Lora's arm against her own, it's comforting. She thinks about refrigerators, cool and white, stocked with the usual things: bottles, cartons of milk, packets, coffee beans in fragrant paper bags, eggs lined up quietly in their shells. Vacuum cleaners, chromium-plated taps, bathtubs, a whole store full of bathtubs, soap in pastel wrappers, the names of English herbs, the small routines.

■

Lora's still talking. But Rennie can't concentrate, she's getting hungrier and hungrier. She wonders when it will be morning.

Surely they will bring something to eat, they'll have to, her stomach is cramping and she hopes it's only the hunger.

Her eyes feel gritty, she's irritated because she hasn't slept more, it's Lora's fault, she needs more sleep and she's thirsty too. It's like the time she was trapped all night in a bus station, by a blizzard, on her way home for Christmas, some town halfway there, the snack bar isn't open and the toilets don't work, there's a bad smell and no prospect of a bus out until dawn, maybe not even then, they have to wait for the wind to go down before they can plow the roads, people yawning and dozing, a few grumpy children, the coffee machine out of order. But it would be tolerable if only the woman packed beside her on the bench would quit talking, in a maroon coat and curlers, no such luck, it goes on and on, triplets, polio, car crashes, operations for dropsy, for burst appendixes, sudden death, men leaving their wives, aunts, cousins, sisters, crippling accidents, a web of blood relationships no one could possibly untangle, a litany at the same time mournful and filled with curious energy, glee almost, as if the woman is childishly delighted with herself for being able to endure and remember so much pointless disaster. *True Confessions*. Rennie tunes out, studies the outfit on the woman asleep on the bench across from them, her head sideways: the corsage with the Christmas bells and silver balls and the tiny plastic Santa Claus held captive on her large woolen breast.

"You aren't listening," says Lora accusingly.

"Sorry," says Rennie. "I'm really tired."

"Maybe I should shut up for a while," says Lora. She sounds hurt.

"No, go on," says Rennie. "It's really interesting." Maybe soon they will come to question her, isn't that what happens? And then she can explain everything, she can tell them why it's a mistake, why she should not be here. All she has to do is hang on; sooner or later, something is bound to happen.

■

Rennie is walking along a street, a street with red-brick houses, the street she lives on. The houses are big, square, solid, some with porches, some with turrets and gingerbread trim painted

242

white. These people take care of their houses, they are proud of their houses. Houseproud, says Rennie's grandmother, who is.

Her mother and her grandmother are with her. It's Sunday, they've been to church. It's fall, the leaves have turned, yellow, orange, red, a few drift down on them as they walk along. The air is cool, cold almost, she's so glad to be back, she feels safe. But nobody's paying any attention to her. Her hands are cold, she lifts them up to look at them, but they elude her. Something's missing.

Here we go, says her mother. Here are the steps. Easy now.

I don't want to die, says her grandmother. I want to live forever.

The sky has darkened, there's a wind, the leaves are falling down, red on her grandmother's white hat, they're wet.

■

The window above them gets brighter and brighter, now it's a square of heat. Rennie thinks she can see mist rising from the floor and walls and from the red bucket. The lights in the corridor are still on. Lora's asleep, her head thrown back into the corner where she's propped, her mouth is open a little, she's snoring. Rennie has found out she talks in her sleep, nothing intelligible.

Finally there's a shuffle in the corridor, the clink of metal. A policeman is here, unlocking the door; in two-tone blue and a shoulder holster. Rennie shakes Lora's arm to wake her up. She wonders if they're supposed to stand at attention, as they used to in public school when the teacher came in.

There's another man with the policeman, dressed in shoddy gray. He's carrying a bucket, red, identical to the one that's fermenting by the door, and two tin plates stacked one on the other and two tin cups. He comes in and sets the bucket and the plates and cups down on the floor beside the first bucket. The policeman stays outside in the corridor.

"Hi there, Stanley," Lora says, rubbing her eyes.

The man grins at her, shyly, he's frightened, he backs out. The policeman with him locks the door again, acting as if he hasn't heard.

On each of the plates there's a slice of bread, thinly buttered.

Rennie looks into the bucket. The bottom is covered with a brownish liquid that she hopes is tea.

She scoops some out in a tin cup, takes that and a plate over to Lora.

"Thanks," says Lora. "What's this?" She's scratching her legs, which have red dots on them, bites of some kind.

"Morning tea," says Rennie. It's the English tradition, still.

Lora tastes it. "You could've fooled me," she says. "You sure you got the right bucket?" She spits the tea out onto the floor.

The tea is salty. They've made a mistake, Rennie thinks, they've put salt in it instead of sugar. She pours the tea back into the bucket and chews the bread slowly.

■

The cell heats up. Rennie begins to sweat. The stench from the bucket is overpowering now. Rennie wonders when she'll stop noticing it. You can get used to almost anything.

She's wondering when someone in authority will arrive, someone she can talk to, someone she can inform of her presence. If they only realize she's here, who she is, they'll get her out. The policeman did not look like someone in authority. She's convinced of her right to be released, but she knows that not everyone will see it exactly that way.

About midmorning, judging by the sun, two other policemen arrive outside the door. One is black, one brownish pink. They seem friendlier than the first one, they grin as they unlock the door.

"Take the bucket and come with us," says the pink one. Rennie thinks they're talking to her. She comes forward.

"I wonder if I could see the supervisor," she says.

"We not talking to you," the black one says rudely. "She the one."

"Hi there, Sammy," Lora says. "Hold your horses."

She goes out with them, carrying the bucket of piss.

Lora is gone a long time. When she comes back she has a clean bucket. Rennie, who's been imagining atrocities, says, "What happened?"

"Nothing to it," says Lora. "You just empty out the bucket.

There's a hole in the ground out there. I saw some of the others, they were doing the same thing." She sets the bucket down in its old place and comes over to the dry corner to sit down.

"Prince is on the floor above us," she says. "They're fixing it up for me to see him, maybe in a couple of days." She's happy about this, she's excited. Rennie's envious. She would like to feel like that.

"Guess what?" says Lora. "They got Marsdon."

"Oh," says Rennie. "Is he in here?"

"I mean he's dead," says Lora. "Somebody shot him."

"The men on Ste. Agathe?" says Rennie. She thinks of Marsdon running through the scrub, up the hill in his slippery leather boots, nine or ten men after him, while the police boat comes into the harbor, they'd want to get him while they still had time.

"No," says Lora. "The story is it was the cops. Ellis."

"I thought he was working for the CIA," says Rennie. "I thought he was an agent."

"There's a lot of stories," says Lora. "The CIA, Ellis, what's the difference? Anyway Ellis didn't want him talking about how he set it up, Ellis wants everyone to believe it was real. Nothing like a revolution to make the States piss money, and they've done it already, Canada just gave a great big lump of cash to Ellis, they told me, it said on the radio. Foreign aid. He can use it to finance his dope trade." She pauses, keeping an eye on Rennie. "Some of them are saying that Paul shot Minnow," she says.

"You don't believe that," says Rennie.

"Who knows?" says Lora.

"Why would he do that?" says Rennie.

"CIA," says Lora. "He was the one bringing in the guns for Marsdon, eh?"

"Come on," says Rennie.

Lora laughs. "You believed it once," she says. "I'm just telling you what they're saying. Guess what else?"

"What?" says Rennie, not wanting to.

"They think you're a spy," says Lora. She chuckles, a little insultingly.

"Who does?" says Rennie. "The police?"

"Everyone," says Lora, grinning. "Just, they haven't figured out who for yet."

"How did you hear all this?" Rennie says. "It's ridiculous."

Lora looks at her and smiles. From the pocket of her skirt she takes out a fresh package of cigarettes, Benson and Hedges, and a box of Swedish matches. "Same place I got these," she says. "I told you I had my ass covered."

Rennie's tired of guessing games. "How?" she says.

"I'm a dealer, remember?" says Lora. "So I made a deal."

"Who on earth with?" says Rennie, who can't imagine it.

"Those two cops, the ones who came just now?" says Lora. "Morton and Sammy. I knew they'd be here sooner or later; it took them a while to work it out but now they're in charge of us. They don't want us in with the others. They were selling for me on St. Antoine, they were my protection. Nobody knew except Paul. They sure as hell don't want anyone else around here finding out about that." She lights one of her new cigarettes, tosses the match onto the damp floor. "They were in on the shipments. They knew what was coming in and when, they knew the guns were coming up from Colombia along with the grass, they knew what was in Elva's boxes, they didn't know all about it but they knew enough, and they didn't tell, how could they without blowing their own act wide open? Ellis wouldn't like that. He'd think that was treachery. A little dealing he could understand but not that. Dealing, they'd just get canned. That, they'd get offed. So I've got them by the nuts."

"Can they get us out?" Rennie says.

"I don't want to push it," says Lora. "I don't want to make them jumpy, they're jumpy enough already. Anyway they want me here, they can keep an eye on me better. They don't want anyone else to get hold of me and start squeezing; who knows, the first hot cigarette on the foot and everything might come squirting out. They'll take good care of me though, they know I won't go down alone, I told them that. If I go I take somebody with me."

"What's to stop them from just burying you quietly in the back yard?" says Rennie.

"Nothing at all," says Lora. She finds this funny. "Pure bluff. I told them I had someone on the outside who's checking up on me."

"Do you?" says Rennie.

"Well," says Lora, "there's always Paul. Wherever he is."

Neither of them wants to talk about that.

They're eating, lunch, cold rice and chicken backs, boiled, Rennie thinks, but not enough. Pink juice runs out. Lora gnaws with relish, licking her fingers. Rennie doesn't feel too well.

"You can have the rest of mine," she says.

"Why waste it?" says Lora.

"Maybe we could ask them to cook it more," says Rennie.

"Ask who?" says Lora.

Rennie hasn't thought about it. Surely there must be someone to ask.

"It could be a lot worse, is what I always say," says Lora. "Where there's life there's hope. It's better than a lot of the people get at home, think of it that way."

Rennie tries to but without much success. Lora is eating the rest of Rennie's chicken back now. She aims a bone at the bucket, misses, wipes her hands on her skirt. The nails are gray, the skin around them nibbled. Rennie looks away. Now they will have stale chicken to smell, as well as everything else.

"We could ask them about the tea," says Rennie.

"What?" says Lora, her mouth full.

"The salt in the tea," says Rennie. "You could tell them they made a mistake."

"Hell, no," says Lora. "That wasn't a mistake, that was orders. They're doing it on purpose."

"Why would they do that?" says Rennie. The poor food she can understand, but this seems gratuitous. Malicious.

Lora shrugs. "Because they can," she says.

■

It's dusk. They've had supper, a piece of bread, the salty tea, water which tastes like rancid butter, a cupful each. The mosquitoes are here. Outside the grated window they can hear the pigs, up there in the yard; as Rennie watches, a curious snout pokes through.

Neither of them is saying anything. Rennie can smell their bodies, unwashed flesh, and the putrid smell from the bucket, Lora is out of cigarettes for the time being, she's picking at her fingers, Rennie can see her out of the corners of her eyes, it's an irritating habit, they've both run out, run down. She's having trouble remembering which day this is, they should have begun when they got here, scratches on the wall, perhaps this is the day her ticket expires, her twenty-one-day excursion. Maybe now someone will come looking for her, maybe she will be rescued. If she can only keep believing it, then it will happen.

She hopes they'll do it soon, she's deteriorating, she knows this because right now she's daydreaming about food, not even real food, not spinach salads with bacon and mushrooms and a glass of dry white wine, but Kentucky Fried Chicken, McDonald's hamburgers, doughnuts filmed with ersatz chocolate and shreds of stale coconut, thick nasty cups of ancient coffee, the dregs, her mouth's watering at the thought of it, potato chips, candy bars from subway magazine stands, Mars, Rowntree's coated raisins, silently and voluptuously she repeats the names, how can she? She sleepwalks along Yonge Street, into one franchise after another. *No-frills Snak Pak.* Maybe she's delirious.

She switches to a jigsaw puzzle, in her head, the top border, the ones with the flat edges, it's always the sky, one piece fits into another, fits into another, interlocking, pure blue.

■

"Try getting a comb for us," says Rennie. "If you can."

"I tried before," says Lora. "People slash their wrists with them. They don't want any funny deaths in here, not if they can help it. Some church or other is poking around."

"How about a brush?" says Rennie.

"You got any money?" says Lora, with a small laugh.

Rennie looks at her, she's thinner now and filthy, there's no other word for it, the white blouse is gray, the purple skirt is damp and greasy, dark moons under the eyes, they both smell, there's a sore on Lora's leg that won't heal, her hair is matted. Rennie knows how she herself must look. She thinks they should do exercises, but when she suggested it, Lora said, What for? and Rennie doesn't have the strength to do them by herself. What she really wants is a toothbrush. A mirror. Someone who could get them out.

"I could braid it," she says.

"What?" says Lora. It's harder and harder to keep her attention.

"I could braid your hair," says Rennie. "At least that would untangle it."

"Okay," says Lora. She's restless, she's out of cigarettes again, the flesh around her nails is raw. "I wish we could get some news in here," she says. "You can't trust what they tell you. I'm tired of this place."

Rennie doesn't remember hearing her complain before. It seems like a bad omen. She begins on the hair, it's like pulling strands of wool apart.

"Go easy," says Lora. "At least we don't have lice."

"Yet," says Rennie. Now they're laughing, it's idiotic, they can hardly stop. There's no reason for it. When they finish, Rennie keeps going with the hair. She's making it into two long frizzy braids. "What do you dream about?" she says to Lora.

"Lots of stuff," says Lora. "Being on a boat. My mother. Sometimes I dream about having a baby. Except I never know what to do with it, you know? I think I'd like it though. When I get out of here and I get Prince out maybe that's what we'll do. They think it's funny here if you have a baby after you're about twenty-five though. For them that's old. But I don't care, let them laugh. Elva will like it, she's always bugging me to have a son for Prince."

Rennie finishes with one of the braids and starts on the other. "If we had some beads," she says, "I could do you up like a Rasta."

"Tin foil," says Lora. "Some of the girls use that on the ends. When you get out, can you do something for me?"

"What makes you think I'll be out any sooner than you?" says Rennie.

"Oh, you will," says Lora. She says this wistfully, fatalistically, as if it's just a fact of life that everyone knows about.

Instead of cheering Rennie up this makes her anxious. She winds the two braids around Lora's head. "There," she says. "You look like a German milkmaid. Except I've got nothing to pin them with."

"Tell someone I'm here," says Lora. "Tell someone what happened."

Rennie lets go of the braids. "Who should I tell?" says Rennie.

"I don't know," says Lora. "Someone."

Lora's face is streaked with dirt. Perhaps later they can take turns wiping off each other's faces with the salty tea.

■

Rennie can't remember what people are supposed to think about. She tries to remember what she herself used to think about, but she can't. There's the past, the present, the future: None of them will do. The present is both unpleasant and unreal; thinking about the future only makes her impatient, as if she's in a plane circling and circling an airport, circling and not landing. Everyone gripping the arms of the seat, trying not to imagine the crash. She's tired of this fear, which goes on and on, no end to it. She wants an end.

She wants to remember someone she's loved, she wants to remember loving someone. It's hard to do. She tries to conjure up a body. Jake's body, as she has before, but she can hardly remember what he looks like. How does she know he ever existed? There's no proof. Acts of the body, of love, what's left? A change, a result, a trace, hand through the sea at night, phosphorescence.

Of Paul, only the too-blue eyes remain. They don't talk about Paul much; nothing has been heard, according to Lora, nothing has been said on the radio. He's disappeared, which could mean anything. Rennie does not want to think about the noises behind her in the harbor, the machine-gun fire, the explosion. She doesn't want to think of Paul as dead. That would rule out the possibility of rescue. She would rather know nothing. Possibly she is the last person he touched. Possibly he is the last person who will ever touch her. The last man.

She switches to a yoga class she once went to with Jocasta.

Feel the energy of the universe. Now relax. Start with the feet. Tell your feet, Feet, relax. Now send your mind into your ankles. Tell your ankles, Ankles, relax. Go with the flow.

She thinks about Daniel, Daniel eating his breakfast while listening to the news, which he doesn't really seem to hear, since his knowledge of world affairs is more or less nil, Daniel caught in rush hour, Daniel getting his feet wet because he didn't listen to the weather forecast. Daniel in surgery, a body spread before him, his hands poised for incision. Daniel leaning across his desk, holding the hand of a blond woman whose breasts he has recently cut off. Who wants to cure, who wants to help, who wants everything to be fine. You're alive, he says to her, with kindness and duplicity, compelling as a hypnotist. You're very lucky. Tears stream silently down her face.

Daniel moves through the day enclosed in a glass bubble, like an astronaut on the moon, like a rare plant in a hothouse: a fluke. Inside the bubble his life is possible. Normal. Outside, what would become of him? Without food or air. Ordinary human decency, a mutation, a freak. Right now she's on the outside looking in.

From here it's hard to believe that Daniel really exists: Surely the world cannot contain both places. He's a mirage, a necessary illusion, a talisman she fingers, over and over, to keep herself sane.

Once she would have thought about her illness: her scar, her disability, her nibbled flesh, the little teethmarks on her. Now this seems of minor interest, even to her. The main thing is that nothing has happened to her yet, nobody has done anything to her, she is unharmed. She may be dying, true, but if so she's doing it slowly, relatively speaking. Other people are doing it faster: At night there are screams.

Rennie opens her eyes. Nothing in here has changed. Directly above her, up on the high ceiling, some wasps are building a nest. They fly in through the grating, up to the nest, out through the grating again. Jack Spaniards, Lora calls them. In memory of what war?

Pretend you're really here, she thinks. Now, what would you do?

■

It's another morning, time has a shape even here. When the guards come, they have names, Sammy and Morton, and she knows now which name belongs to which, Morton's the pink one. Rennie stays in the background. She still has difficulty understanding what's being said, so she lets Lora deal with it. They have a hairbrush now, though not a comb; which is better than nothing. Rennie would like a nail file, but she knows better than to ask, it's too much like a weapon. Lora doesn't need one, her nails are bitten down to the quicks anyway.

"Try for some chewing gum," Rennie says to Lora. Where there are cigarettes there must be gum. It will give the illusion of toothpaste; her mouth feels as if it's rotting. Lora goes out with the bucket.

She's gone longer than usual, and Rennie begins to worry. At the back of her mind is the fear that Lora won't be able to restrain herself, her temper, that she'll do something or say something that will tip the balance, put them both in jeopardy. She herself, she feels, would have more control.

But when Lora comes back she's the same, there are no cuts or bruises, nothing has been done to her. She sets the empty pail on the ground and squats over it. Rennie knows that smell, the smell of bloodheat, seaweed, fishegg. Lora wipes with a corner of her skirt, stands up.

"I got your chewing gum," she says. "Next time I'll try for some toilet paper."

Rennie is disgusted. She thinks Lora should have more self-respect. "No thanks," she says coldly.

Lora looks at her for a moment. "What the shit's eating you?" she says.

"You're worth more than a package of gum," Rennie says. How many of them, she wants to ask, one or both? One at a time, or both? Lying down or standing up? It isn't decent.

Lora is bewildered for an instant. Then she laughs. "Goddamn right I am," she says. "Two packages. I got one for myself too."

Rennie doesn't say anything. Lora sits down and opens the gum. "Women like you make me sick," she says. "Tightass. You wouldn't put out to save your granny, would you?"

"Let's not talk about it," says Rennie. There's no point. They're in this room and it's a small one and there's no way out. All she can do is try to avoid a fight.

"Why in hell not?" says Lora, chewing. "What's wrong with talking about it? What makes you think it's any different from having some guy stick his finger in your ear?"

"It is," says Rennie.

"Only sometimes," says Lora.

Rennie turns her head away. She feels sick to her stomach. She doesn't want to watch Lora's grubby hands, her bitten fingers as they strip open the pack of cigarettes, the cigarette between the drying lips, the corner of her mouth.

But Lora is crying, Rennie can't believe it, convulsive sounds from her throat, her eyes clenched. "Fuck it," she says. "They've got Prince in here. They won't let me see him, they keep promising. What'm I supposed to do?"

Rennie is embarrassed. She looks down at her hands, which ought to contain comfort. Compassion. She ought to go over to Lora and put her arms around her and pat her on the back, but she can't.

"I'm sorry," she says. *Women like you.* She deserves it. It's a pigeonhole, she's in it, it fits.

Lora sniffles, stops now, wipes her nose on the back of her hand. Grudging, resentful, forgiving, a little. "How would you know?" she says.

■

Rennie doubles over, stumbles for the bucket, crouches. It's sudden, she can feel the sweat dripping down her back, she's dizzy, she hates pain. She's been invaded, usurped, germs taking over, betrayal of the body.

She lies down on the floor, even though it's wet. She closes her eyes, her head is the size of a watermelon, soft and pink, it's swelling up, she's going to burst open, she's going to die, she needs water, even water tasting of chlorine, Great Lakes poisons, her sense of irony has deserted her, just when she needs it, any kind of water, an ice cube, sugar and fizz from a machine. What has she done, she's not guilty, this is happening to her for no reason at all.

"You okay?" says Lora. She's touching Rennie's forehead, her fingertips leave dents. Her voice comes down from a great distance.

Rennie tries hard. "Make them get a doctor," she manages to say.

"For that?" says Lora. "It's only *turistas*. Montezuma's Revenge, the tourists call it. Everyone gets it sooner or later. Take it from me, you'll live."

■

It's night again. Someone is screaming, quite far away, if you tune it down it sounds like a party. Rennie tunes it down. She can sleep now in the light from the corridor, she goes to sleep quite peacefully, no one has done anything to her yet, she goes to sleep hugging herself. The screaming is worse when it stops.

Rennie is dreaming about the man with the rope, again, again. He is the only man who is with her now, he's followed her, he was here all along, he was waiting for her. Sometimes she thinks it's Jake, climbing in the window with a stocking over his face, for fun, as he once did; sometimes she thinks it's Daniel, that's why he has a knife. But it's not either of them, it's not Paul, it's not anyone she's ever seen before. The face keeps changing, eluding her, he might as well be invisible, she can't see him, this is what is so terrifying, he isn't really there, he's only a shadow, anonymous, familiar, with silver eyes that twin and reflect her own.

Lora is shaking her, trying to wake her up. "For Christ's sake," says Lora. "You want every cop in the place down our necks?"
Rennie says she's sorry.

■

It's noon, Rennie can tell by the heat and the angle of the light, and then the rice arrives. How much she's come to depend on it, that tin plate. The day ends when it's empty and another day of waiting begins, right then, with the scrape of the bones into the red bucket. Her life is shrinking right down to that one sound, a dull bell.
Outside in the courtyard there's something going on; all of a sudden there are harsh voices, shouts, a shuffle and clank. Then there's a scream. Lora gets up, her plate drops and spills. "Christ," she says, "they're shooting people."
"No," says Rennie. There haven't been any shots.
"Come on," says Lora. She bends, holds out her cupped hands.
"I don't think we should look," says Rennie. "They might see us."
"Maybe it's Prince," says Lora.
Rennie places her tin plate carefully on the ground. Then she puts her foot in Lora's hands, is lifted, clutches the bars.

There are people in the courtyard, five or six men in uniform, the two blues of the police, then another group, they seem to be tied together, arm to arm, they're being pushed down, to their knees, among the dry weeds and snarls of wire, the police have sticks, cattle prods? The ones kneeling have long hair, long black hair standing out from their heads; at first Rennie thinks they're women, then she sees they are naked from the waist up, they have no breasts.

One man still wears a woolly tea-cozy hat; a policeman snatches it off and the hair tumbles out. A pig runs in panic through the archway, it zigzags among the men, standing and kneeling, the policemen laugh, two of them chase it with cattle prods while the others watch, it dashes under the gallows platform and then back through the archway again. The kneeling men turn their heads, follow it with their eyes.

Now Rennie sees that one of the policemen has a rifle, he's raising it, for a minute she thinks he's going to shoot them all, the whole line of them. He hesitates, letting them believe this, do they? But he detaches the bayonet and walks slowly around to the back of the line with it, strolling, hips rolling, taking his time, luxuriating. He's not doing this just because he's been ordered to: He's doing it because he enjoys it. *Malignant.*

"What's going on?" says Lora, whispering. Rennie doesn't answer.

The policeman grasps the hair of the first man in the line, gathers it almost lovingly into a bunch, a handful, then suddenly jerks the man's head back so that the throat is taut, it's going to be worse than shooting. Butchery.

But all he does is saw at the hair, he's cutting the hair off; that's all he's doing. Another man follows him with a green garbage bag, for the hair. It's chilling, this tidiness.

"What is it?" says Lora. "What're they doing?"

He's at the second man now, the courtyard is oddly silent, the noon sun beats down, everything is bright, the men's faces glisten with sweat, fear, the effort of keeping in the hatred, the policemen's faces glisten too, they're holding themselves back, they love this, it's a ceremony, precise as an operation, they're implementing a policy, he pulls the head back like a chicken's, the hair is gray, he slices again with the bayonet but he's not careful enough, the man howls, a voice that is not a voice, there are no teeth in his opened mouth, blood is pouring down his face. The man with the bayonet stuffs the handful of hair into the bag and wipes his hand on his shirt. He's an addict, this is a hard drug. Soon he will need more.

The kneeling man continues to howl. As if they've been waiting for it, two others come over and one of them kicks the howling man in the stomach. A third throws water over him from a red plastic bucket. The man falls forward, he's kept from hitting the pavement by the ropes that link him to the other men, one of the policemen jams the cattle prod in between his legs, he's flung back, now it's a scream. Not human.

"Pull him up," says the man in charge, and they do. They continue along the line, the hurt man's face is on a level with Rennie's own, blood pours down it, she knows who it is, the deaf and dumb man, who has a voice but no words, he can see her, she's been exposed, it's panic, he wants her to do something, pleading, *Oh please.*

"Let me down," says Rennie. The best they can do is avoid calling attention to themselves. She leans against the wall, she's shaking. It's indecent, it's not done with ketchup, nothing is inconceivable here, no rats in the vagina but only because they haven't thought of it yet, they're still amateurs. She's afraid of men and it's simple, it's rational, she's afraid of men because men are frightening. She's seen the man with the rope, now she knows what he looks like. She has been turned inside out, there's no longer a *here* and a *there.* Rennie understands for the first time that this is not necessarily a place she will get out of, ever. She is not exempt. Nobody is exempt from anything.

"Good God, what is it?" says Lora. She's still whispering, her hands on Rennie's shoulders.

"Prince isn't there," says Rennie. "They're cutting their hair off."

She kneels, picks up the chicken back Lora spilled, wipes the dirt from it with her fingers, puts it on Lora's plate. "You should eat it," she says. "We need to eat."

■

In the middle of the morning, at the usual time, the two guards come again. Today one of them is new, he's too young, skinny body, thin wiry arms, face smooth as a plum, eyes innocent. Rennie takes one look at him and sees that he knows nothing at all.

Morton is frightened, he's got his arm across his chest, almost touching his pistol, things are no longer under his control. It's the innocence of the other one that frightens him.

They unlock the door. Lora's watchful but she bends over anyway to pick up the smelly red bucket.

"Her turn today," says Morton, pointing at Rennie with the hand. "You been doin' it every time."

Rennie isn't prepared for this, she knows what will be expected of her, she's going to dare him. "Why?" she says. "Where's Sammy?"

"I don't mind which one," says the boy. He's heard something then, he wants part of it, he knows what but not what for.

"Shut your mouth," says Morton. He's afraid of being caught out, the young kid's smart enough to figure it out but he's a fool, he'll tell, maybe not deliberately but one way or another. He wants Rennie to go rather than Lora because it's safer, that's what he thinks. "Sammy's grandmother got sick," he says to Lora.

"Yeah," says the young boy. "She sick bad." He has a high nervous giggle. "What you need Sammy for? I just as good."

"I'll go," says Rennie. She doesn't want a squabble, something's about to go wrong.

"No," says Lora. The barred door's partly open, she yanks it and pushes out into the corridor. "What's happened to Prince? Is that it? You don't want me to know, you don't want to tell me. Oh shit. Where did you put him?"

She's got Morton by the arm but he's the one who's sweating, it's not her, she's tight and cold. The young boy's looking at both of them, trying to untangle this. He giggles again. "Prince?" he says. "The big man, Prince of Peace? He never in here at all, man."

"Shut your damn mouth," Morton says to him.

"You tell her he still alive?" says the boy. "He dead a long time ago, man." He thinks this is a joke. Rennie wonders whether he's stoned, it's a possibility.

"When?" Lora says quietly, to him alone, not to Morton. She's dropped her hands down, she's no longer holding Morton's arm.

"What you need to tell her that for?" Morton says with disgust. The boy has completely blown it.

"He caught in the crossfire," the boy says. He giggles some more. "That what it say on the radio. You tell her you got him in here, make her work hard for you, eh? Get some for your own self. You are a bad man." He's laughing now, not just giggling, this is the funniest thing he's heard in a long time.

"You pig," Lora says to Morton. "You knew all along. You were just afraid I'd crack up if I heard about it, right, and then they'd find out what you were up to. They shot him in the back, right?"

Morton puts his hand on her arm, soothingly, like a doctor almost. "You go back in," he says. "I doin' the best I can for you. You lucky you alive."

"Fuck you!" Lora screams. "I'll tell everyone about you, nobody screws me around like that, they can shoot you too for all I care!"

Tears are running down her face. Rennie heads toward her. "Lora," says Rennie, "there's nothing you can do," but Lora is beyond her. Morton is pushing her now, back toward the door.

"Fucking pig," she says, "take your fucking hands off me!" She kicks at Morton, aiming for the groin, but he's too fast for her. He catches the raised leg, lifts, tips her backward toward the boy, who's quick enough, he's not stoned after all, he catches her and jerks her arms behind her. Morton knees her in the belly, he's knocked the air out of her. Now nobody needs to hold her arms and after the first minute she's silent, more or less, the two of them are silent as well, they don't say anything at all. They go for the breasts and the buttocks, the stomach, the crotch, the head, jumping, My God, Morton's got the gun out and he's hitting her with it, he'll break her so that she'll never make another sound. Lora twists on the floor of the corridor, surely she can't feel it any more but she's still twisting, like a worm that's been cut in half, trying to avoid the feet, they have shoes on, there's nothing she can avoid.

Rennie wants to tell them to stop. She wants to be strong enough to do that but she isn't, she can't make a sound, they'll see her. She doesn't want to see, she has to see, why isn't someone covering her eyes?

■

This is what will happen.

Rennie will be taken to a small room, painted apple green. On the wall there will be a calendar with a picture of a sunset on it.

There will be a desk with a phone and some papers on it. There will be no windows.

Behind the desk there will be a policeman, an older man, with short graying hair. In front of the desk there's a chair. Rennie sits down in the chair when the policeman tells her to. The policeman who's brought her here will stand behind her.

She is asked to sign a release form saying that while in custody she has not been harmed in any way and has not witnessed any other detainee being so harmed. She thinks of Lora, her pulped face. She understands that unless she makes a mark on this paper they may not let her out. She feels that she has forgotten how to write. She signs her name.

They have her suitcase here, from the hotel, and her purse. The older man says that perhaps she would like to change her clothes before meeting the gentleman from the Canadian government who is here to see her. Rennie feels this would be a good idea. She's taken to another small room, much like the first except that the calendar is different, it's a white woman in a blue bathing suit, one piece, again no windows. She knows the young policeman is standing outside the door. She opens her suitcase and sees her own clothes, the clothes that used to be hers. Alien reaction paranoia. She starts to cry.

Rennie knocks on the inside of the door, which opens. She walks out. She's just as dirty but she feels less dirty now, she feels decent, she's wearing a cotton dress, faded blue, and her hair is combed, as well as she could do it in the mirror from her purse. She's carrying the suitcase in her right hand, the purse is over her left shoulder. Her passport isn't in the purse or the suitcase either. So she's not really out, not yet. She's decided not to ask where her camera bag is.

She is taken up some stairs, along a stone hallway, then into a much larger room, one with windows. She can hardly remember what it's like to be in such a large room, to look out of windows that are so huge. She looks out. What she sees is the muddy field where the tents were; now it's empty. She understands that this is one of the rooms that are usually shown to tourists, the room where they were going to sell the local arts and crafts, a long time ago. There are two wooden chairs in the corner, and a man is standing beside them waiting for her. He's still got the tinted glasses and the safari jacket.

He shakes hands with Rennie and they sit down on the wooden chairs. He offers her a cigarette, a black one with a gold band, which she refuses. He smiles at her, he's a little nervous. He says she certainly has given them some uneasy moments. There wasn't a lot they could do when the region was destabilized and the government here was so panicky, overreacting he says, but the situation is normalizing now.

The government can't make a public apology of course but they would like her to know unofficially that they consider it a regrettable incident. They understand that she is a journalist and such things should not happen to journalists. It was an error. They hope she's prepared to consider it in the same light.

Rennie nods and smiles at him. Her heart is beating, she's beginning to think again. Of course, she says.

To tell you the truth, says the man, they thought you were an agent. Of a foreign government. A subversive. Isn't that absurd? It's the common charge though, in countries like this.

The man is uneasy, he's leading up to something, here it comes. He says he realizes she's a journalist but in this instance things are very delicate, getting her out of here has been more difficult than she may suppose, she doesn't know how these small southern countries operate, the people who run them are quite temperamental. Irrational. For instance, the Prime Minister was very angry because the Americans and the Canadians didn't send in their armies and their navies and their air forces to support him, over, let's face it, a completely minor insurrection, doomed even before it started. The Prime Minister seemed to feel that Rennie should be kept in a cell because these armies had failed to materialize. As a kind of hostage. Can she imagine that?

Rennie says she can. I suppose you're telling me not to write about what happened to me, she says.

Requesting, he says. Of course we believe in freedom of the press. But for them it's a matter of saving face.

For you too, thinks Rennie. Have you any idea of what's going on in here? she says.

The Council of Churches made an inspection and was satisfied

260

with the conditions, he says, too quickly. In any case we can't interfere in internal matters.

I guess you're right, says Rennie. She wants her passport back, she wants to get out. Anyway it's not my thing, she says. It's not the sort of piece I usually do. I usually just do travel and fashion. Lifestyles.

He's relieved: She understands, she's a woman of understanding after all.

Of course we don't make value judgments, he says, we just allocate aid for peaceful development, but *entre nous* we wouldn't want another Grenada on our hands.

Rennie looks out the window. There's a plane, coming down at a sharp angle across the oblong of sky, it flashes, silver, up there in the viciously blue air. It must be the afternoon flight from Barbados, the one she came in on, only now it's on time. The situation is normalizing, all over the place, it's getting more and more normal all the time.

Actually I'd like to forget the whole thing as soon as possible, she says. It's not the sort of thing you want to dwell on.

Of course not, he says. He stands up, she stands up, they shake hands.

■

When they're finished, when Lora is no longer moving, they push open the grated door and heave her in. Rennie backs out of the way, into the dry corner. Lora hits the floor and lies there, limp, like a bundle of clothing, face down, her arms and legs sprawled out. Her hair's all over, her skirt's up, her underpants ripped and filthy, bruises already appearing on the backs of her legs, the heavy flesh of her thighs, massive involvement, or maybe they were there already, maybe they were always there. There's a smell of shit, it's on the skirt too, that's what you do.

The older one throws something over her, through the bars, from a red plastic bucket.

"She dirt herself," he says, possibly to Rennie, possibly to no one. "That clean her off."

They both laugh. Rennie's afraid it isn't water.

They go away, doors close after them. Lora lies on the floor, unmoving, and Rennie thinks *What if she's dead?* They won't be back for hours, maybe not until the next morning, she'll be alone here all night with a dead person. There should be a doctor. She picks her way carefully around the outline of Lora, the puddle on the floor, blood mixing with the water, it was only water after all. She looks out through the bars, down the corridor, as far as she can see in either direction. No one's there, the corridor is empty and silent, the lightbulbs hang along the ceiling with loops of wire in between, at regular intervals. One of them is burned out. I should tell someone, thinks Rennie.

■

Rennie is in the kitchen, making herself a peanut butter sandwich. There's a radio on somewhere, a soft blur of noise, or maybe it's the television, a blue-gray oblong of mist in the living room where her grandmother sits propped in front of it, seeing visions. Rennie cuts the sandwich in four and puts it on a plate, she likes small neat ceremonies like this, she pours herself a glass of milk.

Her grandmother comes through the doorway between the dining room and the kitchen. She's wearing a black dress printed with white flowers.

I can't find my hands, she says. She holds out her arms to Rennie, helplessly, her hands hanging loose at the ends of them.

Rennie cannot bear to be touched by those groping hands, which seem to her like the hands of a blind person, a half-wit, a leper. She puts her own hands behind her and backs away, into the corner and along the wall, maybe she can make it to the kitchen door and go out into the garden.

Where is everybody? says her grandmother. She starts to cry, screwing up her eyes like a child, scant tears on the dry skin of her face.

Rennie's mother comes in through the kitchen door, carrying a brown paper bag full of groceries. She has on one of her shopping dresses, navy blue.

What's going on? she says to Rennie.

I can't find my hands, says her grandmother.

Rennie's mother looks with patience and disgust at Rennie, at her grandmother, at the kitchen and the peanut butter sandwich and the groceries she's carrying. She sets the bag down carefully on the table. Don't you know what to do by now? she says to Rennie. Here they are. Right where you put them. She takes hold of the grandmother's dangling hands, clasping them in her own.

■

The sunlight is coming in through the little window, it falls on the floor in squares, in one of the squares is Lora's left hand, the dirty blunt fingers with their bitten cuticles curled loosely, untouched, they did nothing to her hands, shining and almost translucent in the heavy light. The rest of the body is in darkness, in water, the hand is in the air. Rennie kneels on the wet floor and touches the hand, which feels cold. After a moment she takes hold of it, with both of her hands. She can't tell from holding this hand whether or not Lora is breathing, whether or not her heart is still moving. How can she bring her back to life?

Very carefully, this is important, she turns Lora over, her body is limp and thick, a dead weight. Dead end. She hauls Lora over to the driest corner of the room and sits with her, pulling Lora's head and shoulders onto her lap. She moves the sticky hair away from the face, which isn't a face any more, it's a bruise, blood is still oozing from the cuts, there's one on the forehead and another across the cheek, the mouth looks like a piece of fruit that's been run over by a car, pulp, Rennie wants to throw up, it's no one she recognizes, she has no connection with this, there's nothing she can do, it's the face of a stranger, someone without a name, the word *Lora* has come unhooked and is hovering in the air, apart from this ruin, mess, there's nothing she can even wipe this face off with, all the cloth in this room is filthy, septic, except her hands, she could lick this face, clean it off with her tongue, that would be the best, that's what animals did, that's what you were supposed to do when you cut your finger, put it in your mouth, clean germs her grandmother said, if you don't have water, she can't do it, it will have to do, it's the face of Lora after all, there's no such thing as a faceless stranger, every face is someone's, it has a name.

She's holding Lora's left hand, between both of her own, perfectly still, nothing is moving, and yet she knows she is pulling on the hand, as hard as she can, there's an invisible hole in the air, Lora is on the other side of it and she has to pull her through, she's gritting her teeth with the effort, she can hear herself, a moaning, it must be her own voice, this is a gift, this is the hardest thing she's ever done.

She holds the hand, perfectly still, with all her strength. Surely, if she can only try hard enough, something will move and live again, something will get born.

"Lora," she says. The name descends and enters the body, there's something, a movement; isn't there?

"Oh God," says Lora.

Or was that real? She's afraid to put her head down, to the heart, she's afraid she will not be able to hear.

■

Then the plane will take off. It will be a 707. Rennie will sit halfway down, it will not be full, at this time of year the traffic is north to south. She will be heading into winter. In seven hours she'll be at the airport, the terminal, the end of the line, where you get off. Also where you can get on, to go somewhere else.

When she's finally there, snow will be on the ground, she'll take a taxi, past the stunted leafless trees, the slabs of concrete, the shoebox houses, they'll stop and she'll give the driver the correct amount of money and she'll walk up the stairs and through her own front door, into the unknown. She doesn't know who will be waiting for her, who will be there, in any sense of the word that means anything. Perhaps nobody, and that will not be fine but it will be all right. Wherever else she's going it will not be quietly under.

She's drinking a ginger ale and thumbing through the inflight magazine, which is called *Leisure*. On the front, up at the top, there's a picture of the sun, orange, with a smiling face, plump cheeks, and a wink. Inside there are beaches, the sea, blue-green and incredible, bodies white and black, pink-brown, light brown, yellow-brown, some serving, others being served, serviced. A blonde in a low-riding tie-dye sarong, the splotches reddish. She can feel the shape of a hand in hers, both of hers, there but not there, like the afterglow of a match that's gone out. It will always be there now.

The ginger ale tastes the same as it used to, the ice cubes are the same, frozen with holes in them. She notes these details the way she has always noted them. What she sees has not altered;

only the way she sees it. It's all exactly the same. Nothing is the same. She feels as if she's returning after a space trip, a trip into the future; it's her that's been changed but it will seem as if everyone else has, there's been a warp. They've been living in a different time.

There's a man sitting beside her. Although there's an empty seat between them he moves over, he says he wants to see out the window, one last glimpse as he puts it. He asks if she minds and she says she doesn't. He's standard, a professional of some sort, he's wearing a suit and drinking a Scotch and soda, he's selling something or other.

He asks how long she was down for and she says three weeks. He says she doesn't have much of a tan and she says she's not all that fond of lying around in the sun. She asks what he does and he says he represents a computer company. She wonders if he really is who he says he is, she'll wonder that about everybody now.

"Vacation?" he says.

She could pose as a tourist but she chooses not to. Working, she says. She has no intention of telling the truth, she knows when she will not be believed. In any case she is a subversive. She was not once but now she is. A reporter. She will pick her time; then she will report. For the first time in her life, she can't think of a title.

He asks her if she's a secretary. "I'm doing a travel piece," she says, and gets the usual reaction, a little surprise, a little respect, she's not what she looks like. She tells him where.

"Where they had the trouble?" he says. He says he's been there and it doesn't have a tennis court worth mentioning, and she agrees that it doesn't.

He asks her if she travels alone much and she says yes, she does, her work requires it. He asks her to dinner and she wonders what to say. She could say that her husband is meeting her at the airport or that she's a lesbian or that she's dying, or the truth. She says unfortunately she doesn't have enough time, she has to meet a deadline, and that's the end of him, he feels rejected, he's embarrassed, he moves back to his own seat and opens up his briefcase, it's full of paper.

She looks out the window of the plane, it's so bright, the sea is below and there are some islands, she doesn't know which ones.

The shadow of the plane is down there, crossing over sea, now land, like a cloud, like magic. It's ordinary, but for a moment she can hardly believe she's here, up here, what's holding them up? It's a contradiction in terms, heavy metal hurtling through space; something that cannot be done. But if she thinks this way they will fall. *You can fly,* she says to no one, to herself.

There's too much air conditioning, wind from outer space blowing in through the small nozzles, Rennie's cold. She crosses her arms, right thumb against the scar under her dress. The scar prods at her, a reminder, a silent voice counting, a countdown. Zero is waiting somewhere, whoever said there was life everlasting; so why feel grateful? She doesn't have much time left, for anything. But neither does anyone else. She's paying attention, that's all.

She will never be rescued. She has already been rescued. She is not exempt. Instead she is lucky, suddenly, finally, she's overflowing with luck, it's this luck holding her up.

ABOUT THE AUTHOR

MARGARET ATWOOD, whose writing has been widely acclaimed by critics in the United States, Canada, England, and Europe, is the author of five novels—*The Edible Woman, Surfacing, Lady Oracle, Life Before Man*, and *Bodily Harm*—as well as nine books of poetry.